BOUND

Other Books By Alexandrea Weis

To My Senses
Recovery
Sacrifice
Broken Wings
Diary of a One-Night Stand
Acadian Waltz
The Satyr's Curse
The Satyr's Curse II: The Reckoning
The Satyr's Curse III: Redemption
The Ghosts of Rue Dumaine
Cover to Covers
The Riding Master
The Bondage Club
That Night with You
Taming Me
Rival Seduction
The Art of Sin
Dark Perception: The Corde Noire Series Book 1
Dark Attraction: The Corde Noire Series Book 2
His Dark Canvas: The Corde Noire Series Book 3
Her Dark Past: The Corde Noire Series Book 4

By Alexandrea Weis with M. Clarke

Behind the Door

By Alexandrea Weis with Lucas Astor

Blackwell, Prequel to the Magnus Blackwell Series

Forthcoming from Vesuvian Books

By Alexandrea Weis

The Secret Brokers
Realm

By Alexandrea Weis with Lucas Astor

The Chimera Effect
Death By The River
4 For The Devil

BOUND

A MAGNUS BLACKWELL NOVEL: BOOK TWO

Alexandrea Weis with Lucas Astor

▼

Bound
A Magnus Blackwell Novel, Book II

This is a work of fiction. Names, characters, places, and incidents either are the product
of the author's imagination or are used fictitiously.
Any resemblance to actual persons, living or dead, or locales is entirely coincidental.

Cover Credit: Original Illustration by Sam Shearon
www.mister-sam.com

ISBN: 978-1-944109-61-5

VESUVIAN BOOKS

Published by Vesuvian Books
www.vesuvianbooks.com

Praise for the Magnus Blackwell Series

Awards

2018 Feathered Quill Book Awards
Gold (1st Place) Winner—Mystery—Blackwell
Silver (2nd Place Winner—Adult Fiction—Blackwell

2017 FOREWORD REVIEWS: Indies Book of the Year
Finalist: Horror—Blackwell (Winners TBA June 2018)

2017 International Book Awards
Finalist—Blackwell

2017 Readers' Favorite
Honorable Mention—Fiction—Supernatural—Blackwell

2017 Best Book Awards
Finalist: Horror—Damned

Praise

"I love the storyline ... The author throws fire on many pages through vibrant dialogue and fantastic scene writing ... far from predictable, and so satisfying and rewarding." *~Feathered Quill Book Awards* Judges' Comments

"... an intriguing, dark tale complete with vividly drawn characters ... Readers will be engaged from the start of the story to its climactic ending." ~Melanie Bates, *RT Book Reviews*

"A dark story of passion and revenge ... A guilty-pleasure read that kept me captivated ..." *~New Orleans Magazine*

YOU CAN'T ESCAPE
THE DARKNESS

Chapter One

A hard, steady rain blurred Lexie's view out the window. She shifted in her seat, silently cursing her uncomfortable wooden bench. She wanted to get the hell out of there. Hospitals held too many bad memories of ER visits and the horrible day her father had died.

She peered down at the long, marble-colored cane in her hand, her fingers running over the fire-breathing head of a dragon carved into its handle. Warmth radiated through her bones. The pearl changeling stones in the cane's eyes glowed in the hazy fluorescent lights, soothing her jittery nerves.

A nurse walked out of room 802. "She's ready, Mrs. Bennett." She examined Lexie's long white dress and red turban. "Keep your visit short, please. Too much stimulation tires her out."

Lexie opened the heavy hospital door.

Daylight filtered through closed, short curtains along the far wall. A steady, slow beeping kept time with a green glowing

1

monitor above the bed. The squiggly lines rolling across the screen meant nothing to Lexie except to tell her the person she came to see was still alive. Several bags hung from an IV pole next to the bed, amplifying her distress. She slipped into the oversized vinyl chair set at the unconscious woman's bedside, questioning if she should have come at all.

"Do I know you?" The woman's smoky voice surprised her.

"I'm glad you're awake." Lexie forced a smile.

The woman's white hair neatly piled atop her head, coffee-colored skin, and sharp, uncanny blue eyes had Lexie thinking the old bird looked pretty good for someone knocking on death's door.

"Your son asked me to come, Mrs. Braud." Lexie's grip tightened on her magical baton juju, reassuringly rubbing her thumb along the dragon's snout. "He said you wished to speak to your spiritual leader."

Mrs. Braud raised her eyebrows. "You're the new mambo?"

Lexie gritted her teeth. She'd been asked the same question many times since assuming her role. She didn't understand. She'd found her calling, fulfilled her purpose in life, and discovered a passion that made her soul sing. Why didn't everyone else see it, too?

"I can assure you I was appointed by the Queen to oversee—"

"I know what you are, but it's not who you are." Mrs. Braud placed her willowy hands over the white sheet covering her lap. "You have not taken the title into your heart."

Lexie leaned back in the chair, reminding herself not to start a confrontation with the frail woman. "I am mambo in words and deeds. I've come, according to custom, to make you ready for the great journey."

A slight smile crossed her pale lips. "I know where I'm going. Do you?"

Lexie's frustration nibbled at her. "I'm not sure why your son asked me to—"

Mrs. Braud coughed, winced, and held her hand against her chest. "When you're at the end of life, some things become very clear." Her voice became melancholy as she reclined on her pillow. "You haven't crossed the bridge to death. For people like me such understanding only comes with death, but for you … well, you're special. You must live in both worlds—the light and the dark. Are you ready to do that, Lexie Arden?"

Lexie fumbled with the cane in her hand, unsure of how to answer. "My last name is Bennett, Mrs. Braud, and I can assure you I do reside in both worlds. More than you can possibly imagine."

"Are you speaking of me, dear girl?"

A light flashed, and a man with broad shoulders, dressed in a sharp black coat and a vibrant red vest appeared by her side.

Magnus Blackwell cut a handsome figure, even if he was a ghost.

She glanced at him briefly before focusing again on Mrs. Braud. Magnus was her spirit guide and never far from her side. At times, she found his constant presence annoying. Then there were moments, like this one, when the sight of his vivid green eyes set her mind at ease.

"It seems I'm in constant communication with the darkness."

A playful smirk spread across Magnus's thin lips. He pressed his hand to his chest. "Darkness? Me?"

Mrs. Braud looked over her ghost with fleeting interest. "You speak with the dead. Everyone has heard of your gift. But there's more to being a mambo than calling to the departed."

Lexie gripped her cane as she summoned her strength to stand. She didn't need this crap. Not today.

Magnus held up his hand to her, calling for calm. "Don't give credence to what she says. She's not well."

She smoothed out her features and sat back in her chair. The cane vibrated, reinforcing her tranquility.

"I have worked with many people who needed me in the city. My position is to guide and encourage others. To be a spiritual leader and advisor."

Pain riddled Mrs. Braud's face, and she sucked in a labored breath. "Noble words, but you haven't done what the spirits want. They're your true masters. You must listen to them because soon they will demand your attention."

Lexie's cheeks flushed. "Which spirits are you talking about?"

"What did I say about calm?" Magnus arched an eyebrow. "You look like you're about to explode."

Mrs. Braud closed her eyes. "You should listen to your Mr. Blackwell."

Lexie inched closer to the bed. "You can see him?"

"I see all the dead." Her voice grew dark, husky, drawing Lexie in.

She shook her head and concentrated on the task at hand. "Why did you ask for me, Mrs. Braud?"

The white sheets covering her quivered with her rapid breathing.

"The spirits have a message, Mambo. Prepare. The darkness wants you." Right after the words left her lips, Mrs. Braud relaxed.

The monitor's constant beep slowed. Lexie reached out to touch her arm while the older woman peacefully slept.

The door flew open.

"You should go now." The nurse stood framed by the light in the hallway. "She's had enough activity for one morning."

Lexie glanced at Magnus. He nodded and then disappeared.

In the hallway, Lexie approached the nurse. "Thank you for letting me see her."

"I hope you weren't too disappointed." She clicked her pen

4

and wrote something on the chart in her hand. "Mrs. Braud hasn't responded to anyone."

Lexie stumbled forward but caught herself. "What are you talking about?"

The woman glanced up. "The tumor in her brain. She's been in a coma for over a week now. The doctors say she doesn't have long, but still, it's a difficult process to watch. Were you good friends?"

Lexie stifled her shock. "Ah, no. Her son asked me to visit as a spiritual advisor."

The nurse glimpsed the cane in her hand. "I see."

Hushed whispers erupted from the other nurses working on the hospital floor as they took in Lexie's dress, turban, and baton juju.

"Thank you for helping me," she mumbled and rushed to the elevators at the end of the hall.

She breathed easier when she made it to the grand lobby. A glass and steel homage to the modern skyscraper, it had crisscrossing metal bars set into monstrous two-story glass windows overlooking Prytania Street.

Doctors in long white coats darted around her as visitors and hospital staff bustled in and out of the lobby. Lexie's hurried footsteps carried her across the white-tiled floor and past rows of plastic bucket chairs and uncomfortable couches.

God, she hated this place.

Steps away from exiting the hospital, Magnus reappeared.

"You're angry." He tapped his ghostly dragon cane on the floor, but it made no sound. "You can't be surprised by what occurred."

Lexie glanced around, making sure no one was near. "I don't have a problem with her being in a coma. But what did she mean by the darkness wants me? I thought I already belonged to the darkness." She held up her cane. "Isn't that what this is for?"

"Do not be so upset by the ramblings of a dying woman. You came to see her. You've fulfilled your duty and done a great service."

"My duty? Which is what?" Her insecurity rocketed to life. "For months, I've struggled with being mambo. I thought once I held the baton juju, everything would fall into place. Shit like this makes me feel like I've made no progress at all."

"Language, please." Magnus motioned for her to head toward the doors.

She stopped at the wall of windows lining the front entrance. The rain had let up, turning into a light drizzle, but her despair had not receded with the storm. She'd pushed for months to make herself heard among the citizens of New Orleans, but despite her efforts, she still felt like an interior designer from Boston in over her head. She wanted nothing more than to share her gift and to fulfill her ardent desire to be a guiding light to others.

Magnus stood next to her. "It takes determination and courage to win over those you must lead. They will believe in you in time."

She rested her head against the glass. "That's the problem. No one believes in me. Emile Glapion can't get anyone at the NOPD to work with me. I've got some steady clients and the trust of a handful of priestesses, but no one else."

Her teary blue eyes gutted Magnus, but the doubts she harbored, words would never soothe. He understood her misgivings. In the beginning, hope drove them. But as the doors of other voodoo practitioners closed to them, their enthusiasm waned.

"You're trying too hard. Sometimes people will only see the truth when they're ready."

She sniffled and retrieved her keys from her purse. "People can be a real pain in the ass."

He gave her a cruel grin. "There's the Lexie I know. I'll see you back at the shop."

She dashed into the rain and across the parking lot. He watched her go, entertained by her zigzagging course, attempting to dodge puddles.

He regretted keeping what he'd sensed from her. The shadowy disturbance came over him the moment they had set foot in the hospital. It tainted the air like a sour mist soaked with unhappy souls. Mrs. Braud's comments had unsettled him, and he didn't want to add to Lexie's anxiety about the strange meeting.

But the darkness was there—and it had made its intentions known.

Something bad is coming.

Magnus clenched his cane and disappeared.

Tourists clogging Royal Street jostled Lexie as she walked along the uneven sidewalk. The clip-clop of horse-drawn carriages, the roar of traffic, and the peppery scent of Cajun food wafted through the air. When she stood below her red *Mambo Manor* sign, she smiled with pride.

She considered her little shop the personification of her role, announcing to all the world she'd embraced her sacred charge with gusto. But despite her efforts, no one seemed to understand how much her work meant to her. Her driving passion for using her gift for good felt satiated the moment the Queen had placed the coveted baton juju in her hands. Would they ever see her as anything more than an oddity?

With a firm hold of her cane, she opened the door and went inside. The hint of burning sage tickled her nose. Glass shelves covered the white plaster walls filled with an assortment of bells, drums, shrunken plastic heads, incense burners, and a plethora of voodoo dolls. Display cases alongside a wooden counter held silver jewelry and gemstones of clear quartz, moonstone, citrine, green aventurine, amethyst, and rose quartz for divination and spellcasting. A high wall of bookcases to the right offered a wide selection of references on voodoo and magic. A few individuals perused her titles, making her glad she'd insisted on carrying the books to educate the public about her religion.

She stepped onto the shop floor, and a jazzy tune filtered through the speakers built into the roughhewn beamed ceiling. A balmy, early fall breeze blew through the open door, rustling a rack of T-shirts touting various mottos associated with New Orleans.

"Mrs. Favaro is already waiting for you in the workshop." A petite young woman came up to her.

In a matching white dress, her shop assistant, Nina, helped Lexie with the day-to-day management of her store.

"Thank you." Lexie inspected Nina's smooth café au lait skin. "Everything okay while I was gone?"

"Your next appointment rescheduled, and I got confirmations from the three other clients you have spirit sessions with later this afternoon. The phone hasn't stopped ringing. Everyone wants to meet the new mambo."

Lexie sighed as Mrs. Braud's words came back to her. "I'm nothing more than another French Quarter attraction."

Nina folded her arms; her stunning chocolate brown eyes

steeped with curiosity. "You're hardly that. Marie Laveau knew what she was doing when she picked you."

"Thanks, Nina. You always make me feel better."

She nudged Lexie's arm. "Isn't that what you pay me for?"

"Excuse me." A woman with orange hair came up to Lexie, holding out a shot glass. "What is this symbol?"

Lexie examined the half-circle marked with crosses through it and etched in black on the side of the glass. "It represents one of the spirits or loa in voodoo. Each guard a realm in our world. The glass you're holding represents Kalfu, the god of death and chaos."

"Harvey!" the woman called across the shop to a man in Bermuda shorts. "We need to buy a set of these for your sister. She's into the occult, isn't she?"

Nina winked at Lexie and stepped in to help the woman select more shot glasses from the display.

Lexie admired Nina's swift handling of the customer. The young woman strangely appeared one rainy evening shortly after she'd opened her store. Lightning had ripped across the sky, and a second later, Nina arrived. Lexie took it as an omen.

She snuck behind a red door in the corner of the shop with *Private* painted in gold across the front. Crystal sconces lined the long, narrow hall, which led to the rear of the building. She passed a storage room, piled high with boxes and used to keep the inventory for the store.

Lexie pushed on through the claustrophobic corridor until she arrived in a small kitchen with white cabinets, an uneven stone floor and french doors opening on to a courtyard. The aroma of freshly brewed coffee called to her, but she eased through the doors, anxious to get to her appointment.

Shards of light from the afternoon sun stretched across the weathered cement of the courtyard and caught in the small pond, shooting sparkles across the murky water. Along the high bricked walls surrounding her, banana trees, potted hibiscus, and a few fat ferns offered a tropical paradise in the heart of the city.

Out of nowhere, a flash of gray sprinted across the courtyard to the ledge on the pond.

Lexie put her hand on her chest, frightened by the intruder. "Don't you have a home?"

A gray Maine coon cat sat on the edge of the pond, inspecting her. It's green eyes flickered, and the tip of its fluffy tail thumped in a steady rhythm. Then it leapt from the ledge and disappeared into the shadows.

She headed to the corner of the courtyard where a rusted tin potter's shed waited beneath the shade of a single-story yellow carriage house. Her husband, Will, had insisted on converting it into a workshop or atelier for her client meetings. Lexie was grateful he had gone to the trouble. She'd witnessed many wonders inside the small shed, and she questioned if today's session with Gus Favaro's widow would offer her another glimpse into the world of the dead.

She paused at the plywood door as images of Mrs. Braud popped into her head. The woman's words circled her mind like a persistent vulture.

"What else do the spirits want from me?"

Shaking off the strange encounter, she took a deep breath and focused. It was time to get to work.

The flickering white candle in the center of the wooden worktable rocked and swerved. Lexie waited for a sign from the spirits, but nothing came. She searched the rows of wooden shelves, crammed with books and potted plants, and an ache of confusion lodged in her gut. The air smelled of basil, thyme, and sage, but there was no aroma of smoke, cologne, or anything else supernatural. No charge of electricity and nothing to indicate a spirit manifested in the room. The room seemed peaceful and not the hub of spiritual activity she'd seen in the past.

Why can't I detect anyone?

A woman across the workbench from her in a blue Chanel dress clutched her Louis Vuitton purse to her chest. Her upswept golden hair complimented her red lips. Her small brown eyes remained glued on Lexie.

"Are you getting something?"

Lexie flashed a tolerant smile. "Not yet, Mrs. Favaro."

Her full lips thinned to a straight line. "You're my last hope, Mambo. Detective Glapion's search for clues has run dry. He hoped you could give me an explanation about my poor Gus's death."

Magnus stood behind her client. His gaze reflected the question rolling around in her head—*Why can't I sense anything?*

"Let me try again."

She rubbed her hands together, digging down once more into her center. The familiar white light shone brightly in her mind's eye, but it seemed a little off. Black specks marred its pristine surface and shadows lurked in the distance, expanding with every breath.

Never saw that before.

A jolt of sharp pain rocked through her chest. She gritted her teeth to keep from crying out. Her head remained bowed as she realized this wasn't something physical, but spiritual. It was like a door slamming in her face, smothering out the light.

The darkness wants you.

Mrs. Braud's smoky voice echoed inside her.

11

The pain intensified and Lexie didn't know if she could take much more. Swirls of black and white filled her mind. An explosion of light resonated in her ears and then an odd emptiness slithered through her. It was a cold, hollow sensation, blotting out the last traces of white light in her soul.

Chapter Two

Lexie opened her eyes and glanced around her workshop. Nothing appeared out of place. The bookshelves crammed with her collection of voodoo books, herbs, and reference materials on loan from her mentor, Titu, were untouched.

A tug at the center of her being snapped her back.

"What is wrong, dear girl?" Magnus's dark-blond hair bobbed in an ethereal breeze while his sights locked on her.

The white ribbon of energy flowed between them, but the connection she shared with her ghost grew fainter with every passing second like her spiritual well was running dry.

Ellen Favaro tapped her finger nervously on the worktable. "Is something wrong?"

She took a deep breath hoping to keep it together. "No, Mrs. Favaro. The spirits are reluctant to come forward. Perhaps you should tell me more about your husband's activities the night of his death. Is there anything else you can remember? Anything that might explain the how he ended up in the swamps?"

Ellen's voice became thick with tears. "I have no idea why anyone would kill him. Gus was a good Christian man. The detective told me someone at Tulane looked at the carvings on his chest." She took a handkerchief from her bag and wiped her eyes. "He said they were used in rituals for voodoo, but I never heard any more. We don't know any voodoo priestesses. I never met one until I came to see you."

Magnus scowled at her. "You're not concentrating on the ribbon between us."

"I'm concentrating," she argued. "Something is blocking me."

"What is blocking you, Mambo?" Ellen looked up. "Is my Gus being difficult? He was always difficult."

Lexie was about to answer when a breath of cold air enveloped her. A mist rose from the cement floor, barely visible at first it bubbled up in spurts and then swirled and gathered around her feet. It crept across the floor, eerily covering the ground until it was no longer visible.

Her eyes flew to Magnus. The horrified expression on his face snuffed out his handsome features.

A tentacle shot up from the mist, wriggling like a snake as it rose to the height of a person. The thin cone of air widened into a golden gown. From the Victorian era, the dress had a bodice done in gold silk, an underskirt and full sleeves composed of antique lace, and gold ribbon sewn into the fabric. Hands reached out, delicate and ashy, from the end of the sleeves. Then a black rope bound the woman's hands together at the wrists. A neck rose out of the lace collar. Two small gold doves sat like a crown on top a mass of honey-blonde curls.

"Katie?" Magnus whispered.

But the ghost did not register Magnus's remark. She had a dainty oval face and a slightly dimpled chin. She entreated Lexie with tearful blue eyes. Something wasn't right with her. Her lips moved but did not make a sound. She gave the impression of fighting to form words, but her mouth wasn't cooperating.

"I'm here to help," Lexie said to the ghost. "Tell me your name."

She convulsed with fervid shivering, and then raised her bound hands in front of her, acting as if she fended off an attacker.

"Katie, it's me." Magnus slid out from behind Ellen.

"Ah, what's going on?"

Lexie slowly got to her feet, rattled by the encounter. "Are you Katherine Blackwell? Were you married to Magnus Blackwell?"

"Who's Katherine Blackwell?" Ellen's designer handbag dropped on the table.

Katie thrashed about the workshop. Her eyes rolled back, sinking into the sockets and changing into black holes. The color drained from her cheeks, turning her skin a deathly gray, then her head rocked far back, arching her neck back to the point of snapping in two. Her mouth opened wide, resembling a deep hole. Something grabbed her wrists and yanked her forward like a dog on a leash.

The air grew thin. Lexie wanted to run to Katie's side and free her, but her rational mind kicked in, calming her. The ghost had appeared for a reason, and she wanted to know why.

Another voice, a threatening one, came from Katie.

"The others from our realm will not cross the threshold to join you, Lexie Arden. The departed are not at rest and will never be until you join them. You are no mambo. Your gifts are false and your power fleeting. Your days are numbered."

Katie's mouth closed, and her cheeks pinked. The black in her eyes drained and reclaimed their vivid blue color. She appeared dazed, but as she came to her senses, her features pulled back in a look of terror.

"I'm trapped! Help me, Magnus! Please!"

Her figure ballooned and then burst into a fine mist, erasing every trace of her. It dropped to the floor and hovered around Lexie's feet. Then the light fog drained into the cracks in the cement until every last speck disappeared.

His dragon cane flung to the side, Magnus rushed to the center of the workshop. He crashed to his knees, patting the ground. "Katie!"

"Will someone please tell me what's happening?"

Lexie went around the table and took Ellen's elbow, helping her from the bench.

"We will have to postpone your reading for another day, Mrs. Favaro. The spirits are upset."

"But I need to find out what happened to my husband." She shirked off her grip. "I was told you were the best."

"I am the best, Mrs. Favaro. I will help you find out what happened to your husband. But not today."

Her high heels clipping on the floor as she went, Ellen stormed from the workshop.

Lexie sagged against the flimsy door as her tired eyes found Magnus searching the bookshelves and tin ceiling. The deep lines marring his face sickened her.

"Was it her?"

His hand over his mouth, he faced her. When he connected with Lexie, he raised his head and collected himself. His lips pressed tightly together he picked up his cane from the floor.

"It wasn't her voice." He avoided her gaze. "My Katie was a spiritualist in my day, and spoke with spirits frequently, but what we witnessed … It frightened her."

"Hell, it frightened me." With a confident stride, she eased closer to him. "Did you recognize the voice?"

He hesitated. "No, I did not."

Her eyes scrunched together as she tilted her head. "Why don't I believe you."

"Forgive me, but the entity's anger was directed at you, not me. Perhaps I should be asking you the same question."

The slight upturn of his lips and the cock of his left eyebrow told her whatever he knew, he wasn't going to share it.

He bowed. "If you would excuse me, my dear. I think I will disappear for a time. You don't need me anymore."

He vanished before Lexie could question him further.

The pearl-colored eyes of her dragon cane called her back to the table. Looking for reassurance, she clasped the snarling dragon's head handle, and a tingle surged through her.

The rush of peace and warmth refreshed her. Like recharging her batteries, the cane always grounded her. It lifted her up when down, righted her frame of mind when scattered, and guided her on the right path to serve the inhabitants of the city. She closed her eyes and reached into the center of energy in her chest—her lifeline to her ability.

The ribbon with Magnus glowed up to a certain point, but beyond, appeared frayed and dull. She could hardly make out Magnus as he floated in his misty world. She knew he was there, had seen his existence when not linked to her earthly plane, but now, he felt far away—too far.

Something's wrong.

Lexie stood and clenched the cane, praying its power would rejuvenate her connection to Magnus.

It didn't.

Tendrils of panic threaded through her, as a bitter taste

swept through her mouth. What would happen if this was permanent? She had a business to run, clients to care for, a city to oversee.

"Shit!" She paced the floor of her atelier.

It had only been a few months since the Queen had given her the dragon cane at the *haute défi*. Her skills in voodoo kept evolving on a daily basis. Were hiccups in one's ability expected in the voodoo realm?

She pushed the door open and stepped into the courtyard. A few quick breaths of air cleared her head but did little to offset the twisting mass of dread in her gut.

A flash of inspiration pushed her dark thoughts aside. Titu Hebert was an experienced voodoo priestess. She would know what to do.

Lexie glimpsed the two-story Creole townhouse where she lived and worked and hurried across the courtyard to the rear entrance. The tapping of her baton juju on the cement resonated between the structures surrounding her, intensifying the tightness in her chest.

She bounded into the kitchen and rushed along the narrow hall until she came to the red door marking the entrance to her shop. Her hand trembled as she twisted the knob, but she kept an easygoing smile on her face. No need to alarm her customers.

Lexie had not taken two steps into the store when she ran into Nina.

"Why did you finish up early with Mrs. Favaro?"

"Something happened during our session." Lexie eyed the customers milling about.

"She seemed pretty upset when she left. I booked her for next week and offered her a discount."

"Nina, I have to go out for a minute." Lexie headed to the shop's entrance.

"No problem. I'll take care of everything."

On the street, Lexie's edginess quickened her step. Tourists milled about, and traffic filled the streets, but the world didn't feel the same. The ability she'd treasured ever since her initiation into the voodoo religion felt muted. She could not detect the world around her. The sights, smells, tastes, and sensations she could readily tap into in the past had fled. It was as if a black veil had camouflaged her sixth sense and everything beyond her fingertips was out of reach.

She halted in the middle of the sidewalk as fear gripped her. The door opened by her initiation had become an essential part of her in a short period. To have the flow of information cut off without any preparation was like a kick to the gut.

How can I be mambo without my sight?

Upended, she took off for Burgundy Street. But the more she thought about being separated from the flow of information, the faster she rushed across the cracked and uneven sidewalk. Soon, she was running for Titu's home, praying the experienced priestess could fix her.

Despite the mild weather, sweat trickled down her back and along her temples when she reached Titu's front door.

Her shaking hand pressed the doorbell. "I've gotta be the world's worst mambo ever."

"Lexie!" Titu's smile fell as she examined Lexie's appearance. "What is it, child? You're soaked through."

Lexie rushed in the door and shut it behind her. "Titu, something's happened." She gulped in a deep breath. "I was doing a reading, and this spirit appeared. Magnus said it was Katherine and—"

Titu held up her hands. "Calm down, child. Come inside, let me make some tea, and you can start at the beginning. Tell me everything."

19

The tea helped, so did telling Titu the entire story, but uncertainty still tormented her.

"I detected a change in the air this morning." Titu put her teacup down on the kitchen table. "I've also felt my abilities weaken."

A pair of black cats trotted into the room, hissing at each other.

"Behave." Titu snapped her fingers at them. "Never seen a couple fight like these two."

"Considering what Helen did to her husband, he's entitled to be mad at her." Lexie sipped her tea. "Any ideas who's behind this?"

"Only the blackest magic can make a priestess lose her power, but a mambo, that's sheer evil at work."

Lexie's hands trembled, almost dropping her teacup to the floor. "What are you talking about? What evil?"

Titu rose from her chair and shuffled to the stove. "The law of voodoo is you must not do to another what you're not willing to receive. It keeps the practitioners of our art in the realm of white magic—good magic. But to inflict harm on another is black magic or evil."

"*Les droits des noirs* is black magic, and Renee did it. But she's not evil; Bloody Mary manipulated her."

"No, she belongs to the darkness. You can feel it in her. It's like a sickness possessing her soul. It can sit for the longest time and not ask a thing of you. Then, one day, it will awaken, and you're helpless to resist it. I think the darkness has finally claimed her."

Lexie slumped in her chair. "I never got that impression.

She's always seemed confused and absentminded with me, not possessed. Makes me feel sorry for her in a way."

"Believe me, child. You now belong to a world where you don't need proof for something to be real. There's no science to voodoo. No explaining how or why it works. Belief gives it power; good and bad."

She'd seen many strange things since entering the religion of voodoo, but none of it had felt odd or wrong to her. The power of her cane and the magic she practiced sat right with her soul, but somehow the warning against dark magic enticed her.

"How do I stop someone from performing such black arts on me?"

Titu lifted the kettle on the stove and then took it to the sink. "To fight evil you must become evil, but to allow the darkness in will change you. Evil must have a sacrifice. One cannot embrace the darkness without giving up something of the light." She flipped on the tap and filled the kettle.

Intrigued, Lexie stood from the table and came closer. "What would I have to give up?"

"Who knows? It's different for every soul. But you're Mambo of New Orleans, and should never take on the darkness."

"But if I'm to be respected, should I know the dark magic, too? Be like Renee and the others who embrace it. Seems to me as long as they control such power, I will never be able to compete with them."

Titu slammed the tea kettle on the countertop. "No, you shouldn't ever consider such things. Those who practice the dark side of voodoo are, in the end, consumed by it. You might get some insights in the beginning, but the dark spirit will toy with you, tease you, and eventually turn you to its way of thinking."

Lexie cautiously approached the counter. "How do you know? Maybe things will turn out different for me."

Titu blanched as she shook her head, unable to look at her. "Marie Laveau's daughter felt the same way you did. Marie Katherine embraced the darkness. It's the main reason her mother passed her over and gave your baton juju to my ancestor, Simone Glapion."

Her serious expression needled Lexie's curiosity. "Have you ever tried the black side of magic?"

A glint of sadness stirred in Titu's eyes. "No, but I know someone who did." She carried the tea kettle to the stove top. "When I was a little girl, I got very sick. Turns out, I had a rare blood disorder. The doctors told my mother I would die." She set the kettle on a burner. "My mother had no husband, so, she did the only thing she knew. She gave herself to the dark side to make me well." Titu flipped on the burner and the blue flame burst to life. "I got better. The doctors were amazed. But I knew what my Momma had done. My sister, Lia, was just a baby at the time. She never saw the change in our mother, but I did." She shuffled back to the table. "The signs were subtle at first. She would get angry easily, or her demeanor would go from sunny to downcast in the blink of an eye." Titu sank into her chair. "Lia was three when my grandmother took us from the house. My mother worked spells in the swamps by then. She was a powerful priestess before she changed, but her dark spells made her even more powerful."

Lexie's breath hitched. "What happened to her?"

"When I was seven, they found her in the swamp—eaten by the crabs. My grandmother said it was the drink that killed her. I knew better; the darkness killed her." Titu raised her head; her face a mask of sorrow. "That's what it does in the end. It takes you. So never be thinking about handing yourself over to it, child. It will kill you."

A pulse of fear erupted from the center of Lexie's being. It wasn't the same sensation she got from her gift. This feeling terrified her.

"What does your ghost say about this?" Titu sat back. "Have you told your Mr. Blackwell you're interested in dark magic?"

Lexie shook her head. "After he saw his wife, he went back to his world. He's upset."

A shrill whistle cut through the air. Lexie rushed to the stove, switched off the flame, and removed the kettle from the burner.

"Someone is threatening you by using his wife," Titu said behind her. "It's one way of ensuring your ghost is rendered powerless. With him out of the way, you're vulnerable."

She arched her back and spun around. "Vulnerable? How?"

"Mr. Blackwell is your protector. He watches out for you and makes sure no harm comes to you." Titu raised her eyebrows. "What else did you think a spirit guide is for?"

"Whoever sent his wife wishes to harm me?"

Titu pushed herself up from the table. "Harm you, or get you out of the way. I think someone isn't pleased about your being mambo. I know several priestesses in the city who have spoken against you. This may be the beginning of a backlash."

The possibility of opposition had occurred to Lexie, and she'd hoped any resistance to her appointment short-lived. It seemed she'd overestimated the energy in the dragon cane, and underestimated the loyalty of the priests and priestesses in the city.

Her rigid posture deflated, and she sank against the counter. "What do I do?"

Titu came up and patted her forearm. "First, we size up the competition. Next week is your first council meeting of the voodoo leaders in the city. We can get a better idea of who may be against you there. Then we can plan."

Plan? Lexie paced the kitchen floor. "There must be

something else I can do. Some spell or ritual I can perform to find out who's behind this."

Titu chuckled. "After all these months, you still haven't learned the fundamental rule of white magic."

Lexie frowned at her. "What rule?"

Titu lifted the kettle and brought it to the kitchen table. "You can never use your magic on yourself. White magic is for the benefit of others. To discover the person behind this attack, you will need black magic. Someone who's skilled in the art, and trustworthy enough to make inquiries among the dark priests and priestesses."

Lexie waited behind Titu as she refilled their teacups with hot water. "Do you know anyone like that?"

Titu grinned over her shoulder. "Her name is Kalila La Fay. You two must meet, and soon."

Magnus had stayed in his shadowy world of gray mist as he followed Lexie to Titu's home. The nothingness of his surroundings added to his misery over seeing Katie. There was no light, no dark, only a constant sensation of weightlessness. He often found the place oppressive, craving the life surrounding him when he spent time with Lexie, but after Katie's pitiful cries for help, the atmosphere became unbearable.

When Lexie confided to Titu she'd lost her powers, Magnus punched the fog around him. He should have known.

He registered the strange change in her the moment Katie appeared. There had been something else, too—a whoosh like a flow of energy had entered him. His senses came alive, and his mind filled with images he did not understand. He picked up people walking out on the street, heard their conversations, and even felt their emotions. Several blocks away on the Mississippi River, he perceived the large freighters maneuvering the water and the chug of their engines. First exhilarated by the occurrences, they soon exhausted him, and he'd disappeared into his world to absorb what had happened.

But it was Lexie's compulsion for the dark side which distressed him more than anything else. He'd sensed her attraction to black magic many times in the past and wrote it off as childlike curiosity. Magnus feared for their future together if she pursued her compulsion and delved into the diabolic abyss.

His darling Katie's delicate face and the way it had morphed into the horrid black cavern replayed in his mind. The agony of seeing her again he'd not expected. He believed her lost to him forever. Now she was back, but not as a ghost with which he could seek amends, but as a puppet used to dispense the sadistic vengeance of another.

Who had removed her from her peaceful slumber? He pictured the culprit's head squeezed like a melon in his hands.

Magnus vowed to keep Lexie safe from whoever sought to do her harm. He had lost one woman he cared about to another's bloodlust and wasn't about to let Lexie follow his descent into a life of sin. He'd tasted enough misery for both of them.

Chapter Three

"Let me get this straight," Will said, sitting at their kitchen table. "You're mambo, but Titu wants you to meet with this other voodoo priestess to find out who's messing with you?"

Lexie brought a chicken pot pie to the table, a spiral of smoke rising from its blackened crust. "Kalila La Fay. She knows about dark magic. Titu said she can be trusted."

Will motioned to the dish. "How could you burn this? I said heat it up. Not set it on fire."

"I don't know." Lexie tossed her oven mitts to the table. "I put the oven on three-fifty like you said."

Will chuckled as he got up from the table. "So why does Titu trust this woman?"

He went to the refrigerator and fetched the box of breadsticks he had brought with the premade casserole.

"She worked with her on a few cases for the police. Emile knows her, too." She had a seat.

Will joined her at the table and removed a breadstick from the container. "Well, that doesn't make her trustworthy." He took a bite.

Lexie picked up a serving spoon. "Yes, but she has a pretty impressive clientele."

"But if she works black magic, and you don't, won't that put you at a disadvantage?"

Lexie dug the spoon into the casserole, and the aroma of charred crust wafted past. She fought not to wrinkle her nose. "Titu doesn't think so."

She scooped a mixture of black crust and congealed creamy vegetable and chicken goo on to Will's plate.

"How do you feel about it?" Will poked his fork at the concoction.

Magnus appeared at the table. "I can't believe you are serving such a vile thing. You might poison the man."

The blood rushed to her cheeks with a combination of relief and anger. Without him at her side, she'd felt a little lost. Instead of letting him know of her feelings, she barked, "Where have you been all day?"

Will glanced up at her. "What do you mean where have I been?"

Her lips pinched together, and she pointed at Magnus. "He's back."

Her husband's jaw clenched. "I thought he agreed to stay in the shop and not enter our home."

"I agreed to nothing of the kind!"

"Stop it, both of you." She banged the serving spoon on the table. "Magnus, Will's right. You agreed to stay in the shop, so go back there. We'll talk about this tomorrow."

Her ghost had never been the easiest man to read, but at that moment, the pained stare he gave her spoke volumes.

Will dropped his fork. The clatter of silverware jarred her, compounding her regret for the way she'd treated her spirit guide.

"I want to enjoy a quiet dinner with my wife, not her ghost."

Magnus scowled at him. He headed toward the door, mumbling as he went.

She wanted to call to him, apologize for the rift, but Lexie had Will to keep happy. Sometimes juggling the needs of both man and ghost wore her out.

Magnus reached the door to their apartment and walked right through the dark wood.

"You cater to him too much." Will picked at his dinner.

Lexie tentatively fingered her fork. She wasn't hungry anymore.

"I shouldn't have been so forceful."

"Somehow I find it hard to believe a man with Magnus's past would be easily offended." Will redirected his attention to his plate. "I think you forget who you're dealing with sometimes."

"Normally, I would agree with you, but today was difficult for him. He saw his wife, Katie, during a session."

Will lifted his napkin and wiped his chin. "What happened?"

Lexie avoided his eyes as she pushed a pea around on her plate. "We were supposed to be contacting a murder victim, but nothing came through initially. Then Katie appeared. She was terrified of something and …"

Will cocked an eyebrow, waiting for her to continue. "Go on."

Lexie shifted in her chair. "Then something took over her spirit. It contorted her figure in this weird way and spoke through her. Scared the shit out of me, and, I think, Magnus."

Unimpressed, Will selected a forkful of food. "What did she say?"

"Something about the dead not crossing over to join me. The voice claimed I wasn't mambo, and my powers were fleeting. It said my days were numbered. The funny thing is, it called me Lexie Arden, not Bennett, like it knew me before I married you. The whole thing was pretty upsetting, especially for Magnus."

With a worried wrinkle in his brow, Will put his fork down. "That sounds like a threat."

"Yeah, Titu felt the same thing. But who would threaten me?" She scooped up a pea.

"I don't like this. I can see why Titu is worried." He calmly rested his arms on the table and folded his hands. The bulging vein in his neck, however, hinted at his underlying concern. "When are you going to see this woman she knows?"

Lexie popped the pea in her mouth, debating the question. "I don't know. I guess sometime after the council meeting next week."

Will reached for her hand and squeezed it. "Don't wait. You need to talk to her before your big meeting. We need to get to the bottom of this."

"Why? What difference will it make?"

He let go of her hand. "I've just got a feeling you can't let this simmer for too long."

"You've got a feeling?"

He bobbed his eyebrows as he lifted his fork. "Yeah. You must be rubbing off on me."

The following morning, Lexie called Titu to set up an appointment to meet with Kalila La Fay. By the afternoon, she was in Will's BMW heading along I-10 to the swamps outside of the city.

She followed Titu's directions to the letter, but when she exited the highway and found herself on a shelled road surrounded by cypress trees laden with Spanish moss, Lexie suspected she'd made a wrong turn. Patches of swamp crowded in on either side, increasing her anxiety. Snapping turtles sunning themselves on fallen limbs in the water were the only signs of life she encountered while maneuvering the narrow road.

"Shit, I'm lost."

"I must agree with you," Magnus said manifesting next to her in the car. "I don't like this place."

There was no jut of land to turn her car around, compelling Lexie to continue. The trees along the shoreline grew thicker, blotting out the afternoon sun. Shadows loomed ahead, and in their distorting glimpses of light and dark, she envisioned hands beckoning her onward. Butterflies fluttered in her depths as she drove on, praying the way would open up, or a turn off would allow her to head back to the main highway, but the deserted road went on and on.

Black clouds gathered in the sky, adding an ominous vibe to her journey.

She was about to check the directions on her phone when the end of the road came into view.

"You've found it, dear girl."

Cypress trees smothered a rusted tin roof as thunder rumbled in the distance. The road narrowed, becoming a driveway covered in broken white shells. Thunder clapped as lightning flashed in the sky, illuminating the circular driveway and house behind it.

The hair stood on the back of her neck.

Lexie switched off the engine and grabbed her dragon cane from the passenger seat—Titu had insisted she bring it. She shoved open the door and climbed from the car.

Amid the pungent aroma of the stagnant swamp, a single-story, dingy gray, cypress Acadian cottage with a rickety screened-in porch and two slanted stone chimneys beckoned. Dried cypress needles covered parts of the tin roof and accumulated along the cracked and sagging steps leading to the porch. Dark windows on either side of a black-painted door gave Lexie the impression of unholy eyes scrutinizing a newfound meal.

She ventured through the dead, brown grass and cypress knees dotting the front yard. Beside her, menacing green long-leafed plants with prickly edges flapped in the breeze heavy with the promise of rain.

Another jagged stream of lightning landed just behind the house and the crack of the thunder shook Lexie. Her accelerating heartbeat urged her to head back to her car, but then the front door creaked open.

Magnus searched the swamps around them, deepening the lines in his forehead. "There are other spirits trapped here."

Lexie stopped halfway to the house. "Can you see them?"

"I can hear them. Why can I hear them now? I've never encountered this before."

A shiver snuck through her. "I don't know, but I'm hoping Kalila can help figure it out."

Lightning blinded her. When her vision returned, a woman stood in front of the open door.

A cold draft encircled Lexie as she stared at her. All in black, she wore a veil and long, baggy dress.

Go to her.

The voice in Lexie's head was not one she recognized, but she felt compelled to heed it.

"I want you to stay by the car, Magnus."

"I'm not going to wait out here like a dog!" His indignant delivery rattled her. "I need to be with you. I'm your protector, and I can't protect you from the car."

Her agitation strengthened her certainty for Magnus to remain behind. She couldn't explain why, but Lexie knew he could have no part of what she was about to encounter.

"I have to do this alone."

He glared at her, but then the small lines between his eyes relaxed and his features smoothed over with indifference.

"Very well." He faded from view. "But I am coming back if she threatens to turn you into a toad."

About to step away, raindrops pelted her face.

"Perfect." She took off running toward the house. "The things you get yourself into."

In his foggy world between the living and the dead, Magnus watched as she darted through the rain.

The power emanating from the woman awakened a revolting burning sensation deep in his essence. He could make out the black cloud enshrouding her soul and cutting off any light from getting through. He didn't approve of the woman and was uncomfortable with Lexie seeking her help.

Nothing good can come from this.

Chapter Four

Once safely on the porch, Lexie attempted to get a peek at the woman's face through her veil. The tinkle of rain on the tin roof added to her growing unease.

"You made it." She had a melodious voice. "Titu said you would be on time."

"Are you Kalila La Fay?"

Pallid hands tossed the veil aside. A lovely face appeared. With skin the color of a shimmering pearl, her sloped nose and wide mouth complimented her long, regal neck. Her black eyes, however, intimidated Lexie. They seemed to absorb light and not reflect it. The way they glossed over her face and figure reminded her of a hungry animal.

A slow smile spread across her anemic lips. "I see you brought your baton juju, Mambo." She dipped her head.

Tendrils of Kalila's energy tickled her skin. The woman harnessed immense power, making Lexie feel like a kindergartener on the first day of school.

"You're a *Purs de Coeur*, aren't you?"

Lexie nodded. "So I'm told."

"You wouldn't be holding the Queen's baton juju if you weren't pure of heart. It's the reason the changeling stones are pearl. It means you're unfettered by the darkness possessed by most voodoo priestesses." The woman's eerie gaze lingered on the cane. "Amazing staff she gave you, and one with a unique history."

Lexie glimpsed the dragon head caught in a fierce roar. "Yes, I know. It goes back to the Queen."

"It goes back farther than that." Kalila stepped down from the porch and stared across the shelled drive to the swamp next to her home. "There are legends around every baton juju ever created. Each represents a spirit god. They have been passed down for centuries from one mambo to the next. Yours arrived from Haiti on a slave ship."

"How do you know this?"

Kalila waved off the question. "The spirit inside your cane wants to speak to you."

Lexie raised the cane and reached out with her power to see what she could detect. She zeroed in on the pearl inlaid eyes, and the dragon blinked.

Overcome with astonishment, Lexie almost dropped her cane.

"He knows you feel him." Kalila came up to her. "The first moment you held him, he reached out to you and blessed you with his power."

"Who?" Lexie struggled to regain her composure by biting her lip. "Who blessed me?"

Kalila wore a smug grin. "Your staff was created by the mighty Damballah. He's the peace you feel radiating from your cane. He lives among the branches of the Sacred Tree. Your cane was carved from its branches."

"I thought the cane came from the Sang Noir Tree in Holt Cemetery."

"It was. The black blood tree and the tree of life are one in the same."

"How is that possible?"

"Everything is possible in magic. You should visit the Holt Cemetery to learn the truth for yourself. You will find answers and also questions."

Thunder boomed around her, and electricity charged the air. A thin mist poured from the swamps on the side of Kalila's home. It slinked over the dead grass and around the inhospitable plant life in her yard. When the malevolent mist reached the porch steps, goose bumps broke out on Lexie's forearms.

Since becoming mambo, she'd seen many strange things, but the blackness crowding in around her mind's eye while standing on Kalila's porch terrified her. She'd tapped into the dark force before when helping clients touched by evil but never had she been so caught up in its overwhelming embrace. She couldn't detect anything on the other side of it, but the tickling in her tummy hinted at something forbidden and wild waiting beyond.

Do you like what you feel?

The deep, smoky voice sent a shockwave of dread running through her.

"I rarely see people in my home, Mrs. Bennett."

Kalila's voice snapped her back from the images crowding her head.

"I keep appointments at my business address in the French Quarter."

"Please, call me Lexie." Her clammy hands held on to her cane, eager for its reassuring warmth.

Kalila shook her head. "I should call you mambo."

"Do you recognize me as mambo, Kalila? Or are you opposed to me?"

Her face held not a breath of emotion. "Come inside." Kalila motioned to the driveway. "Best not to talk about business outside. The swamp listens and remembers."

An overhead fixture flickered on, and a living room with red-velvet mahogany furniture came to life. On the hardwood floor in front of a stone hearth sat a tasteful coffee table made from the trunk of a huge cypress tree. Lexie eased her grip on her cane, settling down as she examined the ordinary room.

Indulging her curiosity about the furniture, she went to get a better look at the sofa, loveseat, and settee. The slight outward flare of the arms and the Cabriole legs with decorative carvings meant the furniture was not only antique but expensive.

"Georgian Chippendale. Haven't seen this in a while."

Kalila raised her black eyebrows, seeming impressed. "You know your furniture."

Lexie moved into the room. "I used to be an interior designer. Furniture was a passion of mine. I was mad for anything Louis XIV.

The exquisite oil paintings of green plantation fields and the hand-woven Oriental rug told her the priestess did very well selling her dark spells.

Kalila dropped the balled-up veil onto the sofa. "Titu didn't send you here to question my loyalty, did she?"

Lexie rubbed her arms, bothered by a chill in the room. Titu had warned her of Kalila's power, but she wasn't sure how much the strange woman knew about her gift … or lack of it.

"I need your help unraveling a problem with a dark spirit."

Kalila held up her index finger and waggled it from side to side. "No, the reason you're here is because you can't see anymore. You're scared. I can sense it."

36

She removed a clip from her head, and her long white hair fell around her shoulders. Her pasty skin and stark hair contrasted against her onyx eyes.

Lexie lowered her head, hiding her wide-eyed reaction.

"This is why I'm not mambo. To lead, to teach, to help, you must be like those you're meant to save." Kalila dropped the clip on the sofa. "The Queen knew what she was doing when she chose you. She selected someone who could build her religion up, not tear it to pieces."

Lexie raised her chin. "Do you know anything about the spirit who contacted me?"

"The spirit you saw is controlled by another. Someone very dark. The person hides from my sight, which means they're powerful, and that troubles me. Only one kind of spirit can hide from me—a duppy." Kalila set out across the room.

"What's a duppy?"

She stopped before the mantel. "The Obeah believe each soul has two spirits: one good, one bad. The good leaves the body when someone dies, but the bad is bound to it. It must stay with the body for three days and then it can join its good half, but if the body is burned or destroyed and not buried before the third day, the evil spirit is set free and can appear as a duppy."

"So, you think this malevolent spirit is a duppy?" Lexie held back from venting her frustration and put on a fake smile. "Is there anything else you can tell me?"

Kalila reached for two silver goblets sitting on the mantel. "The one controlling the spirit is angry. The young woman possessed—Katie Blackwell—was chosen for a reason." She carried the goblets back to Lexie. "Mrs. Blackwell conducted séances in her home and considered herself a proficient spiritualist. Unfortunately, she opened a door with her encounters; a door she went through when she died. The one controlling her has the key to that door."

Lexie squinted her eyes, feeling a little lost. "How do you know all this?"

Kalila handed her a goblet. "Kalfu speaks to me. He told me of Katie Blackwell's summoning of the dead."

Lexie took the goblet and then rested her baton juju against the sofa.

"Kalfu speaks to you? I didn't think the great voodoo spirits associated with mortals. Not directly, anyway."

Kalila set her goblet down on the end table next to her. "Kalfu is close to all who practice black magic. Those possessed by him display a dark fire in their eyes and shed black tears."

"Is he the one who seduced you with the darkness?"

Kalila tipped her head to the side. "You're curious about the darkness, aren't you?"

Uncomfortable, she fumbled with the goblet in her hand. How did she describe her interest without hinting at her eagerness to discover more about the other side of voodoo?

"I want to learn all I can about all forms of magic."

Kalila's faint smile changed the light in her eyes. They glinted with suspicion for a second, and then it was gone. She glided across the room to a cypress hutch.

She retrieved a bottle from a top shelf and carried it back to Lexie.

"I was very much like you when I began studying voodoo, but somewhere along the way, I lost my compassion. Handing myself over to Kalfu felt more right to me than wrong."

Kalila shook the bottle, and the liquid inside sparkled in the light.

"What's that?"

"Rum." Kalila cracked a red wax seal on the bottle. "Laced with gunpowder. It's Kalfu's favorite drink. We must each drink to honor his spirit and ask for his help."

Lexie searched for a label, but there wasn't any. "How can Kalfu help me?"

She lifted the bottle and tipped the lip over the edge of the goblet in Lexie's hand. "The person blocking your powers wants revenge. You took something from them. He will help you find out what."

Lexie was at a loss for words. What had she taken? She scanned her memories for any misstep, any injustice. Then she remembered the *haute défi*.

"Is it Renee Batiste?"

Kalila poured the contents of the bottle into her goblet. "Renee is dark, but she's too weak to block powers. No one fears her."

The liquid in her glass had an odd sheen.

Queasy at the notion of drinking gunpowder, she demanded, "Is this safe?"

Kalila snapped up her goblet from the end table and filled it with the rum. "To appeal to the spirits for help, you must honor them. They prefer songs, dances, symbols, and ...," she set the bottle down, "special beverages. To accept Kalfu's help, you must take him into you." She drained the goblet.

The liquid drizzled down her chin and neck, leaving its silvery gleam on her white skin. She placed the goblet on the end table and leveled her gaze on Lexie.

"Drink it. If you refuse, you'll offend the spirit, and he may hinder your search for answers."

Lexie wished she'd brought Magnus with her. She could almost hear his condescending voice in her ear urging her to put the drink down. But he wasn't there, and the tie binding them together had been severed. She wanted it back, and if consuming the nasty libation could reestablish her bond with her ghost then she had to take the chance.

She lifted the rum to her lips and wrinkled her nose at the pungent aroma. In three deep gulps, she emptied her drink.

She gagged as Kalila took the goblet from her hand.

"The taste is terrible, but it's an effective way to meet with the spirit."

The burn of the liquor hit her stomach. Lexie bent over, expecting to vomit.

Kalila regarded her as if waiting for something to happen. "How do you feel?"

Lexie stood upright, glad her nausea had passed. "I'm fine."

"It might take longer on you."

Out of the corner of her eye, the deep red velvet in the furniture bled from the cushions. The stains meandered across the hardwood floor to the fancy rug, seeping into its wool and pooling like the crime scene of a gruesome murder. The paintings on the walls moved, their colors undulating as if viewed underwater, rolling and swirling until the fancy landscapes disappeared for good. Smoke clogged the room, and the air grew thin.

"What's happening?" Lexie clasped her throat. "I can't breathe."

Kalila placed a cool hand on her forehead. "It's all perfectly normal. He's making you ready."

Lexie dropped to her knees, retching. "Ready for what?"

"The possession."

She lay on her back, floating on a bed of clouds. A thick, endless mist of shadows surrounded her. Everything reeked of rum and something sweet like gardenias. She didn't know if she was still in the swamps or some other place. Light came and went in flashes above her, but she could never discover the source. There was no moon, no sun, no stars, just an endless expanse of gray.

Her head throbbed. It was as if a drum played in a steady, unrelenting beat. Her eyelids begged to close, but she fought to keep them open. She had to stay awake, aware of her surroundings. An unsettling itch tweaked in her belly. She sensed she wasn't alone in the ghostly world.

"Lexie!"

The man's smoky voice sounded familiar, but she didn't see him. The last thing she remembered was drinking Kalila's God-awful concoction.

"Lexie Arden, can you hear me?"

She couldn't answer him. Every effort to move or breathe exhausted her. She wanted to crumple into a ball and sleep, drifting off to the rhythm pounding away in her head. What was happening?

"Be calm; the feeling will pass."

This voice wasn't Magnus's. The caring, soft lilt was unlike the ghost she had come to know.

"No harm will come to you."

The dense fog shifted and rolled in front of her creating an opening. She could not see anything ahead of her. No recognizable shapes or forms grounded her. There was just mist and bursts of light. The heaviness in her limbs eased, and she was able to sit up. She rubbed her temples and the thumping in her head dulled into a tolerable ache.

Through the parted mist ahead, the silhouette of a man appeared. He floated on a bed of clouds as if taking a stroll. He didn't have Magnus's stiff and formal gate or even his cane. There was something familiar about him, but she couldn't fathom what.

He came across as transparent and undefined. She could not make out any features, or distinguishing marks. He resembled one of the gray clouds around him. A lump of mist taking the shape of a man.

Her heartbeat sped up. She got to her feet and gulped back a dry swallow.

"Who are you?" she finally got out.

"A friend."

He came closer, and the mist creating his figure cleaved away like flesh from the bone. A solid form emerged. No longer transparent, his details took shape. With every step, he became more human.

Lexie tensed and curled inward, but the confusion in her mind cleared as if what she was witnessing made perfect sense.

"Where am I?"

"My world of shadows."

He came right up to her, and in his last few steps, his presence solidified. He resembled any regular guy she'd encounter on the street.

Lexie gasped and stepped back. If this was a ghost, it was like no other she'd encountered.

With tousled blond hair, he had a long face and a chiseled jawline and cheekbones. In faded jeans, with a white T-shirt clinging to his broad chest and thick arms, the confidence and power he exuded perturbed her, but it was his uncanny blue eyes that struck a chord—she'd seen them before.

"You asked for help, Lexie Arden. I'm here to assist you."

She rubbed her temples. "It was you at the hospital that day. In Mrs. Braud?"

"I told you to prepare." He snapped his fingers, and the fog disintegrated.

She stood in Kalila's living room, the red in the velvet

cushions shimmered under an ethereal light coming from above.

Lexie raised her head. There was no ceiling, only glorious blue skies.

"What are you?"

He went to an armchair and had a seat. He didn't have any shoes, and his unusually long toes confounded her.

"I'm not a what, but a who. I'm Kalfu. You already know what I do."

Lexie's clammy hands pressed against her chest. "You're … you're the devil."

"Devil, Satan, Kalfu … You may call me, Kal. Your world is too hung up on names, and not so much on meanings. I never did get that."

She held up her head, pushing back the bitter taste of terror in her mouth. "Why am I here?"

He sat back, his eyes taking in her figure like a cattleman analyzing a prized heifer. "When you drank from the cup my servant gave you, you took in my essence, making this meeting possible."

Lexie gritted her teeth. Kalila had tricked her.

"This is no trick," he said, reading her mind. "I wanted to meet you. I always like to associate with important people, especially a gifted mambo, such as yourself. The chosen of Marie Laveau. You've created quite a stir among my circle."

She never budged from her spot on the floor, not sure how to deal with the spirit. "You want something from me, don't you? You wouldn't have set up this meeting otherwise."

He clapped his hands. "My, you are clever."

"Tell me what you're after."

"Isn't it obvious? The darkness wants you." He stood, and the light in the room dimmed. "You've felt its desire since you first opened your soul to the spirit world. I can teach you how to use it, show you dimensions beyond your wildest dreams, and I can give you back your power."

He sauntered up to her. With his every step, the lights in the living room flickered. When he was inches away, the sweet aroma of him hit her. Like a field of freshly cut grass, he didn't come across as a sulfur-breathing demon. His aura was intoxicating, but the power he gave off, the electric atmosphere filling the room and controlling the lights, made her insides crawl.

"How … how can you restore my power? Do you know who took it?"

His blond brows lifted as his head tilted to the side. "This was an introduction. We'll see each other again, Lexie Arden, and will talk more about your powers."

In a ball of white light, Kalfu vanished. Lexie peered around the living room. The furniture remained, but the clouds above dropped and blanketed the room. They twisted together into a solid ceiling. Lexie could not tell where the wood beams of the structure began, and the clouds ended.

Slowly, she detected other things—the creak of the hardwood floor, mustiness blended with the humidity of the swamps, a ticking clock, the hum of some appliance, and the nudge of a firm cushion under her head.

"Did you see him?"

Seated next to her on the sofa, Kalila's white hair and dark eyes startled Lexie.

She bolted upright and placed her feet on the floor, grounded by the sensation. She took a moment to tap into the center of her being, searching for any hint of her power, but it wasn't there.

"Did you see Kalfu?"

Lexie wobbled, dizzy from her travels. "You drugged me?"

"All I gave you was rum and a pinch of gunpowder. The

vision was all the spirit's doing."

She rubbed her hand across her damp face. Her mouth tasted like sandpaper. "Why didn't you warn me?"

"You wouldn't have believed me. You needed to meet him."

Lexie got up from the sofa, itching to get out of the house. "I didn't meet anyone."

Kalila rose, folding her arms across her chest. "The spirit wants you to serve him. It's an honor. You should accept."

"I serve no spirit." Lexie marched toward the front door.

"You'll need Kalfu," Kalila asserted behind her. "You won't be anyone's mambo unless you can master the darkness and the light together. The other priestesses will never respect you until you do."

Lexie halted at the door. "But I was appointed by the Queen!"

Kalila's deep chortle filled the air. "There's no question you've won the job. Now you must learn how to keep it."

Chapter Five

Magnus waited outside the cottage, anxious for Lexie. Vulnerable because he was cut off from her, he grieved the loss of the connection they shared. He'd known the moment Katie appeared something had changed between them. Since then, the thoughts, emotions, and even the actions of the living left impressions in his head. In the beginning, he'd only connected with Lexie; now it appeared as if every person he encountered touched him in some beguiling way.

Confounded by what was happening, Magnus went to the green water at the swamps' edge along the side of the house. Raindrops created ripples on the stagnant water. Their concentric circles grew, intersecting in swells, releasing voices in their wake.

Magnus paced at the slimy green bank, attempting to make sense of the strange sounds. The cries of men, women, and children rose up and overwhelmed him.

"Save us!" a woman shrieked.

"Please, help me. I want to be free," a man's husky voice entreated.

"Take me away from this hell," a high-pitched wail begged.

The voices built around Magnus, crowding his ears, imploring him to rescue their tormented souls. He had never heard such noises from anyone.

A vision of his Frannie hurtling over the cliff's edge at Altmover Manor replayed in his head. The sound she made as she toppled to the rocks below resembled the pitiful cries of the spirits around him. Magnus closed his eyes, disgusted by the memory.

When his eyes opened, he scampered backward. In the boggy water, hundreds of bodies floated in various stages of decomposition. Arms, hands, legs, and torsos bobbed on the surface. The woman in black he'd seen with Lexie stood at the water's edge, calling to the dead to wake from their soggy tombs.

Horrified by the agony he saw on their contorted faces, Magnus wanted to obliterate the vision by returning to his shadowy realm, but he couldn't tear himself away. The images of body parts and broken souls held him captive as bitter waves of anger and anguish rolled off the water.

"Your master's in danger."

Magnus spun around.

A little girl in a long white nightgown trimmed in yellow ribbon stood next to him. Down the front, a stain of burnt red went all the way to her bare feet. She held a dirty teddy bear in her arms, but when she peered up at him, a gaping wound across her throat exposed the bone underneath.

Magnus didn't know if he could believe the phantom before him. Spirits had never reached out to him before. This was Lexie's realm. Why did he suddenly have her gift?

"Are you real?"

"Yes, sir. Very real, just like you."

He knelt down beside the child. "What is your name?"

"Mattie. I died in the swamp when I was six. The mistress has me enslaved to do her bidding."

He touched the nose of the teddy bear in her arms. His fingers passed through the toy. "What mistress?"

"The Lady La Fay. The one who called your master to her side."

Magnus examined her gray skin and sunken eyes. "I don't have a master."

She pointed to the cottage. "You're bound to the woman who went inside. She's your master and the one who controls your fate. We are all bound to those who work the dark realm. You'll see."

Magnus was about to question the child when her eyes went black and rolled back into her head.

Her mouth opened, and her lips stretched, expanding painfully beyond her chin and cheeks. The gaping, black hole spread and almost split her face in two. It covered her entire face, leaving only her flowing brown hair untouched.

Alarmed, he stood up. Then the child dropped the teddy bear and held her arms out to her sides.

He searched the swamps for an escape. He found the souls in the water, their dismembered bodies rising from the surface, coming toward him. A parade of legs, arms, torsos, and heads covered with algae and muck approached his spot on the shore.

He faced the girl, her toes floating above the boggy ground.

A soulless, wretched cackle came from the blackness covering her face.

"Welcome, Magnus Blackwell," a woman's whiny voice echoed from the darkness. "Welcome to my world."

Lexie rushed out of the Acadian cottage and stumbled down the slippery porch steps. She ran through the rain clutching the dragon cane in one hand and her car keys in the other. By the time she reached her car, her soaked white dress clung to her figure.

Her tightly pressed lips told Magnus it hadn't gone well.

"What happened?"

"Would you give it a fucking rest?" She shoved her cane into the front seat and tumbled into the car.

Magnus sat in the seat next to her and angrily thumped his cane on the floor. "What have I told you about cursing?"

Lexie sagged in her seat. "Sorry."

Her head rocked back. The act unsettled him. The wall existing between them offered no glimpses inside her, no moment of clarity. All he sensed was an unrelenting distance.

"What has made you so upset? This woman was supposed to help you."

"Well, she didn't. She insisted I drink some nasty tasting rum, and now I've got a bitch of a headache."

"Rum? Why did she want you to drink rum?"

"I don't know. But it gave me visions. Weird ones about a strange guy in the clouds." She ran her hand over her brow. "It's all blurry."

Magnus fingered his ghostly cane as he debated a way to tell her of his suspicions.

"What is going on, Lexie? I can't feel you anymore. The connection we shared was always there, pulsating inside me. Since I saw Katie, you are a million miles away."

Lexie started the car, avoiding his scrutiny. "That warning from Katie did something to me. My powers are muted, blocked … I can't feel anything, sense the world around me, or see the dead."

"And yet, it seems I have the power you've lost."

She pulled the car into the drive. "What are you talking about?"

"While you were inside with Kalila La Fay, the dead rose from the swamps—hundreds of them. Souls she keeps prisoner to do her bidding."

She hit the brakes. "You saw them? But you don't see other spirits. How can this be happening?"

Magnus rubbed his chin. "I've been asking myself the same question. The only explanation is because of our connection, I believe your ability came to rest in me. I have felt and seen things I can't explain, but they're the same things you once told me about. Perhaps this transference is a way to keep your power safe until you can tap into it again."

She wiped the droplets of rain from her face while a grim line spread across her lips. She did not speak for the longest time, her focus remaining on the road ahead. Then she let up on the brake.

"I'm relieved to know my power is with you." The car eased forward. "Tell me more about these spirits. What did they say to you?"

"It seems your hostess likes to collect the dead. There are bodies submerged in the swamps around her home. She controls their spirits. Uses them to do her bidding, and they're not too happy about it."

Lexie stopped the car at the end of the drive. "Kalila La Fay does this? Are you sure?"

"I could see their deformed bodies rising from the waters and hear their cries for help. You need to stay away from her. She's dangerous."

Lexie gripped the steering wheel. The only sound inside the car was the rain plinking on the roof.

"When I was under the spell of the rum she gave me, I met a

voodoo spirit named Kalfu."

He studied her profile, daunted by her pensive stare. "Did he say anything to you?"

"He promised to restore my powers, if I open myself up to him."

Magnus was all too familiar with what awaited those who gave into the lure of wickedness.

"Don't let him in. If you do, you'll never be free of him. Let my life, my deeds, be a warning to you. If you give yourself to such a detestable spirit, you will end up like me."

"I won't consider it until I have to."

"Then let's find a way to make sure it doesn't come to that."

Her lower lip trembled. "What if I don't get my powers back? What will I do? This is my calling. The idea of living life this way makes me want to …"

The tears building in her eyes destroyed him. In the months they had been together, he'd seen her endure so much, but the abject hopelessness confronting him was new.

"There has to be a way to figure this out," he said, sounding upbeat. "You solved the mystery of the dragon cane; you can tackle this, dear girl."

"Then all I had to contend with was you and Jacob O'Connor." She stomped on the accelerator and the car jerked forward. "This is something completely different."

Magnus raised his head as they traveled along the narrow road. "Whatever it is, we'll solve it, together."

Furious black clouds, fat with rain, hung low over the French Quarter as Lexie's car cruised along Chartres Street.

Once safely in the private parking lot Will rented, thunder reverberated through the narrow streets. She climbed from her car and checked the sky. A raindrop landed in her eye. Within seconds, heavy droplets smudged the sidewalk around her.

She clasped her baton juju and covered her head with her gallon-sized purse.

"It's like the rain is following us."

"You should carry an umbrella," Magnus scolded.

Her wet white dress molded to her slim figure by the time she ducked beneath the cover of a jutting balcony. The french doors of her shop, Mambo Manor, were just ahead.

"I'm not sure it would help."

A dazed look overtook Magnus's face. He stood on the sidewalk as people dodging the rain passed through his image. His eyes appeared glued to something; his mouth spread into a grimace.

"What is it?"

He said nothing but nodded ahead.

She checked the open doors of the shops neighboring hers and examined the laughing faces of tourists running in the rain.

"I don't see anything."

He stared at Lexie with a quizzical wonder. "You can't see them?"

"Who are you talking about? The people on the street?"

"No, the ghosts." He motioned to the street, the storefronts, the sidewalk. "They're everywhere."

Lexie squinted at the façade of her building but couldn't detect a single spectral being.

Wispy creatures climbed out from the stucco on the buildings, floated in front of doorways, and drifted along the street. Dressed in an array of clothing covering the gambit of the city's three hundred years, he couldn't find the words to describe the wonders unfolding in front of him.

A woman in the yellow damask regalia of a pampered southern belle dipped her head to him and flashed a flirty smile. A column of men, sabers at their sides and red-sashes across their gray uniforms marched down the center of the street. A dark-skinned woman in a slip of a petticoat strutted past him. A man in a long black coat with high brown boots chased behind her. To his right, a child in rags held up a brush and shoe paste, his brown eyes sunken, and his hands and neck sported black burns. When he shifted his head, Magnus cringed at the burnt flesh on his face.

"You wanna shoe shine, mister? I can polish them boots up real good."

"Ah, no, thank you."

The boy's black, charred lips disappeared when he smiled.

"Bad things are comin', mister."

In front of the door to Lexie's shop, an ethereal being manifested. The smoke thickened and congealed into a solid shape. Color plumped slender arms, and then an oval face dawned. In the same stunning gold dress she'd worn on that fateful night, Katie beckoned to him.

Incapacitated by disbelief, Magnus waited as Katie floated up to him, her gold slippers hovering above the sidewalk. She giggled, her blue eyes lit from within, and the bubbly demeanor he'd grown addicted to when they'd first courted blossomed before him.

"Are you happy to see me, Magnus?"

He longed to reach out to her. Then he remembered the meeting in the workshop and the bliss of seeing her again tarnished. His frosty demeanor returned.

"Why are you here, my dear?"

Her bright eyes dimmed, and her happy glow vanished. She paled as a shadow rose between them. The ominous shade took no shape or form.

Magnus analyzed the mass with his newfound ability. The vile, blind rage emanating from it was a bottomless black hole. It was similar to what he felt from the rotting corpses of the spirits trapped in the swamps, but the intensity reminded him of the violent nor'easters he'd experienced at his beloved Altmover Manor.

Then the umbra twisted into a slender tornado. The compacting funnel arched over Katie, and as her head rose to meet the phenomenon, she opened her mouth to scream. But the mist poured into her mouth before she could utter a single peep. Her eyes widened, her back arched, and her fists clenched as she filled with the unearthly entity.

Frantic, Magnus wanted to call for help, but to whom? They were ghosts among the living and beyond saving.

Katie's head bent all the way back, and her lips stretched into a gaping yawn. Sickened beyond measure at her torture, he prayed for the hideous display to end.

"Tell your mistress I will have my vengeance." The nasty voice coming from the black void in her mouth wasn't Katie's. "I will destroy what she loves, and make her followers despise her. You fool! Eternity at your fingertips and you put your faith in a silly girl."

A diabolical laugh rang out. The cackle sounded familiar to Magnus. He'd heard that laugh before.

Chapter Six

The rain continued, and by late afternoon water collected in the French Quarter streets. The flooding chased away the tourists and Lexie's evening appointments canceled. The other shops on Royal Street closed early, and she decided to do the same.

Once upstairs in her apartment, she settled on her sofa, eager for a few moments of peace. The pelting rain against her windows nudged her eyelids closed. Perhaps a short nap before she had to prepare dinner. It might take away the uncomfortable edginess plaguing her.

She instantly found herself in the foyer of Altmover Manor.

Leftover glasses and dinnerware from a party lay strewn about the foyer. A massive floral arrangement of white roses and pink carnations covered a round table in the center of the room. Paintings of landscapes hung on the walls, and the lotus-shaped sconces burned bright with flickering flames.

"What am I doing here?"

On the second-floor landing, a woman materialized. She picked up the dragon cane.

Emily Mann, in a green gown gathered at the shoulder in a bow, descended the marble inlaid black steps. The sinister sneer on her thin lips added a ghoulish glow to her sallow complexion. Her glasses and mousy brown hair shimmered in the foyer candlelight.

"I'll show you, Jacob O'Connor."

Emily's cackle carried throughout the great house.

The apparition approached Lexie but never registered her presence. She passed through her and then, as if blown by a single puff of wind, the candles on the walls went out. With a bang, the leaded-glass front doors flew open, and daylight flowed across the white marble floor. Workmen dressed in beige coveralls clamored into the home, their heavy boots tromping the floor. They carried boxes, brown paper, and string. Emily Mann stood by the staircase and directed them to different corners of the home. In a dowdy black dress with a collar of black lace hugging her slender neck, she shouted orders. She stood by as furniture, paintings, clocks, tables, and box after box packed with mementos left the home in the arms of the men.

The images came and went like snapshots. Lexie heard Emily's soft voice as she paced the foyer, banging the cane on the floor as if to command the attention of the workmen. When darkness seeped through the doors, Emily set the bolt and headed up the stairs.

A series of sunrises and sunsets poured through the glass doors, Emily Mann came down the grand staircase dressed in black and carrying the baton juju. She floated across the marble floor and then disappeared down the hallway, the tapping of her cane echoing throughout the house. At night, she would climb the steps once more; sometimes she would stop at the top of the stairs, staring at the herculean chandelier with a smug grin. Each day blended into the next, and the sounds of her thudding through the home remained constant.

Lexie was unable to change her vantage point in the vision. She longed to see Altmover Manor before the ravages of time had taken their toll.

Wooden crates bursting with straw and stamped with addresses in England, France, and Egypt accumulated in the foyer. The packages amassed in tall stacks until Emily finally opened them.

The fading afternoon light twinkled through the front doors as she unpacked each of the boxes, and piled the contents on the floor.

Books, dozens of them. Lexie peered over the woman's shoulder and read the titles.

The Spirits of Voodoo: A Compendium of Tales, by K. Bernos, *Ritual Magic and Voodoo Lore*, by G. Voss, and *Famous Voodoo Queens, Priestesses, and Practitioners* by H.E. Llamos.

"I'll be damned."

They were the same books Lexie had found in the box from the Mount Desert Island Historical Society.

Emily Mann sat on the floor of the foyer in her long black dress and leafed through the books.

"This is how you got the collection," Lexie mumbled to the image from the past.

She read spells out loud from the books. The enthusiasm in Emily's mealy brown eyes worried Lexie.

Was this the moment when she went mad?

Time sped up, and while still in the foyer, Lexie caught glances of Emily Mann moving through Altmover Manor. She aged—her mousy brown hair grayed, and her dependence on the support of the baton juju grew more noticeable.

An invisible wind rose beneath her feet and carried Lexie into the living room. She neared the door and spotted the glowing fire in the hearth. In a white and peach floral chair set in front of the fireplace, an old woman sat. On closer inspection, Lexie identified Emily Mann. Her face had sagged with age, her hair had gone white, and her once stout figure appeared frail.

The old woman smiled as she gazed up at the portrait of Magnus Blackwell above a mantel decorated with carved rosettes.

"I wonder if you will ever know all I've done for you."

Her voice weak, she wasn't the assertive woman Lexie had seen directing the moving men.

"Will you ever know the sacrifices I have made? Will you care? Probably not." She laughed, and then a fit of coughing overtook her.

She settled back, out of breath. "I did it all for you, Magnus. Maybe in that next world, you'll notice me. I hope so. I wish I could have told you once how much I loved you." Emily closed her eyes.

Lexie waited by her chair, watching the rise and fall of her chest, and her pity for the woman's life brought a tear to her eye.

Then she slumped over, and the hand resting on her lap slipped to the floor.

"Have you seen enough?"

Lexie backed away, stunned by the voice resonating around her.

Emily Mann's spirit climbed out of her corpse. She wore the green gown from the first time Lexie had seen her on the staircase after Jacob's death. Young, energetic, and with a familiar blackness in her eyes, she glared at Lexie.

"It was a sad life, don't you think?"

Her face lengthened, her hair got lighter, and the dress she wore shrunk.

"You don't want to end up like her, do you, Lexie Arden?"

Her face and figure dissolved into the blond haired, blue-eyed Adonis, Kalfu.

No longer in jeans, he bedazzled in a dark blue double-breasted suit.

"Women love a man in a suit." He ran his hand down the front of his jacket. "What do you think?"

She gestured to the living room. "Why show me this? Why show me that sick woman's life?"

"She belonged to me, just as you will, soon."

Kalfu's laughter burned her ears. The living room vibrated with the sound, and then everything changed.

The walls paneled in a rich oak with rosettes sprinkled along the seams became soft peach plaster with posters of New Orleans. Vines of roses circling the border of the ceiling dulled and withered. Elegant white and peach floral furnishings morphed into Lexie's green sofa, dinged round coffee table, and entertainment center. In the hearth, the fire died, and the portrait of Magnus contracted into the framed wedding photo of her and Will she kept on her sealed fireplace mantel.

She spun around taking in her apartment. "What did you do?"

"Wake up."

She cupped her hands over her ears, not wanting to listen to his voice anymore.

"Lexie!"

Her eyes flew open.

Will arched over her with an apprehensive frown rumpling his face.

"You scared me, baby." He sat down next to her on the sofa, stroking her thigh. "I've been trying to wake you for several minutes."

Relief quieted her galloping heart "I must have dozed off."

Will lifted her chin. "How long have you been asleep?"

"I'm not sure. What time is it?"

He checked his stainless watch. "A little after nine."

She swung her legs off the sofa. "I had the weirdest dream."

"No wonder." He snapped up a book on the coffee table. "If you read stuff like this before sleeping. *The Spirits of Voodoo: A Compendium of Tales.*" He snorted. "Where did you dig up this one?"

"I don't own a copy of—?" She shut her mouth. How did the book get there from her dream? "Ah, how could I have forgotten about that?" She sheepishly smiled. "I was reading a bit about the spirits of voodoo—doing my homework. I've still got a lot to learn."

He kissed her cheek and then stood. "Don't you have enough spirits in your life?"

She touched the book, not sure how it got there. "You would think so, but the voodoo spirits aren't like Magnus."

Will undid his yellow tie as he went to their bedroom door. "How are they then? These spirits."

After a brief stretch, she followed him into the bedroom. "They're part of the voodoo pantheon. Spirits control a variety of elements and are responsible for certain events. Kalfu, for instance, is a spirit credited with chaos and destruction."

He had a seat on their king-sized bed, which took up most of the cramped bedroom. "Is he any relation to Magnus?" He kicked off his loafers. "If you ask me, your spirit is pretty good at creating chaos wherever he goes."

Her hip against their antique Queen Anne dresser—a wedding present from her mother—she gave him a glassy stare. "Magnus isn't so bad. He saved your life, after all. You should get to know him."

BOUND

With a humph, he stood from the bed and unzipped his pants. "I'm not the Mambo of New Orleans." His trousers dropped to the floor.

His blue boxers made her smile. "Pity. Maybe you'd make more headway than me."

He kicked his pants away and unbuttoned his shirt. "What are you talking about?"

At the bed, she sat down. "I have my first council meeting next week. I'm afraid of going. What if they don't accept me as mambo?"

Will tossed his shirt to a chair already piled high with their clothing. "Lexie, you were chosen by Marie Laveau to lead the voodoo faithful of this city. I was there, remember? There are times I can't explain what happened, but it did. The people on your voodoo council will listen to what you have to say, and they'll respect you."

"Respect me?" She flopped back on the bed. "I'm beginning to wonder."

He climbed on top of her and curled his arms around her. "Well, I respect you. As the mother of my children, I sort of have to."

"I'm not the mother of your children yet."

He nuzzled her neck. "When are we going to do something about that?" His kisses explored her chest. "With my firm taking off and you settled in as mambo, all we need is a baby to make everything perfect."

Perfect? She reached for him, clinging to him, hoping to smother her distress. She had no powers, a voodoo spirit wanting to blacken her soul, and all right before her first big meeting as mambo. She couldn't imagine being pregnant, too.

"Perhaps it's not meant to be for—"

"Of course it's meant to be." He sat up and rested on his

elbow while his free hand pushed up the hem of her dress. "We have the life we want, and a kid would only add to our happiness."

"But we have no room for a baby."

His hand slipped inside her thighs. "I got word on a condo today. It's in the Warehouse District. Close to the Quarter for you, a few blocks from the business district for me. It's three bedrooms and has loads of space. We could put an offer in and be moved in by mid-October. What do you say?"

She pushed his hand away and sat up. "It's not a good time. The shop's in a slump, with all the rain and bad weather the last few days, I've had no customers, and my private sessions have dried up. Then there's the council meeting and whatever drama that brings. There's too much going on right now for me to throw moving into the mix."

He laid back on the bed. "It sounds to me as if you're putting voodoo ahead of us."

"That's not fair. You know how uncertain I feel about my role. I've been struggling to understand what's expected of me in a religion I know little about. People look to me for answers, and most of the time I have no idea what I'm doing."

He traced her chin with his finger. "I thought all those special powers you got at your initiation were supposed to help you."

She sat back on her knees and dropped her head with shame. "I lost my powers."

Will sat up. "Lost them? How?"

Her lower lip trembled. "When the spirit I told you about showed up—Magnus's wife, Katie—and then … poof."

"Is Magnus behind this?"

"No." Lexie frowned at him. "I don't think he is, directly."

"But indirectly?" Will wrapped her in his arms and kissed her forehead. "I'm sorry about your powers, but you have to admit, ever since he came into our lives it's been one disaster after another."

She scrambled out of his embrace and stood from the bed. "It's not his fault!"

Will sighed and climbed out after her. "Then why do you and I keep paying the price for his past mistakes?"

She didn't have an answer. Fate had tied her to him, and his problems had become hers, but if she'd never become bound to Magnus, would she have been happy?

"But if he never made those mistakes, never haunted Altmover Manor, never ended up with me, where would I be?"

Will's arms went around her. "You'd be happy with me, in Boston with a baby in your arms and a house in the city. Isn't that what you always wanted?"

Was it? Lexie would never be sure again. Her eyes had opened when she entered the mysterious world of voodoo. She'd never been so alive, and the idea of returning to the life she'd lived before left her empty.

The same satisfaction she experienced with her calling, had frustrated Will. His traditional ways grounded him. She didn't need special powers to know Will was eager to have a normal life. Sooner rather than later, her wants would clash with his.

"So much has changed for us. I believe for the better." She nestled against his chest. "Let me unravel what happened to my powers and put everything in order. Then we can find a new place."

"Don't take too long. I don't want to spend the rest of my life wishing we had lived instead of waiting for the right time to start living." He dropped his boxers.

He threw his arms around her waist and smothered her in a deep kiss. She took in the aroma of his faint cologne blended with the smell of his skin and her spirits rallied. The touch of his rough hands, the way he teased kisses down the right spots on her neck, used to chase away her worries, but this time Will's magic wasn't powerful enough to make her forget her visit to the swamp, her powers, or even the relentless rain.

His kiss deepened, and her desire died.

A baby? Was she ready? How could she be a mambo and a mother?

While he wrestled her dress over her head, Lexie ached to tell him to stop. She'd embraced the idea of motherhood in the past. Now it struck her as foolish.

He tossed her clothes to the floor and lifted her into his arms, then, as he gave her a long kiss, he carried her to the bathroom.

She kicked her legs in protest. "I don't need a shower."

"Who said anything about a shower? It's baby making time."

Panic erupted in her belly. "Put me down!"

His smile crumbled, but he never let her go. "What's wrong?"

She wiggled out of his embrace. "Have you thought this through? I tell you I've lost my powers and all you can say is let's have a baby."

His posture stiffened. "But we want a baby, right?"

"Yes, we want a baby." She refused to meet his eye. "Just not right now. Until I find out who or what has taken my powers, I won't be able to focus on anything else. And if I don't get my powers back, we might have to leave this city. I couldn't stay here and not be mambo. I've never felt so fulfilled. I would be devastated if I wasn't able to serve my followers."

He blew out a long breath and lowered his head. "If that's what you want."

Desperate to appease him, she flung her arms around his

neck. "I want a baby with you. All I'm asking for is a little time."

He unwound her arms; the pain of rejection in his eyes formed icicles on her heart. "I married you, Lexie. Not the Mambo of New Orleans, and not the woman who sees the dead. I can't wait forever for you to figure out what's more important— me or your job."

Without a second glance, he marched into the bathroom and slammed the door.

The *thud* sent a shudder through Lexie. She bit her lower lip not wanting to cry, but the sadness weighing on her made her eyes tear up.

She snapped up a sweat suit from under Will's shirt on the chair and wrestled it on. She tied off her pants and ran from the bedroom to the balcony entrance.

Outside, she breathed in the night air, seeking solace from her raging emotions. Raindrops covered her face, and the urge coursing through her veins to run away from her home, her husband, and her life escalated to a full boil.

It wasn't until she descended the back steps to the courtyard, her burning hunger to leave fizzled out. Shaking her head, she hugged the wooden post supporting her balcony. When she could not take it anymore, she let go of her tears.

Magnus observed from his world as she cried. Her sobbing twisted his soul and brought back a thousand memories of the other women he had made cry. He'd hoped to be immune to the sound as a ghost—he wasn't.

He pushed the veil of his world aside and stepped through the mist. He brushed his hand against her cheek and moved a tendril of honey blonde hair from her eyes.

Lexie gasped, uncoiled her arms from the post, and wiped her face.

"I didn't know you were here."

He sighed at the red rimming her eyes. "I heard you crying, and I came."

She sniffled and wiped her nose with the back of her hand.

"You should carry a handkerchief, dear girl."

Lexie's gruff laughter filtered through the courtyard. "In my moment of need, I can always count on you to tell me what I'm doing wrong."

The harsh comment upset him. He'd never heard such malice from her. She'd teased and joked with him, but his Lexie had never been ugly.

"Did you argue with Will?"

She peered up at the stormy clouds. "Do you think it will ever stop raining?"

"Before you lost your powers, I would have known what's bothering you. I don't like having to guess."

Her shoulders sagged and warily glanced back at him. "Yes, we had a fight. He wants a baby. I want to wait."

"Ah, I see." He touched his ascot tie, searching for something to comfort her. "I can't say I know your husband very well, but it seems to me pressing for children when you are in a crisis seems unreasonable."

"Did you ever want children?"

The question sparked a memory for him. "I'd never entertained the idea of children until I met Katie."

Lexie hugged herself. "She wanted kids?"

He smiled as he remembered a morning shortly after arriving at Altmover Manor following his whirlwind honeymoon. "Katie professed a desire to become pregnant early on in our marriage.

66

The first time she broached the subject was right after our honeymoon. We were taking breakfast in the dining room when she announced she intended to get pregnant right away and fill our home with several children."

Lexie's voice softened. "What did you say?"

"I think the color must have drained from my cheeks because she asked me why I had gone pale, and then I pushed my plate to the side." He shook his head. "The notion of one child, let alone a houseful, terrified me."

"Do you believe you would have made a good father?"

Magnus stiffened at the thought. "I never had a good example in that department, at least from my father. He considered children a nuisance."

"You were afraid you would turn into him. I get it." Her heavy sigh lingered in the courtyard. "I've spent my whole life trying not to be my mother."

He softly chuckled at the notion of Lexie turning into the abrasive Angela. "Yes, we fear becoming our parents most of all. I used to imagine holding my child. Then Reynolds Blackwell would pop into my head. I would hear his voice, relive the cold disregard he gave me, and my resolve not to be a father would harden."

"You're not your father, Magnus."

"And yet, with every passing day of my mortal life, I became more like him. I hurt Katie just as he hurt my mother. In the end, my father and I were all that remained of our family, and we could not stand to be in the same room." He paused and reflected on all the years he'd spent angry with his father. "Perhaps it's a good thing I died when I did. I spared any son of mine the same fate."

"In time, you would have strived to be different from your father."

Pictures of his atrocities floated across his mind. "If you say so."

She gave him a slight smile. "I'll see you in the morning."

Lexie went back up the back steps to her balcony, and he waited until the door to her apartment closed.

"Poor girl, you never thought it was going to be this difficult." He willed the clouds from his world to roll in and cover the courtyard. "Neither did I."

Chapter Seven

In a brighter mood, and humming a jazzy tune, Lexie descended the winding spiral staircase built into the back of her apartment. At the base of the steps, she entered the modest kitchen in her shop.

With a few green cabinets, and a small fridge set below the tiled countertop, the room barely accommodated two people. The sultry aroma of coffee hung in the air encouraged her to set her baton juju against the counter and grab a mug.

"You seem better this morning."

Magnus appeared next to the counter, eyeballing the coffeemaker.

"Ah, yes. Thank you for last night." She adjusted her red turban. "You helped me."

"What else is a spirit guide for?" He nodded to the full coffeepot. "Pour yourself a cup so I can live vicariously through you. I do so miss my coffee and chicory."

She reached for the cabinet above her head. "What else do

you miss? You never mention anything."

He raised his nose and gave her his best condescending sneer. "I'm dead, lamenting anything I enjoyed in life is a futile occupation."

"You must have loved something other than coffee." She selected a mug and lifted the coffeepot. "We've shared so much, but there are times I feel I hardly know you."

"Who are you talking to?"

In her long white cotton dress, and holding an empty coffee mug, Nina stood in the arched entrance to the room.

"I'll work on those questions for you." Magnus snickered and faded away.

Lexie put on a broad smile, determined to hide any hint of trouble. "I was just going over my day."

Nina raised an eyebrow. "I thought maybe you were talking to another one of your ghosts."

She replaced the pot on the warmer. "I only speak to the dead when I'm with a client."

"Could have fooled me." Nina approached the counter. "You look wiped."

"The storms kept me up." Lexie sipped from her mug.

"Just the storms?"

The question made her stomach churn. She'd hired Nina to run her shop, but that didn't mean she trusted her. She couldn't afford for anyone to find out about her lost powers. It would ruin her. With the council meeting coming up, and the constant obligations of her clients, she needed to find a way to get her ability back and fast.

Nina filled her mug with coffee. "I read somewhere the ability to communicate with the dead is stronger during a storm. Perhaps that's why you couldn't sleep; the dead were keeping you up."

Beads of sweat sprouted on Lexie's upper lip. "The dead never keep me up at night; people do."

"I see. Then Will kept you up last night." Nina blew on her coffee. "Why didn't you just say so?"

How could she respond without adding fuel to the fire? She had to watch what she said to her assistant.

Coffee mug in hand, she was about to walk through the archway when she came to a halt. The gray Maine coon cat lay stretched out on the small, circular table in the corner of the kitchen.

"What is the cat doing in here?"

Nina walked up next to her. "Damballah? He always hangs out with me in the morning."

"You named him after the voodoo spirit?"

Nina's smile warmed her eyes. "I can think of no fitting name. Damballah protects our shop bringing peace and balance. The same way he oversees the universe."

The mention of peace and balance made Lexie glance back at her baton juju leaning against the counter. She grasped the dragon-head handle, and the flow of energy passed from the cane to her.

The cat's fluffy gray tail pounded on the table.

"He's waiting for his milk." Nina went to the counter and set her coffee to the side. "I always give him some in the morning."

Lexie approached the cat. "Is it a him or a her?"

"It's a him." Nina opened the small refrigerator.

Lexie slowly reached out, hoping not to scare him. She touched his silky fur, and he purred.

"He likes you." Nina set a saucer of milk next to Damballah. "And he doesn't like just anyone."

Lexie rested her cane against the table not far from where the cat lay. She used both hands to stroke the feline as it stood and

71

sniffed the milk.

"There was a cat at Altmover Manor—the house I told you about. He looks very similar to the one I knew there."

"Cats do have nine lives. He could be spending his with you."

Lexie watched the cat lap up the milk. "Not unless this guy has got frequent flyer miles to get him here from Maine."

The cat stopped drinking and sat back on its haunches. Its green eyes stared at the cane.

Intrigued, Lexie wondered if the rumors about animals and their psychic abilities were true.

The staff moved along the edge of the table. It wasn't much, but the motion spooked her. She was about to reach for her cane when it lurched closer to the cat. The dragon handle came to rest within inches of Damballah.

"See?" Nina picked up her coffee mug, appearing unimpressed. "Damballah approves."

Lexie stepped back, troubled by the event. "The cat or the spirit in my cane?"

"Maybe they're one in the same."

The cat leapt from the table, knocking the empty saucer to the floor. The noise of the dish shattering into pieces made both women flinch. Lexie's baton juju slipped from the edge of the table and landed next to the broken remains of the saucer.

"Damn!" Nina knelt to pick up the shards.

Lexie stooped down to help her. "It's no big deal."

"No, it's a sign. Damballah isn't happy."

The towering oaks along City Park Avenue spread their

welcoming branches to hold back the steady drizzle from cars and pedestrians. The blacktopped street glistened in the light from automated lamps switched on by the ever-present cloud cover. People darted in the rain, some with umbrellas and some without. Most hurried toward the community college located next door to an old cemetery.

"Are you sure this is a good idea?" Magnus asked from the seat next to her in the car. "I know you're curious about the origins of your cane, but traipsing around Holt Cemetery alone is not what I would consider safe."

She scanned the street for the cemetery entrance. "There may be a connection between Holt Cemetery and my missing powers."

"Or perhaps Renee Batiste is behind the loss of your ability. She could be hiding her true intentions by showing the world a confused, weak woman, while on the inside remaining resolute. She had the power to control Remi. What else is she capable of?"

Lexie found the unmarked cemetery entrance and drove down a slender asphalt road hugging the side of a packed student parking lot for the college.

"I don't see it. Renee is weak, a hermit, almost a joke in the community."

Magnus nodded ahead to the end of the road. "Appearances can be deceiving."

She pulled the car up to an archway welded from black iron with *Holt Cemetery* weaved into the metal. No creamy marble statues marked the entrance, no high wall of white plaster outlined the perimeter. There wasn't even a parking lot. The open field beyond the gate had no high mini-mausoleums or rows of exotic tombs—only brown grass speckled with occasional headstones.

"This is sad."

"This is the way things were." Magnus tugged at his jacket sleeves. "The poor blacks of the city were given this lot of land to avoid having their funerals pass through the center of town."

Lexie ached for the people buried in the desolate field. "Good God. How cruel."

"God has nothing to do with the cruelty of man. He's simply a witness."

Once inside the open gate, a guardhouse covered with yellow boards proudly displayed a shiny brass plaque designating the cemetery a historic landmark. Lexie searched for a guard in the window of the small house, but no lights came on, and no one waved them through.

She continued on a slick, narrow asphalt road weaving through the cemetery. They didn't pass any cars or people.

The wipers drummed frantically to clear the rain from her windshield as she got an up-close view of the graves.

Square plots outlined in either rickety wooden fences, uneven stone walls, or small iron railings dotted the landscape. Some headstones were awkwardly set into the ground, slanting to the side, others had fallen over completely. Only a few were stone; most were nothing more than boards of wood with a name and date of death carved or hastily painted on them. Many of the plots didn't have a marker. Instead, tokens and family mementos adorned the graves.

On one a rusted bicycle stood upright without any tires. Another had naked plastic dolls covered with muck and faded plastic red and purple daisies. Bleached flamingo lawn ornaments stood guard over one grave, while farther along, broken plastic lawn chairs sat next to a headstone made of plywood. One gravesite had no marker, only a rusted and battered barbeque grill.

Unprotected from the elements, the items left behind had

74

weathered and scattered about the grounds. Against the backdrop of the dreary skies, the simplicity of the grave markers, and the poverty of the people buried there broke Lexie's heart.

"I feel I know more about the people buried here than in the other cemeteries with their elaborate stone structures." Lexie came to a crossroad and stopped the car. "Do tourists come here?"

"Doubt it. They come for the food, jazz, carnival atmosphere, or architecture. History doesn't appeal to many of them." Magnus pointed to the road on the right. "What we are looking for is up ahead."

Toward the back of the cemetery, they stopped in front of a towering oak tree with heavy limbs sagging to the ground.

Lexie wiped the fog building on her windshield. "Is it our Sang Noir tree?"

"There's only one way to find out." Magnus faded from the front seat.

Lexie opened her door. "I hate when he does that."

An inhospitable cold breeze wrapped around her as she climbed from the car. The sensation made her want to leave the desolate cemetery far behind. She pushed on, wiping the raindrops from her face as she stepped off the street and onto the brown grass.

An overwhelming sense of hostility consumed her as soon as the soles of her shoes touched the grass. The cane in her hand hummed. The intense vibration shimmied up her arm and spread, warding off the malice around her and taking away her unease.

The tip of her cane lifted off the ground and pointed toward the giant tree, shaking as if excited to be home.

This must be the place.

She headed out beneath the black skies to the top of a slight rise covered with old stone grave markers to the only tree in the vast cemetery.

The gnarled, leafless, and monstrous woody plant waited before her. Intertwined light and dark colored bark covered a massive trunk riddled with gouges and scars composed of letters and wiggly lines. All the markings appeared manmade and blackened with age. The maze of twisting limbs crisscrossed and linked together making it impossible to discern where one branch began, and another ended.

Along the ground, leading to the tree, a hodgepodge of graves required some careful maneuvering. Enamored with the headstones dating back to 1879, she almost tripped twice on ugly roots spreading between the markers.

Deep puddles of black water greeted her as she neared the edge of the tree's massive reach. The interlocking array of bent branches above her head offered a respite from the rain, but the ground beneath her was slick with green algae and ruts of mud, making it an arduous trek to the top of the rise.

"This may not have been such a good idea."

Magnus surfaced under a thick branch holding up his marbled dragon cane against the matching tree bark.

Distracted, he squinted at the cemetery behind her.

Lexie edged closer, dismayed by his change in color. "Is something wrong?"

Beyond, standing in the downpour of cold rain, hundreds of people—men, women, and children—posed atop the field of graves. They faced the mighty tree and stared at Magnus with lifeless eyes as if waiting for him to command them into action. In an array of clothes ranging from fine long gowns fashioned in

BOUND

another century, top hats and tuxedos, to rags barely concealing their nudity, the outfits represented several different eras, but the people remained the same—all had dark skin, gaping mouths, and sunken faces displaying the same hopeless mask.

A cacophony of voices rose around him, but the lips of the dead never moved.

"Save us," a woman's voice shrieked.

"Make him send us on our way," a man bellowed in a baritone.

"Ask the spirit to free us," a child pleaded in his ear.

Their souls cried out, deafening Magnus, and forcing him to drop his cane and cover his ears.

The voices became a jumbled mess in his head. He concentrated and tried to tell them he was one of them—an equal, but the dead of Holt Cemetery would not listen.

Lexie darted in front of him. She said something he could not hear. Magnus attuned himself to her voice, anxious to catch her words.

"What is it? What do you see?"

He backed into a tree limb, shaking with relief as her voice carried above the cries of the dead.

"They're all here, unable to leave." He waved to the cemetery. "The dead are imprisoned in their graves."

He retrieved his cane just as the rain picked up, depositing heavy droplets on the ground. A rumble of thunder echoed across the field followed by a ribbon of lightning cutting a path through the sky. The souls of the cemetery never faltered and continued to call to him.

Lexie turned to the mass of graves. "Why are they trapped?"

"Because The Baron will not let them leave."

The booming, grave voice of a man came from behind him. Magnus spun around to confront the intruder.

77

At the back of the tree, where the thicker branches clumped together and blocked out most of the light, several slanted headstones rested amid a quagmire of knotty roots. On a branch dipping to rest right above one of the old stone markers, a man reclined on a bed of green moss.

In a top hat, black tailcoat, and dark glasses, he had cotton plugs stuffed up his nose. With brown skin and a very tall frame, Magnus wasn't sure if he was a spirit or human.

"Can you see him?"

"Yep." Lexie squinted at the strange creature. "But he isn't human."

"If you can see him, he must be human." Magnus feared what would happen if she stayed in the cemetery. The atmosphere around them wasn't friendly. "You need to leave here, now."

"Look what he's holding," Lexie whispered. "Do you see it?"

A long cane with a staff intricately carved to represent a human backbone blended with the marble coloring of the tree. The skull recreated in the handle had blood red stones in the eyes while the jaw hung open as if caught in a silent scream.

"Ah, the lovely Lexie Arden." The man swiftly climbed down from the branch, never missing a step. "The spirits are buzzing with your name."

His laughter rolled around in his chest, and the ground trembled at the sound.

"Did you see the reception committee I summoned for you?" He held his staff out to the field of graves. "The dead needed to pay their respects."

Shaken, Magnus stepped forward. "Who are you?"

A maniacal glint sparked in his eyes as he held up his cane. His features melted into nothing but haunting black eye sockets and white bony crevices. When he tilted his head, his dark skin, full lips, and those freakish amber eyes appeared back in place.

"I carry a baton juju, Mr. Blackwell, same as you." He twirled the cane, and his ruthless smile grew. "But mine is prettier and much stronger."

"He can see you," Lexie whispered.

"Of course I can see your ghost, Lexie Arden. I see all the dead." He swept his walking stick over the gravestones as if he were casting a spell. "Return to sleep, my children."

The spirits hung their heads and floated beneath the shade of the enormous tree. With one last doleful glance, they knelt in the mud, facing away from their headstones, sinking slowly into the mire covering the ground.

Magnus stepped in front of Lexie, brandishing his cane.

The other man scowled. "You dare to disrespect me on my land?"

Magnus lowered his cane. "How do you know our names?"

The intruder's face changed again. The skull with the bottomless black holes for eyes reappeared, obliterating his human features. The jaw slackened, offering a glimpse into the dark hollows of his mouth. The cheekbones honed as sharp as a knife's blade, the teeth white and gleaming, all seemed to accentuate the stranger's vile appearance.

He pointed his cane at Magnus. "Do not challenge me, ever."

Roots from the tree shot from the ground and wrapped around Magnus, encasing him as if caught in a spider's web. He struggled, but the shoots around him tightened, keeping him in his place. He tried to warn Lexie to run, but the power holding him kept him silent. He feared they'd walked into the very pits of Hell.

"Do you smell that?" Lexie muttered with a grimace. "It's like bad rum and cigars."

The man tapped the ground with the tip of his cane, and the branches above him swayed.

The roots enveloping Magnus fell away, and he dropped to his knees, fighting to find the strength to stand.

"I am Baron Samedi. Guardian of the dead."

He bowed to Lexie, ignoring Magnus as he struggled to his feet.

"I was wondering when you would pay me a visit, Mambo." The Baron tipped his top hat to her. "The Queen speaks highly of you."

"If you know the Queen, then you've heard what's happened."

Baron Samedi drummed his fingers on the skull-shaped handle of his cane. "All the spirits are aware of your plight. You wish to recover your powers, but to do so, you must become part of our world. The things you hold dear—your gift, your desire to help others, your love—must evolve before you can cross the threshold."

Lexie stepped forward. "Evolve how?"

The Baron grinned at her enthusiasm. "You must want your gift above all things. To be the strongest, you must sacrifice."

"I'm lost without my ability. It filled my soul with such joy, but now it's empty. I will do anything to have my power back."

He nodded, appearing pleased with her answer. "Then what you will become will weave the fabric of your soul and create your afterlife." He flourished a hand down Magnus's figure. "Like your ghost here. His misdeeds fashioned his afterlife and changed your course."

Lexie pursed her lips. "But what does Magnus's fate have to do with my lost powers?"

"It has everything to do with it. Your life is his afterlife, and he's still making amends."

Magnus frowned. "Another spirit who speaks in riddles."

"Riddles are clues, my dear boy," he said, mimicking Magnus. "The job of a spirit is to guide, to coax, to influence but never to do. The actions of the living are their own to make."

"Perfect!" Lexie tossed up her hand. "So you won't tell me who took my powers then."

Baron Samedi held up his cane. "I cannot. This is your journey, my girl. Fate will not let me interfere."

"This creature will be of no use to us," Magnus spat out the words with all the venom of a cobra.

"What about my baton juju?" Lexie lunged forward. "What can you tell me about it?"

Baron Samedi twirled his cane in his hand as he stepped over to the gnarled tree roots. "The tree of life is found among the dead. It takes the life force of those buried close to it." He waved to the graves tucked beneath the tree.

The way the labyrinth of roots wound throughout the tombstones made it easy for Magnus to believe the tree must have absorbed something from the dead.

"Is this the Sang Noir tree?" Lexie asked.

"The Black Blood Tree." Baron Samedi patted the branch next to him. "It's the most powerful blood there is."

Magnus smirked. "And why is that?"

Baron Samedi tapped his cane into the boggy ground. Moss covered branches dipped and swayed overhead as the wind grew cold.

Smoke wisped from an unmarked grave, slithering, growing, its tendrils rising, creating feminine curves. The female's hips swayed as if dancing to music.

Dark flesh covered the figure, embellishing her supple legs, slim hips, tiny waist, and filling out her breasts. Her face materialized, the blush of youth still rosy on her cheeks. She faced

Baron Samedi, bowing to him while showing Magnus her perfectly formed backside.

Samedi's eyes flickered with delight. "Does any of her look familiar to you, Mr. Blackwell?"

"Who is she?" Lexie muttered, coming up to Magnus.

He avoided her gaze. "I have no idea what you're talking about."

"Think back." Baron Samedi raised his cane, twirling it in the air, and the woman slowly rotated with it. "To Madam Simone's and the girl you took there—Evangeline."

Magnus recoiled. The girl had been one of Madam Simone's whores, and untouched to his kind of pleasure. He'd spent several hours with her, fascinated by the smoothness of her ass and the way it felt around his erection. Madam Simone had given her coke oil to use to dull the pain. He remembered being displeased with the concoction; now, disgust over what he had done to her tunneled through him.

The ghost floating above the grave turned to Magnus. Her eyes popped open when she spotted him. For a brief moment, her memories were his. He experienced the degradation she'd suffered while he thrust into her again and again.

"You ask why these people." Baron Samedi's voice became somber. "Because where there is great suffering, there is great strength. Such is the power that gave birth to the tree of life and keeps it strong."

Baron Samedi snapped his fingers, and the ghost of Evangeline wriggled back into the wet ground.

"What happened to her?" Magnus looked on as her spirit dissolve to dust.

"She died a few months after you left New Orleans." Baron Samedi leaned against a branch. "The fire you started at Mahogany House left her unemployed. She accepted the offer of a former customer to become his lover. He put her up in a house for a time. Then when he wanted a new lover, he strangled her while she slept. Actions are like ripples on a vast ocean of time, Magnus Blackwell. And your ripples are catching up with you."

"He's made amends for his past," Lexie called out, coming to his defense.

Baron Samedi's eyes honed in on her. "Has he?"

He approached Lexie, gliding on a pocket of air.

Magnus's knuckles whitened as he clenched his cane, wanting to lash out at The Baron for getting too close to his charge.

"No matter what may come." Baron Samedi's voice deepened. "Protect the Queen's baton juju. Guard it against evil. It's more than a symbol of your power; it's the source of it. As long as you hold on to it, you shall remain mambo." He turned to Magnus. "And good luck with your guide. Trust me; you'll need it."

The ground shook as he chuckled, and then his laughter bloomed into a deafening roar. The sound became a boisterous wind in the cemetery, rattling the headstones and rustling the branches of the great tree.

The spirit's presence suffocated Magnus. It coiled around him and squeezed.

A bolt of lightning struck not far from their spot beneath the tree.

Magnus spun around right as Baron Samedi vanished.

The earth beneath them stilled, the wind died, and the cemetery became the quiet, desolate place they had first encountered.

"I've talked to a lot of spirits, had a number of visions, but I've never seen anything like this." Lexie rested her hands on her knees, catching her breath.

Magnus glared at the place where The Baron had stood and wiped his coat sleeve as if to rid himself of the experience. "Yes, but what did we learn?"

A deep rosy color burned her cheeks. "Whoever took my power, wants us both out of the way."

"That should narrow down the field considerably."

"Any ideas who could hate us both." Lexie moved away from the tree.

He checked the still falling rain. "Not a clue."

Lexie kept her gaze on the ground as they walked through the graves. "Is it true?" Her voice sounded small. "What he said about the women, Evangeline, was true it true?"

"You know about my past. You saw it when we were joined at your initiation."

"No, I saw images." She pointed at the poor woman's grave under the tree. "I've never met one of your victims."

He bristled at the comment. "She wasn't a victim. She was paid handsomely for her services."

"She didn't volunteer for her position, Magnus. Men like you made women whores because you couldn't accept them as anything else."

He swallowed his hostile retort. Magnus didn't need another reminder of his sins.

"This isn't the time or place. Let's get back to the car before you catch your death."

She shook her head. "All this time I thought I was being punished. That I was the one someone wanted to hurt. But it's you."

"Are you saying this is my fault?"

"The answer is in your past!" She pointed her baton juju at the giant tree. "Don't you remember what Baron Samedi said, 'Actions are like ripples in a vast ocean of time.' Your sins, your ripples, are still wreaking havoc in my world."

Magnus looked back at the tree. "But I returned the rightful mambo to the city. I paid for my crime by being bound to you."

Lexie sighed. "Maybe there's something else we're missing."

The wind picked up, and Magnus checked the sky. "Well, we're not going to figure it out in the rain. Let's get back."

He waited by her side as Lexie maneuvered through the slime and bent headstones.

She slipped once and almost toppled to the ground but caught herself before diving headlong into a pile of mud. Once out from the shade of the tree, the dead grass made the going easier for her, and soon she arrived at the asphalt road.

Before Magnus moved inside the car, he took one more look at the mighty Sang Noir tree, its gnarled limbs touching the ground and curling around, hugging its trunk. The tombstones beneath were undetectable from the road, and the unearthly world they had encountered vanished from view.

The slam of Lexie's car door made him turn away. While she settled in the driver's seat, memories of meeting Baron Samedi replayed in his mind.

If Lexie losing her powers was his doing, he needed to find a way to fix it before it was too late for both of them.

Chapter Eight

Rainwater flooded the French Quarter as Lexie drove her car to the parking lot down from her shop. Standing water swirled around her wheels as something scurried along the sidewalks.

"What the hell?"

Rats. Hundreds of fat, brown vermin dashed across the cracked walkways, darting around tourists, street signs, and the occasional dog on a leash. A woman squealed next to Lexie's car as she avoided a gang of rodents rushing between her feet. The determined creatures climbed in doorways, on windowsills, even up poles leading to second-floor balconies to get away from the deep water.

She pulled into her reserved spot in the lot. "They're everywhere."

Lexie rushed through the rain, dancing to avoid the creatures as she hurried to her store.

"I can't believe this."

Magnus floated next to her, grimacing at the rats huddled together on a corner. "They must be coming out of the sewers."

She ran the last steps to her store's entrance, but the handle on the french door wouldn't budge. While she fought with it, getting soaked in the process, two brown rats with long fleshy tails landed on the doorstep and glared at her with their black eyes.

The door to the shop swung open, and the rats were swept out of the way with a broom.

"I saw them." Nina waved Lexie inside. "Hurry, before more show up."

Lexie bounded in the doors. Nina locked them behind her.

"Oh, God." Lexie slapped at her legs and ankles. "I hate fucking rats."

Magnus glided past her. "Please, dear girl. The language."

"They were trying to come in the doors. I had to lock them." Nina put the broom to the side.

Lexie rested her baton juju against a glass display case. "When did this start?"

"Not long after you left." Nina went to the stack of T-shirts and picked up a towel. "Here."

Lexie took the towel and wiped her arms and face.

"Ms. Carol from the candy store two doors down ran out of her shop shrieking. I went outside to see what was up, and that's when I saw them—coming out of the drains."

Magnus cringed as several rats ran by the door. "All this rain must be overwhelming the system."

Nina turned away. "Yes, it has."

Lexie stared at her assistant's back, not sure what to make of her comment. "What has?"

Nina paused at a selection of smudge sticks of sage, basil, thyme, and rosemary. "The rain? You said it's overwhelming the system." She selected a short wand of sage.

Magnus held up a finger to his lips, urging Lexie not to say anything.

Nina sniffed the air. "There's bad juju all around. The universe is out of balance. You can feel it. So can the rats. We need to cleanse the store with sage."

Nina went to the burning white candles set up on a display alter. She lit the sage, allowing the fire to singe the tip, and then blew the flame out.

Magnus hovered close to Lexie. "I concur with your girl. I've been sensing unease but could not make sense of it until now."

Crestfallen from being cut off from her sixth sense, Lexie cast her eyes to the ground. "I can't feel anything."

"But you're our Mambo." Nina went to the front door. "You should be tapped into all the energy around us."

Lexie silently berated her slip. She needed to tell Nina something, anything to keep her problem hidden a little longer. She couldn't afford to let her secret get out. It would cost her the credibility she'd worked so hard to establish.

"I meant something has been off with me, too. How did you know the balance of the universe is out of line?"

Nina fanned the tendril of smoke all around the doorway. Once she'd completed her task, she faced Lexie.

"My grandmother taught me everything in the universe is about good and evil and the continued struggle between the two forces. When either force pulls ahead, life is out of balance. When a never-ending rain falls, pestilence rises, and people become angry, the dark side has taken over."

Lexie considered the smoking sage in her hand. "In other words, there will be more ahead for us than rain and rats."

Nina glided up to her, catlike in her movements. "Evil is fighting for control, and you're the only one who can stop it from taking over. Evil will bow only to a mambo."

Her anxiety churned. *But how can I stop it without my powers?*

"Steady there," Magnus whispered in her ear. "You can handle this."

"I don't know what to do." Her voice sounded more strained than she'd expected.

Nina smiled and waved her wand of sage from Lexie's shoulder to her ankles. "The spirits will guide you. They will show you the way."

"She say anything else?"

Lexie stood in Titu's entryway dripping water on to her shiny pine floors.

"Isn't that enough? She scared the shit out of me, talking about spirits guiding me. I've had my fill of them lately."

Titu handed her a towel. "What do you know about the girl?"

"Her social security number, birthdate, and address. What else do I need?"

"You should find out a little more about your employees, child. You're too trusting." Titu clucked and folded her arms over her bright yellow muumuu. "Why did you come rushing over here to question me about what your shop assistant said? Why not ask her?"

"I didn't want to ask her too many questions." Lexie slumped against the exposed brick wall, wiping her face with the towel. "I got scared she'd find out I lost my gift."

"Your gift isn't lost," Magnus spoke up next to her. "I have it."

Titu raised her head to the ghost. "What did he say?"

"He has my gift. He's been seeing the dead since I lost my abilities."

Titu's brows went up on her smooth forehead. "How long have you known?"

Lexie fidgeted with the towel in her hands. "The first time was outside Kalila's home. He saw spirits she keeps imprisoned in the swamps."

"He found out about that?" Titu took the towel from her and dropped it on a bench. "I'd heard rumors she imprisoned the dead, but I never could pick up anything."

"It happened again when we went to Holt Cemetery. He saw the dead stranded there."

"Holt Cemetery?" Titu headed deeper into her home. "What were you doing there?"

Lexie followed her to the living room, her wet tennis shoes squishing as she walked.

"I went to see the Sang Noir Tree." Lexie glanced at Magnus standing next to a painting of St. Louis Cathedral. "When I was there, I met Baron Samedi. He knew a great deal about my baton juju and the origin of its power."

Titu shuffled across the hardwood floor to the plush yellow sofa. "Are you sure it was his spirit?"

"He told me his name. He also spoke in riddles mostly. All the spirits I meet lately seem to do that."

Titu reached back for the sofa and slowly sank into the cushion. "What other spirits have you met?"

"At Kalila's, there was another." Lexie sat next to her. "She gave me a drink of rum, nasty tasting stuff, and the next thing I remember was meeting this attractive man. His name was Kalfu and—"

"The dark spirit?" Titu shook her head. "I should have known she would try something. She arranged an introduction to the spirit without asking your permission. That was wrong."

"It wasn't such an awful experience. Kalfu was attractive and far from menacing."

Magnus floated across the room to the sofa. "You never said he was attractive."

Titu wiggled a finger at him. "What's wrong with your Mr. Blackwell?"

She shifted her gaze to Titu, giving Magnus the cold shoulder. "Meeting all these other spirits has upset him."

He appeared in front of her. "What are you up to?"

Titu struggled to her feet and went to the fireplace mantel. "You need to be careful with Kalfu. He only shows you what you want to see. It's what clever spirits do; they hide their true ugliness. Then once they make you a part of their world, they change you."

Magnus sat next to her on the sofa. "I don't like where this is going."

Titu peered up at the portrait of Simone Glapion in her flowing white gown. "Kalila La Fay once was a beautiful woman. She had the smoothest skin and brightest eyes. But when she embraced Kalfu, her skin changed, and her eyes became black." Titu sucked in a raspy breath and faced her. "The same fate awaits you if you embrace him."

He pointed the tip of his cane at Titu. "You need to listen to her."

Lexie glared at him and went to the mantel. "But what if I had both elements of light and dark? I could bring balance to the universe."

Titu patted her arm. "You have no idea what it would do to you. Best not to go down that road."

"But what if the darkness can help restore my powers?"

Magnus scrambled from the sofa. "Are you insane?"

Titu cupped her face. "Stop talking nonsense, child. All this rain has gone to your head." She shuffled for the arched entryway leading to the kitchen. "No mambo has tamed the darkness: it has only overwhelmed them. You cannot repeat such a mistake. I'm sure your Mr. Blackwell will agree with me."

After she left the room, Lexie turned to Magnus. "I already know you agree with her."

He strolled up to the mantel and rested his elbow on the corner. "What more can I add? You've barely learned how to perform white magic; how can you conceive of tackling the black?"

"Five months ago, nobody believed I could find your dragon cane." She checked her wavering voice and reined in her aggravation. "At every turn in my life, I've been told what I can't do, and then I did it to prove everyone wrong. This is no different."

He eased closer, uncertainty stamped into his smooth brow. "This is a challenge you can't win, no one can. You heard Titu, other mambos have tried and failed. You will, too."

The hope her ghost would stand by her retreated, dragging down her confidence.

"How can you be so certain?"

He slammed his fist on the mantel. "Because I know!"

"Get in this kitchen, child," Titu called.

"Coming." Lexie cautiously approached her ghost. "What is it? What aren't you telling me?"

He nodded to the kitchen entrance. "Go on. I can feel she's getting impatient."

"You never answered me."

His heavy sigh added to her suspicions. He wasn't admitting

everything he knew.

"The universe put me with you on this path, but if you change direction, I might not be allowed to stay. Do you want to risk losing me?"

She'd never imagined her interest in darkness might cost her the ghost who had been at her side day and night for the past few months. Lexie couldn't succeed without him. But if she didn't reconnect with her powers, she wouldn't have a chance of succeeding at all.

The shops were closing up for the evening as Magnus and Lexie made the trek back to her home on Royal Street. The rains had stopped, but the humidity clung to her skin, chilling her to the bone. Numerous puddles covering the uneven sidewalk added to her discomfort by soaking her white tennis shoes. Lexie never thought she'd miss the heat of summer, but now she longed for it.

The party capital of the country, the French Quarter never emptied of revelers. Tonight, however, she encountered more rats than people scurrying about.

"There's something I've wanted to ask you." Lexie sidestepped a pair of rats fighting on the sidewalk. "It's about Emily Mann."

"Emily?" He stopped mid-stride. "What about her?"

Lexie halted next to him. "You told me once she spoke with you when she haunted Altmover Manor. She would discuss the house and the running of it."

"Yes, she interacted with me as if I were alive. Even after my death, she remained my devoted secretary."

"What about the voodoo books, and the cane? Did she ever mention any of those to you?"

Magnus continued along the sidewalk, floating just above the cement. "I remember her reading out strange incantations to my portrait in the living room. She'd ask me what I thought, and if they made me feel any different." He shook his head. "They were gibberish to me."

"When she died, she had her ashes spread around Altmover Manor. You never saw her ghost or spoke to her?"

He stopped beneath a flickering gaslit lamp. "Never. I only detected O'Connor."

Lexie raised her head to the three-story mansion next to them, pretending to admire its wrought-iron balconies while plotting her next question.

"I find it hard to believe you had no contact with Emily whatsoever after her death. You sure you two never crossed paths?"

"The afterlife is not a park! We don't bump into each other while strolling the grounds. Why are you interrogating me about her?"

She slouched against the mansion wall. "In my visions, I saw the dreariness of Emily's life and the change in her when the voodoo books arrived. I saw her spending hours huddled over the books and speaking the spells. In all the time you observed her, did you see her change? Titu spoke of Kalila changing when she took on the dark mantle, did Emily change when she became obsessed with voodoo?"

The question tormented Magnus. He still held so much guilt

about Emily, where did he begin?

"You asked me before how I could be so certain you wouldn't win against the darkness. I know because I've seen it before with Emily." He raised his head and lost himself in the swirls and curves of the balcony above. "She spent endless hours poring over her voodoo books and telling me of her plans. I realized she'd gone mad after a few years locked away in Altmover. Her physical changes seemed to mirror the blackness filling her soul."

Lexie pushed away from the building. "What did you do?"

"What could I do as a ghost?" The hopelessness of his supernatural existence at Altmover Manor inundated him. "Near the end of her life, I barely recognized the eager, soft-spoken woman I'd confided in. There were times I blamed myself for her end."

"Makes you wonder what drove her over the edge: the blackness she embraced, or her love for you?"

The question gnawed at his soul. "I never understood how she felt until after I was a ghost. If I'd known as a man, I would have sent her from my employ."

The ethereal face of a woman darkened the window of a dwelling behind Lexie. Creole with deep-set eyes and an alluring smile, she winked, offering him an invitation to enter the home. Then, her face tensed in terror, her smile disappeared, and an offensive cackle rose from her lips. The horrid sound cut through the night, troubling Magnus.

Emily had laughed in a similar way night after night while sitting before his portrait at Altmover Manor. It was the same laugh he'd heard coming from his Katie when the darkness overtook her in Lexie's workshop.

Lexie moved in front of him, blocking the ghost in the window. "And you think the voodoo changed her?"

He retreated to the sidewalk, eager to get away from the mansion. "Emily wasn't a rational person. She didn't need voodoo to turn her dark; she was already well on her way by the time O'Connor and I found ourselves haunting the halls of my home."

Lexie fell into stride beside him, tapping her cane in unison with his.

The sound of wood hitting cobblestone echoed between the buildings on the narrow street.

"I believe you, Magnus." She brushed her hand along the first black posts of the iron fence around St. Anthony's Garden. "You would never have been the kind of man to cater to the whims of an irrational woman."

His cruel grin was back. "Then again, I have catered to you, my dear. That should account for something."

When he turned to admire the garden located behind St. Louis Cathedral, Magnus froze.

Spirits in white cassocks, and a few in the brown vestments of monks, floated through the azalea bushes or sat on the white stone benches. Dozens of apparitions crowded a cement path or stood at the rear of the garden facing the back wall of the cathedral. They did not seem to acknowledge each other, and all the ghosts had their heads bowed in prayer. Their mumblings lingered in the air, and then a single, clear voice with perfect pitch rose above the din.

The image of a monk in his drab brown robes with a white rope around his waist materialized in the alley to the left side of the cathedral. With his head of gray hair rocking back and forth, he sang a Latin prayer to God, praising his works.

"Are you okay?"

Lexie waved her hand in front of him, and the image of the singing monk vanished, along with his captivating voice.

"What are you staring at?"

He cleared his throat and resumed their stroll. "It's nothing. I just got lost in the lyrics of a familiar tune I heard once as a boy."

"What song?"

He kicked out his legs, heading in the direction of her store. "A hymn I heard in church. Praising God in Heaven, and all his spiritual creations."

"You went to church?" She giggled. "I can't picture it."

"It was another lifetime," he admitted. "Before I discovered I preferred sin over the promise of Heaven."

"Knowing what you know now, would you have stayed in church?"

"Church wouldn't have saved me. It's a tool for finding inner wisdom, but when it comes down to it, Sunday sermons will never replace the guilt instilled by experience. A man must choose to save himself. No one else can do it for him."

Lexie smiled at him. "Did your time as a ghost teach you that?"

He raised his head to the overcast sky. "No, you did."

Chapter Nine

"**I**'m sure I'll be home early." Will kissed her cheek, his briefcase tucked under his arm.

"Me, too." Lexie ran her fingers through his stubborn cowlick. "Things have been dead in the shop the past couple of days."

"Why don't we go out for dinner, if it's not raining?" He set out for the back steps leading to the courtyard.

"I thought you hated going out?" Lexie peered over the railing outside their back door.

He continued down the stairs. "I thought we could celebrate. Five months of wedded bliss today."

"You remembered." She smiled down at him. "How about Stella's? You love their crab cakes."

"I'll make a reservation for us." He waved at her. "Love you, baby."

She waited for him to emerge from beneath the back stairs

and head along the carriage alleyway to the gate on Royal Street. She smiled as his footfalls echoed around her. When she heard the gate open, Lexie stepped back toward her apartment door.

"What the hell?" Will hollered.

She hurried toward the stairs. "Will?"

He didn't answer.

Numb with panic, Lexie trotted down the steps still wearing her slippers and robe.

"Will!"

He still didn't reply.

Images of him being beaten or robbed weakened her legs as she ran. All the nightmares she had kept to herself gushed forth. Was the blackness haunting her, turning on her husband? Or worse, was someone coming to claim him as payment for her becoming mambo?

Her slippers skidded on the wet cobblestones when she leapt from the stairs to the carriage alley and ran to the gate.

With shaking hands, she opened the gate and tore onto the street.

Will stood motionless, his briefcase still tucked under his arm.

Relief rushed through her, and she placed her hand over her pounding heart. Lexie took a deep breath and gagged. The scent of rotting flesh hung heavy in the air. She covered her nose and mouth and followed his gaze.

Splayed along the wet sidewalks, huddled in doorways, lying squished by cars in the middle of the street were dozens of dead rats. The rains from the night before had moved many of the carcasses toward the drains, but the bloated varmints had blocked the ability of the water to recede. Lexie shuddered at the overwhelming presence of death—this was a sign.

A smattering of people ventured along the walkways. Some

had their mouths covered and averted their eyes from the carnage. The more adventurous among them took pictures of the rats huddled in piles in the street. One fool had propped up a few around a beer bottle not far from the entrance to her shop.

"Oh my God." Lexie stepped closer to Will.

He put a protective arm around her and ushered her back through the gate. "Get inside."

"You okay? You're not hurt?" The frown lines around his mouth deepened as he put his briefcase down. "I'll call someone with the city. Get them to send a sanitation truck or something."

Lexie tugged her robe's sash tightly around her waist. "Nina said there would be more bad things in the city."

"Nina, your shop assistant?"

"Yeah. I've been getting a lot of messages from outside sources lately. Since my powers have dried up, I keep seeing …"

Magnus popped up alongside Will. He tapped his cane, getting her attention.

"I'd refrain from worrying Will with your other spiritual encounters. The man might lock you away in a nunnery."

"What are you seeing?" Will gripped her arms. "More ghosts?"

She glared at Magnus. "Spirits, actually. Spirits with agendas."

Will let her go and gathered his leather case. "Doesn't sound any different from Magnus. I've never heard of a specter with more of an agenda than that asshole."

Magnus glowered at him.

"He's standing next to you, Will."

He mumbled something she couldn't make out. "Stay upstairs until the city cleans up this mess. I don't want you exposed to God knows what diseases those vermin carry." He kissed her cheek. "I'll call you when I get to the office."

Magnus scowled as Will shut the gate behind him. "Why does he continue to be so hostile toward me?"

Lexie set the deadbolt, securing the carriageway. "I have no idea."

"You need to speak with him." Magnus followed her to the stairs. "He can at least be civil in my presence."

"He doesn't know when he's in your presence, and I've already spoken to him. It won't help."

Lexie had reached the top landing when Magnus appeared in front of her. "I cannot abide by—"

He seemed to look right through her to the courtyard below. "What is it?"

He raised his finger to his lips and then pointed to the pond.

Lexie spun around, and before she cried out, covered her mouth.

Sweeping gowns of green, red, and yellow moved in unison with white Spanish military uniforms trimmed in gold braid and wearing red sashes. Drab, torn, dirty tunics and petticoats of former slaves circled a pair of shiny Lycra pants topped with a sparkly silver shirt. Even children's white nightgowns mixed in with the fray. But none of the entities had faces or limbs; only their clothes were visible to Lexie as they moved in time to a tune she could not hear. Like colorful dancers at a Mardi Gras ball, men and women's outfits from centuries past swirled around the fountain in the courtyard.

"I can see them!" She gripped the railing. "My powers must be returning."

"No, I think this is something else." Magnus faced the door to her apartment. "Yesterday, when we were coming back from Titu's, I spotted ghosts along the way. At first, there were flashes of faces here and there, but at St. Anthony's Garden, the dozens of priests and monks buried on the grounds appeared to me."

Weary of it all, she rubbed the back of her neck. "What does it mean?"

Magnus peered down at the scene below. "The rain, the rats, maybe the dead are rising as well. Perhaps the negative energy is calling to them."

She tucked her hands under her arms. "If this is happening here, what about the rest of the city?"

Magnus grimaced. "I'm afraid we will find out soon enough."

Magnus's words came true the following morning.

Customers crowded the shop, demanding something, anything, to help protect them from the evil that had brought the rain and pestilence to the city.

Haggard faces and bloodshot eyes told of sleepless nights, and every person she met reported feeling the same sensation of doom.

"The world is coming to an end," one woman cried on her shoulder.

She didn't know what else to do to dispel her customers' fears. Not being able to use her ability to help those in need was the cruelest cut of all for Lexie. The lack of power ate at her day and night, leaving her a frazzled jumble of nerves.

She tried to make amends by running herself ragged to offer her clients everything from amulets blessed with protection spells to holy candles, juju bags to ward off evil spirits, and key chain trinkets touting voodoo symbols for good luck.

"Mambo, is there anything else we can do to keep the evil away?" an older woman asked as she clutched her rosary beads to her chest.

Lexie grimly shook her head. She picked up her coffee mug from the counter and took a sip. "The spirits are challenging each other, as they do, but everything will settle soon."

"You hope they settle soon." Magnus arched an eyebrow while her customer debated between two holy candles. "Have you ever considered what will become of these people if the balance is not righted?"

"Good always prevails," she muttered.

"Does it? I'm not so sure anymore." Magnus gestured to the people combing through her store. "Look at them. They know what's coming. We all do. Evil is at hand, dear girl, and you're the only one who can stop it."

She ignored her ghost. How in the hell was she supposed to stop anything?

Nina came out from behind the cash register. "This is getting out of hand."

Lexie coolly curled her hand around the mug and placed it against her chest. "I realize that, and if I could wave a magic wand and make it go away, I would."

Nina lowered her voice as a customer pilfered through the display of protective talismans.

"People are frightened. They're coming to you for comfort. Is there nothing you can do to help them?"

The weight of her responsibilities pressed down on her. "I'm not sure—"

A couple wearing *Bourbon Street Badass* T-shirts scampered up to her, breathless and very pale.

"Our hotel concierge told us this was the place to go for help." The young woman rapidly spoke as she wrung her hands. "Last night, we kept seeing people walking around in our hotel room at three in the morning. Not real people, ghosts."

ALEXANDREA WEIS WITH LUCAS ASTOR

Lexie smiled, biting back her growing apprehension. "It's a very haunted city."

The man yanked at the collar of his T-shirt. "Me and my wife are from Ohio. We don't have ghosts there. Here, they're in our hotel room, around the corner at a bar. I swore I saw an old woman in a red antebellum dress with a red umbrella strolling down the street."

Her fingers tightened around her coffee mug. "Perhaps she was a street artist in costume."

"I thought the same thing." His wife came up to her, dropping her voice to a whisper. "Until a car drove right through her."

How could she fend off an antsy public while trying to figure out what had happened to her? Could it get any worse?

She set the mug down with a decided thump. "I'm sorry, but ghosts are part of the city."

The man stepped closer. "So, you ain't gonna help us? What kind of bullshit is this?" His voice cracked. "We shelled out a boatload for this trip to this half-assed city, and so far, all we've seen is rain, dead rats, and now we can't sleep in our overpriced hotel room because of a ghost."

Lexie's agitation boiled over. The incident brought back too many memories of pretentious clients who bitched about their gold bathroom wallpaper clashing with their imported Italian marble sink. She was about to tell the asshole where he could shove his attitude and his expensive vacation when a shimmering light appeared.

In the center of her store, the light bent and shifted. The couple retreated. Their mouths dropped open, and the woman bit her knuckles, her pallid face wracked with fear.

"You never address this lady in such a manner." Magnus made his presence known, flaunting a scowl, guaranteed to terrify

104

the living. "Otherwise, you will have to deal with me."

The young man took off, barreling out the shop, leaving his trembling wife behind. With bulging eyes, the woman backed away from Lexie. She bumped into the rack of T-shirts before she made it across the store. At the door, she fumbled with the latch.

The sound of the door swinging open and bumping off the doorstop echoed throughout the shop.

She stumbled outside, and then took off running.

The other people in the shop focused their attention on Magnus. Lexie expected them to make a beeline for the exit. Instead, they gave a cursory glance to his black coat, black boots, and the cane in his hand, and then continued to browse the items on her shelves.

"Well, well." Nina scurried out from behind the register. "So you do have a ghost. People keep asking me about the mambo's ghost."

Lexie stared, dumbfounded, at her assistant. "People ask you about him?"

"Now I get why you talk to yourself all the time. You've been talking to him."

Lexie ignored the comment. "Nina, this is Magnus Blackwell."

Magnus bowed his head but said nothing.

"Great special effects," a customer commented as they passed by Lexie and Nina. "He almost looks real."

The last of the customers left, and Lexie rushed to the front door and locked it.

When she wheeled around and faced Nina, Magnus had disappeared.

She headed to the counter but stopped when the gray Maine coon cat trotted out the open red door and across the floor to her assistant.

Nina picked up the cat. "Why didn't you tell me about him?"

"You know why. You saw the reaction of that couple. It would have been yours had I mentioned him from the get-go." She crept closer to Nina while the cat tracked her with its intelligent green eyes. "Who told you I had a ghost?"

Nina set the cat on the floor. "There are people in this town watching you. Seeing if you are cut out to be mambo. Some think you aren't experienced enough; others believe in your ability."

Lexie's eyebrows rose. "And which one are you?"

Nina's mouth twisted into a knowing smile. "I believe you're the true mambo. It's why I took this position. I want to keep you safe from the others in the voodoo community who want to overthrow you, and take away your baton juju."

Lexie's mouth hung open, stunned by the news. "How do you know this?"

"My grandmother is a voodoo priestess and has heard rumors. She's the reason I came to work for you. She refuses to initiate me into the religion, so I decided would learn about the art from our mambo."

Her shoulders drooped with relief. "I thought I couldn't trust you."

Nina looked away. "I didn't tell you the truth before because I figured you would fire me. I grew up reading every book I could on the Queen. When I was little, I wanted to be her. I hoped learning voodoo from her chosen mambo would be the next best thing."

"I knew I liked her." Magnus reappeared at Nina's side.

Nina inspected him from head to toe. "My grandmother told me about you. Did you do all the bad things people say?"

The gray cat on the counter hissed at Magnus.

"A gentleman never discusses his past." He pointed at the

cat. "Why does that beast look so familiar?"

Nina strolled to the counter where the cat lay, preening himself. "You've probably seen him before. Cats get around."

A nagging idea struck Lexie as she took in the interaction between her shop assistant and her ghost.

"Why can everyone see and hear you now, Magnus?"

Nina tickled under the cat's chin. "For the same reason people see ghosts everywhere, and rats fill the streets—the bad juju. It opens the door between the living and the dead to create chaos."

"I have to concur with your associate. I've seen my kind everywhere lately. I thought it had to do with your ability and how it had …," he cleared his throat, "rubbed off on me. It seems other forces are at work."

A rapid knock on the door startled Lexie, and the cat leapt from the counter.

"What the hell?"

Lexie retrieved her cane as she crossed the room to the door. She put her hand on the knob, and for a split-second, a cloud of fear enveloped her. She understood what it meant—things were about to go from bad to worse.

No sooner had she shot back the bolt when an older gentleman barged his way inside.

"Can you help me?" Otis Landry wiped the droplets of rain from the gray jacket with a trembling hand. "All hell has broken loose, Mrs. Bennett. I never thought in all my days I'd be coming to you for help, but I don't know where else to turn, or who would believe me." He lowered his head and whispered, "I have a ghost problem."

Lexie looked around for Magnus, but he had vanished.

"Mr. Landry, this is my assistant." She directed him to Nina while she shut the door. "You can speak freely in front of Nina.

She knows all my secrets."

Otis Landry scoured the empty store. "I know what people say about you, Mrs. Bennett. It's one of the reasons I rented you this shop. But in my house on Conti Street, I've had frightful activity. I'd heard stories about a slave girl who hanged herself from the balcony, but never saw her. Over the past few days, it seems she's come back with a vengeance."

Lexie glanced over her shoulder at Nina. "Tell Mr. Blackwell I might need his assistance." She took her landlord's arm. "Let's go deal with your ghost."

Chapter Ten

I n a desolate spot on Conti Street, snuggled between two dark, abandoned buildings, Otis's gray two-story Creole townhouse waited. Closed black shutters over the windows added to the depressing aura surrounding the home.

Lexie stood on the sidewalk, wanting to get a vibe from the structure, but the more she reached out with her mind, the greater her feeling of gloom. While she concentrated, a mist seeped from the bricks laid into the steps in front of the entrance and dangled like a spider.

"How long have you lived here?" She ignored the mist and peered up at the second-floor balcony.

"Ten years, and never a problem." He removed a set of keys from his pocket. "Then, the other day, I was sitting in the living room, watching TV, and heard a woman's cries. When I went to investigate, I found all the contents of my fridge on the kitchen floor."

She stood by as he unlocked the front door.

"Pictures have been ripped off the wall and damaged. Every morning I wake to find the kitchen in disarray, the appliances unplugged, and at night doors slam, and my bed shakes."

"Someone sounds angry."

He held the door for her. "But why now?"

She opened her mind as she entered the home, hoping her gift would kick in, but her hands fluttered with disappointment around her baton juju when the cold emptiness in her center remained unchanged.

The first room, a stuffy, dark living room done in drab tones of beige and brown, touted American Federal furniture upholstered in a rusty red pattern of interwoven olive branches. When two Hitchcock chairs cropped up against the wall, Lexie closed in on them.

She ran her hand lovingly over the detailed stencil work. "These are originals. Not machine made, but designed by hand."

"You know your furniture, Mrs. Bennett. Lambert Hitchcock originals." He came up to her. "How is it a woman running a voodoo shop knows about antique furniture?"

Lexie smiled as she stood. "In another life, I was an interior designer."

"You gave that up to come here?"

The incredulity in his voice astounded her, but she tempered her reaction. "I was called here, Mr. Landry. I have no regrets about leaving my other life behind. I want nothing more than to be what I am for as long as I can."

A high-pitched scream shattered the silence.

Lexie grabbed her chest, almost dropping her baton juju.

Otis shook his head, unfazed by the interruption. "It came from the courtyard. It usually happens every day about this time."

The crisp draft teased her skin. The hair stood on the back of Lexie's neck. She held on to her cane, willing the energy it

110

emitted to strengthen her.

She closed her eyes and tried to tap into her ability. Lexie pictured the ribbon with Magnus and called to the spirit with her mind. But all she detected was her emptiness.

"Can you sense what the spirit wants?"

Insecure and ashamed, she avoided his gaze. How could she help the man or the spirit plaguing him?

"Tell him the spirit is distressed over being brought back to the scene of so much misery," a familiar voice whispered in her ear.

"Magnus?" She searched the living room. "I can't see you."

"Neither can your landlord. I'm in my world to avoid being seen, but because I have your ability, I can still speak with you."

"Who's Magnus?" Otis frowned.

"My spirit guide." Lexie went to the pocket doors at the end of the room. "Does this lead to the courtyard?"

He opened the doors for her. "This way."

The pungent scent of mothballs clung to a narrow hallway decorated with drawings of New Orleans. They wove their way through to the cramped kitchen at the back of the house.

French doors with four panes of glass filtered the dreary daylight onto an old brick floor, adding to the oppressive atmosphere.

Otis charged ahead to the doors. "Out here."

They stepped into a courtyard shaded by high buildings all around. Warped balconies circled on all four sides; some of the railings were cracked, broken, or in desperate need of fresh paint.

"The buildings on either side are being renovated for apartments," he explained. "It's usually noisy during the day, but the work stopped because of the rain."

Brown ferns in black sugar cane melting pots decorated the courtyard. In the center, a willow tree's black, withered tendrils dipped onto the courtyard's gray tiles. A wrought iron table sat tucked away in a corner covered with dead leaves.

"What happened to your plants?"

Otis picked off a few leaves of the fern next to him. "Started dying about the same time the ghost showed up."

A whisper caressed her cheek. "Look up at the balcony."

Lexie followed Magnus's advice and stepped into the courtyard. She braced for the sickening sight of a woman dangling at the end of a rope against the gray plaster wall at the back of the townhouse.

There was nothing but a chipped blue-painted railing above. No one was there.

"Do you see anything?" Otis tracked her gaze.

"There's a woman in a white wedding dress," Magnus mumbled.

Lexie's jaw slackened. "Why is she in a wedding dress?"

Magnus gauged Lexie's reaction from the confines of his murky world. He feared crossing over, in case he scared her client away, but the vision before him tugged at his compulsion to be at Lexie's side.

The beautiful woman's long white gown, trimmed in lace and flowing with yards of muslin, had a corseted waist, with sleeves gathering at the shoulder, ballooning at the elbow, and tapering at the wrist. The effect was breathtaking, but with her deathly complexion and long, wavy dark brown hair, Magnus found her appearance disconcerting.

"Why can't the living see you, dear lady?"

A light breeze lifted her hair and brushed the fabric of her dress. She floated from the end of her rope made of white bedsheets, trapped forever in her last moments of life.

"I don't have the power." The ghost's black eyes darted across the courtyard. "Who are you? How can you hear me?"

He struggled to find words she would understand. He didn't have a lot of experience speaking with his kind.

"It's difficult to explain, but I am like you—no longer in the body."

Otis squinted up at the balcony. "I don't see anything. You say she's in a wedding dress?"

Magnus ignored her pushy landlord and spoke to Lexie. "She doesn't have the energy to appear to you. And this woman isn't your landlord's reported spirit. This is someone else."

He refocused on the distressed woman in white and asked, "Do you have a name?"

"Rebecca."

"Why are you haunting this house, Rebecca?"

"Because of my fiancé, Daniel." Her voice faltered. "I was waiting for him to return from the war, but he didn't. I remember seeing him in my house after we got word he'd died on the battlefield. His ghost begged me to join him in death, so I did." Her image faded in and out as if fighting to stay in the physical world. "Where am I? Is this a dream?"

Magnus shuddered at the comparison. He'd lived the same dream before Lexie walked into his former home, waxing and waning in and out from his world to hers.

"Are you sure someone's there?" Otis stepped closer to the balcony.

Lexie pounded her baton juju on the patio floor. "Would you stop your incessant questions, Mr. Landry." She stuck her open hand in front of her landlord's face. "My spirit guide's in contact with your ghost, and I can't hear him over you."

Magnus longed to rescue her from the obnoxious man, but explaining his presence would make the situation even more difficult.

Otis narrowed his gaze at her, angering Magnus.

"I was under the impression you talked to the spirits directly, Mrs. Bennett. Everyone around town says you have the gift."

Lexie's lips mashed together, and she wielded her cane in both hands.

I'd better step in.

Before Magnus could cross the curtain of mist, the figure on the balcony shifted and blurred. Her head swung from side to side, slow at first and then it sped up. It was as if Rebecca attempted to fight off something, or someone, unwanted.

The gray clouds hovering in the sky above the courtyard darkened. Thunder shook the ground, and the wind picked up, sweeping up the dead leaves beneath the willow tree.

"Magnus?" Lexie called to him. "What's going on?"

A whirlwind of dead leaves climbed to the balcony where Rebecca helplessly swayed. It lifted her dress, and as the fabric billowed, the leaves spiraled around it, changing the white muslin into gold. The ghost's hair rose and as if tended by invisible hands piled atop her head and lightened to an attractive shade of honey blonde. Her dark eyes bulged, and the irises faded from black to a scintillating blue.

Magnus almost toppled forward as the apparition became his Katie, resplendent in her gold party dress. Seeing his wife sucked the energy from his spirit—he could not move or even speak.

"Oh shit," Lexie exclaimed when Katie's ghost revealed itself on the balcony.

"That's not a white wedding dress," Otis said in a reverent whisper.

A sense of urgency pushed aside the blow of Magnus's grief,

114

and he plowed through the misty curtain into Lexie's dimension.

"Katie?" Lexie called. "Katie, do you remember me?"

Magnus arrived in the physical realm his focus drawn to Katie's trembling lips. Fear ratcheted up in his soul as a dark cloud dipped from the sky settling right over her head.

"Why am I here?" Katie cried to the cloud while tears stained her cheeks. "Why are you doing this?"

"Is this my ghost?" Otis asked.

"No, not your ghost." Lexie moved closer to the balcony. "Someone else's."

Magnus rushed toward Lexie just as Katie's eyes rolled back in her head and a barrage of horrific seizures overtook her.

"Lexie, stay where you are. Don't go near her!"

Lexie's hand went to her mouth. "Dear God, not again."

Katie's head jerked back extending her mouth into a black cavern bereft of any light. The hole gaped wider and wider until the whites of her eyes, and even her forehead, became overrun by the blackness.

Katie's suffering dropped Magnus to his knees. He blamed himself, blamed his past deeds for the hell she now endured. Until that moment, he'd never wanted to take back the crimes he'd committed. All the misery he'd caused came to light in Katie's twisted, ugly image.

"Get him out of here," Magnus called to Lexie while pointing at Otis.

But Lexie didn't budge. Glued to Katie's presence, she stared, wide-eyed at the balcony as if mesmerized by a voice Magnus could not hear. Spellbound, she and Otis remained at the mercy of the dark essence taking over Katie's soul.

"I warned you." A whiny voice resonated throughout the courtyard. "The dead are rising and will never rest. Plague and pestilence will terrorize this city until you leave. You were never meant to be mambo."

The blackness covering Katie's face undulated and buzzed like a million bees avenging a threat to their hive. A wave of black rose from her mouth. The wave broke apart and transformed into a mass of flies. They swarmed over her dress until they covered every inch of gold and lace.

"Magnus! Please, help me!"

Magnus struggled to his feet, desperate to reach her, but an odd humming stopped him. He winced as the noise grew to a deafening roar. A shattering *bang* rocked the courtyard, and after … quiet.

In a panic, he searched for Katie, but she'd disappeared.

The empty balcony stood above him, and then the reassuring sounds of the city returned.

Lexie sagged as if released by some unseen force. Rain trickled from the sky and covered her face.

Beside her, Otis also moved. He wiped the rain from his cheek, his bulging eyes fixed on Magnus.

"Is he … one of them?"

Lexie extended a hand to her ghost. "Mr. Landry, this is my spirit guide, Magnus Blackwell."

Will's arm went around her as they sat on their green sofa watching a Saints game on the TV.

"How did he react to meeting Magnus?"

"Mr. Landry was pretty shaken up by the entire encounter. First Katie's ghost and then Magnus. I think it may have been too much for him."

"It would have been too much for anyone." He cuddled next

to her. "Sounds like this Katie has an agenda. But I still don't get why she's out to get you? You never knew the woman."

"I can't make any sense of it." Lexie nestled her head in his chest. "But now I have more to deal with than a pissed off ghost. Otis Landry knows about me. He heard the black spirit threaten me and the city. What if this gets out? I'll be ruined."

Will kissed her brow. "Otis Landry is hardly tight with the voodoo people in this town. Even if he did know something, which he doesn't, who would he tell?"

"I have no idea, but if it got out, it would hurt my credibility."

"You're the one Marie Laveau chose. How can anyone question her?" A fly whizzed by Will's face, and he swatted at it. "I'm sure it's just a voodoo glitch of some kind." He stood from the sofa.

She glanced up at him, wondering what he meant to do. "Voodoo glitches are called bad juju."

"My secretary said the same thing. She swears the city has been cursed." He went to the kitchen. "If you ask me, she's more concerned about her job. All this rain has put my building projects behind schedule."

Lexie sat up and reached for the remote, muting the game. "Our store sales have plummeted since the rain began. A few shops on our block have shut down for good until things improve. The tourists have left town."

He searched the kitchen counter. "What does your ghost say about all these happenings?"

"He agrees with Nina. Bad juju has descended over the city."

Will lifted a magazine from the counter and rolled it up. "I like Nina, but the way she just showed up at your shop makes me wonder about her intentions. You should get her checked out." He leapt toward the entertainment center, swinging the magazine. "Damn, missed."

"You sound as suspicious as Titu."

"Well, Titu is a wise old bird. If she's questioning Nina's appearance, you need to run a background check. After everything we went through with Bloody Mary, who's to say her supporters aren't plotting against you."

The *bam* of the magazine connecting with the kitchen counter jarred her.

"Would you leave the fly, Will." Another one buzzed past her face. "Shit. There's two of them in here. How did they get in?"

Will went to the doors leading to the balcony. "Do you hear that?"

Lexie got up from the sofa, and as soon as she came up to him, a low buzzing came through their back door.

"What is it?"

Will hooked her waist. "Get behind me."

"Why?"

"Just do it, Lexie!"

She curled into his back with her hands on his shoulders, looking around the nape of his neck while he reached for the door handle.

The buzzing got much louder when he cracked the door.

Her breath coming in quick gasps, she stared out into the night.

A wave of black shot up from the courtyard as if alerted by the light escaping from their door. The humming became deafening. Her eyes adjusted to the dark, and then Lexie became paralyzed with terror.

Flies, thousands of them swarmed like a flock of birds, dipping and rising with a single mind. While poised over the pond, their mass obscured the floodlights from the adjacent buildings.

Aghast, Lexie's nails dug into Will as the swarm pulled into a giant ball. A black wave flowed over the mass, bending and twisting in different directions, forming a shape.

"Have you ever seen flies do that?" Will mumbled against her cheek.

Never taking her eyes off the object, she whispered back, "No. Never."

Right after Lexie spoke, the ball suddenly contracted into a tight, flat orb.

The flies disappeared, but their buzzing remained. Depressions sank into the orb; two eyes, a dip where the nose should be, and a thin line for the mouth.

The face reminded Lexie of a large black skull.

The skull then exploded, and the flies flew off in every direction.

"Holy shit!" Will slammed the doors and set the bolt. "What the hell was that?"

Lexie went around him to the window and peeked outside into the courtyard.

The only things hovering above the pond were a few bright beams from a neighbor's spotlight. The flies had disappeared.

She stepped back, trembling. "It's a warning."

"Any idea who's sending it?"

She rubbed his back, eager to feel his warmth. "No, but I'm sure I will find out soon enough."

"Are you all right?" Magnus arrived in her living room. "I came as soon as I felt the dark presence nearby."

"We're fine." She looked up. "Just spooked."

"Who are you talking ...?" Will's voice faded. "Oh my God. Is that ...?"

Lexie held her breath as Will stared openmouthed at

Magnus. "Can you see him?"

Will closed his mouth and cleared his throat. "Oh yeah."

She rubbed her head, fighting the tension headache coming on. "This is all I need."

"Others have seen me, why not him?" Magnus maneuvered closer. "It's a pleasure to meet you, Will."

Will's cheeks blanched, but he managed a courteous nod.

"Yeah, it's nice to know you're real."

Magnus smugly grinned. "I've always been real."

A long lapse of silence followed as each of the men—well, man and ghost—sized the other up.

Since she'd first met Magnus, she longed for Will to see him, to know he existed. Her wish finally granted, she questioned if seeing Magnus was good for her husband. Will had stayed on the fringe of her world, opting to support her in any way he could, but leaving her to run her responsibilities without his assistance. She'd preferred things that way, seeking guidance from Titu instead of Will. He had his architecture firm, and she her shop. Could they go back to their comfortable existence, or had the tide turned?

"Why is this happening?" Will staggered backward. "Why am I seeing him?"

Lexie rested her hand on his shoulder. "Whatever is going on, whoever brought the rats, rain, and flies, is also waking the dead."

Magnus nodded as if he agreed. "The door between the two worlds is open, and the dead can be seen by the living."

Will stared as if she'd just produced an elephant from her pocket. "Are we talking end of the world shit here, or is this phenomenon limited to this city?"

"I think it's just here."

Magnus pointed his cane at the football game playing on the

television. "Well, it is sunny in Dallas, so it is safe to assume the world is not ending."

"Yeah, thanks for the insight." Will went to the kitchen. "I need a drink."

Lexie followed him. "You've known Magnus is real. Now you can just see him."

"And hear him." Will reached into a cabinet and curled his fingers around a bottle of scotch. "Are there any more ghosts I should know about. Is Jacob coming back, as well?"

"O'Connor is enjoying his eternal slumber, I assure you," Magnus imparted from the living room.

Will set the bottle on the counter. "Good to know."

"Why are you freaking out about this?"

He raised his bloodshot eyes to her, his knuckles white as he gripped his glass and poured himself a drink.

"I don't know, Lexie, let's see? I saw flies turn into a skull out my back door, and then your ghost appears in my living room. I'd say that merits a drink."

"It won't make things any easier to understand, my dear boy." Magnus approached the kitchen.

"First off, I'm not your boy." Will took a healthy sip of scotch. "Second, who is this black presence, and did they orchestrate that crap with the flies?" He polished off the drink and poured himself another. "Lastly, why does my wife have to save the city?"

Magnus stopped next to the counter. "Because Lexie is mambo, and I feel she is the reason the black presence is here."

Lexie marched up to her ghost. "You never mentioned that before."

His lips tilted upward, not quite smiling but as if he meant to. "It just came to me. When I watched the display in your courtyard, I realized it was for you. All of the events we've witnessed have been for you. Someone is attempting to show you their power."

Will's hand trembled while lifting the glass to his lips. "Who's doing this? Is it a person, or another spirit?"

Magnus tapped his finger against his cane. "You've brought up an interesting point. This could be a spirit and not a person."

"But what spirit?" Lexie took a moment to consider the question. "The only ones we've dealt with together are Jacob and Francis. I never interacted with Katie. I would have sensed something from her before losing my powers."

"Valid point." Magnus smoothed his coat sleeve. "Then perhaps it is someone you cannot sense. Someone who has remained hidden."

Lexie fought to the figure out the mystery, but she was numb. The past few days had been challenging for her, and she longed for an escape from her troubles.

"I've intruded enough on your evening." Magnus wheeled around to Will. "Now you know I'm real, let me say, I will always protect Lexie. She will never be harmed as long as I am with her."

Will's deadly gaze looked as if he'd loaded the gun and taken aim at Magnus. "I'm relieved to know she means something to you."

His fading image resembled the time-lapse sequence of a subject in an old photograph disintegrating over centuries, but it only took seconds for Magnus's black coat, red vest, and black boots to melt away.

Will took another deep sip of his drink. His tongue swept across his lips as he peered into his empty glass.

"I can't imagine what kind of man he was. The people he must have pissed off, ignored, or destroyed. I'm sure the list is quite long. Any one of them could reach across time to hurt both of you."

"Let's not think about it now." She didn't want Will to worry. This was her mess. "Pour me one of those?"

Will reached for another glass. "I thought you gave up drinking when you became mambo."

"I did. But after the shit I've seen today, I won't be able to sleep without one."

Will put her glass on the counter and picked up the bottle of scotch. "You and me both, baby. You and me both."

Chapter Eleven

T he full moon's rays kissed the surface of the dark swamp, its fingers of light dipping just below the water and disappearing from view. The air laden with moisture clung to Lexie's skin, but no breeze brought any relief. The crickets' chirp, the insects' buzz, and the hooting of a lone barn owl blended with the constant hiss of swamp gas escaping to the surface and swirled into a single hypnotic refrain.

Lost in the rhythm of life around her, Lexie barely registered the eerie mist cloaking her feet. It crawled across the ground from the waters' edge and climbed the knoll where she waited, but for what she wasn't sure. The mist coiled around her ankles and slinked up to her slender thighs. It caressed the hem of her silk nightgown and brushed the surface of her abdomen, but lingered on the rise of her bosom. The touch against her nipple awakened her from her listlessness. Adrenaline coursed through her veins, but she was unable to move. She seemed tethered to the land—a sacrificial lamb for the gods.

Drumbeats drifted across the water. Sweat beaded Lexie's brow, rolling into her eyes, and her hands curled, digging her nails into her palms. Her eyes fell on the glassy surface of the swamp.

The water—something headed her way across the water.

A cloud of mist rolled and built in the center of the swamp in a spot surrounded by cypress knees rising out of the water in a circle. The fog resembled cotton candy as it congealed to fluffy clouds. Then it moved, heading toward her on the shore.

Lexie's rapid breathing burned her lungs, and a hammer pounded in her head as fear ripped through her gut.

The first glimpse of him came as an outline against the cloud. A trace of a hand, a hint of a face.

He solidified with every passing second. Blond tossed hair lifted in the breeze; concise red lips stood out from tanned skin. The mist carried him closer, and when his face fully formed, the fear cleaving her in two instantly vanished. Back in his casual jeans and fitted T-shirt, Kalfu stepped from the cloud, and his bare feet touched the boggy ground in front of her.

"I told you we would meet again."

He took her hand and an icy dread shot through her core.

The light around him changed, and utter darkness radiated from Kalfu's eyes, turning her stomach. It filled Lexie with a mind-numbing hopelessness and sent her resolve adrift on a dank, dark ocean.

The binds keeping her trapped magically lifted, and she crashed to her knees.

She scurried back from him. "What was that? You touched me and ... I can't describe it."

"You wanted to know me. It's why you're here." He raised his arms displaying a cold, empty grin. "In my world."

"How did I get here, Kalfu."

"Kal. Remember?" He crooked his finger. "Follow me."

He led Lexie from the knoll, and the weight holding her in place disintegrated.

They walked toward a thick cloud. The mist split in the center and parted. A white stone bench and table appeared. Moonlight lit the swamp around them, highlighting the beauty of the clumps of knotted cypress trees, pools of stagnant water, and patches of mossy ground.

Lexie scanned the swamps for any signs of life. Her jaw muscles tightened as her mind raced with how to stay ahead of the evil spirit. She could never embrace such a dark entity, but then the promise of her lost power nudged her determination aside. How could she resist him when so much was at stake? Her power meant everything. It was the only way for her to stay mambo.

He motioned for her to have a seat across from him.

Lexie eased onto the bench, careful to press the rim of her short nightshirt around her thighs.

"Yes, before you ask, you're dreaming."

She rested her jittery hands on the table. "Okay, I'm dreaming, but why here?"

He raised a pointed finger in the air, and the music of the swamp clamored around them. The din of crickets, owls, bugs, even the hissing of water resonated in her ears until it became so loud she could not think. When he lowered his finger, the sounds died away.

Kalfu sat back on his bench, watching her. "I'm at home in the swamps."

She crossed her arms, tucking her hands into her sides. "You should get out more."

He laughed, and the black water around them rippled. The small waves painted with shards of moonlight carried across the swamp for as far as the eye could see.

Lexie admired the play of light and dark, momentarily swayed by the beauty of his imaginary world.

"That is what fascinates me about you, Lexie Arden. Your spirit. It makes you a formidable mambo."

The mention of her title fortified her will. She could not play a passive game with the spirit of darkness. She needed to fight him.

"I can also see through bullshit a mile away. Why am I here?"

His sly grin added a malevolent glimmer to his eyes. "Ah, there is your courage. Once most people see my true inner self, they cower before me, beg me to spare them, or offer some sacrifice to grant their wishes, but not you." He tapped a single finger on the table while keeping up his sinister, vacant stare. "You challenge me."

"You didn't bring me here to kiss your ass. You have something to say, so say it."

He clapped his hands, and the swamp closed in around her.

Four walls sprang up from the moss-covered ground. Painted dark blue and with framed diplomas and certificates on the wall, the room cropping up around her resembled an office.

Her hard bench sprouted into a red leather chair, and her bare thighs squeaked against the cowhide. A cherry desk popped up in front of her. Dark carpeting replaced the grass beneath her feet, and the moon disappeared behind a drab ceiling covered with popcorn-coated sheetrock.

"If we are to talk business ..." Kalfu stood behind the desk in a black pinstripe suit. "We need to set the mood."

She peered around the room, a little overwhelmed by the sudden change of scenery.

He took his chair and locked his fingers together on the

desk. "Tomorrow you will meet with the voodoo council of your city. There you will be challenged. The one who challenges you will not be what she seems."

Lexie fidgeted in her chair as she waited for him to continue, but he added nothing more. Her mouth opened in stunned surprise and she tossed up her hand.

"That's it? Can I get a name?"

"You are not mine yet. If you were, there would be names."

Lexie sat back as the reason for their meeting becoming readily apparent.

"And if I became yours, what would you expect of me?"

His leering smile sent a wave of revulsion through her.

"Does that mean you're considering my proposal?"

She gulped and stared him down, hell-bent not to show an ounce of fear. "Yes."

He dropped his gaze to the desk, his thin lips spread in a smug expression. "If you accept me into your soul, my wants and confidence would become part of your own. You would never have to fear about being powerful enough to serve as mambo; you would be the greatest mambo of all—I suspect even greater than the Queen. In exchange, I could call on you to perform certain duties for me."

"Duties?" She countered, not trusting a word he said. "Can you be more specific?"

He gouged a long fingernail across the surface of the desk, curling up a splinter of wood into a ball.

"Would you prefer it written out in a contract?"

The sight of the scar across the smooth surface of the wood sidelined her wisecrack reply, but she refused to be intimidated.

"Would you stick to the contract?"

He chuckled, but did not answer.

She fidgeted in her chair.

This was a dangerous game with an adversary who could wipe her from the face of the earth with just a thought, but she had one card to play. She was mambo—a position she knew Kalfu respected. She had to make the most of it.

"Ah, I hear you thinking, Lexie Arden."

"My last name is Bennett."

He examined his fingernails, appearing uninterested. "Arden is the name you were initiated under and in my world, it is the name you are known by." He raised his head and listened to the air. "Time to go. Your husband is calling."

Lexie was about to ask him what he meant when Will's deep voice came through the ceiling.

"Wake up, baby."

A burst of light blinded her. Her limbs felt compressed by an enormous burden, and a pressure built in her chest, making her first gasp of air painful.

"Lexie, come on."

She opened her eyes.

Will was there with a white, steaming coffee mug in his hand. The aroma of the Columbian blend wafted by her nose, and she sat up.

Her trembling hands went around the mug.

"Hey, there." He took the mug away and embraced her.

The heat from his body rekindled the spark in her empty spirit.

"You're shaking. What happened? Did you have a bad dream?"

Lexie pulled back from him and connected with his soulful brown eyes. His earthiness grounded her, rousing her from the fog the meeting with Kalfu had left in her. She cupped his cheek and nuzzled his nose.

"Do you know what you mean to me?"

129

Will took her hands in his. "Talk to me. Tell me what's frightened you." He kissed her forehead. "It has to be something pretty bad for you to put me before your coffee."

"I had the strangest dream." She squeezed his fingers as she noticed the dark circles under his eyes. "You don't look like you slept very well, either."

"Don't worry about me. I just have my business to look after; you have the welfare of the entire city."

Lexie rolled her eyes. "Don't remind me."

He patted her thigh. "So, what was this bad dream about?"

Images of Kalfu tempting her faded into a blur. "I met a spirit, a voodoo spirit. We talked in a swamp, or was it an office? I can't remember."

Will combed his hand through her hair while his teeth tugged at his lower lip. "Last time you told me that, Magnus came into our lives. Should I be expecting another spirit to join us?"

She looked away. "No. No more spirits. I promise."

"Hey." His thumb caressed her cheek. "It doesn't matter how many ghosts you bring into our lives. If living with a few meddlesome spirits around is what I have to do to keep you happy, then so be it."

Tears welled as she met his gaze. "You mean that?"

He pulled her close, tucking her head under his chin. "You are my world, Mrs. Bennett. I'd do anything to make sure you're happy."

She reveled in the safety of his arms, wishing to remain with him a little while longer, but as she listened to his soothing heartbeat, she caught sight of her alarm clock.

"Why did you wake me so early? It's not even seven."

"You told me to." He sat back on the bed. "You wanted to get up early and prepare for your meeting."

She tossed her covers aside. "Shit. The council meeting is today."

Will got up from the bed. "Wish I could be there for moral support, but I have back-to-back client meetings all day."

"You sound busy."

He went to the closet door. "I'm not complaining. Bennett Architecture is doing well. One day I'll take on a partner. Make it, Bennett and Bennett Architecture." He glanced back at her over his shoulder. "I was hoping we could get started on making my partner. I want to get William Bennett Junior behind a draft board ASAP."

"William?" She sat on the edge of the bed. "What about Willamina?"

"She will be our number two baby." He removed a black pinstripe suit still wrapped in the dry-cleaning bag from the closet. "After that, I was thinking of going for twins."

She was about to bring up the high cost of raising multiple children when he stepped into the bathroom and closed the door.

She let out a long breath as she came up with a flurry of things to tell Will when he came out of the bathroom. The prime one being—how was she to juggle her life as mambo with motherhood? And children weren't even a consideration until she got her powers back, took care of the city, and set right the imbalance in the universe. Overwhelmed by the list of things she had to do, Lexie flopped back on the bed.

We'd be mad to have a child now.

The side of her bed dipped as the gray Maine coon cat jumped on the comforter and stared at her.

"Where did you come from?" She patted the bed, encouraging him closer. "Come here, Damballah."

The cat padded to her and curled up in her lap. She stroked the creature's thick hair and considered how much this cat

131

reminded her of the one she'd known in Maine.

Lexie became hypnotized by the cat's purring. The cadence of it soothed her and at the same time empowered her being. She became refreshed and energized in an instant—the same way the cane made her feel.

The bathroom door flew open and Will bounded out, freshly shaven with damp hair from his shower.

"That was fast," Lexie said.

"What are you talking about?" He ran a towel over his face.

"You usually take long showers in the morning."

"I did." He held the towel out to the bed. "What are you doing? I thought you had to get ready. Why are you still in bed?"

"I was petting the cat. He's pretty, huh?"

"What cat are you talking about?" He stepped toward the bed and placed a hand on her shoulder. "Are you sure you're all right?"

Lexie's eyes darted around the room, searching for Damballah, but there was no sign of him. Not even a single gray hair stained her white nightshirt.

Will had a seat on the bed. "Maybe you fell back asleep and dreamed about the cat. Could that be it?"

She rubbed her face. "Yeah, maybe so."

Despite the countless hours she spent communicating with spirits, she'd never felt so adrift. Was this a hangover from her dream, or was Kalfu's influence more far-reaching than she imagined?

"What are you going to do after your council meeting?" Will called reentering the bathroom. "Go back to the store?"

Lexie snapped back and considered the question.

"Yeah, I have to. Everyone is freaked out by all the crazy stuff going on. Nina can't handle it on her own."

"I can see why they're freaked out. The floods, the rats, and those damned flies forming God knows what in our courtyard."

"And the ghosts. Everyone is seeing ghosts. It's why the shop's been so busy."

Will stuck his head out the bathroom door while fixing his gray tie. "What are you going to do about it?"

The question hit her hard. She'd been asking herself the same thing, but to hear Will say what had haunted her for days was utterly distressing. It was as if fate now pressed her for a solution.

"I'm not sure I can do anything. Not without my powers."

He came up to her in his dress shirt and blue boxers, the lines across his forehead and around his eyes crinkled in alarm.

"People are counting on you. You're their mambo, their leader. You need to find a way to help them or they may lose faith in you."

Lexie snatched up her coffee mug from the night table as the oppression bearing down on her spirit buckled her self-confidence.

"I've heard some priestesses in the city want me removed as mambo."

"Who told you this?"

"Nina and Titu have heard rumblings. It's one of the reasons this council meeting is so important. Titu insists I must show my strength to the other members to avoid a backlash."

He pushed up the knot in his tie. "How are you gonna do that?"

Lexie nursed her warm mug in her hands. "Damned if I know, but I'll have to figure out something soon before everything turns to shit."

"To pot," Will corrected. "Not shit."

"Pot, shit, hell—what difference does it make? If I can't fix things, we'll be run out of town."

He pecked her lips. "I know you, baby. You're smart and resourceful. You'll find a way. I have faith."

Faith. It seemed to be something she had in short supply lately, but she needed it to take control of the chaos taking over the city. Then, Kalfu's offer floated into her head.

"What if the only way to fix the problem meant you had to give up everything? Would you do it?"

"I'd do whatever necessary to keep you and everyone else I love safe." Will retreated to the bathroom to finish dressing.

Lexie peered into her black coffee, reflecting on a life filled with a similar darkness. Could she handle it?

"I've got a feeling I'm gonna find out soon enough."

Magnus sat on the edge of the pond in the courtyard outside Lexie's apartment as more rain clouds stretched over the tops of the surrounding houses. He ran his thumb over the dragon's head handle of his cane as he stared up at her balcony.

The fitful sleep she'd exhibited the night before concerned him. He spent the occasional night by her bed, keeping watch, but since Katie's appearance, he had stuck close to her side. He'd sensed the trouble to come, and feared leaving her alone at night, making sure to depart before her eyes opened in the morning. Will seeing him posed an even bigger problem for his nocturnal guard duty.

The man will be impossible if he catches me.

While fretting over how to keep close to her now everyone could see him, a flick of something out of the corner of his eye drew his attention to the staircase leading to her balcony. The gray Maine coon cat trotted down the wooden steps.

When the creature spotted Magnus at the pond, he hissed.

"This game of yours is getting old."

The cat took a few steps onto the courtyard and then sat down, his green eyes fixed on Magnus.

"I must admit I was flummoxed the other day when you arrived at the store. You had not changed at all from your time in my old home." He stood from the pond's edge and slowly approached the cat. "When I saw you hanging around Altmover Manor, I never gave you a second thought. But here, in New Orleans?" He set the tip of his cane firmly on the cement and rested his hands on the handle. "The time has come to reveal yourself, or I will insist Lexie trap you and send you packing to the local pound."

The cat's tail pounded on the cement.

Magnus grinned, cocky with the knowledge he was right about the beast.

"I'm waiting, Damballah."

The tail stilled, and the feline inclined his head to the side.

Fingers of light rose out of the ground around the cat, but the animal seemed indifferent. It waited as the opaque funnel of brilliance rose higher and got so thick Magnus detected no hint of gray fur behind the veil. The rays stretched until they reached the height of a man.

Magnus tapped his finger on his cane handle, waiting for the special effects to end. He knew they were for his benefit. Any spirit not interested in putting on a performance would have appeared by now.

The beams of light capped off a few inches above Magnus's head and then retreated. The faint glimmers washed away, sinking into the ground. When the light withdrew, a man stood where the cat had once been.

With ebony skin, a round, jovial face, and bald head, he

wasn't quite what Magnus had expected. The white three-piece suit threw him, along with his white leather shoes.

"Finally, we meet, Mr. Blackwell." The voice was throaty and lyrical. "I wondered when you would figure it out."

Magnus stayed back, not wanting to get too close. "The girl, Nina, is the one who discovered who you are, not me."

Damballah directed his attention to the balcony above. "But your mistress still doesn't know." His green eyes found Magnus. "And she must not, at least, for now."

"She's getting suspicious. She will need to see you soon. Lexie needs your protection and your help."

"She already has it, in more ways than you can imagine." He slipped his hand into the pocket of his white jacket. "She will see me when she has chosen the time. As for the rest, that is up to her and you."

Magnus pouted his lips; he'd hoped for a different answer. "Darkness wants her. You cannot allow him to win her over."

"Kalfu wishes to rule through her, but he's a child. He still believes humans can be ruled. He never bothered to understand the power of will—it's impossible to break, even in the weak. I made it impenetrable like the sun, and as limitless as the stars in the heavens."

"Then spare her." Magnus ached for what he suspected lay ahead for Lexie. "You can restore her power."

Damballah shook his head. "Only she can do that, Mr. Blackwell. Until then, her ability is safe with you."

Magnus squeezed his cane, holding back his anger. "I will not sit by and let her be harmed."

His happy-go-lucky expression sobered. "Nothing hurts more than being helpless to spare the one you love great pain. It's a lesson everyone must endure, even ghosts." Damballah raised his head as if listening to something in the air. "She's coming down."

Magnus bent over his cane, feeling drained. "How will this end for her?"

He strolled over to him, his jovial smile back on his thick lips. "Who said it will end? Life and death are an adventure, my friend, and this is only the beginning."

Chapter Twelve

The squat, slanted roofs, narrow streets, and the white spires of St. Louis Cathedral from the thirty-fifth floor of the One Shell Square building captivated Lexie. She'd never seen the French Quarter from such a vantage point.

"Quite a view," Magnus said to her right. "I've never dreamed of being so high."

The rooftops of the old cottages bunched tightly together reminded her of a village set amid the landscape of towering glass mountains. How the past existed so congruently next to the new puzzled her when she'd first arrived. Now she understood the melding of architectures and cultures was the way of things in New Orleans. Every idea, every structure absorbed into the city's essence, and like a good gumbo, the residents learned to thrive on its uniqueness.

But as she thrilled at the panoramic scenery, the reason for her visit to Krieger and Carson Law Firm brought back the tension crushing her head.

Titu stood on the other side of Lexie, taking in the view. "Our secretary, Jacques Krieger, is a lawyer for the firm. Being one of the council members, we get to use his conference room."

"You have a lawyer on this thing?"

"Those who are leaders in our religion are also leaders in our community." Titu glanced over her shoulder at the others gathering at the oval conference table. "Voodoo encompasses all walks of life, all races, all classes. The council strives to embrace the same diversity as the citizens of our city."

Lexie turned and encountered the hostile glares from the five members of the council in the conference room. The pounding in her head picked up tempo to keep pace with her rapidly beating heart. She swallowed hard, unrelenting in her quest to appear confident.

"I'm beginning to get the picture."

Titu took her arm, guiding her to the table. "There are always six practitioners on each council. Our mambo makes the seventh member. In case any vote is split down the middle, you must break the tie and remain impartial, but in the past, it hasn't always been so. The history of the council is mired more in money than voodoo. You will change that."

Lexie's confidence twisted into knots. "I'll do my best."

A warm electric tingle of energy from her dragon cane eased the discomfort in her head. Ready to address the grim faces around the table, she remembered Queen Marie's faith in her.

Titu let her go. "Remember, after I call the meeting to order, tap your cane three times on the floor and place it on the table."

"Why three times?"

Titu offered her a sly smile. "You'll see soon enough."

"It will be fine," Magnus encouraged next to her. "You are the chosen one."

"I know that, but do they?" She nodded to the table.

139

"Prove their suspicions wrong." He turned to her, arching one eyebrow. "Be the woman who won the cane, and they will see what I already know."

She let out a long breath. "And what is that?"

"You are unconquerable."

His words melded with her soul.

The support of Will and Magnus, compounded by the strength she drew from her cane, gave her determination to face the storm ahead.

Her head held high, she stopped at the conference table.

Here we go.

No welcoming smiles greeted her—only the hungry glowers of cannibals ready to tear her flesh from the bone.

Each member sized her up, and Lexie compared the intrusive glances to the uncomfortable experience of a gynecological exam—nerve-wracking and highly personal. Titu had prepared her for some rancor among the members, but not the abject antagonism staring back at her.

At that moment, she was thankful for the loss of her power. To be able to tap into the psyches ripping her to shreds would have only destroyed her morale.

Once urged to the head of the table by Titu, Lexie had a seat and waited as her mentor settled in next to her.

Magnus took up position behind her.

She could tell by the curious glances, the council members could see her spirit guide. The acknowledgment of his presence comforted her more than she realized. Her ghost had become a vital part of her mystique.

At the other end of the table, a man in a blue suit stood up. His ebony skin added a luminescent tint to his teeth when he smiled.

"I call this meeting of the elders of the New Orleans Voodoo

Council to order," the man announced in a deep baritone. "The record will show all members are present." He dipped his head to Lexie. "Mambo, if you will."

Trepidation tingled her fingers as everyone observed her. Mindful of every move she made, and praying she didn't screw up, Lexie stood from her chair.

With a firm grip on the openmouthed dragon head handle, she banged the tip of her cane on the floor. The thud echoed through her as if the staff amplified the sound. After the third one, she gently rested the baton juju on the table and held her breath.

For several seconds, nothing happened, and Lexie feared the council would turn on her. Then, the staff vibrated; very slight at first, but soon it bounced on the table, filling the room with a frenzied clattering.

When the tip of the baton juju moved, she gripped the edges of her chair and eyed the others at the table. No one else appeared alarmed.

The wiggling tip reminded her of a snake's tail. The slithering motion climbed higher. The scales carved into the wood of the staff plumped as if filling with water. The scales undulated, coming alive on the back of a serpent. The marble color of the wood darkened to a deep almost black green, resembling the flesh of a lizard.

Lexie's eyes watered, and she had to remind herself to blink. So overwhelmed by what was happening to her cane, she pinched the skin on her hand to make sure she wasn't lost in another dream.

The tail of the creature coming to life on the table curled around, coiling on itself. The vibrant hue of dark green flushed up the entire length of the cane, reaching the head. When the color touched the tip of the dragon's snout, its lips peeled back exposing its long white fangs and bright pink gums. A red tongue jutted in and out, and the creature rose up, standing as if ready to strike.

The one thing confounding Lexie were the changeling stones. They remained two iridescent pearls. The dragon, now fully materialized, rocked from side to side, inspecting the faces of the council members. When the uncanny eyes settled on Lexie, she almost bolted from her chair.

"Now there's something you don't see every day," Magnus muttered.

Titu placed her hand on Lexie's forearm. "Stay calm, child."

The dragon writhed on the table, dipping closer to Lexie, and baring its sharp fangs.

Sweat dripped down the back of her white dress. Edgy at not knowing if she was going to be attacked or revered by the dragon, she looked to the others at the table, hoping to find reassurance.

With an exuberant grin, Titu raised her head to the council members.

"Damballah is with us. He approves of our mambo."

Lexie relaxed, but never took her eyes off the dragon still weaving in front of her.

"Is it supposed to do that?"

Titu angled closer and covered her mouth with her hand so only Lexie could here. "The cane has been missing for over a hundred and fifty years. No one knew what to expect."

The dragon uncoiled itself and extended out over the table, darting its red tongue as it went. The dark green drained from its skin, and the marble color of the wood reappeared. The scales shrunk back into carved shapes while the head of the creature curled around. Its eyes gleamed as the mouth opened, showing its razor fangs. It petrified, and the light of life left the dragon's being, changing back into the baton juju Lexie had come to know.

Magnus arched over her shoulder. "I never imagined it could come to life."

"The legend states Damballah must appear and call the meeting to order before we can begin." Titu slouched in her chair. "When the baton juju turns into a serpent, it means the god approves."

Lexie touched the end of the cane, testing it to see if it was safe to pick up. "What did you do all those years without the baton juju?"

"Hoped Damballah approved and went on with our business."

She raised her eyebrows to Titu. "What if he hadn't appeared today?"

Her dry chuckle drew the attention of the others at the table. "Just be thankful he did. No one will question your appointment after that display."

Her cane at her side, Lexie settled down in her chair, the acid churning in her stomach.

"Why didn't you warn me?"

"Because if I had told you what to expect, you would have seen what was expected. The mind must remain open for the eyes to see the truth."

"Mambo, I am Jacques Krieger," the man in the blue suit proclaimed. "And I welcome you to this meeting as our leader."

Titu, Jacques Krieger, and another on the council gently patted the table, offering their support. Three individuals—a man, seated between two women—did not join in.

The man's skin reminded Lexie of Kalila's. It had the same shimmering pearl color. His features struck Lexie as handsome with a square jaw, high forehead, and thin lips, but it was his black eyes—a telltale of his affiliation to the darkness—which bothered her most.

The women flanking him were even more off-putting. One had onyx skin and the other stark white. They had similar pouty thick lips, round faces, and the same blank expressions. They even shared the same curly, fiery red-gold hair. Their vacant faces made her wonder if they were high on some drug, but their milky white eyes, bereft of any hint of color, disturbed Lexie most of all.

Magnus dropped his head, turning away from the others, and placed his lips close to her ear.

"Any idea who they are?"

Titu tapped the arm of her chair, drawing her attention. "I see you admiring the Chez sisters, Helen and Corinne. They were born together but had separate fathers, and since they were small have served the voodoo spirit, Maman Brigitte. They only speak to recite her prophecies; otherwise, they're mute. Maman is the wife of Baron Samedi and a death spirit, but unlike the others in our religion, she's a white Irish woman with fiery red hair. Hence the reason for their bad dye job."

"What about their eyes?"

Titu's nostrils flared. "Their mother sacrificed their sight to Kalfu when they were children. Madeline Chez was a crazy bitch who lived in the swamps and surrounded herself with evil companions. She sat on the council for years and was always stirring up trouble."

Her language surprised Lexie. "Doesn't sound as if you cared for her."

"No one did. Madeline's daughters have followed in her footsteps, so watch yourself around them."

"And the man?"

Titu's voice hardened. "Harold Forneaux. He's a power-hungry priest who would love to rule the council through you."

Harold's intrusive gaze met hers.

His face clouded over with mist. His features dissolved and someone else manifested in the smoky essence. Lexie blinked thinking it was a trick of the light, but then Kalfu's face appeared. *Remember what I told you. You will be challenged. The one who challenges you will not be what she seems.*

"Normally, we would discuss items related to territory issues between priestesses." Jacques' loud voice made the cloud hovering over Harold's face evaporate. "As y'all know the job of the council is to resolve disputes and assign control over regions. But there's a more pressing issue—the events in the city."

She stared at Harold, biting her lower lip and grasping what she'd seen.

A whoosh of white appeared in her peripheral vision, distracting her. Then Magnus's unhappy frown edged in front of her.

"Trouble has arrived."

A woman's screech rattled the windows in the room overlooking the city.

"I have a challenge to put to the council!"

In a red silk robe covering her long white dress, Renee Batiste stood in the open double doors to the conference room. Her legs spread apart in an assertive stance, her eyes shined with a black light as they haphazardly darted around the room. Her long black, disheveled, frizzy hair accentuated the translucent glow on her coffee-colored skin. She weaved unsteadily on her feet, coming across as a confused Amazonian warrior searching for the battle.

This was not the woman Lexie had encountered in previous meetings. Always cordial, a little timid, and never overzealous, Renee had become known around town as a tragic figure—a shadow of her former self.

"Damn." Titu's knuckles shone white against the dark wood

of her chair's arm. "What's she doing here?"

Jacques pushed his chair away and was quickly on his feet. "You're not a member anymore, Renee. You were removed when Bloody Mary lost the *haute défi*."

"I demand to be heard." Renee scurried toward the table, her face frozen in a manic, glossy-eyed expression. "Your mambo has no power!"

Panic overpowered Lexie's rational thinking, and her rage took control. She wanted to choke the living shit out of Renee. How could she do this to her now? In the middle of her first council meeting?

A gentle breeze grazed her cheek, grounding her. She glimpsed Magnus's ghostly white hand pulling away.

"Remember who you are. Show no regard for her ravings, and they will have no reason to doubt you."

His words rattled around her head, driving away all the cobwebs created by her fury.

"That's a baseless claim." Jacques' voice echoed throughout the room. "You have no authority here. Go home."

Renee banged both her fists on the table, imitating the temper tantrum of a five-year-old. "I've heard from her landlord; she has no power. Otis Landry is my client, and he came to me concerned when Lexie Arden could not rid him of a spirit."

The energy in the room shifted, and even without her power, Lexie could feel the annoyance of the crazed woman's appearance abating. A prickle of disbelief rose around her.

She opened her mouth, hesitating as she formulated her reply, but Renee swept down to her end of the table. She pointed at Lexie and bared her white teeth.

"Bad juju is sweeping through the city because of her loss of powers. You've all felt it. The break in the peace between light and dark has touched each one of us."

Before Renee could continue her wild rant, a woman with long white hair and withered dark skin rapped on the table with her gnarled hand.

"I have something to say." She stood, rising slowly from her chair. "You all know me. I've practiced the art for fifty years, but my powers have faded. I have felt the shift in the universe. Bad times are upon us."

Jacques hunched forward as he placed his hands on the table and stared down each member of the council.

"Madame Henri is right. A bad juju grips the city. I, too, have lost my powers. We must do something before things get worse."

"See?" Renee rested her hands on her hips, and defiantly raised her chin resembling a maniacal dictator. "This would have never happened under Bloody Mary's reign. It's because of her the universe is not happy."

"I've heard enough!" Titu wiggled her finger at Renee. "How dare you walk in here speaking against the woman who saved us from Bloody Mary—your friend whose evil suffocated this city for years."

Renee closed in on Titu, her movements more animal than human. The strange tone of her skin, enhancing the diabolical glint in her eye.

"Your powers are gone too, Titu Hebert. Admit it. All the white magic is being sucked out of the city. The spirits do not want a charlatan as mambo."

All eyes at the table turned to Lexie.

"Careful." Magnus was in her ear. "She's not herself. She's possessed."

"No shit," Lexie mumbled.

The Chez twins, who had never uttered a sound before this moment, raised their hands in unison and rolled back their heads.

They swayed, rocking side to side in a trance, their fiery hair churning like angry waves on an ocean.

"The darkness in the priestess grows tired of waiting."

They spoke as one in a breathless female voice, tinged with a distinctive Irish accent.

"He yearns to blacken your bright light. Hurry with your answer, dear lady. He wants to replace your wrong with his right."

Their words added to Lexie's troubles. She'd seen many things in her short tenure as mambo, but never two women speaking as one, and in a voice not belonging to either. The message of the rhyme was clear to Lexie: Kalfu's patience would not last for long.

Madame Henri bowed her head. "Madam Bridget has spoken. We must adjourn this meeting."

Harold Forneaux wrapped an arm around each of the Chez sisters. "Until we can find a way to put the universe in balance, we must disband the council."

"That's bullshit, Harold, and you know it!" The *crack* of Titu's open hand hitting the table cut through the tense atmosphere in the room. "You've wanted to control the council for years, so you can continue with your nefarious operations in the swamps without answering to us. Bloody Mary let you get away with your drug business, but Lexie will not. So don't sit here and spout your holier than thou attitude for the spirits. This is about your bottom line."

"That's slander, Titu Hebert!" Harold dropped his arms from the twins and kicked back his chair.

"Good." Titu smirked at him. "You can hire Jacques to sue me."

Jacques held up his large hands to the group, urging calm.

"We can't disband. The Queen forbade it. The council will

remain, and an approach to the problems in the city will be agreed on."

"How can we fix anything when a deceiver rules?" Renee insisted.

Pushed beyond her limits, Lexie sprang from her chair, white anger boiling her brain. She gripped her cane, bolstered by the feel of wood in her hand. She was the rightful mambo, and she'd be damned before she let Renee take her title away.

"I'm the Queen's chosen, selected after a long line of untrue priestesses took over. Bad juju has hung over New Orleans since the death of Simone Glapion. It changed when I arrived."

Madame Henri raised her head to Lexie, scolding her with a pair of liquid brown eyes.

"But your ghost killed Simone Glapion with the very cane you hold in your hand."

Magnus's mouth dropped, and his focus shifted to Lexie. "How did she know that?"

Madame Henri shuffled closer to the ghost, showing him a craggy-toothed smile. "Everyone knows what you did, Mr. Blackwell. The spirits have spoken of it for many, many years. Why would fate tie you to any mambo of this city? You're the bad juju haunting us. You should be cast out."

"You will not touch my ghost!" Lexie faced down the older woman, adamantly banging her cane on the floor. "I am what I am because of him."

"They're pitting you against me." Magnus stepped behind her. "I don't like this."

"Where do your loyalties lie, Helen?" Titu let out a long sigh, appearing bored with the conversation. "None of us in this room dare reverse the Queen's judgment. Ms. Marie has spoken—Lexie is Mambo."

"But we can appoint someone else until another *haute défi* is called." Renee slinked closer to Titu's chair. "Someone with their power still in place. It can be done."

"That can never happen!" Jacques' gruff voice climbed higher, almost to the point of breaking. "There will not be another *haute défi*. The Queen has made her choice. We must support our mambo. All of us." His hands rose in the air, pleading with the others on the council. "How can we maintain peace in the city when we can't even reach an accord amongst ourselves?"

"The spirits don't want peace. They want revenge." Renee let loose an acidic cackle eliciting a grimace from almost every face at the table.

The horrible sound vibrated through Lexie, echoing in the hollow place where her energy used to reside. Pain filled her, cruelly throbbing as if the laughter had awakened it to action.

Trembling, she grabbed her chest.

What the hell was that?

A river of dread coursed through Magnus as Renee's twisted laugh rang in his ears. He recognized the sound. He thought it familiar the first time it had come from his sweet Katie in Lexie's atelier. Now, he was positive.

How had she followed him from the past? He believed death had separated them forever, or he'd hoped it would.

"Magnus, did you hear her laugh?"

The terror etched into Lexie's features tore him apart.

"Yes. The same darkness using my Katie has Renee."

"We're not going to get anywhere today." Jacques drooped against the table. "I suggest we postpone any discussion on the bad juju in the city until more research is done. Until a cause can be discovered."

"I second the motion." Titu reached for Lexie's hand. "Let's get out of here."

Renee rushed toward her place at the table.

Magnus barred her way by floating in front of Lexie's chair. The black light in her fiery eyes slithered through him as he took up a guarded stance.

"You know better, Magnus."

The voice coming from Renee was his Katie's but tinged with a fury she'd never possessed in life. He almost didn't recognize it except for the way she sweetly spoke his name.

He held his ground and did not budge.

Renee's lips pouted. "Magnus, please."

It was Katie's voice, sounding how he remembered her.

"I don't like this game."

The guilt her words awakened nearly made him crumble to the floor. On a night when his anger had overpowered him, he'd abused his wife and hurt her. He closed his eyes, haunted by the moment when his love for her had died.

"Magnus? What is it?"

With Lexie's voice in his ear, he opened his eyes.

Renee had left the conference room.

He dashed to the open double doors leading to a beige-colored hallway.

"Where did Renee go?"

Lexie came up to him. The wrinkle between her eyes hinting at her distress.

"She left. She stormed out as soon as Jacques closed the meeting."

Magnus rested his hand against his brow, collecting himself. The arrogance he held in life had faded, but for once he wished he could be the man he was—indifferent to others, and immune from their suffering.

Titu joined them at the doors, giving Magnus a cursory going over.

"What's up with your ghost?"

Lexie checked the nearly empty room. "The dark spirit I told you about before. The one I encountered in my workshop when all this mess started, it's in Renee. Magnus recognized it, too."

"It seems things are worse than we believed. Renee Batiste is no friend of mine, but she's a priestess of the art." Titu rubbed her chin. "We have to find a way to free Renee of this spirit."

"How does she propose we do that?" Magnus knitted his brow. "Call an exorcist?"

Lexie scowled at him. "How do we free her from this evil?"

"Possession isn't about evil, but about need." Titu stepped into the hallway outside. "The spirit needs the body for something. We just have to figure out why this dark entity wants Renee, the purpose for possessing her. When we have the answer, then we can banish it."

Lexie followed Titu out of the conference room. "Since we don't know who or what the spirit is, banishing it may be impossible."

In the hallway, Titu paused and adjusted her black shawl. "Perhaps, but there's another way. A spirit can be trapped for a few seconds in a body it possesses if the person is rendered unconscious or killed. We could knock Renee Batiste out with drugs, and this spirit would be at our mercy. Once trapped, we could send the spirit across the bridge to blackness and banish it from this world forever."

Magnus nervously peered down the corridor, afraid others may be listening to their conversation.

"We should move along."

Lexie paid no attention to him and stopped. "How do you send a spirit across the bridge to blackness?"

"You must stand in the middle of the bridge holding on to the spirit. Then you proclaim, 'I cast you across this bridge to blackness, and call them by name. For all your sins, may you never know peace." Titu shrugged. "It's not hard."

"Doesn't seem to be. But how do you get to the bridge?"

Magnus sighed, growing frustrated with their dawdling. "Why do I feel there's a catch coming?"

"The bridge exists in another dimension." Titu's lips lifted in a forced smile. "To get there takes a great deal of power. And if you ever do get to the bridge, some believe you will never be the same." A hollow hitch resonated in her voice. "It haunts those who have visited it, lingering in their nightmares and blackening their souls."

The curiosity alight in Lexie's taut features bewildered Magnus. How could she be so interested in something so terrifying?

"Have you ever seen this bridge?" Lexie asked.

Titu patted her hand and headed down the hall, leaving the question unanswered.

Chapter Thirteen

T he following day, the dreary gray skies descended and cast a woeful shade over the French Quarter, which eventually made its way inside the doors of Mambo Manor.

"It's been ages since I've seen the sun."

Seated on a stool behind one of the glass counters displaying various amulets, necklaces, bracelets, and rings, Nina rested her head on her hand releasing long sighs.

A distant roll of thunder added to the patter of rain against the window.

Lexie wanted to scold the young woman for sitting around, but there was nothing to do. They had conducted their weekly check on the inventory in the storeroom, gone through the website emails and product orders, and cleaned the display cases, plus dusted the bookshelves. Since they had opened, there hadn't been a single customer. Lexie doubted she'd seen more than a handful of people walking the street.

"Maybe we should close for the day," she said, sounding

more despondent than she'd intended.

"Nonsense," Nina insisted. "Things will turn around."

Lexie removed her red turban-shaped hat. "After yesterday's council meeting, I'm wondering if I should give up being mambo." She ran her hand through her honey-blonde locks.

"I heard Renee Batiste showed up and spilled the beans about your power."

"How did you know?"

"The rumor mill is working overtime in the city."

Lexie chewed on her thumbnail. "What else are people saying?"

Nina got up from her stool. "Being mambo isn't what you expected, is it?"

"I didn't know what to expect. I came to New Orleans to find this." She held up the baton juju. "Instead, I found my calling. I always wanted to help people, to give comfort to the lost and helpless, but when I became mambo, I discovered I could do so much more—be so much more. I became fulfilled for the first time in my life. Funny thing, I didn't even know what a mambo was until Titu explained it to me. Even then, I had no idea of the responsibility attached to the title, but now … I wonder if the Queen made a mistake in choosing me."

"Marie Laveau would never have selected you unless she was sure you could handle it. She set the bar high for others who followed, and she waited until the perfect candidate came along to continue her work."

"I agree with Nina." Magnus materialized in the open doorway to the street.

Nina gasped, and her hand went to her chest. "Does he always just appear like that?"

"My dear girl." Magnus sauntered into the store, swinging his cane. "You will survive this hiccup."

"Your Mr. Blackwell is wise, and a little creepy, but he's got a point." Nina tossed up her hand. "No more talk about giving up being mambo. You would anger the universe if you did."

"And we can't have that," Magnus added.

A bright beam of white light sprung from a spot on the floor next to him. It reached up to the low ceiling and obscured a section of the shop wall on the other side. A shadowy specter appeared in the light, twisting and bending as if trying to break free.

"Lexie?" Nina edged closer: her unblinking eyes took on a watery sheen. "What is it?"

The dark shape in the light robbed Lexie of her speech. It moved as it congealed from a smoky presence to a solid form. A woman's hips shone through, along with the curve of a face, and long hair swept up in a soft breeze.

"You need to be careful, Mambo."

A female voice, melodious and distinct, came from the figure.

"She's after you and will not rest until she has your power, and your ghost."

Lexie squinted, anxious to find the owner of the voice. She sounded so familiar, but the way the light shifted made it difficult to see her.

Then the figure stopped moving, and Kalila La Fay briefly came into focus. Her face no longer shimmered with its brilliant pearl color but was a smooth café au lait. Her eyes were a muddy brown, and the black fire distressing Lexie at their first meeting had died out. It was as if the woman Titu had mentioned—the one before Kalfu claimed her—stood in Lexie's presence.

"He means to have you, and change you forever."

The light blazed, and Lexie covered her eyes. Intense rays spread into her shop and their force pushed her back against the wall. Then the light got sucked in one intense blast into the ceiling. The impact knocked the wind out of her, sending her plummeting to the floor.

"Lexie, are you okay?"

Flat on her back, and staring up at the ceiling, the burning in her chest told her to breathe, but she couldn't. The commands from her mind went unheeded by her body. She couldn't move and as the seconds ticked by her need for air created a horrible panic. Then she thankfully gasped, hungrily sucking in a breath.

Magnus's face appeared above her. "Are you all right?"

She scooted into a sitting position, holding her chest as the burning ebbed.

Nina slipped an arm around her waist, helping her from the floor.

"What happened?"

Her lower lip throbbed. Something trickled down her chin, and she wiped it away.

"Is that blood?"

Nina held on to her as she stared at her hand.

"You bit your lip when you hit the wall."

Lexie's legs wobbled as Nina escorted to the stool behind the display case.

Nina sat her down and raised her head to get a better look at her lip. "I'll get you some ice for that." She took off for the kitchen.

Magnus was at her side, eagerly checking her cut lip. "Are you hurt anywhere else?"

Lexie squirmed on the stool, wincing slightly. "No, I'm good."

He raised his hand to her lip, appearing as if he wanted to touch her. "You scared the hell out of me. One minute you were talking with us, the next you launched across the room."

She peered over his shoulder at the red door, checking on Nina's whereabouts. "I saw Kalila La Fay. She was in the shop, standing next to you. Didn't you see her?"

Magnus stepped back, staring blankly at her. "No. All I saw was you tossed across the room."

A sense of doom engulfed Lexie.

"Something's happened to Kalila. Her spirit reached out to me."

"Did someone hurt her? Did she tell you how she died, or why?"

Lexie banged her fist on the counter. "No. I didn't get anything like that."

Magnus turned to the window behind the counter. She was about to ask him what he sensed when red and blue flashing lights danced on the walls of her shop.

By the time she stood at the window, the door of a police car parked on the street opened. Emile Glapion climbed out with his jaw clenched and his eyes cast downward.

Lexie forced back her tears, knowing her suspicions about Kalila's death were right.

"Watch what you say to the detective." Magnus slowly faded from view. "You have a habit of saying too much to the police."

"We found her in the swamp right outside her home." Emile put his glass of iced tea on her kitchen table and eyed the faint light trickling in her balcony windows. "Aunt Titu said you went to see her the other day. Did she mention anyone being after her? Happen to give you any names of people she might be feuding with? Is there anything you can remember that struck you as odd?"

Lexie removed the white towel filled with ice from her lip. "My whole visit was odd, but we only talked about me. I went to her to see if I could find out who's stealing my powers."

Emile's gaze grew colder than the ice in her towel. "Did you think Kalila stole them? Is that why you went?"

Her anger came to life, and she threw the towel from the table to her kitchen sink. "Are you saying I'm a suspect?"

His face remained impassive as he rested his hand on the revolver clipped to his waistband. "I'm trying to get to the bottom of a murder investigation."

"Well, I didn't kill her!"

Emile pointed at her lip. "How did you get that?"

Her hand went to her mouth. "I tripped over something and ran into the wall."

He frowned, not appearing too convinced. "No one hit you, or attacked you, or you didn't cut yourself with a sharp blade?"

"No!" Lexie set her hands on her hips and glared at him. "Your aunt sent me to Kalila because she believed she could help me. She was rumored to have a lot of influence with the dark side of magic."

Emile rested his arms on the table. "I'm afraid when we found her, she wasn't alone in the swamp. We found several other bodies in the water. One was a small child—a little girl around six or seven. Her throat had been cut. Know anything about that?"

Lexie covered her face with her hand, overcome with the loss of a child. When she could look at Emile, she kneaded her knuckles into her thighs, angry with herself for not being forthright.

"The souls of the bodies you found were bound to Kalila."

The lines across his brow deepened. "Say again? Bound to her? How?"

"Kalila would bind spirits of the dead to her and use them to do her bidding."

"After killing their bodies?"

"I don't know." Lexie slumped in her chair, fed up with his questioning. "We never discussed anything other than my situation."

Emile sat back. "Do you think the same person she said was after you, could be after her?"

"Not a person, a spirit."

"Spirits don't carve up a woman and leave her face down in the swamps. In my experience, only people do that—people who practice dark magic."

A rush of nausea came over her. "Carved up? How?"

"Like my brother, Remi." He briefly turned away. "But the symbols were different this time. I showed Titu the pictures from the crime scene because we needed help IDing Kalila—we couldn't find any family. She recognized the symbols right away, and told me about the spell used on her."

Lexie braced herself against the edge of the table. "Go on."

"It's called a draining spell. *Prendre le pouvoir* Titu called it. Black voodoo practitioners carve certain symbols into the victim's chest and back, and then drain their blood. It's supposed to give the person performing the spell the victim's magical power once they drink their blood."

Lexie closed her eyes, revolted by the image of Kalila's final moments. "The poor woman."

Emile pushed his iced tea glass away. "Whoever killed Kalila La Fay meant to show everyone in the voodoo world they're in control."

"But why her power? What could they do with it?"

He casually tossed up his hand from the table. "You got me."

Lexie's eyes flew open as a thought hit her. "Whoever killed her may have muted my power. Maybe they're collecting it for something."

Emile stood from his chair. "That was Titu's thinking. Someone is out to take control."

"Then they won't stop with Kalila. You have to find this person before they hurt anyone else."

He brought his glass to the sink. "Because of the similarities to other murders in the city, we're working with the Lafourche Parish Sheriff's Department on this one. I've got men interviewing Kalila's neighbors and others who practice voodoo in the swamps, but we think the person who reported the crime committed it. A call from a woman at ten fifteen this morning to the local 911 operator said Kalila's body was floating in the swamp around her home." He poured out his tea and set the glass on the counter. "The call was traced back to Kalila's cell phone. And spirits don't use those."

Spirits she could deal with, but an angry person …?

Lexie dashed across the kitchen, determined to get more out of Emile.

"Why are you telling me this? You wouldn't share any of this without a reason."

"I know you." He careened closer, getting right up in her face. "You'll go looking for answers, just like when you went hunting for your baton juju. But you can't do that this time. Understand?"

Lexie nodded but had no interest in his advice. "Thanks for coming by, Emile."

He kissed her cheek. "I'll see myself out."

After she closed her apartment door, she paced her living room floor.

"Who could do such a thing?"

"You know who." Magnus appeared with a deep line of

worry marring his brow. "Renee made her intentions very clear at the meeting. She wants control and will take the power of other priestesses to get it."

"I don't buy it. I know Renee, and I can't believe she killed Kalila." Lexie collected her baton juju leaning against the kitchen counter. "I need to go and see her. Find out for sure."

"Are you out of your mind!" Magnus stood in front of her. "Emile just told you a killer is out there, possibly after you, and you want to confront the lead suspect?"

"It wasn't Renee. She's a quiet woman who wouldn't hurt a fly. At the meeting, we all recognized the same dark spirit who hijacked Katie in her. If I can speak to Renee, when the spirit isn't possessing her, maybe I can get some answers."

"What if the spirit forces her to go after you?"

"I'll take that chance."

Lexie went to the table by the front door and snatched up her keys.

Magnus floated across the room to her side. "You should bring someone else with us, someone human. A witness."

She opened the door while considering his question. "I'll close the shop and take Nina with me."

"Do you think that's wise? You barely know the girl."

"Yes, but everyone else I know would try and stop me, including Titu. I have to check on Renee, and I need someone with me she won't see as a threat."

He came toward her, his lips a thin, angry line. "You haven't thought this through. I must protect you, and I can't do that when you insist on running into the jaws of danger like an overzealous guppy."

She calmly met his gaze and put the dragon head of her cane in front of him.

"If I'd listened to you and Will, I wouldn't be the Mambo of

New Orleans. But I am, and I have every intention of keeping my job for a very long time, but on my terms. No one is going to bully me, or force me to hide away." She strutted through the door, ignoring his glum expression. "That's not who I am."

"Are you sure you want me to come?" Nina asked, rushing behind her on the sidewalk.

Lexie darted through the drizzle, dodging puddles.

"You're all I got. My husband would probably insist Emile lock me up if he knew."

Waves of buzzing flies rose and fell around them as Lexie used her cane to shoo the insects away when they passed the occasional bloated rat carcass on Royal Street. She pinched her nose as she did some fancy side-stepping to avoid the minefield of dead creatures. Crews from the city had cleared the streets of the carrion days before, but still, the unfortunate varmints kept showing up, keeping the air saturated with death and despair.

Nina hurried to her side as they approached Renee's shop. "Why don't you leave her for the police?"

Lexie came to a halt in front of the closed doors. "Because Renee's been docile as a kitten for months, and now she wants me out? It doesn't make sense."

"People never make sense." Nina blinked up at the doors. "Especially serial killers."

"I must add my two cents." Still wearing a scowl, Magnus solidified next to Nina. "You should reconsider this folly. Go back to the shop and let Emile handle Renee."

"What kind of mambo would I be if I ran away from every challenge?"

"The alive kind," Nina muttered when Lexie marched in the doors.

Magnus attempted to follow Lexie in the building, but a force held him back. A curtain covered the entrance barring his kind from entering. He struggled to wedge his way inside the establishment, but the energy pushing him back was too strong.

"Lexie!"

She stepped inside with Nina, and then shut the doors.

Magnus scoured the street for another way in the shop.

He went to a shuttered window and reached his hand through the thick wood, but the force was there, blocking his attempt.

He remembered the ability he'd gained from Lexie. Holding on to his ghost cane, he opened his inner core to the building, searching every crevice for a gap he could squeeze through, but the structure was locked up tight behind a solid wall of magic.

He punched the air, furious at being left behind. "Dammit!"

A bell above the entry rang as they walked inside. The front of the cozy shop done in deep red with black-painted floors catered to the tourist trade with many of the same things Lexie sold—T-shirts, voodoo trinkets, books, with a few added amulets thrown in.

"We should get some of those." Nina gravitated toward a display of spirit boards.

"We didn't come here to compare inventory."

The thump of the dragon cane called Nina back to Lexie's side.

"Keep your eyes open."

A curtain of red beads hanging before a door at the back rustled. Then hands pushed the beads apart.

In a bright red dress cut off at the ankles, red turban, and white sash tied at the waist, Renee Batiste entered the room.

"Can I—?" She came to a halt when she spotted Lexie. "Mambo? What a surprise." She sped to Lexie's side with her head bowed low. "What are you doing here?"

Lexie lifted her chin and the dark circles and vapid brown eyes, void of any menacing black light, were the first indication of Renee's suffering.

Her sallow skin had none of the luster seen at the council meeting. The pronounced folds around her mouth made her resemble a deflated balloon. Even her carriage seemed bereft of any vivacity as she struggled to stand next to Lexie, grunting as she straightened her back. With stooped shoulders and a protruding collarbone, she came across as a sad caricature of a once imposing priestess.

"Renee, are you sick?"

A smile barely registered as if the effort pained her. "It's nothing to concern yourself about."

Lexie cautiously approached, searching for the slightest hint of the black light returning to her eyes.

"I came to speak to you about the council meeting."

Renee's hands twisted together, and the lines around her mouth stretched taut, deepening their cut into her skin. "Why? I don't belong to the council anymore."

"But you were there the other day." Nina charged up to them. "You burst into the room and denounced Lexie."

Her face crinkled in a confused expression. "But I was never at the council meeting."

Lexie wasn't sure whether to believe her, but she remained eager to push on for the truth. "You came to the meeting, barged in, and told everyone I have no power. You wanted me removed as mambo."

Renee dropped to her knees at Lexie's feet.

"I never did such a thing." She jutted her praying hands above her head, her voice rising with her sobs. "The day of the meeting I was unwell and spent the entire morning in bed. I've had terrible dreams lately, and sleep very little. I swear it wasn't me at the council meeting." When she glanced up, tears streamed down her cheeks—black tears.

Lexie's revulsion made her back away, but then she stopped. Renee was a lost soul who needed her support, not her ridicule. She put her arm around Renee's waist and helped her from the floor.

"I believe you."

"You're kidding!" Nina taunted her with a deadpan stare. "She's lying. She's putting on a great performance, real Academy Award material, but she spoke to your landlord and used it against you."

"It's not a lie!" Renee's eyes darted from side to side. "I can't remember the day of the meeting. In fact, I can't remember a lot of things lately. And yes, I spoke to Otis—we're family—but I never told anyone what he said. I don't think I did. It must be the nightmares making me forget. I have so many of them. They frighten me."

Lexie noted her shaking hands. "What are your nightmares about?"

Renee wiped away a tear. "I'm drowning in a black cloud. It covers me, goes into my mouth and nose, I can breathe, but I can't speak or cry out. Then nothing. I wake up and find strange things have happened."

Nina quirked a questioning eyebrow at Lexie.

"No, it's true."

Renee grabbed Lexie's hands, squeezing them.

"I wake up in different clothes, and my hair ..." She touched the turban on her head. "It's down. I never wear my hair down in the shop. The tourists expect it to look like the Queen's."

Renee crossed herself as another tear fell. "You must help me, Mambo." Her pitiful cries drowned out the sounds of the French Quarter. "I am possessed. You must rid me of this evil spirit."

Lexie put her arm around her and caught a glimpse of Nina's quivering lower lip.

"Before I can do that." Lexie gripped her arms. "I need you to contact a spirit for me."

"A spirit?" Renee wiped her eyes. "But you have your spirit guide. He can—"

"He can't," Lexie edged in. "Not this spirit. It's his wife."

Shown to an open door in a dim, narrow hallway, Lexie had to take a minute to allow her eyes to adjust before entering Renee's spirit room.

"Are you sure about this?"

She glanced past Nina to the empty corridor. "Where's Magnus?"

"I have no idea. Maybe he doesn't want to witness this part."

Concerned, she scrutinized the hallway. "It's unusual for him not to butt in."

Nina stood in the doorway to the room, barring her way. "Renee isn't very stable, and I'm not sure how much help I'll be if furniture starts flying."

"Nothing dramatic will happen." She held up her cane. "I have this. We'll be fine."

She sighed. "If you say so."

No bigger than a broom closet, the spirit room was lit by a single white candle on a round table surrounded by four chairs. The walls were the same deep red color as the shop but had no pictures or decorations. The heavy aroma of burnt leaves hung in the air.

Nina sneezed as she had a seat at the table. "What's that smell?"

Renee sat across from her. "Mallow. I use it to call benevolent spirits to our realm and ground them for better communication."

"The spirit we want isn't good." Lexie settled in next to Nina. "Perhaps we should use something else."

Renee shook out her hands. "No, it will offer us some protection from evil if it comes." She clasped Lexie's hand and then Nina's. "What's the spirit's name?"

She could hardly make out Renee's face in the sketchy light. "Katherine, Katie, Blackwell. Wife of Magnus Blackwell."

Renee rocked her head from side to side. "Give me a moment to contact her."

Lexie kept her palms down on the table inches from the candle as Renee had instructed, but she felt foolish. Communicating with spirits for her had never involved such theatrics. She believed in a more practical approach—straight up talking to them.

"Katie Blackwell," Renee called out. "We want to speak to you. Can you come to us?"

Lexie worked to awaken her powers, but the black veil covering her inner eye remained.

"We will not harm you." Renee raised her head, as if listening to the air. "We're friends of your husband's. Magnus sent us."

Seconds ticked by. Lexie's hopes of making contact sputtered. Then something in the candlelight caught her attention

Strange images appeared in the flame; faint ones she had to squint to make out.

The exterior of Altmover Manor came forth, looking similar to the day she and Will first arrived. The beauty of the abandoned home became obscured by darkness, then the vision changed and the living room floated before her. Magnus, resplendent in his black coat, black boots, and red vest, descended from his painting above the mantel. A perfect recreation of their first meeting, and then the flash of pictures in the candlelight sped up. Her search for the mystery of the dragon cane flickered as a series of snapshots. Her trip to New Orleans and her growing bond with Magnus all came and went.

"He likes you."

The high-pitched voice came from a corner of the room.

"He never liked many people."

Her heart thudded in her chest. "Did you hear that? The voice?"

"What voice?" Nina dipped her face into the stream of candlelight.

"My words are for you, Lexie Arden."

She sounded closer, right over her shoulder.

"Is it her?" Renee demanded.

Lexie held up her hand, asking for silence. "Katie?"

The candlelight rose into the air becoming a balloon of yellow light.

Inside the anomaly, Katie materialized, decked out in her gold gown a ghostly breeze sent wisps of blonde hair floating around her face.

"I should have heeded all the warnings from others about my séances. They marked me. They damned me." Her face flushed a bright pink, making her seem almost human. "I never had your power. She wants to possess it, you know."

Lexie's nails dug into the wooden table. "Who does? Who is the black spirit controlling you?"

Katie's lovely smile dipped, and her eyes watered. "I don't mean to do bad things, but she makes me. I have no wish to hurt my Magnus. He looks happy. Is he happy?"

"Katie, tell me who is doing this and I can help you."

She sniffled as a black rope descended from above and slipped around her wrists, binding them tightly together.

"She hates you just like she hates me. She plans to grab up as much power as she can to fight you and destroy you. Be careful, Lexie Arden." Katie raised her head. "I must go. She's coming back for me."

The balloon of light fizzled and disappeared. Right before the candle on the table went out, a woman's bloodcurdling scream shook the room.

"What was that?" Nina spun around in her chair.

Renee touched Lexie's hand. "You made contact with her, didn't you?"

Lexie came out of her fog. She rubbed her head, making sense of what she'd experienced.

"She said the dark spirit is a woman wanting to possess my power."

The overhead lights came on.

Lexie winced and covered her eyes.

"Is it another priestess, perhaps?" Renee stood by the light switch at the door.

Lexie struggled to put the pieces of the puzzle together, desperate for an answer, but something kept nagging at her about what Katie had said. She got a sense she knew the spirit.

"No, it's not a voodoo priestess."

Nina's brow scrunched together. "How can you be certain?"

Renee returned to the table. "Because taking the power of another priestess would mean certain banishment across the bridge to blackness." Her gaze settled on the smoke rising from the candle. "Whoever's doing this is risking certain nothingness. No member of our voodoo culture would attempt such an abhorrent act. We may squabble amongst ourselves, but there are certain boundaries we do not cross."

Nina stood and confronted her. "But you committed the *les droits des noirs* on poor Remi Glapion. You killed Titu Hebert's nephew."

"I killed no one." Renee held her head up high. "Yes, I performed *les droits des noirs*, I admit it. But I never killed him. Helen had her thugs take care of him."

Her nerves strained past the breaking point, Nina's outburst severed the last slender thread of control in Lexie.

She punched the table and shoved back her chair. "Dammit. Enough!"

A stunned silence settled around her, and Lexie lowered her voice, fighting to regain her calm.

"It's the past. We must focus on what's in front of us."

"Just don't trust her. She's a liar." Nina hurried to the door, yanked it open, and fled the room.

Lexie slouched as her responsibilities bore down on her.

"Thank you, Renee."

"She's wrong, Mambo. I can be trusted."

She sighed, not sure whom to trust anymore. "I hope so. It will prove to be your undoing if you ever cross me."

Lexie left Renee in the dark spirit room, anxious to return to the comforting light of day.

Chapter Fourteen

A red-faced Will paced the floor of their living room, the squeaking of the floorboards grating against her nerves. She waited for him to explode after telling him of her afternoon adventure at Renee's. Lexie chewed her nails, her feet curled under her on the sofa, as her anticipation mounted.

"For the love of God, do you know how reckless it was to visit that woman? She's a murder suspect, and you go waltzing over there with a ghost and shop assistant for back up."

Lexie glared at her husband. "I had to go. I had to find out if Renee was okay. I had to see her and question her myself."

"And what if she had drugged you, stabbed you, or shot you? What would you have done?"

She shook her head. "Renee wouldn't do that. I know her, and the woman Emile suspects of killing Kalila is not the woman I met today. She's shattered by whatever dark spirit possesses her."

Will ran his hand through his thick brown hair. "Emile

173

called me after he left here, suspecting you would do something dangerous. I should have listened to him." He emphatically pointed at the front door. "Someone is out there going after priestesses, and you could be next. Doesn't that register with you?"

Her voice grew dangerously low. "You don't have to keep reminding me I'm a target. But I can't stand by and do nothing or show the world I'm afraid. I have to set the out of whack order of things right again, no matter the cost."

"The cost? Do you hear yourself?" His sharp voice echoed off the walls. "You could end up dead, Lexie, and then …" Instead of continuing, he charged toward the sofa and sat down.

"If anything happens to you, I don't know what I would do," he whispered. "I love you so much, and I couldn't go on without you."

"I'm sorry. I didn't think. I never think. I'm a bulldozer, remember?" Melting into him, she hooked her arms around his thick bicep and sighed into his shoulder.

His warm embrace chased away all her fight and her fears.

"How could I forget? You scared the shit out of me." His lips grazed her cheek. "Please try not to do it again."

She snuggled against his chest. "I would promise it will be the last time, but you know me."

He softly chuckled into her hair. "Yeah, I know you, but I don't want to spend our days arguing about what you should or shouldn't be doing. I'm not married to the mambo of this damned town; I'm married to you."

"This is bigger than you and me. It's always been."

He cupped her face and raised her head to him. "Not for me. I'm in this for you, not for the city, or the voodoo, or even the people. You're all that's mattered to me since the first day I saw you on the Williamson job. I get you have responsibilities, and I support you completely, but I have to know we matter. You and me."

Lexie was torn—her life with Will did matter, but her calling mattered more.

She wanted happiness with her husband, a family, and a future together, but her power had satisfied her in a way no domestic bliss ever could. She needed it and was addicted because it was the only thing that ever made her feel completely alive. How could she tell Will of her passion? She couldn't. He would never comprehend the heights her ability had taken her to, and she would do anything to get such exhilaration back—whatever the cost.

He reclined, taking her with him, against the sofa. "Promise me if you plan to go out on any more dangerous escapades, you'll call first and discuss it with me."

She patted his chest and sat up. "I will if I get it in my head to visit any more crazed voodoo priestesses."

"Why don't I feel assured." He shook his head and got to his feet. "I'd better check the meatloaf, make sure you're not burning it."

"Very funny. Bring the scotch when you come back."

"Things must be getting to you." Will strode to the open kitchen on the other side of the living room. "I might have to spring for another bottle at this rate."

"He doesn't believe your promise, and neither do I." Magnus manifested tugging at the sleeve of his black coat.

She rolled her eyes at her ghost. "Where have you been?"

The intensity of his scowl softened. "When you went into Renee's shop today, a force kept me from entering. You should have left the minute you realized I wasn't with you."

"I had to see Renee. After her display at the council meeting, I had to make sure she was all right."

"It's quite obvious she's not right in the head, but at this moment my issue is with you."

"What issue?" Will strolled back into the living room and spotted Magnus. "Why is he here? He promised to stay downstairs?"

"I am here to speak with your wife," Magnus replied, his tone thick with indignation.

Lexie stepped in before the situation escalated "He came because he's angry with me. I left him outside when I visited Renee."

"Why did you do that?" Will set the glasses in his hands on the coffee table. "I'm not happy with you visiting a murder suspect, but I would have preferred Magnus was with you when you went."

Magnus hooked the handle of his cane on his arm. "See? He agrees with me."

Will opened his mouth to reply, but Lexie stepped in.

"Renee didn't kill anyone. When I spoke to her today, she had no memory of her outburst at the council meeting, and I believe her. The woman I saw was sick and wasted."

"It could have all been an act?" Will withdrew to the kitchen. "After the stunt she pulled with Bloody Mary at the cemetery that night, I wouldn't believe a word out of her mouth."

"It seems we share the same sentiments." Magnus stood in the center of the living room. "I told you not to trust her."

Will stepped into the room, carrying a scotch bottle in his hand. For a brief moment, ghost and husband stood shoulder to shoulder, peering down at her.

She folded her arms, uncomfortable with their scrutiny.

"I contacted a spirit when I was at her shop. No one else, just me." She hesitated, knowing what her disclosure would do to Magnus. "It was Katie."

Magnus groaned and dropped his head.

Lexie cursed under her breath. "I had to talk to her. See if she could tell me who's behind this mess."

Will put the scotch on the coffee table. "And what did she say?"

"This spirit wants my power. It wants to possess it and destroy me. Katie said, 'she hates you like she hates me.'"

"She?" Will shrugged his broad shoulders. "She who?"

Lexie tilted her head, contemplating the endless sorrow in her ghost's eyes. She'd seen it before whenever the dark spirit contacted them, always igniting her curiosity about what he wasn't telling her. His reaction confirmed her suspicions.

"You know who she is, don't you?"

Magnus remained silent as he examined his cane. He gripped the handle and set the tip on the floor with a dull *thud*.

"It's Emily Mann."

Will almost knocked the bottle over on the coffee table. "Your secretary?"

"How did you figure it out?" Magnus asked.

"The way Katie spoke about her, she knew her. From what I knew of Emily Mann and her fascination with voodoo, it wasn't hard to guess. When did you know?"

"I heard Katie's maniacal laugh when she first appeared to us and speculated, but at the council meeting when Renee laughed, I was certain."

Lexie aimed a scolding gaze across the room. "You should have said something before."

"I'd forgotten how she was." Her ghost went to the mantel. "For years after my death, she roamed the halls of my mansion. Every day she would talk to me, ask me about the cane, ask me about where I had stolen it from. She discovered the power in it after Jacob's death. She became addicted. It was then she bought all the voodoo books. She devoted years to their study, practiced their spells, and became very powerful. Emily longed to go to New Orleans and do more research, but she never wanted to leave Altmover Manor."

The visions, her suspicions, and her association with the dark spirit all added up.

The answer Lexie had searched for now revealed, a new problem nagged at her. How did she get rid of Emily Mann?

"I don't get it." Will poured out a glass of scotch. "Lexie losing her powers, the rain, the rats—it comes down to a jealous secretary back from the dead to get revenge on Magnus?"

"No, she wants to possess Magnus." Lexie reached for the drink. "She wants my power as mambo, and she assumes that includes my ghost."

Will lifted the mouth of the bottle over the second glass. "But how can a ghost become mambo?"

"She won't be a ghost if she possesses someone." She rolled her glass in her hands, considering the question. "She can inhabit Renee's body, we've seen it already. But to remain, she needs an awful lot of power. Draining some from Titu and me, plus a few others on the council wasn't enough. That's why she killed Kalila La Fay. She was able to collect all of her power and keep it. Emile told me of the spell used to drain her."

Magnus nodded, approaching the sofa. "Which is probably the spell she will try to use on you."

"Over my dead body." Will snapped up his glass. "What do we do to stop her?"

"I have no idea." Lexie sat forward, her mind racing, when an odd cramp gripped her center. She put her drink aside and rubbed her chest. "I have to find a way to stop her before she becomes too powerful."

Will sipped his drink and then frowned. "How are you going

to do that without your ability?"

Heeding the twinge, she rose from the sofa and went to the bookcases along one wall of the living room.

The collection of rare leather-bound books crinkled with age called to her. Her discomfort eased as she read a few of the titles.

"I bet the answer's in here. With a little research, and a whole lot of help from Titu, I should be able to come up with something."

"That doesn't sound like much of a plan?" Will's brow ridged, accentuating his intimidating stare. "Should I be hiring spiritual hit men?"

"That won't be necessary." Magnus aimed his cocky grin at Lexie. "We already have the chosen one on our side."

Patchy beams of moonlight trickled through the balcony doors as Lexie sat on her living room floor. A dozen open books lay arranged around her to catch the light from a nearby reading lamp.

"Hey, it's after midnight," Will said from their bedroom doorway. "Come to bed, baby."

Lexie spied him through the haze the lamp created, admiring his muscular chest. She chided herself for not being fast asleep in his strong arms.

"In a while. I just want to check a few more things."

Will's footfalls made the old floor moan. He had a seat next to her and gleaned a few of the open pages.

"Do you think there's a spell to get rid of her spirit?"

Lexie shrugged while arched over a thick tome. "Titu doubts it. She said she never heard of a spirit collecting power from the living. The *Prendre le Pouvoir* performed on Kalila is meant to be done by a living person. She believes Emily Mann has found a way to bend the rules of voodoo."

"Then you must bend the rules of voodoo to your advantage and beat her."

She glanced up from the book. "It's not that easy. There are checks and balances in magic. When forces move things out of balance, bad things happen. One must obey the rules to turn things around; otherwise, the magic may not stick."

He scooted closer to her. "Lexie, magic is nothing more than the will of a person to change their stars. It's no different from prayer or wishing. The belief behind the hope is the true magic." He placed his hand on the center of her chest. "You have more hope, more magic in you than anyone I've ever known. Believe in that, not a spell, not a ritual, believe in you, and bend the universe to your desires."

She rested her hand over his and tears gathered in her eyes. She never thought Will paid attention when she spoke about voodoo. He'd affirmed from the moment they walked into Altmover Manor ghosts and magic weren't real. Now, here he was, believing in her and her ability.

"Wow, I never expected this."

His arms went around her. "Well, you can't be married to the Mambo of New Orleans and not pick up a few things here and there."

"I always supposed you thought what I did wasn't important."

He pulled back and stared at her. "Of course, it's important. You help people; you keep them safe. I was there at the cemetery that night when the Queen chose you. I saw strange and wonderful things I never thought existed. You opened my eyes to a whole new world. I'm in awe of what you can do. I can't believe

I'm married to such a remarkable woman."

A single tear trickled down her cheek. "Really?"

He cupped her face and wiped her tear away with his thumb. "That's how I know you're going to beat this spirit. You have an incredible gift, but you're also tenacious as hell. It's the reason you're here. You never give up."

Lexie wrapped her arms around his neck.

His support, and his strength, never mattered to her more than at that moment.

Will kissed her cheek and pulled away. "Come to bed. Even a mambo needs her rest."

Tucked in bed with Will spooned behind her, she handed herself over to sleep. But her eyes had barely closed when the tingle of a presence entering her bedroom danced across her skin.

A hot wave radiated from her core, taking her by surprise. It branched to her fingers and toes. The same sensation she used to experience tapping into the white ribbon she once shared with Magnus, she hugged herself, overjoyed at the prospect of her power's return.

A white ribbon of light gushed from her center, pulsating in time with her rapid heartbeat. It twisted and curled across the bedroom only to disappear into a dark corner. She squinted, eager to see Magnus at the other end, but no one was there.

About to climb from the bed, she stopped when the cord changed from a pure luminescent white to dark blue. The fire in her chest subsided, and a bone-chilling cold replaced it. Then her lifeline to the spirit world faded from blue to an ashy shade of gray. The gray withered turning black. The light-sucking color held no hint of life, and then the ugly blackness seeped closer to her. It wiggled along the ribbon, eagerly reaching for her.

Horrified, Lexie went to sever the grotesque thing from her body, but when her fingers passed through the dead connection, her skin shrank away becoming the same lifeless black color. She yanked her hand back and inspected it. Her skin plumped with a youthful glow.

"Don't look for light when dark will do."

His seductively smoky voice came from where the ribbon ended. She knew who it was. His image still haunted her.

"Why are you here, Kal?"

Kalfu stepped out of the shadows. In only jeans, his sculpted abs glistened in the light drifting in from the courtyard. His defined arms, chest, and broad shoulders looked straight out of a romance novel.

"Just coming from the gym?"

He raised his hands, his blue eyes flickering with mischief. "One does what one can to keep their followers happy."

She sat up on the edge of the bed. "Why are you in my dream?"

He stopped a few feet from her. "Who says this is a dream? I don't need dreams to come to you."

"Why come to me at all? I never summoned you. I don't worship you."

"I'm still hopeful."

His devious smile sent a chill through her. It was as if thousands of ravenous black beetles consumed her soul.

"What do you want?"

He rocked his hands behind his back. "It's what you want. You have the means, all that remains is the desire."

"What are you talking about?"

"The spirit, the one who teases you, I can give her to you, and all her power."

A prick of suspicion caressed her arms. "But I would have to follow you, right? Pledge my loyalty to you?"

His slow sashay toward the bed exuded confidence; whatever

game he played, he knew he would not lose.

"I would require much more than loyalty."

"Forget it." Heat burned her cheeks, and she scrambled from the bed, eager to put some distance between them.

"Very well." He closed the gap between them. "But I promise a time will come when you need me."

Part of Lexie wanted to give into him, hand herself over to his alluring power, but her practical mind refused, bolstering her resolve. But for how much longer? She couldn't remain mambo without any power, and if her ability didn't return soon, she might be forced to consider his offer before New Orleans fell into ruin.

Kalfu disintegrated into a thousand specks of light, dancing and circling, and then they dropped beneath the floorboards of her room.

She stared at where he had stood.

The cold his appearance stirred in her center remained, tempting her, teasing her to join him. She ached to feel whole, powerful, intact, and in tune with everything around her. But could he give her that, or would his side of magic still leave her hollow? And if she became his, what of her will, her desire to help her city? Would he control those as well? Doubt plagued her, stirring the anger in her veins.

Shit!

She wanted to strangle Emily Mann for putting her in such a precarious position.

If I ever got my hands on her …

When she crawled under the covers, Will rolled over to her.

His embrace chased away her conflict. She nestled against him, his musky aroma tantalizing her senses. His warmth eradicated the cold of Kalfu's visit. With him, all the bad she'd experienced was wiped clean. Will brought her back to a world of light, goodness, and love.

"Who were you talking to?" He nuzzled her neck, his hands rubbing up and down her back.

"I'm sorry." She kissed his chest. "I was thinking out loud."

He let her go and sat up, wiping his sleepy eyes. "What is it? What's bothering you?"

She rested her hand on his chest, hoping for his energy to pass on to her, giving her strength.

"How to set things right again? What do I do?"

Will kissed her forehead and pulled her to him. "Don't think about it now. Tomorrow something will come to us. Our demons always seem bigger in the dark." He brought her back to the bed with him. "Get some sleep."

He was about to let her go when she held his arms. "Don't. I feel better when you hold me."

"I'll never let go of you, baby." He tugged her close, his head pressed into her neck. "Not even after the stars burn out."

Chapter Fifteen

The afternoon sun made a brief appearance, breaking through the constant cover of black clouds over the city. The respite was so appreciated by everyone, that many took to the streets to enjoy the warmth.

But the heaviness in the air promised more rain was on the way. Lexie didn't join the other shopkeepers around her, marveling at the comforting light. Instead, she stayed in her shop, sitting on the floor with Nina and going through the reference books she'd brought down from her apartment.

"You think the answer is in here?" Nina flipped through a few pages.

"Not the answer, but perhaps a spell I can use to bring the spirit under my control."

"What does Titu advise?" Nina set her book to the side.

"I called her this morning and left a message. I haven't heard back from her yet."

Magnus appeared, poised over the books on the floor.

Nina startled when she saw him.

"You shouldn't sneak up on the living."

"How else would you suggest the dead arrive?"

A change in the light darkened the windows. Lexie rose from the floor, attracted to the shadows reaching across her shop.

Outside, black clouds rolled in, smothering the sun. The people milling about quickened their step as thunder shook the buildings. The wind rushed down the emptying street, and the burgeoning clouds descended from the heavens, hovering above the ground.

Litter drifted in the wind, scattering along the sidewalks and street. The swirling air thinned, and the clouds twisted into shapes of people. Shadowy figures, of men, women, and children paraded in front of Lexie's shop door. They clung to the stucco of buildings, stretched across the cement, and some crowded in corners, but these ghosts had no faces, no features to make them appear human. Like whirling drifts of smoke, they clogged her window and blotted out the last vestiges of daylight.

Magnus appeared at her side. "They're not supposed to be here."

"Aren't they the ghosts you saw before?"

"No. These are different. I'm not sure what they are, but this isn't right."

Sickened by the sight, she clenched her fists. "I have to put a stop to this."

"I agree." He never looked away from the lost souls on the street, the empathy for their suffering reflected in his eyes. "But I fear the cost you will have to pay to bring order back to this city. You dark friend is reputed to be a wearisome taskmaster."

She studied his profile. "You saw him last night?"

"I felt the change in the atmosphere around you. I went to your bedroom to check on you and found him loitering in the corner. I wanted to warn you, but he stopped me."

"He stopped you? How?"

Magnus turned to her with a brooding look on his face. "I am a ghost, and he's a powerful spirit. If he commands me to stay back, I cannot refuse him. In the same way, I can't deny you."

Outside the window, the spinning shadows of the dead amplified the heaviness settling over her.

"Perhaps we should get someone more experienced with voodoo to help us."

"There is no one else. Only you and your power can help them."

He eased up to her, adding a soothing tone to his voice.

"You can do this. I believe in you."

"But I'm just an interior designer from Boston. I'm not a good cook, I'm a terrible housekeeper, and my bookkeeping skills are nonexistent." She anxiously twisted her fingers together. "I'm in over my head."

"You are not what you do, Lexie Arden Bennett. You are what's inside of you. This is your calling. Good or bad, right or wrong, this is why you're here. You must find the courage to face this. There is no running away from destiny."

"Hey, Lexie?" Nina called across the room. "I think I found something."

Lexie backed away from the window and crossed the room with Magnus following close behind.

Nina pointed to an open book. "In here, I found a spell. It's called *une fois était*, or *once was*. From what I can tell, it's used to upset the balance of the universe. Shift it toward either good or bad."

Lexie perused the page in the book, her mouth moving as she read the spell. "This requires an awful lot of energy. 'To cast the balance of fate in the desired direction, the power of three experienced practitioners must be collected.'" Lexie lowered the book. "Three?"

"Kalila makes one." Nina stood from the floor, wiping the front of her white dress. "It would explain why she was drained of her power."

Magnus came closer, gleaning the open page in the book. "She needs two more to perform the spell."

"I'd better call Emile." Lexie handed the book back to Nina.

She strode across the room to the register and opened the drawer below where she kept her purse.

Once she had her cell phone in hand, she dialed Emile's number.

"Lexie, where are you?" Emile's voice had an edginess she'd never heard since meeting the detective.

"I'm at the shop. Why?"

"Stay there. Is anyone with you?"

Lexie glimpsed Nina and Magnus at her bookshelves. "Yeah, Nina is with me."

"I'm sending a car to you. The officer will check in when he gets there. Don't leave the shop or go anywhere without a police presence. Do you understand?"

A tingle of dread climbed up her back. "Emile, what's wrong?"

Seconds ticked by as Emile's long pause compounded her fear.

"Jacques Krieger was found dead in his office this morning by his secretary. I'm at the scene now."

Lexie gripped her knees. "He sits on the council."

"I know." His heavy sigh rang in her ear. "His murder resembles Kalila's. The carvings are identical. The bloodletting, all of it."

Her eyes drifted back to the book in Nina's hands. "That's

BOUND

two powerful voodoo practitioners."

"Yeah, I realized that." The anxious clip in Emile's voice vanished.

The impact of her actions sent an avalanche of guilt pressing down on her. The deaths of Jacques and Kalila were her fault. If she'd never come to New Orleans, sought out the dragon cane, and took her place as mambo, none of this would be happening.

"What can I do? There must be—?"

"Don't do anything. Don't go anywhere, don't leave your shop." Emile's adamant tone rang in her ears. "At night, lock yourself in your apartment. I'm going to make sure the other members of the council have surveillance until we catch this person."

Person? Lexie wanted to tell Emile what she knew about Emily Mann and her dark intentions, but he was a cop. He needed facts, and living people to pursue, not ghosts.

"What about Titu? I tried calling her but I never—"

"I have a car on the way to her place right now," he cut in. "She's fine. I just got off the phone with her."

Lexie's relief cascaded through her. "Thank goodness."

"I'll keep you posted on what we find. In the meantime, stay put. Call Will and let him know what's going on. He'll want to be with you."

Lexie hung up the phone, and her hope for the future became a distant speck of light on a black plane.

It seemed the darkness was everywhere, crowding in around her, and pressuring her to join its ranks. How could she hope to save anyone in time without giving up her soul to Kalfu's malignant world?

"What is it?"

Magnus stooped over her, his twinkling eyes grew listless with apprehension.

189

"Jacques Krieger from the council is dead. Killed just like Kalila La Fay."

Nina gasped. "He was a formidable priest. If the person who stole his power took Kalila's, they only need one more to perform this *once was* spell."

A flash of red and blue lights sent Lexie to the window. A police car pulled up outside her door.

"Detective Glapion's detail has arrived." She faced Nina, trying her best to appear confident. "Take the rest of the day off. There's no point in staying open."

Nina's pensive gaze reeked with her disapproval. "Fine. I'm not going to argue with you." She went behind the counter to get her purse. "You call me if you need me to come back."

Nina smiled contemptuously at Magnus. "Keep an eye on her."

A blur of white, she darted out the door and closed it before Lexie could say good-bye.

Lexie went to the door, anxious to check on Nina as she navigated the countless souls clogging the street.

When she stepped outside, the quiet overwhelmed her. There wasn't a ghost or dancing shadow in sight.

The door of the police cruiser swung open, and the officer climbed out.

In his pressed blue uniform, the lanky officer strolled up to Lexie, his hands hiking up his gun belt and a cordial smile spread across his pasty lips.

He stopped before reaching the door, his gaze tracking Nina as she walked quickly down the street.

He tipped his hat to Lexie and then to Magnus in the doorway. "Ma'am. Sir. Detective Glapion sent me to keep an eye on things. I'll be right outside in the car."

She went inside and closed the shop door as the officer

meandered back to his car.

Lexie faced Magnus. "You need to tell me everything you know about Emily Mann. There's got to be a way to find her weakness, something we can use to shut her down."

He went to the display case by the window and rested his elbow on the glass.

"I never knew much about her when I was alive. What I picked up after her death you already know."

"What about her family? Her relationships after your death?"

"She didn't have relationships with anyone. The only person she communicated with was Katie's father, Miles Parker. Her correspondence with him was related to the upkeep of the house, nothing more."

"She must have had someone else in the house with her."

"Yes, she did. Me."

Lexie was about to interrogate him further when her cell phone rang. Will's name flashed on the caller ID, and her apprehension eased.

She hurried to pick up the call desperate to hear his voice.

"Emile just called me. Are you okay? Did the detail show up?"

She cupped the phone against her cheek, wishing he were with her. "They're here. Parked right outside."

"Stay put. I'm coming home."

"What about the firm? You need to be there?"

"You can't honestly believe I'm going to worry about my company when a psychopath is going around carving up priestesses, and my wife may be next? I'm going to bring a few days of work home with me, so I can stick close to you."

Tears clouded her vision. "You'd do that for me?"

"Lexie." His voice dropped when he said her name. The sound tossed a warm blanket of calm around her. "I'd do anything for you. Don't you know that by now?"

"Yeah." She sniffled. "I know."

"I'll be home in twenty minutes." He hung up, and Lexie stared at her phone.

"I gather he's on his way."

She tossed her phone on the counter. "Yes. He's scared. So am I." She reviewed everything she learned about Emily Mann when they'd lived at Altmover Manor, which wasn't much.

"After Emily Mann died, the caretaker at the historical society on the island told me she was cremated, and her ashes spread around the house."

Magnus rolled his eyes. "The stupid fool wrote instructions in her will for her ashes to be thrown over the cliff where I died. I was terrified she'd end up as another ghost haunting me for eternity since she was so damned adamant the service take place within forty-eight hours of her death. She requested her lawyer say something at the ceremony in French. Considering she barely knew the language, it surprised me."

A prick of suspicion caught in her chest. "What words? Can you remember them?"

"Something about setting her soul free. I never paid much attention to what was said."

The discomfort in her chest mushroomed into an unpleasant burn.

"And she never haunted Altmover Manor."

"Not once."

Lexie tapped her finger against her lips. Emily had a purpose planned for her funeral, why else leave detailed instructions?

Magnus floated up to her. "What are you thinking?"

"She wasn't bound to the house like you and Jacob, but she never moved on to where Katie and Francis went. Kalila mentioned something about a spirit torn in two at death. One

B O U N D

part goes to heaven, and the other remains on earth. She called it a duppy." She rechecked her cell phone. "I need to speak with Titu about this. Maybe I should go to her."

Magnus eyed the police officer sitting in his car outside her door. "Not a good idea. You need to stay where the police can keep watch over you. And Will is on his way. Go with him, not alone."

"But why hasn't she called me?"

A chilly wind brushed past, tickling her skin and she shivered.

She glanced up to see if the door to the shop had opened, but it remained closed.

"Lexie." Magnus glided closer, pointing his cane at the stack of books by the shelves. "Look over there."

The book on top of the pile magically open and the frigid breeze in the room fanning the pages.

Entranced, she padded closer to the stack. She reached out to touch the open page of the black leather-bound book when a voice called to her.

"Read, child."

Lexie gasped, and her hand stood poised above the page. The voice was unmistakable.

"Magnus, did you hear that?"

He stood next to her, scouring the room. "She's here. I heard her."

A tightness gripped Lexie's throat. "Do you see her?"

Red and blue flashing lights came through the window, sending a stream of colored patterns throughout the shop. A car engine roared to life, and screeching tires blasted through the air.

Sick to her stomach, she ran to the window just as the police cruiser took off down Royal Street.

"Titu!" She bolted for the door.

Magnus appeared, his long arm stretched across the threshold.

"You can't go. You need to stay here. It isn't safe."

She fought with the handle. "You heard her voice. She's in trouble. I have to go to her."

Lexie was out the door before he could say another word.

Magnus spun around, desperate to come up with any means to get her back inside. She'd left her baton juju leaning against the counter, and the sight of it raised alarm in him. She was out there powerless and alone.

"Shit!"

On the sidewalk, he summoned the strength of his newfound power and held his hand over the door, willing it to close.

Slowly, inch by inch the door moved toward him. When the latch clicked into place, he sagged with fatigue.

Ahead, Lexie turned at the end of the block on St. Ann Street.

"It would be my lot in death to be bound to such a stubborn creature."

He caught up with her instantly. "Lexie, please calm down. You can't—"

"Shut up, Magnus." Her arms pumped as she kept on running past the smattering of tourists braving the rain. "She's in trouble. I know it."

She tripped once on a broken curb, almost tumbling to the ground, but rushed on.

He sensed how all her emotions washed together similar to an array of different colored paints going down a drain. He ached to counsel her but understood her well enough to stay back and let her go. She never listened to reason half the time and made decisions based more on her heart rather than her head. It's what he adored about her; the eccentricity of her nature, and the ardent passion of her soul.

She made it to Burgundy Street, and her paced slowed.

Up ahead, police cars with their bright lights flashing sat parked at odd angles in front of a Creole townhouse—Titu's home.

Lexie stopped to catch her breath while inspecting the array of cars. The sheer terror throbbing in her every cell implored him to help her, but he could do nothing. What lay ahead he could offer no shield for, or soften whatever blow may come. The experience of living was hers; all he could do was bear witness to the upheaval it created.

Before he could encourage her to return to the shop, she ran toward the police cars.

An officer lining a perimeter with yellow tape stopped her, hugging her around the waist and keeping her from going past the line of cars.

"Ma'am, you can't go up there."

"But Titu's my friend!"

The shriek of madness in her voice cut Magnus in two. Never had he heard such a sound from her.

The police officer struggled to hold her. She wiggled in his arms, a crazed look in her eyes.

When another officer came forward, he assisted in getting her under control.

Her arms secured by her sides, the two officers moved her behind the yellow tape lying in the wet street.

"I've got to see her. I have to know she's all right." Her cries carried through the air.

"You can't see her, ma'am. She's gone."

One of the officers set her down on the curb, his hand on her shoulder holding her in place.

"I'm very sorry."

Perched on the dirty curb, she had her legs splayed and did not move a muscle; her blank expression mirrored the shock Magnus sensed numbing her mind. A slight drizzle fell from the sky at the moment her first tear slipped down her cheek. Magnus had a seat next to her in the rain, preparing himself for what would come.

The stretch of agony overtook her features after the shock evaporated, and the guttural cry she made brought back the anguish of his brother's death and his mother's last breath. He wished to every force in the universe to be able to hold her at that moment, but he could do nothing as she crumbled to the sidewalk, and convulsed with sobs.

"Lexie, please."

He tried to comfort her, but she was momentarily held hostage by despair.

"You must not do this. Titu, would not want it. She is at peace."

"You need to listen to your friend, ma'am," the young officer advised while hovering over her.

He gave Magnus an assertive nod before turning away and heading back to the others in his detail.

Magnus watched over her as the sobbing came and went. He could not think of anything else to do but stay with her in the rain and offer comfort.

A familiar face came around the side of the police cars, his determined stride appearing a little slower than Magnus remembered from previous encounters. Emile stood over them, the shiny badge attached to his belt speckled with raindrops, and his face a blank mask of stone.

"Lexie." He wrapped her in his arms.

She came out of her lethargy and held him close. Her white knuckles pressed into his back, her shoulders shuddering with her sorrow.

"Tell me she's okay, Emile. She's not dead. She can't be."

Emile buried her head in his chest and whispered something in her ear Magnus was not privy to. Her heartbreak rang out after he spoke to her, resonating in the street and draining every last dreg of Magnus's energy.

Police officers around them lowered their heads and backed away, eager to give them some privacy.

While Emile held her, rocking back and forth, Magnus joined the officers.

A voyeur to their misery, he could no longer comprehend the magnitude of their loss because he knew what awaited the dead—it wasn't sorrow, but joy.

Chapter Sixteen

Covered with their white bedspread, Lexie sat propped up on a corner of her green sofa, gripping an untouched mug of lukewarm chamomile tea.

The tea no longer sloshed around in her mug—her shaking had subsided—but the numbness overtaking her limbs and her mind had not receded. If anything, the black hole filling her thoughts had expanded, sucking in every ounce of will she possessed.

"Emile said it was the same as the others." Will tucked in the edges of the comforter, nestling her in even tighter. "The officer sent to her house found her. When she didn't answer the door, he broke in and …"

"She has three now." Lexie peered into the mug of tea. "She'll make her move."

"Who?"

"Emily Mann. She's behind the murders." She put her mug down on the coffee table.

Will rubbed his chin. "You're not making any sense, baby."

She closed her eyes wishing to wake from her nightmare. How she wanted to go back in time. Stop Will from buying Altmover Manor, keep him away from Maine, and never let Emily's foul plot pan out.

"I'm tired." She got up from the sofa, staying wrapped in the long comforter.

Will slipped his arm around her. "Go lay down. I'm going to make a few calls."

She plodded to her bedroom door, rethinking every decision she'd made, analyzing the path bringing her to this city, and eventually taking the life of her mentor. How could she exist knowing Titu's death was her fault?

In her bedroom, she stopped short of closing the door all the way and peeked through the narrow opening at Will.

He stood in the middle of the living room, his hands wrapped around his head, appearing as lost as she felt.

Poor man. What have I done to him?

Of all the characters in the play of her life, Will had suffered the most. His dream had died in the ashes of Altmover Manor, and he had packed up and moved to New Orleans, starting a new business because of her. Lexie cursed what she was. She hated the gift for bringing so much sorrow to so many.

On the bed, she never bothered to kick off her shoes. She sank onto the sheets and rolled over on her side, cocooning herself in the comforter. Dried tears made her cheeks feel rough against her pillow. Fighting to get the comforter closer, still bothered by the cold, something Titu once said rolled across her mind.

Death comes for all of us, child.

Child. Lexie would always equate the endearment with her friend.

All Titu's wisdom—the things she'd taught her and the spells she'd explained—Lexie forced herself to remember, anxious to never forget any of her teachings.

Her eyelids drooped, and she welcomed the embrace of sleep, hoping to dream of the first friend she'd made after arriving in New Orleans.

Something startled her awake.

Everything was black, and the light beneath the door from the living room snuffed out. But she'd only fallen asleep minutes ago, how could it be so late at night?

She sat up, her muscles aching with every movement. She untangled herself from the comforter and then felt the mound beside her.

Will was asleep in bed next to her. Everything was as it should be. But the bliss of forgetfulness washed away, and the horror of Titu's murder rained down on her.

"You shouldn't grieve for me, child."

Lexie clamored from the bed, peering into the darkness for Titu.

"Where are you?"

An orb of light floated by the bathroom door. Akin to a beam from a streetlight, the soft ray grew bigger. A figure composed of smoky tendrils weaved and bobbed. The smoke thickened into a human shape, and then the outline of clothes manifested.

First a silver muumuu and turban, then a smiling Titu came into focus. Her brown eyes shimmered with an ethereal inner light.

All the love Lexie had known from the woman, shone from her eyes, basking her in warmth and curling around her in a ghostly hug.

"Can you see me, child?"

"Titu? You're here." But then her happiness dwindled. "What happened? You must tell me."

Titu's chest rose and fell as if caught in a contemplative sigh. "Such matters are no longer important. I am where I need to be, but you have work to do."

A fiery anger rose from Lexie's depths, obliterating her sadness. "The only work I have is to catch your killer. I swear to you, I will destroy whoever hurt you."

Titu's *tsk-tsk* reverberated in the room. "You don't need to seek revenge for me. I am at peace. What the spirits want from you is to perform your duty as mambo. Set what is wrong right again."

Lexie rested her head in her hands. "How do I do that without you?"

"You don't need me to fulfill your purpose." Her hand waved over the ground next to her. "You need what is here. Remember what I showed you?"

An image surrounded by pale light materialized of the books she'd left piled on the floor of her shop. The one on top of a stack magically opened and the pages flipped as if lifted by a breeze.

"The answer you need to fix everything is here."

The light around the vision dulled until it became one with the darkness in her room.

The fear of losing Titu again spread through Lexie, setting off a wave of trembling in her limbs.

"Will you stay with me like Magnus?"

Titu shook her head, and her image faded along with the light surrounding her. "It's not my purpose, child, but I am with you. We never leave the ones we love."

Titu's spirit faded, and then she was gone.

Lexie raised her head to the ceiling, and whispered, "I love you, too."

She did not allow herself to cry; she'd done enough of that. Instead, her heartache became the fuel to drive her cause—to find out who killed her friend. Determination replaced her sorrow, and she became reenergized. Lexie would be the best-damned mambo the city had ever seen, and she would start tonight.

She set out for the back steps off her balcony, wanting to bury herself in the book Titu encouraged her to read.

Still in her nightshirt, she descended the spiral staircase to the kitchen at the back of her shop.

"What are you doing?"

Magnus stood at the bottom of the steps.

"Titu appeared to me and showed me something in a book I was reading before I got distracted by the police car. I have to find it."

Magnus hurried behind her as they traveled the narrow hall to the front of the store.

"Lexie, you need to go back to bed and rest."

"Bullshit!" She spun around to him. "I'm not helping anyone sitting around feeling sorry for myself. My job is to find the asshole killing people and fix this goddamned city. It's time to end this."

"And you think this is the message Titu gave you?"

Lexie flipped on the lights in the shop. "Knowing Titu, absolutely."

Her ghost halted in front of her; his usual smug grin wiped clean. "When my brother died, I swore I saw him at night in my room, asking me to play with him. But Edward never haunted Altmover, just as Titu isn't haunting your apartment. She's moved on. I've felt it."

"I thought you of all people would understand." She marched through his apparition.

Across the shop, stacked next to the reference books she and

Nina had pulled from the shelves, the open black tome waited.

Lexie perused the pages, the words suddenly took on a whole new meaning. A shiver sailed through her—this spell could give her the chance to take control.

Titu had guided her to the answer, and the profound gratitude she felt somewhat eased her sadness.

Settled on the floor, she fell into a trance, mesmerized by what she read.

Magnus stood close by, tapping the toe of his black boot and occasionally sighing.

She was about to tell him to be quiet when something on the page spoke to her.

"Holy shit!" She gathered up the book in her arms. "It's a spell for sending someone across the bridge to blackness."

Magnus snapped to attention. "The same place Bloody Mary threatened to send you?"

"Yep. And according to this, you can't send anyone there without this spell. It locks them in; otherwise, they could come back. Titu taught me the words, but there's more to it."

Magnus tried to read over her shoulder. "What else are you going to need to perform this spell?"

She read on, and Lexie's hopes fell as quickly as they had soared. "Apparently, a whole hell of a lot of power."

The police precinct where Emile Glapion worked wasn't far from Lexie's shop—only a few short blocks on Royal Street. She set out from her courtyard gate in the early morning sprinkle without an umbrella. She planned on dodging anything heavy beneath the safety of the balconies positioned along her route. The dark clouds still hung over the city, an ever-present reminder of the work she had to do. Fortunately, no more dead rats cluttered the street. Even the flies had departed.

Magnus strolled next to her, a perturbing smirk on his face.

"I have to agree with Will; this isn't a good idea."

"I'm only going a few blocks. There was no reason for him to take time away from his company to walk me in the rain when I have you."

"He's your husband, and wants to protect you."

Lexie tightened her grip on her cane. "I love him, but he's smothering me. Since Titu's death, he hasn't left my side. I needed a break, and so did he."

Lexie's footsteps echoed along the empty street. A few shops had opened, and their bleary-eyed attendants busied themselves setting up sidewalk signs and window displays. The only reassuring presence, the delectable aroma of coffee and chicory coming from every open shop door.

"It's a ghost town."

Magnus raised his cane to a woman up the block from them. "Quite literally."

With a pink parasol in one hand, she wore a matching pink hoop-skirt dress dotted with white rosettes. Her gold hair hung in ringlets around her face and bounced ever so lightly as she spun in circles on the sidewalk, searching for something or someone.

She headed their way and pursed her pink lips as her sky-blue eyes anxiously searched the street.

"Have you seen him?"

Her breathy voice overtook them when they were almost on her.

Magnus politely dipped his head in greeting. "Have I seen who, Mademoiselle?"

"Etienne Tournier. He was to meet me here." The blush

deepened on her cheeks. "He is my betrothed. We are to wed in a week."

Lexie stepped closer to the fretting woman. "Is your name Leda Avequin?"

"Mais oui."

Her French accent added to her alluring beauty.

"Have we met, Madame?"

Lexie shook her head and tried to smile. "Etienne left word. He's waiting for you at his home. He will see you there."

The relief in her fluttering eyelashes was palpable. "Merci beaucoup."

She took off down the street, her small leather shoes not making a sound on the sidewalk.

"How did you know her?" Magnus asked.

"Leda Avequin was betrothed to marry Etienne Tournier until he was killed in a duel after a card game. Grief-stricken, Leda was said to roam the city in her Sunday best searching for her lost love. She eventually went mad. Her father had her locked away in a convent until she died. Her ghost roams the French Quarter asking strangers if they have seen Etienne."

In a small way, Lexie envied the spirit. Over two hundred years and her devotion to her great love still burned.

Magnus frowned at her. "How do you know this?"

"Remember those ghost tours Will took me on to learn about the city? He thought it would be romantic."

"You didn't agree as I recall."

"No. All the stories were of broken hearts, murder, and bitter feuds. Every ghost came from conflict or loss." She ached as she thought of Titu. "Are there any happy spirits, Magnus?"

"Those who die happy, do not need to haunt the earth. They're at peace." In corners, beneath the shade of balconies, the disconcerting shadows reappeared. "Or they used to be at peace.

I'm afraid no one will have any rest until Emily is sent on her way."

They arrived at the front door of the neoclassical, three-story pink building set on a corner and topped with a white balcony railing set off in four corners by large decorative urns. Police officers in dark blue uniforms congregated out front, sitting either in their cars, sipping coffee or smoking cigarettes, or huddled beneath the large portico covering the entrance.

Lexie strolled through the glass front doors, acknowledging a few officers as she went, with Magnus close on her heels. Once inside, dozens of people stopped her progress as they stood packed into the small police station waiting area.

"You'd better take a number," a short man in jeans suggested. "There at the desk."

Lexie studied the high front desk with several officers tending to frantic residents.

"Why are all these people here?"

"Muggings, robberies, ghosts, take your pick," the man explained. "The city is going nuts, and the police don't know how to help."

Lexie thanked him and then pushed her way through the crowd.

A sour-faced officer with a bald head and sweat stains around his collar glowered as she stood on her toes to speak to him.

"Take a number."

"Emile Glapion? He's expecting me."

The grumpy officer offered an audible *humph* while waving her on to the inner workings of the station.

After getting buzzed through bulletproof glass doors, Lexie maneuvered through a rush of uniformed officers to Emile's office.

In the main room of the station, dozens of plain-clothed

officers sat at desks manning the phones. The men and women all wore frustrated frowns, and the hum of conversation deafened Lexie.

When she put her hand on Emile's door, she hoped his office would offer a respite from the noise.

"Lexie?" Emile rose from his desk, holding his phone. "What are you doing here?"

"I need to talk to you."

He held up his hand, asking for her patience.

"I understand your problem, Mrs. Halen, but all our officers are getting around the city as best they can. We will get to your complaint, so please do not worry. And yes, you keep your ghost locked up in your attic until our officers get there."

Emile hung up and exhaled. "The calls haven't stopped since I got in this morning."

"When you told me you would be here, not even two days after … I thought you were insane."

Emile angrily tossed the pencil in his hand across his desk, not hiding the hollow emptiness in his eyes.

"No, insane is sitting in a house surrounded by crime scene tape and questioning your reality." He grimaced and set his closed fist on his desk, coming across as Dr. Jekyll fighting to contain his Mr. Hyde. "Here I can be useful. I've got a murder investigation to solve." His attention turned to Magnus standing behind her. "Who's the guy in the costume?"

Lexie had forgotten about everyone's ability to see her ghost.

"Ah, this is Magnus Blackwell. My spirit guide."

Emile backed up from his desk, ran into his chair, and flopped clumsily into the seat.

"How do you do, Emile." Magnus extended his hand and approached the desk.

Emile stared at him, his mouth ajar. "We've been getting

calls in for over a week about ghost sightings, the dead walking the streets, dead loved ones breaking into their homes, but I never saw anything funny until now."

Magnus sat on the corner of his desk. "And you never noticed the strangers in the street, dressed in costume?"

"It's New Orleans; everyone dresses in costume." He rolled his chair to his desk, wiping the gleam of sweat from his brow. "I'll admit, I've seen what I thought were ghosts around town. I just didn't want to admit I was seeing them."

Magnus edged closer to Lexie. "He needs to know."

"Know what?"

Lexie set her cane to the side. "What if I said a ghost killed Kalila, Jacques and ..." She could not find the strength to say her name.

Emile's jaw clenched. "If this was anyone but you, I would have thrown them out of my office by now. Go on."

"I think a departed spirit, a duppy, is creating chaos in the city. The ghosts, rain, even the crimes are because she wants evil to reign."

His brown eyes widened. "She?"

"A woman of my former employ named Emily Mann. My secretary."

Emile waggled his finger at Magnus. "Your secretary is causing all this crap in my city?"

"And is the one behind the murders."

Emile remained silent as he sized up Magnus. "I'm sorry, Mr. Blackwell, but ghosts don't carve up people, and then drain them of their blood."

"Not blood, but what the blood represents," Lexie edged in. "Power."

"But why here? Why now?"

"I haven't figured that part out, precisely." She ran her

fingers across her tense brow, then she straightened up, remembering what she had to do. "I only know we have to end this. We have to rise above our emotions and do what is needed, not what is wanted."

He sat back in his chair, observing her for the longest time, his face an impenetrable mask.

"Now, you sound like a mambo."

Magnus leaned across the desk and whispered, "So tell her what you know."

Lexie stared at her ghost, ready to throttle him.

How dare he use his ability. She'd never asked him to plant suggestions in Emile's head to get him to talk. It wasn't what she'd come to the station to do.

Emile sat up in his chair and nodded. "I'll tell you what I know." He opened his desk drawer and pulled out a folder. "A ghost didn't kill Jacques Krieger, Kalila La Fay, or my aunt. A woman did."

She examined a single sheet, a lab report, clipped to the outside of the folder.

"Prints at all three crime scenes are Renee Batiste's."

She pushed the folder back across the desk, not impressed. "Renee possessed by the spirit of Emily Mann killed them, but Renee was not the mastermind, only the tool."

"No one cares about spirits or possession in a court of law." Emile opened the folder and flipped through a few of the papers. "Her fingerprints were at every crime scene, and on the bodies. She was pretty sloppy about leaving her DNA all over the place."

"But Renee didn't do it!" Lexie insisted.

Emile put a hand to his head, appearing disoriented.

He took a few seconds, and when he saw the open file on his desk, he slapped it closed.

"What am I doing? I shouldn't have shown you that file."

Emile stood up. "You need to go."

Lexie went around the desk. "You must listen. Emily will never let you take Renee. She won't give up her conduit until she has what she wants—my power, my title, my cane, all of it."

He abruptly arched away from her, his bobbing Adam's apple hinting at his agitation. "Whatever you claim is inside Renee Batiste is going to have a hard time busting out of a prison cell. Once my men pick her up, she will never see the light of day again."

Dread locked up her stomach. "When are your men going to arrest her?"

Emile sagged against this desk. "There's a patrol car on the way to her shop on Royal now."

"No, Emile." She clasped his arms, pleading with him. "You have to let me handle this." Her mind flooded with different ways to buy time for Renee. "Let me confront Emily Mann and end her dark influence."

Emile removed her hands and escorted her around the desk.

"There are some things I can't do. And one of them is impede justice. Renee Batiste will be prosecuted for the murders, and no defense of ghosts or possession is going to stop her from getting convicted. I'll make sure of that. I want her to pay. Can you understand that?"

She did understand his reasoning, but she couldn't embrace it. "Then I will have to do this without your help."

"Don't interfere with this investigation, Lexie." His cold voice sounded different from the Emile she knew. "I can't protect you if you overstep your bounds."

She retrieved her baton juju and ran her finger over one of the pearl eyes gleaming under the fluorescent lights. She answered to a higher power than Emile's badge.

"I don't need your protection. I've got the spirits on my

side."

Lexie raced out of the police station.

A steady rain greeted her when she stepped on the sidewalk. She took off in the direction of her shop, banging her cane on the cement as she marched along, venting her frustration.

"Where are you going?"

She never broke her stride when he appeared, floating alongside her. "To Renee's shop, to warn her. Emile is a fool. He's denying forces he—"

"Forces he doesn't understand," Magnus cut in. "Forgive me, my dear, but I've been one of those forces people fear for quite a while. I'm used to being ignored and denied. Emile is embracing what he knows. All humans do when faced with the unknown."

"Well, I don't!"

He shook his cane at the sidewalk ahead of them. "No, you go running headfirst into the unknown."

"It's what I'm expected to do as mambo."

Magnus smirked. "If you say so."

Aggravated, she raced ahead, impervious to the rain. She was glad no one was on the walkway with her, she might have pummeled them with her cane if provoked.

Up ahead on Royal Street, flashing blue and red lights glinted in the rain.

"If they take Renee away, we might never get a chance to contact Emily Mann." She broke out in a jog.

When she got closer to the police cars, she discovered a crowd of onlookers on the other side of the street from Renee's yellow Creole cottage, peering into the open doors. A few held up cell phones videotaping the event.

Shop attendants in neighboring stores even ventured out into the rain, eager to see the cause of the commotion.

Two police officers, thick as tree trunks, came rushing onto the street from Renee's Shop of Divination. Renee wasn't with them.

The murmurings of the crowd grew, and the flashes from a few phones went off as the officers quickly climbed into their cars.

The police sped away, their tires leaving tracks on the wet street.

Lexie slouched against her cane. "She got away."

Magnus raised his head as if picking up something in the wind. "She's hiding. Emily knows the police are after Renee. She will take Renee somewhere safe."

The crowd in front of the shop disbanded and Lexie moved in closer to him. "Do you have any feeling about where she'll go?"

He shook his head. "I can't sense her, but she will come for you. It's only a matter of time."

Lexie surveyed the people remaining on the corner, reviewing what they had captured on their phones.

"We have to prepare."

"How?" Magnus asked.

"Titu knew how. She showed me in a book."

The moment they reached the door to Mambo Manor, a burning sensation erupted in the center of Magnus's being. Something was amiss.

Across the first floor of the building, a black fog seeped from the closed windows and its wisps snaked out from under the front door. The villainy throbbing from within frightened him.

Lexie sidestepped him, keeping her eye on the shop door. "What is it?"

He put out a hand, urging her back. "A blackness has settled over your shop. It wasn't there when we left."

Lexie stretched her raised hands toward the building. "I don't feel anything." She removed her keys from her dress pocket. "We have to go inside and see what's wrong."

Magnus stepped in front of her. "Let me go first. You wait here."

He pushed through the closed door, passing through layers of paint, dark wood, and emerged on the other side.

Once in the shop, he paused, listening for any movement. When he tried to ease his way inside, something blocked him. He glanced down at an object in his path, and his anger boiled.

The T-shirt rack lay upended at his feet, torn shirts scattered everywhere. Tossed books, their pages ripped from the spine and shredded to confetti, covered the floor. Glass display cases were broken or cracked as if hit with a massive blow while shattered shot glasses remained untouched on their display stand.

It was Emily Mann's handiwork all right, but he guessed it was also a warning. One Lexie would never heed. She'd view the destruction as a challenge.

Damn woman is going to be impossible after she sees this.

A key jiggled as Lexie unlocked the bolt.

She dashed inside, shoving the door out of the way and came to a grinding halt beside him.

"Fuck!"

Classic Lexie.

She set her cane down and trekked through the debris, stooping down to inspect a piece of broken glass or the shredded hem of a T-shirt. Her face red with rage, her hunched figure exuded the hostility of a nest of riled hornets.

He was about to offer a few words of solace when she raised her white knuckles into the air.

213

"I am going to destroy that bitch!"

"Mambo?" came from the open shop door.

In his black robe with his hands reverently folded together, Harold Forneaux waited. In the light of day, his luminescent skin offered a peek of the road map of veins in his face and neck. The large trident-shaped one in his forehead pulsed in a dark shade of blue.

Behind him on the sidewalk outside, the Chez twins stood, with their heads cocked to the right they had their insipid white eyes raised to the heavens. Their fiery red hair, more orange than red in the daylight, came across as garish as it bounced around in the breeze tearing through the streets.

Magnus suspected the three together meant only one thing—trouble.

"We demand an audience." Harold walked up to Lexie. "We have matters to discuss."

The Chez sisters came into the store with their hands hidden beneath their black robes.

They were able to navigate without a cane or any other assistance, puzzling Magnus.

"How … how do they get around?"

Harold's black eyes seared into him. "They see with their minds. Kalfu gave them great inner knowing."

"Sounds like something he would do," Lexie said under her breath and then fixed her attention on Harold. "What matters do you wish to discuss?"

He scanned the decimated store. "It seems you've had visitors."

"Did you know about this?" she snapped.

His features showed all the emotion of wet concrete. The only thing Magnus found intimidating about the man was his towering height.

"This was not my doing." He cocked his head to the side. "It's the same spirit spinning trouble all over the city."

"Is that why you're here? Because of the spirit?"

"You have no power, Mambo." Harold angled closer to her, infuriating Magnus. "The city and its people suffer from your inability to take control. I am here to ask you to step down as leader of the voodoo council. We must appoint another. One able to reverse the tide of events."

Lexie opened her mouth to speak, but Magnus hurried to her side before she let loose more obscenities. He'd dealt with enough hostile takeovers when alive to know what to do to protect Lexie's interests.

"She will not step down." Magnus floated forward, meeting Harold's hostile gaze. "Lexie has a plan to contain the situation, and you will let her implement that plan, or you will be considered a threat to the stability of the council. I'm sure members of the voodoo community, if informed about your proposed takeover as they would be by their true mambo, would also be upset, creating an uproar. Do you want to be responsible for the widespread civil unrest in the city?"

Harold blinked several times, seeming unsure of what to say.

"No one has recognized you, ghost."

Lexie widened her stance, readying herself for battle. "He's my spirit guide and can speak anytime he likes for me."

Magnus smirked.

Lexie collected her baton juju and pointed it at Harold.

"I am mambo. The baton juju is mine, given to me by The Queen, and I will carry out my duties until she, and only she, tells me to stop."

Harold's nostrils flared as his voice dropped to an angry growl. "You have no power. How can you hope to remain our spiritual leader?"

Lexie lifted her chin. "I will get my power back."

A cool breeze from the street entered the shop, lifting scattered pages torn from books, and rustling scraps of fabric.

Magnus turned his head to the wind, sensing an essence of danger. He was about to suggest they shut the door when the twins broke out in a fit of strange convulsions. Their hands shook, their heads rocked back, and their eyes changed from white to black, and their hair billowed upward.

"Darkness rushes to its end, eager to overtake the sky." They spoke as one in the same breathless, feminine Irish accent. "It will rend seed from the soil, and the light in the mother will die."

Not sure what to make of the twins' prophecy, Magnus sought Lexie's reaction for guidance.

Her upper lip curled, and then her steely gaze connected with her adversary.

"Who are you going to get to replace me as mambo? You, Harold?"

"If need be, yes!" His massive hand sliced through the air. "Titu and the others are dead. They must be replaced for the council to function."

"And they will be replaced when the problems of the city have been addressed." She gestured to the open door for him to leave, but he ignored her.

"How are you going to help the city when you cannot even lift a grain of sand with your mind?"

"I don't need my mind to move a grain of sand. Bulldozers only need their strength, and I have more than enough to carry this entire city." She banged the cane's tip less than an inch from his black loafers. "You tread very carefully from this point on, Harold Forneaux, or I will shut you down if you ever cross me again."

Magnus almost broke out in applause. He expected the man

to balk at her threat, but he didn't.

Harold backed up, and the hard line across his lips eased.

"You have forty-eight hours, but after that, I will take the sacred baton juju of Damballah."

He reached out to within inches of the handle, but then the dragon's pearl eyes flashed, and its jaws snapped at Harold's fingers.

Harold yanked back his hand, holding it to his chest, and staring, dumbfounded, at the cane. Lexie crinkled her brow as Harrold's peculiar expression.

Magnus could not believe what he'd witnessed, but by the look on Lexie's face, she'd not seen the dragon come to life.

Harold lowered his hand to his side. "If you refuse me, I will banish you from this city. You will be cast out of the voodoo religion, cursed by the priestesses, and your name will be left unspoken in the record of mambos for all time." He stiffly bowed. "Until then."

The twins backed out the doorway, never taking a misstep.

Harold hurried after them, his black robe flapping behind him.

"I think you are about to face a coup, dear girl."

Lexie did not say a word. She paced back and forth on a spot free of debris. The steady *tick* of her cane on the floor set the tempo of her movements like a metronome guiding a musician.

He waited for her to work out her dilemma, and when she was ready, seek out his advice. But as the minutes passed, and her pacing continued, Lexie didn't turn to him.

For the first time since arriving on the doorstep of Altmover Manor, Lexie wasn't reacting with her usual blustery gusto.

She stopped in the middle of her pacing and darted to the pile of books she'd left on the floor.

"She destroyed the book Titu left open for me." Lexie rifled through the torn pages scattered on the floor. "She knows I've read the spell to get rid of her."

"Do you know how to perform this spell?"

She stood up. "Without the book, I have no idea."

"What do we do?"

Lexie's lips lifted into a coy grin. "We need to make a new friend."

Chapter Seventeen

"I'm not surprised you came to see me, Mambo. I've been informed of Harold's intentions to oust you."

Madame Henri showed Lexie into a cozy living room surrounded by ash oak paneling and overflowing bookcases crammed with an assortment of paperback and leather-bound books. A double-tiered brass chandelier above cast a hazy glow while a fire crackled in the hearth. Family photos set in silver frames covered the walls, and above a mantel of carved roses, a portrait of Madame Henri, wearing a white voodoo priestess dress and turban, a white skull in her hands.

Lexie took a seat in one of the two green high back chairs placed in front of the fireplace.

"He means to take over the council." Lexie set her cane to the side.

"He's always wanted it. Practitioners of the black arts have never gotten along well with those of us in the light. He's using Titu's death and your loss of power to seize control."

Madame Henri slowly settled into a matching chair next to her.

"I'm very sorry for you and Emile. I know Titu mentored you, guided you, and her absence has left a void in your heart and mine. She was a good friend. We may not always have seen eye to eye, but we respected each other."

Lexie rubbed her fingers over a hole in her armchair, concentrating on the softness of the worn fabric.

"Thank you, Madame Henri. I want to do everything I can to bring whoever did these things to Kalila, Jacques, and Titu to justice."

"Justice?" Madame Henri's eyebrows rose. "That's a word for the living; the dead don't need it."

Lexie eased back in her chair, lifting her damp shoes to the fire. "The ghosts I have dealt with always seem hell-bent on revenge."

"The ghosts you've dealt with, are just that—ghosts. Pieces of a soul which have left the body. The part of a person filled with anger, suspicion, revenge, and fear will remain on this plane, especially if they died in pain or anger. Traumatic deaths, lives filled with great suffering, will bind a ghost to this world. But the goodness of the person will move on—a sort of spiritual cleansing. The bad remains while the good departs. We call what is left behind a duppy."

Magnus scowled as he came around Lexie's chair.

Lexie ignored him. "Are all ghosts a duppy?"

"Yes. The spirits arising on the streets lately are such duppy." She motioned a gnarled hand at Magnus. "But you're different, Mr. Blackwell. You're whole. Your soul never split after death. The universe had other plans for you."

"Why is Magnus different?"

Magnus arched over the side of Lexie's chair. "This I must

hear."

"Isn't it obvious?" Madame Henri motioned to the ghost. "He's here for you. To be a spirit guide he needs his love, not just his hate. To be whole and make decisions based on both sides of his emotions—the good and the bad."

"What about the black shadows on the streets?" Lexie folded her hands in her lap, comforted by the warmth of the fire. "What are they?"

"Shadow spirits: they tie soul and body together. It's what we see when we walk in the sun. When we die, our spirits depart, our bodies disintegrate, but the shadows remain—a testament to the life lived by the joining of a body and soul. We never see them, not directly. They sometimes appear out of the corner of our eye. Something we think we saw, but aren't sure. Eventually when a person is forgotten by kin and by time, and their body has faded to dust, their shadow returns to Damballah, their creator." Madame Henri warmed her hands in the firelight. "But someone has taken these shadow spirits from the sacred place Damballah keeps them. As long as they walk among the living, there will be chaos."

Lexie recalled what she'd learned from her spell books, and wanted to broach a way to share her findings with Madame Henri. She needed advice and the help of a practiced priestess.

"I might have found a way to send these spirits back to their world."

"You've found a spell?"

Lexie debated about trusting another priestess, but at this point, she figured she didn't have much of a choice.

"Soon after Titu died I found a spell in one of my books. It's meant to banish a soul across the bridge to blackness. Do you know it?"

She sat back in her chair taking in the fire's glow. "Powerful spell. Very powerful indeed, and can only be performed by a mambo."

Lexie twisted her wedding ring. "But my book describing the spell was destroyed by … a duppy. She means to stop me. I believe she's the reason chaos has overtaken the city."

"You know this duppy?"

Magnus stepped forward. "I do. She was my former secretary, Emily Mann."

The older woman sat in silence, analyzing the ghost. "What did you do to incur this woman's wrath?"

"I have no idea. She lived on my estate, ran my affairs, and kept to herself. She was an excellent secretary, and other than that, I knew little about her."

"She was also in love with him." Lexie sighed and folded her hands in her lap. "He never knew when he was alive."

Madame Henri gave a curt nod and then asked, "What else?"

Magnus frowned. "There's nothing else. As I said, I barely knew the woman. I didn't realize she was in love with me until after I became a spirit."

Something in his languid tone didn't sit right with Lexie—he kept something from her. There was more.

"But this woman knew you, Mr. Blackwell." Madame Henri peered into the fire. "Your habits, your preferences, and even your appetites. There must have been something, an act so upsetting it stirred the anger to feed her duppy. Love unrequited does not instill such power; only loathing can create it."

"She's angry with me, not Magnus." Lexie fidgeted in her chair. "She's jealous of my bond with him, and my having the baton."

"Oh, she hates you." Madame Henri adjusted the shawl around her shoulders. "But the fuel for her hate doesn't come from jealousy. The incentive for everything begins in her life and her time with Mr. Blackwell. Think, Mr. Blackwell."

Lexie cast her gaze to her ghost. "What haven't you told me about Emily?"

His nostrils flared and his green eyes seethed. "I never touched the woman!"

She stood and put her hands on her hips. "I never said you did. Is there some way you treated her? Some way you spoke to her? Anything she would resent you for?"

Magnus went to the fireplace, keeping his back to her.

"Don't you think I've tried to recall some memory which could explain all of this?"

The fury in his voice convinced Lexie she was right—he had a secret.

Madame Henri struggled to get out of her chair. She went to the fireplace and confronted Magnus.

"Think of the little things, Mr. Blackwell. The day-to-day trivialities, and there you will find your answer."

Magnus thought a moment.

"There is one thing. I had forgotten about it. At the time, it seemed ..."

Knowing his past, Lexie dreaded what it might be.

"Forgotten what?"

Magnus scrubbed his face with his hand. "I had dalliances with my maids—and Emily was the one to procure them for me. When I was done with them, she would send them on their way."

"She was your pimp?" Shock, anger, and a wish he were alive so she could punch the shit out of him, coursed through Lexie.

Madame Henri's boisterous laughter bounced around the room. "I don't think such a word existed in Mr. Blackwell's time."

Magnus fondled his ascot tie, appearing uncomfortable with the subject. "She acted as my head housekeeper, in addition to being my secretary. It was a common practice in my day."

Lexie's disgust churned. "What did you do to your

housemaids?"

"You know what I did!"

"I think we found the reason for your spirit's anger." Madame Henri shuffled back to her chair and with a heavy sigh, eased into her seat. "People can tolerate many things, but when they witness someone hurting or demeaning another, very few stay silent. And the ones who do are haunted by that silence. It eats at them and twists their thinking until one day it turns to anger. Lexie saved you from an eternity of stewing in yours. Who does Emily Mann have?"

He faced the two women, holding his head high, but his blank features lacked his usual arrogance. "I never gave what I did a second thought at the time."

"Every action in life sows the seeds of the afterlife, Mr. Blackwell. It would seem you're still paying for your sins, as are we all."

"Like ripples in the ocean." Lexie resumed her seat, drained of energy. "I'm going to send her over the bridge to blackness as soon as possible. We must end her reign of terror."

"Are you prepared for the consequences?" Madame Henri asked. "If you banish a soul tortured by the actions of your ghost to an eternity of nothingness, you will carry that guilt with you for your eternity."

"My concerns are not important. The lives of others are my priority."

"Spoken like a mambo." Madame Henri's smile dipped. "Unfortunately, the spell you speak of is a show of force. Your power against your enemy's. You must stand with them in the center of the bridge, and when the wall of wind appears, it will carry them into the blackness on the other side. Make sure you're the powerful one because if you're not, the other person will be able to send you across the bridge instead."

Lexie drooped in her chair. "How can I challenge Emily if I don't have any power?"

"You must find some. You cannot go up against such a strong duppy until you do."

Where could she turn for help? How could she find enough power to send Emily across the bridge? Her hope dried up. It was as if she stood at the edge of a cliff, knowing, eventually, she'd have to jump.

"Lexie?" Magnus stepped in front of her. "We have a problem."

"No shit we have a problem. How can I—?"

"It's not that," he interrupted. "I have an odd sensation."

She massaged her forehead, not sure how much more she could take.

"What is it?"

"I can feel Will. He's in trouble."

"Will?" Panic quickened her heart, and the room closed in around her. "My Will?"

Magnus floated to the living room entrance. "We must leave."

Lexie was almost to the door when Madame Henri spoke.

"Be careful. She's going to try and force your hand. Don't let her. Remain in control."

Her words followed Lexie out of the room. When she stepped through the doorway and into a hallway with gold-framed mirrors, Magnus charged in a blur past her.

"Hurry, Lexie."

Her throat tightened as she ran through her dark green gate finally home. She tore along the carriageway, her rapid steps echoing in the narrow alley. In the courtyard, she yelled for Will, but her voice croaked and barely registered. She glanced at the phone in her hand while heading to the back steps to see if he'd answered any of her dozen texts or calls.

Please, dear God, not my Will.

"Upstairs," Magnus called down from her balcony. "Now."

On the back steps, she tripped on the hem of her long, wet dress, and clawed at the fabric desperate to get to her husband. At the top of the balcony, the gaping door to their apartment sucked the life out of her.

"Will?"

Her leg muscles quivering, and her heart hammering in her chest, she stumbled through the door.

Her upended sofa and coffee table lay shoved up next to her untouched bookcases on one side of the room. The contents of her altar strewn over the floor—melted white candles, a broken jar of distilled water, and a mound of crushed basil—appeared purposefully trampled. A trail of papers from the altar led across the room to Will's open briefcase.

Oh, God. No.

Her spinning head made her squat on the floor.

In the sea of destruction before her, she knew only one thing was gone.

Will had been taken from her.

She crawled to the leather case she'd bought him when he opened Bennett Architecture.

Magnus's boots stood before her. "Don't panic. We'll find him."

She snapped up his keys and wallet not far from his briefcase and held them to her chest.

Her lower lip quivered. "She took him, didn't she?" Tears welled in her eyes. "Where is he?"

"I don't know." Magnus knelt in front of her. "I can't feel where they have gone. I only sense she is with him."

She climbed unsteadily to her feet and headed toward the door.

"Lexie, we have to think this through. You can't go off half-cocked without a plan."

She imagined Will, hurt, bleeding and calling for her. "I have to find him."

A blinding white light bloomed in the center of the living room, hovering above the debris, opening like a flower touched by the morning sun. Lexie's hand flew in front of her face, and she squinted into the brightness. The light faded and when she lowered her hand, the ghost of Katie Blackwell floated above the room in a halo of yellow light.

"I have a message for you, Lexie Arden."

Still in her gold dress, Katie's face was pale, her mouth twisted in an ugly frown, and her eyes shaded with dark circles. The black rope binding her hands was thicker than she remembered, and the ghost's image filled the room with such dismal hopelessness, it almost sent Lexie to her knees.

"Katie?" Magnus rushed to his wife, reaching out to her. "Why are you here?"

"She sent me." Katie stretched out her hand to meet his. "Forgive me."

Before she could touch her husband, Katie convulsed, arching in vicious trembling. Her eyes rolled back, and her mouth opened, stretching until it seemed her jaw would tear away from her head. The yellow halo around her swirled with black smoke. It filled the open cavern where her mouth used to be and eventually blocked out all the light.

"I have your husband."

The deep whiny voice was back.

"He's an incentive to make sure you comply with my wishes. I have the power of your three friends. More than enough to allow chaos to reign. Bring the cane with your submission to me. I will be waiting for you at Devereaux Plantation for the next two nights. If you do not appear by the third night, your husband will die."

The black smoke evaporated, and the light revived around the ghost. Katie's mouth shrunk back into place. The dainty features on her pretty face resurfaced, but her quaking frown remained.

"Help me," she whispered. "She's so cruel and wants to—"

An enormous black hand swept down from the ceiling and shoved Katie's ghostly image aside. She evaporated into a cloud of yellow light. Then the light twinkled in small dots before it disappeared. But her ghastly cries for help remained, rising higher and higher until they stopped altogether.

"Katie!" Magnus stood beneath the spot where his wife had materialized and searched the ceiling for any trace of her.

Lexie shared his torment. They were both suffering at the hands of a monster, and the utter sense of helplessness Katie had introduced into the room inundated Lexie. The pain was cataclysmic. How could she go on without her Will?

But you have to go on. You have to fight, child.

Titu's voice in her head deftly bolstered her drive for revenge. The resolve in her gut, fed by her anger and anguish, hardened to granite. She would find her husband, and she would send the diabolical bitch ruining her life right back to hell. But to do that, she would need power, and she knew of only one place to get it.

She shook her head, dismayed by the precarious design of fate. No matter how hard she fought against him, Kalfu would get what he wanted—her.

"We should call Emile." Magnus faced her. "Let him know about Will."

Lexie remembered Will's wallet and keys gripped against her chest and ran her finger over the soft leather.

"We can't do that. He will want to go after him, and I can't allow it. She wants me."

Magnus came up to her, his defeated gaze replaced by concern. "Emile can go with you when you meet her. He can have officers ready to pull you and Will out in case anything goes wrong."

"The police won't help us. This is beyond their capabilities." She stiffened her back, her determination eclipsing her despair, and set Will's wallet and keys down on a side table. "I'm going to meet her and beat her at her own game."

Magnus came around in front of her and planted his legs. "How? You don't have any power."

"Not yet." She let out a long breath. "But I will."

Chapter Eighteen

In Titu's living room, below the portrait of Madam Simone, Lexie stood with her overnight bag and her dragon cane.

She'd arrived on Emile's doorstep a few minutes earlier, courtesy of the police car parked outside her shop.

Lexie had planned to take up his offer to stay in his guest bedroom, but only for the night. She needed a place to think and plot her showdown with Emily away from the reminders of Will and what had happened. But after arriving, Emile's crimson face made her reconsider her decision.

"You must tell me where she's holding him!"

He set the drink in his hand on the coffee table with a *thud*, spilling a few drops of the scotch meant for her.

"When you told me what happened on the phone, I thought you were mad even to consider facing her."

"I didn't tell you where she wants to meet because I knew what you'd do." She dropped her bag on the floor and went to get her drink. "You'd lock me in a cell and go off to rescue Will, killing him in the process. We're going to do this my way."

"I have to be involved." He scooped up the other glass of scotch on the table. "There's a warrant out for her arrest. I can't ignore it."

"I'm not asking you to ignore it." She swirled her drink, admiring the amber liquid. "Give me twenty minutes alone with her to rescue Will and rid Renee of Emily's spirit. Then you and your men can come storming in and do whatever you like."

He shook his head. "I can't allow that. You could be heading into an ambush. Renee still has connections with Bloody Mary's old crew of thugs. She'll have them waiting for you."

"So what?" She glanced at the painting above the mantel. "Simone would want me to fight."

"She's not my department head. I've got policies and procedures to follow. If my boss ever got wind of me bringing a civilian along on an arrest, he'd have my badge."

Her mind spinning, she had a seat and set the baton juju to the side.

"Does your boss know about what happened at St. Louis Number One Cemetery during the *haute défi*? How civilians were put at risk?"

Emile coolly lifted his glass to his lips. "You wouldn't dare."

She kept her gaze on her scotch. "Give me what I want, and your boss will never know about any of it."

"Careful, dear girl." Magnus appeared in the corner of the room, resting his shoulder against the door to the courtyard. "You're playing with fire."

Emile bobbled his drink in his hands. "Is that your ghost?"

Lexie tipped her scotch toward her ghost. "You remember Magnus Blackwell."

Magnus gave their host an ever so slight nod of the head.

Emile went to her chair, keeping a watchful eye on Magnus.

231

"If I give you the time you need, there can be no mention of it in my report, you and Will were never there, and Renee will be mine with no interference from you."

Lexie slumped with satisfaction back into her chair. "Deal."

She drained the last dregs of scotch, and the room around her showed through the bottom of her glass. Memories of every long afternoon chat, early morning tutoring session, and late-night lessons on voodoo with Titu came to mind. Her bitterness added to the burn of the drink in her stomach. Titu's death and her husband taken from their home—what kind of dream was this, or was it real?

The relentless, chest-tightening, nauseating anxiety over Will's safety was the only thing keeping her upright. Without it, she would have given in to her urge to curl into a ball and sleep away her nightmare.

Emile rolled his glass around in his hands. "Are you going to tell me where we're going?"

"I'll give you directions on the way there, but until then, no." She sat back in the plush chair, the guilt twisting her gut. "It's my fault Will was taken, and I have to get him back, not you or your men." Her hand closed around the arm of the chair and squeezed, letting go some of her pent-up rage. "This is beyond your world: it's mine."

"Your world?" Emile gulped back his scotch. "I don't understand any of it. I lived most of my life with my aunt. She took care of Remi and I after our mother died, but I never participated in her rituals; never wanted to learn about her religion. I thought it was a lot of BS."

"You can still be a part of it." Lexie enjoyed the warm flush the alcohol provided. "Titu taught me belief is the most important element of magic. If you believe, then you can create."

Emile sat in the chair across from her. "She used to tell me

232

the same thing, but I never bought into it." He glanced up at her ghost. "Until now."

An uncomfortable silence sifted through the room.

Her thoughts gravitated back to Will— how was he, what was he feeling? She tried to reach out to him, hoping some shard of her power remained, but nothing came to her. Horrid images of Will tied up, bleeding, battered, or worse, filtered through her mind, and she quickly knocked back the rest of her scotch.

How much more would she have to go through? Was being mambo worth losing the only man she ever loved?

"Harold Forneaux came to see me earlier today. He wants me to step down." She set the empty glass on the coffee table. "After I get Will back, I just might give him the damned baton juju and be done with it."

"You can't do that." Emile rose from his chair, holding his drink. "No one said it would be easy. And who knows what may happen down the road, but you can never give up. Titu would never let you, and I won't let you. You told me if you believe, you can create. If that's the real magic, then it lives in you, Lexie. You have to believe in you and let nothing else stop you."

His words rang hollow to her. "I did believe in myself when I had my power, and Titu and Will beside me, without them ..." Her voice dried up.

"Marie Laveau placed her faith in you, if you run away from your responsibilities, you will never forgive yourself." He picked up her empty glass. "I know a thing or two about duty. Good or bad, you're appointed to protect the people of this city. So, do it."

"How can I without my power?" She wanted to vent a volley of curse words, but instead, she calmly climbed from the chair, wiping her damp eyes.

"Then get the power you need. Find a way to win. Do

whatever it takes." He walked toward the arched entrance to the living room. "I'll get us some fresh drinks."

After he left the room, Lexie's gaze drifted to her ghost.

"You're awfully quiet."

"What would you like me to say?" Magnus glided toward her. "So how do you plan to get Will back?"

She went to the mantel, and her attention zeroed in on Simone Glapion's painting while her thoughts stayed on her husband.

Is he okay? Is he being hurt?

The urge to go, run to the plantation and be with him, surged through her with a vengeance. But she couldn't lose her head and give in to her panic. If she showed any weakness, Emily would destroy her and Will.

There was only one choice left for her.

"Emile's right. I've got to get the power I need to beat Emily, then Will and the city would be safe."

Magnus drifted closer. "What are you thinking?"

She wasn't sure how to phrase what she had decided. How did she explain how cornered she'd become? She had to get Will back at any cost, even if it meant giving up her soul.

"You most certainly are not going to give yourself to Kalfu! Do you know what he will do to you?"

"I have no choice." Her voice sounded small, broken. "It's the only way to get Will back."

His lips pressed into a white slash as he came at her. "There has to be another way. I know darkness, Lexie. I've lived with it for over a century. It wasn't until I met you I saw the error of my ways, and even then, my soul is still black, still stained with my sins. You are not me. You can't destroy the goodness in you."

"Stop it, Magnus!" She tossed up her hands, not interested in his argument. "I can get the power I need to get what I want.

And I want Will!" Her voice broke. "I can't live with myself if anything happens to him. Coming to New Orleans was my idea; becoming a mambo, my purpose. I will not let him suffer for my mistakes."

"But he loves you and would withstand any horror to make sure you are safe." Magnus gentled his voice. "He would not trade one second of your adventure here for a life without you, and neither would I." His mouth softened from its hard stance, and the corners lifted into a half-smile. "I care for you, Lexie, and I can never agree with the rash commitment you are about to make."

The rare display of affection touched her. She didn't need their ribbon of light to sense his thoughts or share his concerns. She already did.

"I care about you, too, Magnus. But this is my choice, and I don't want you to have any part of it."

He shook his head and stepped back from her. "As you always say, my dear, fuck that! If you insist on doing this insanity, then I'm doing it with you."

She shook her head. "I can't ask you to do that. This is the dark side of magic, and you don't—"

"Where you go, I go." He removed a wisp of hair from her cheek. "Even if it means taking a trip to hell."

Inside the blue guest bedroom she'd once shared with Will, Lexie sat on the king-sized bed and agonized over her husband. The two glasses of scotch she shared with Emile had done nothing to relieve her anxiety.

A warm energy flowed into her hand as she wrapped her

fingers around her baton juju, but the sensation brought little comfort.

The creak of the hall floors let her know Emile set out for his bedroom. When the light under her door finally went out, she stood up and unpacked her bag.

Resigned to her fate, she removed the simple cotton white dress she'd brought with her—the ceremonial one she planned to wear to confront Emily—and set it on the bed. She stepped out of her jeans and slipped the dress over her head.

In front of the mirror mounted on top of the mahogany dresser, she ran her hands over the smooth dress. She glanced down at her hands, surprised not to see them shaking. After so much inner turmoil since losing her power, an odd calm spread through her.

Convinced she made the right decision, Lexie collected her baton juju and headed to the bedroom door.

In the hallway, she padded to the landing and down the stairs, anxious not to wake Emile. The last thing she needed was to explain what she was doing roaming his home in the middle of the night.

From the dimly lit stairs, she made her way to the hallway toward the back of the house. The light from the street outside filtered through the windows guiding her way. The light comforted her, made her feel safe. Would she still feel that way after she became his?

When she passed the kitchen, the bright green eyes of the two black cats sitting on the kitchen counter reflected the street light. They scurried to her ankles, meowing and purring for attention. She urged them away with the tip of her cane, but the cats remained.

Once she stood before the plywood door to Titu's atelier, the cats ran back down the hallway toward the kitchen. A light sweat beaded her brow when she reached for the handle with an unsteady hand.

Damn. The shaking is back.

She clenched her fist, willing away her trembling when a chill rose around her. A funny scent lingered in the air—freesia mixed with something spicy?

"Think what you're doing, child?"

She raised her hand to her mouth, hiding her cry.

Titu.

She scoured the shadows in the hallway, but there were no distortions, no apparitions, no fanciful balls of light, only the shade made by the streetlamps outside.

"I know you're here and, if you know about Will, then you realize I have no choice."

Lexie waited; the only sound she heard was her rapid breathing. She didn't know if Titu's silence meant approval or acceptance, but prayed her mentor understood. And if she couldn't, Lexie didn't care. Titu was gone: Will was alive, and she would sacrifice anything to save him.

She yanked the door open, and a loud creak of resistance rang through the hall. Her stomach grumbled, a result of too much scotch and no food, and then she stepped inside.

The aroma of herbs tickled her nose. On the unfinished floors, an assortment of potted plants wilted in desperate need of water. Dried herbs hung from the wood beams in the ceiling while shelves crammed with jars and pots gathering dust.

She found a box of matches on the worktable in the center of the room and went to the tulip-shaped sconces on the walls to light their melted white candles. Once the glow of light permeated the room, she searched the books on the shelves.

She found the spell she remembered in K. Mandry's *Of Light and Dark: Spells and Rituals for Evocation.*

With the page for conjuring dark spirits open on the table, Lexie went in search of her ingredients.

"How can I help?"

Magnus came to life in front of a shelf of sage plants.

She'd never been so happy to see her ghost. With him at her side, she could do this.

Lexie tapped the open book on the table with her finger. "Read out the ingredients to me."

While Magnus went through the list, she gathered everything she needed: sage, ground human bone, dried oak leaves, rum, gunpowder, and a clipping of her hair.

Once the ingredients sat in a pile in the middle of the table, she obtained a knife with a pearl handle from one of the shelves.

"What's that for?" He cocked a wary eyebrow at the knife.

She stroked the pearl handle. "When the time comes, I have to add my blood to the items on the table to seal the deal."

The last ingredient was a black candle she found hidden away in a cabinet. She lit the candle and stood back, taking in her handiwork.

"That's it?" Magnus asked as he sat across from her.

"Power is in the belief, right?" She wiped her hands together. "No matter what happens, don't interfere."

"May I just state for the record, this is a bad idea."

"I have no other choice. I need power to fight her."

Magnus slowly grinned. "Well then. Here we go."

Lexie held her hand over the pile of leaves, dust, hair, and rum. She swore she detected a ripple of energy floating up to meet her. Encouraged by the sensation, she slammed her hand down. The ingredients squished through her fingers, and a cloud of dust rose to her face.

The musty aroma drifted past her nose. Her skin flushed, and a sense of peace overtook her being. It was as if finally choosing to join Kalfu had released her fear.

She closed her eyes and recited the words she'd memorized from the text.

"Spirit of the darkness, I beseech thee, come to me. Kalfu, travel on the wind of suffering to my door and be in my presence. From this moment hence, thy powers I wish to share for things that need be done. Take me as your servant, and grant me your unyielding strength."

Alert to any creak, any breeze or change in the air, Lexie's senses remained on edge.

"Nothing is happening." Magnus pointed to her hand buried in the muck. "Are you doing it right?"

Her irritation flared. "There's no wrong way of doing it."

"Perhaps you should—" He stood from the table. "Someone is here."

Lexie reached into her core, hoping some smidgen of her power would register the presence, but nothing had changed.

Damn.

A drop in the temperature teased her arms. It was slight at first, but then the growing cold embraced her. With her hand still on the pile of gunk, she shivered as the room became downright freezing. Her breath clouded in front of her as she exhaled one nervous breath after another.

The air contracted. The pressure in her ears rose until the pain made her yank her hand away from the table. She covered her ears, swallowing hard to pop them. The pressure around her kept climbing and soon it was getting hard to breathe.

Something was wrong. She couldn't get any air. Her eyes watered, and flashes of black closed in on her. Petrified by what was happening, she reached for Magnus's ghost, desperate for the comfort of another.

"Lexie!" Magnus put out his hand to her, but it passed right through. "What's happening?"

Life drained from her limbs, overtaken by the cold in the room, and she dropped to her knees. On the floor, she barely had the strength to keep her head up when out of the corner of her eye, a funny black spot appeared.

It hung in the air not far from her head. It got bigger and bigger and soon formed a thick black cloud like the ones over the city. It spread over her, covering her body with a comforting warmth.

She relaxed, her breathing slowed, and she no longer felt afraid. The cloud closed around her, blotting out Titu's atelier, and right before the last remnants of light from the black candle got snuffed out, Kalfu's face materialized.

"Welcome, Mambo. I'm happy you have decided to join me."

Chapter Nineteen

T he black globe swallowed her, engulfing her in utter darkness.

She wasn't sure if she was awake or asleep. Similar to falling in a dream, she tumbled backward deeper into the desolation. There was no order, no sound, no light, nothing to give her senses something to latch on to, or a landmark to gauge how far she'd fallen, or even where she was. The black went on and on.

A hand latched onto her. It held her at the wrist, and her fall slowed. Soon her legs came under her, and her feet gently touched the ground.

"You've arrived."

The light of hundreds of silver candelabras ignited around her. The flickering candles helped to settle her nerves somewhat. Long white sticks sprouted from the ground and their tips sparked with fire. The tapered candles came to life, and she raised her head following the trail of smoke rising from the flames. Blackness greeted her, and she shivered as she gaped upward, dazed by her journey.

The smoke from the candles shifted and surrounded her. Images materialized in the hazy fog, and the glint of gold sparkled in the candlelight.

When the smoke parted, as if swept aside by magical hands, it revealed an exquisite gilded room with life-sized mirrors on the walls and ceiling. Furniture cropped up, appearing out of nowhere, covering the black-tiled floor, and all intricately decorated Louis the XIV pieces, Lexie momentarily forgot about the reason for her arrival, and admired the furnishings, indulging in her love for the period.

She went to a table of solid silver with lions' heads at each corner inlaid with lapis lazuli eyes. The creatures blinked at her, and Lexie stepped back, unsure of what she'd witnessed.

She crossed the floor to an ebony dining room table long enough to seat thirty people. With pedestals of silver with ivory carvings of elephants and giraffes rising from the center, it was a piece she'd seen in books. Her hand went to stroke the head of an elephant, and the animal raised its trunk to her. She gasped and snapped her hand back but found the carved figure was once again an unmoving fixture on the table.

The chairs alongside her were also ebony with ivory arms and silver inlaid in geometric patterns in the backs. The strange designs composed of triangles and squares made her dizzy. It was as if they floated above the chairs, creating a creepy optical illusion.

Her hand to her head, she was uncomfortable in the room. The moving figurines couldn't be real. Maybe it was the smoky atmosphere playing tricks with the light, or perhaps she'd fallen asleep in the workshop.

Letting go of her misgivings and deciding to go with her dream, she became fascinated with a cabinet to the side.

Made in the metal-marquetry technique of brass inlaid over a tortoiseshell design, it glistened in the candlelight. She ran her hands over the detailed of cherubs and feathers, delighting in the contrasting colors and surfaces characteristic of the Baroque style.

"Ah, you picked the best piece in the place."

Kalfu walked up to her from out of nowhere.

In only jeans with an open white, long-sleeved shirt, he seemed almost provincial amid the elegant décor. Predatory in his movements, the ripple of his taut stomach muscles and the expanse of his muscular chest accentuated her vulnerable position.

She had no power to challenge him, physically or magically, and she was in his world, at his mercy. The way his blue eyes glided over her dress intimidated her, which he probably wanted, but she had to stand up to him. She could never let him see her fear.

"Why are you in my dream?"

"This is no dream." He spread out his hands in a welcoming gesture. "This is my world. Your spell brought you here."

Knowing her spell had worked triggered a nervous tremor in her hands. She pressed them against her sides, eager to appear brave in front of the unholy being.

"I would never have guessed your world included Louis the XIV furniture."

His cheeky grin irked her. "I wanted to make sure you felt welcome."

She rested her hand on the cabinet next to her, not acting very impressed. "André-Charles Boulle was the royal cabinetmaker for Louis the XIV. He perfected this technique and artists all over the world tried to copy it. But this, it's a perfect reproduction."

Kalfu leaned in closer, and the aroma of freshly cut grass

wafted passed her. "It's not a reproduction."

She removed her hand from the cabinet and reformulated her approach. "Why are you going to all this trouble? We both know why I'm here."

His musical laughter reminded her of an addicting waltz.

"You are blunt. I like that. But you are also uncertain." Kalfu moved toward the dining table, a place setting for two of glistening gold plates, cutlery, and sparkling crystal appeared. "I want you to submit to me not because you have to, but because you want to. I do not need sycophants." He rolled his eyes. "I've got enough of those. I need an equal, a partner who can work with me to do ... anything I desire."

Her anger flared. "And what is it you desire? To conquer the world, control men's minds, fill the Earth with your dark minions. I won't have any part of that!"

His boisterous laughter shocked her—it almost sounded genuine. He clapped his hands as he took her in with a leering gaze.

"Ah, my dear Lexie Arden. I do not wish to rule your world. It would take up too much of my time and require substantial effort. I'm a creature of pleasure."

"Or of pain," she countered.

He pointed at her with raised eyebrows. "You see? That's what I'm missing. No one would ever speak to me in such a manner. But you would never tell me what I want to hear."

"Are you sure you can handle a woman like me?"

"Oh, I can handle you, make no mistake about that. I adore fire in people, and you, my dear Mambo, have more than enough to keep it very interesting between us." He took her hand. "Let us dine and talk about the wonderful things we can do together."

His touch warmed and comforted her. She thought it odd a spirit associated with death and darkness should have such soft hands. When did he become the diabolical menace she'd expected? This approach was more disconcerting than if he'd appeared as a fire-breathing devil.

"I don't do that," he said as he showed her to a chair. "Breath with fire and brimstone. It's very unbecoming."

Lexie stared at him. "How did you know what I was thinking?"

He pulled out one of the ebony and ivory chairs. "I've known what you're thinking since the moment you were born, Lexie Arden."

At the table, she analyzed his comment while fingering her gold plate and gold cutlery.

"Do you listen to everyone's thoughts?"

He took the chair next to her. "Only those who will be useful to me."

Kalfu reached for a carafe of red wine. "We must drink a toast."

She took the folded napkin from her plate. "What do we drink to?"

The wine sloshing in her glass echoed throughout the room.

"To us. To the beginning of a long and prosperous relationship."

Lexie didn't reach for her glass. Instead, she kept her hands in her lap.

"What will you expect of me in this relationship?"

He filled his crystal wine goblet. "Ah, down to business." Kalfu put the carafe to the side and lifted his glass. "You're to swear loyalty to me. You will represent my interests in your world, be a proponent of my way of thinking, and when I need you to, do my bidding."

"And in exchange? I get what exactly?"

He peered into his wine. "My power. You will be the most

powerful mambo in history. No one will ever be able to overthrow you or challenge your authority."

Her fingers hesitated over the wineglass, disgusted by what he proposed.

"I'm here to save my husband, not strengthen my reign." She lifted her glass. "Ah, but you already know that if you have read my thoughts as you claim."

He sat back in his chair, his keen eyes sweeping her face. "How fortuitous for me your husband was kidnapped. Otherwise, this meeting might never have occurred."

"Did you have something to do with it? Did you plan to take Will to win me?" She took a quick sip of wine, hoping for encouragement.

The unexpected sweetness of it tempted her, but she needed her wits about her.

"Despite what you hear of me, making people do my bidding isn't as easy as you think. The spirit you're dealing with came up with stealing your husband on her own. I would have killed him and had you begging me to bring him back." He sipped his wine and then smacked his lips. "It worked out better this way."

The reality of who she dealt with sank to her depths along with the heady wine. She shakily set her glass on the table.

"What will happen if I refuse your offer? Will you kill my husband then?"

He thumped his glass on the table, a loud hiss escaping from his downturned lips.

"I will cast you across the bridge to blackness. Your soul will spend eternity lost in a black void of nothingness." He edged closer, his gleaming smile returning. "But please me, and I will make you a very happy woman."

Lexie did not return his smile. "My husband makes me

happy."

He folded his hands and sat back in his chair. "The doubting Will Bennett? I find that rather amusing."

Lexie stroked the stem of her wineglass, considering her next move.

"If I agree to your terms, you must stay out of my decisions. I will rule as I see fit, not as you want."

His grin slipped. "You've got a lot of courage coming to my world, as my guest, and making demands." He put his face right in front of her. "I make the demands here."

The sweet aroma around him faded and a hint of putrid decay mixed with a touch of charred flesh wafted past her.

Nauseated by the smell, she struggled to keep her cold stare on him.

"How many who have come to your world have been a mambo? You want me, then I have terms of my own."

His low whistle circled the air. "You are a stubborn little mouse."

She bristled at being called a little mouse but wondered if that's how she'd been acting since becoming mambo.

She'd been overly lenient with the voodoo practitioners in her realm, barely making waves and avoiding conflict, hoping the strategy would garner her acceptance. Perhaps she'd been wrong.

Suddenly all the doubts she harbored, all the criticism she'd endured faded away, and an ironclad resolve to never again second guess herself, or bend her will to please another took hold. She was Mambo, and it was high time she acted like it.

She met his cold eyes, dropping her voice to reflect the anger in her soul.

"Yes, I'm stubborn, but I am no mouse. I have the Queen's blessing, and the baton juju of Damballah belongs to me. I earned it. I fought for it. I am a force to be reckoned with, and I reign over a world you could never control. I come to you asking for power, and in exchange, you will have my gratitude and my ear, but nothing more. My mind, my heart are mine, and if you ever try to take them away, I will use everything I have to fight you."

He sat back, his arrogant grin revitalized, and she knew in that instant, she'd made the right call. Nothing impresses the powerful more than power.

"Finally, the tigress has awakened. You'll be an asset to my organization." He pounded the table with his fist, the dishes and utensils rattled. "Done."

The sound terrified her, but she never moved a muscle.

After a deep breath, she said, "Then I agree."

He pressed his finger to his lips. "There is one more matter we must discuss. I require a sacrifice of all those who pledge their loyalty to me."

Her mouth went dry. "What sacrifice?"

He rolled the wine in his glass. "I take something in payment to remind you of your commitment to me. And no, I will not take your husband. You wouldn't be much good to me if you were mourning him all the time. No, it's never anything so obvious. It's more of a token, a piece of you hardly missed."

Lexie kicked herself for not finding out ahead of time about the sacrifice, but she had committed herself, and getting Will back was in her power, or soon would be.

"What will you take from me?"

"I will decide that in time, but what I need to hear from you right now is you will join me of your own free will. No reservations, no doubts. You commit to me absolutely."

Picturing Will, she lifted her wineglass and held it to him. "Of my own free will."

When he tapped his glass against hers, the clang of church

bells clamored above them.

She glanced up, but the only thing there was darkness. The peeling of the bells blared in her ears. She put her wineglass down, cringing. Then the bells stopped, abruptly, and all that remained was a strange throbbing in her temples.

The pain subsided, and Kalfu stood over her, wielding one of the gold knives in his hand. He held it above her neck, his blue eyes radiating with an eerie light.

A black, icy terror coursed through her. Was she about to die?

"Now commit to me, Alexis Marie Arden." He raised the knife higher. "And then let us seal this contract in blood."

Magnus sat observing the rise and fall of Lexie's chest as she lay slumped over the table. He'd seen her faint before during her initiation into voodoo. Then he didn't fear the unexpected; this time, he did.

Was he doing the right thing?

He asked himself the question a thousand times since she proposed her plans to him. He'd yearned to lock her away and keep her from ever dabbling in darkness. But Lexie wasn't his, and he had no control over her decisions. It was the hardest lesson he'd learned as a ghost—letting someone else make the same mistakes he had learned. He equated it with being a parent. Children never listened, why should Lexie?

The minutes ticked by and he ran through a list of people to contact. He was seconds from heading to the door when her lips moved.

She mumbled a few unintelligible words and then her left

hand rose from the table. It stopped above her head as if someone held it there.

A bright circle of light next to the table took Magnus by surprise.

It twinkled and then lengthened to the size of a man. The shape thickened, and he could not see the other side of the workshop through it. Details came into focus: blond hair, blue eyes, and a callous smile. The man before him dipped his head and greeted Magnus in a smoky voice.

"Ah, Mr. Blackwell. At last we meet."

The stranger held Lexie's hand above her head, but Lexie never awoke from her slumber. The picture presented stirred his fury. How could this man have such control of his Lexie?

"Who are you?" Magnus stood, brandishing his dragon cane.

"I'm the one your mistress summoned." He set Lexie's left hand on the small mound of leaves and dust. "My name is Kalfu."

Magnus knew the name and hated it. "What have you done to her?"

He wiped his hands together. "Nothing. She's in my world and will wake up when our deal is struck."

Magnus lowered his cane. "Your deal?"

"She has committed to me, body and soul."

Kalfu's disclosure burned through him. He had failed to keep her safe from the evil he had once embraced.

"No!" He pounded the table. "She is under duress. She will do anything to get her husband back. You cannot hold her to this bargain."

Kalfu had a seat on Lexie's bench across from Magnus. "And what would you have her do to fight the spirit you created? Emily Mann is your invention, my good man. She needs my power to win."

"She can win without your power." Magnus approached the table, challenging Kalfu with his eyes. "She can do anything she sets her mind to."

Kalfu crossed his arms, studying Magnus.

"You care for her. I thought you were the kind of spirit who cared for no one, especially no woman."

Magnus opened his mouth to argue, but Kalfu stopped him with a penetrating glare.

"I know what you are, what you have done, Mr. Blackwell. You're my kind of creature—dishonest, disloyal, and prone to creating a whole lot of chaos. The things you've done would be a credit to my name."

Magnus examined his cocky smirk and gauged his desire to make a deal. He'd known men comparable to Kalfu: vain, brash, self-absorbed, and eager to put forth their interests—the man he'd once been. So how could he best such an opponent? Magnus had to find a way to spare Lexie his destiny. He could not spend eternity living with the guilt of letting her down.

"You're a businessman, Kalfu, are you not?"

Kalfu nodded, his smirk sagging ever so slightly. "I'm not opposed to deals that promote my interests. Why? Are you going to make me an offer, Mr. Blackwell?"

His sarcastic tone perturbed Magnus. A deal with the devil—he'd made such a commitment when he was among the living. What difference would it make when he was dead?

He leaned over the table, keeping his eyes on his prey. "Don't hold her to any deals she makes under the fear of losing her husband. Even you must admit the universe would not take kindly to such a bargain."

"I do not care for the whims of the universe." Kalfu stroked Lexie's fine blonde hair, infuriating Magnus. "But I am interested in hearing your offer."

"Take me." Magnus arched closer, wanting to distract him from Lexie. "I will swear loyalty to you, if you leave Lexie's soul in peace."

Kalfu let her hair fall from his hand and tipped his head thoughtfully to the side.

"Interesting proposition. You could go far working for me. But I must pass, for now." He stood and snatched up the pearl-handled knife still on the table. "Lexie's commitment to me must be sealed in blood."

To Magnus's horror, he plunged the knife into her left hand.

"No!" Magnus rushed toward her.

But as the blade went through her hand and stuck in the table, Lexie never moved. She never roused from her slumber, never uttered a sound.

Kalfu released his grip on the knife and wiped his hands. "Good evening, Mr. Blackwell. We will meet again, I assure you."

A flash of light blinded Magnus, and he shielded his face with his arm. The light vanished as quickly as it appeared and when he looked again, Lexie remained asleep—her hand pinned to the table by the knife—but Kalfu had disappeared.

She stirred, groaned, and slowly sat up, opening her eyes. She tried to move her left hand and stilled when she spotted the knife.

He was about to tell her to remain calm while he went for Emile when she reached for the blade's handle.

"No, Lexie, don't."

She didn't listen, and he cringed when she ripped the blade from her hand. Lexie dropped the knife to the side, her skin bunched around her eyes in a pained stare, and then she held up her hand, surveying the damage.

No blood spewed from the wound, but Magnus dashed to the shelves anyway, searching the atelier for a bandage or scrap of linen.

When he could find nothing, he rejoined her at the table. But there wasn't any blood on her hand.

She held it up and examined the gash. "It doesn't hurt. Why doesn't it hurt?"

Magnus had no explanation but was sure it had something to do with Kalfu's influence.

"We need to see to your injury. Let's return to the house and find a bandage."

Right after he spoke the words, the laceration became engulfed by a glowing, yellow light. It came from inside the wound, shooting outward from both sides of her hand, and sending rays to the ceiling and the table below.

The radiance brought the torn pieces of flesh together. The skin closed over, and within seconds, it appeared as if no injury had occurred.

Then when the pulsating light shrunk beneath the back of her hand, a thin white scar sealed the wound.

Lexie turned her hand over. "Tell me you saw that."

"I saw it." Magnus pointed to the back of her hand. "He left you a scar. Something to remind you of your pledge to him, no doubt."

She closed her hand, making a fist. "You met him?"

He took a seat next to her, wanting to scold her for what she had done, but didn't.

"Do you know what you're doing? He's evil; evil like I used to be. You can never rid yourself of such darkness."

"You did." She sighed and touched the wedding ring above the scar. "I'm doing this to get my husband back. Will is worth it."

He could not argue with her love for the man. He only wished in life he'd loved with her passion.

"Do you feel any different?"

"No different." She flexed her left hand. "Maybe it takes time for his power to kick in."

A deep rumbling rose from beneath the mud floor. Magnus stood from the bench, spinning around and searching for the source.

The ground trembled, and the table and shelves shuddered. A few potted plants fell, the clay shattering on the floor.

"What's going on?" Lexie backed up from the worktable.

"I don't know." Magnus feared for her safety. "You need to get out of here."

She could barely stay upright while holding on to the table. Lexie fell, landing hard on the floor.

Magnus shot to her side, anxious to make sure she was okay. He stayed next to her on the floor until he caught sight of a black mist wiggling up through the ground.

It moved toward Lexie, wrapping around her legs. Its horrendous color contrasted against her creamy skin as it journeyed along her calf and then maneuvered to the side of her white dress.

She frantically batted at the black vines. "Magnus, what is that?"

He swiped at the object, but his hand passed through her leg. Magnus felt utterly useless. He had to save her, but how?

The winding blackness spread, twirling around her body like a voracious weed. It covered her legs and continued along her torso. She called to him, shrieking for help as she attempted to push it back, but the spindles latched on to her arms and inched higher.

Frantic, Magnus combed the workshop for anything he could use to stop the dark cloud from enveloping her completely.

The mist climbed to her neck, wrapping around as if two hands were strangling her. When it reached her open mouth, a river of black poured into her, cutting off her cries.

The opaque blob obliterated any trace of her. Nestled in her black sheath, Lexie lifted from the floor, carried by an unseen force toward the ceiling. She didn't struggle within the blackness, or at least, Magnus didn't notice.

In an act of desperation, he tossed his arms around the pod, but as soon as he touched it, a shock of electricity lashed out, throwing him to the floor.

Lexie hung in the air. He waited, sick over the prospect of losing her to the darkness.

Then the black mist slowly retreated. The pod descended from the ceiling and gently set down on the floor.

The black peeled back, revealing her blonde hair, then her face, and the top of her white dress. When the thick smoke cleared away completely, its tendrils seeped back into the ground.

Magnus stepped closer, hovering over her, making sure she was breathing.

Seconds later, her eyes opened.

A sense of unease shook him; they weren't their usual brilliant blue. There was something darker about the light they gave off.

"Magnus, what happened?"

She struggled to her feet and for a minute had to hold on to the edge of the table to stay upright. After wiping her forehead, she glanced at her hand.

"I remember the knife and then something strangling me."

He watched her every move, anxious to make sure she was the same Lexie he adored.

"How do you feel?"

She closed her left hand into a fist. "I feel good. Strong." She pushed away from the table, taking in the room.

He inspected the black stains left from the mist on her dress.

"What do you feel?"

"I can feel … everything. The life flowing around me. I can hear the people outside, sense their emotions and their fears. I can smell the coffee brewing at the shop down the street, taste the fried eggs at the late-night diner around the corner, even taste the sugar on the beignets at Cafe Du Monde." She went to the door. "My power is back."

The funny thing was, Magnus could sense the same things. The emotions and conversations of people on the streets, the smells of the restaurants, even the sound of the Mississippi River churning.

"What you feel isn't your power. It still resides in me."

She gripped her dragon cane, and the dragon's eyes blinked. When they opened again, Magnus stumbled back, alarmed by the sight.

He pointed at the cane. "The stones … they've changed."

The right changeling stone remained an iridescent pearl, but the left one was black like onyx. Magnus checked his cane. The stones in his had changed too—one eye black and one pearl.

What he'd feared had come to pass: she was his. The changeling stones were his proof.

Magnus wanted to throw his cane against the wall, furious he had failed to keep her out of Kalfu's clutches, but then the single pearl stone stopped him. She wasn't completely his. There was still hope.

Lexie examined the dragon's face on her cane, but showed no sign of emotion.

His Lexie reacted to everything in her charismatic way, her bright face radiating her special warmth, but this woman's frosty demeanor he did not recognize.

"It doesn't matter." Her voice had a smoky quality he'd never detected before.

"It most certainly does matter." He rushed up to her, desperate to make her understand. "Your cane senses what you have done. Your heart is no longer pure."

Her disconcerting eyes ripped into him with a bitchy voracity he'd never seen.

"I don't give a damn about anything else but my husband."

She yanked open the flimsy door to the atelier, letting in the early morning light.

"Now let's go get him."

She marched out the room, not with her usual stubborn stomping, but with a purposeful, confident sashay.

Where was the lively, endearing woman he'd known? Her voice, eyes, even her walk had changed. A horrid realization seized him—his Lexie had become an undeniably darker creature.

"I hope you know what you're doing, my dear. I pray we both do."

Chapter Twenty

Devereaux Plantation, nestled along the winding path of River Road, remained hidden behind dense brush. It sat across the two-lane street from the high levee charged with holding back the Mississippi River.

Emile's unmarked police cruiser drove through a narrow opening in the brush Lexie had not detected from the road.

They traveled about twenty feet through the gravel road until they reached a rusted iron gate secured with a padlock. Beyond the gate, a smattering of moonlight snuck through the cloudy sky, illuminating grounds covered with high grass and massive oak trees draped in Spanish moss.

"Quite a place."

Emile climbed into the car after popping the padlock on the gate with bolt cutters.

"It used to be." He tossed the bolt cutters in the back seat. "The Devereaux family founded the sugar cane plantation in the 1820s. It remained in their family until the last heir, Lucienne

Devereaux, died in 1958.'"

The car crunched along the shelled road, passing a thick hedge of brush on either side as it eased through the gate.

"Has it been empty since then?"

"No, the home and the fifty acres surrounding it were bought by an oil company." Emile steered the car through a clump of overhanging vines. "They renovated the house into corporate offices in the seventies and eighties, only to be set aside when the company relocated their headquarters to Texas."

She examined the weeds showing up in the headlight's beams. "Who owns it now?"

"A preservation society bought it. They plan to overhaul the entire property and open it as a museum when they get the money."

She lost all interest in the history of the home when the headlights revealed a clearing up ahead.

The road made a sharp right turn, and then red bricked steps appeared out of nowhere.

They rose to a veranda set with round columns covered with peeling white and clinging ivy vines. A door secured with several planks of wood stood behind the steps, the transom above was also crudely sealed with boards splashed with graffiti. The car beams revealed colonial windows on either side of the entrance. The plywood covering them had even more graffiti, but one set of words spray painted in black stood out to Lexie—*Enter and die.*

A beam of moonlight broke through the clouds and shone on the home, illuminating the entire structure. A Greek Revival masterpiece, it boasted six sweeping columns in front and a second-floor balcony wrapped in delicately scrolled wrought iron.

"It's well preserved."

"On the outside, but the inside will be another story, so watch your step." Emile parked the car a few yards from the house and switched off the lights.

Except for the occasional streaks of moonlight, the house remained shrouded in darkness.

"I'm beginning to see why she chose this place." Emile shut off the engine. "We're going in blind here."

"We're not blind." Lexie opened the black, pulsing center of her being. "I can pick up everything around us."

"I thought you lost your powers."

She reached for the door, hiding her eyes. "They came back."

Lexie climbed from the car, letting her eyes adjust to the moonlight. She detected a strange energy around her. It circled the lifeless house, creating a low hum as it went. A white light rose from the shingles on the roof and seeped from the exposed brick on the exterior walls. Orbs zipped across the porch and second-floor balcony, and roamed through the house, bobbing in the uncovered windows. Like the frenzied activity of an arcade game, the display mesmerized her. Then it died away, and ghostly faces replaced the dancing lights.

In windows, on the balcony, and dotted throughout the land, the people who once lived on the plantation were everywhere. In tattered clothes of drab material, most of the images were of slaves. They toiled in the gardens in front of the home, or worked on the veranda, sweeping or scrubbing the entrance. Occasionally, the owners popped up, mostly the women, adorned in anything from hooped skirt dresses, reminiscent of the Civil War, to fitted gowns reflecting the turn of the last century. They supervised the slaves, peered out from their balcony to the passing river, or looked to children playing beneath the massive oaks. Men flitted in and out, in long coats or with wide-brimmed hats, they never appeared to be interested in the running of the home.

Voices rolled her way. She picked up a few names, laughter,

cries of distress or sorrow, and hints of gossip, but none of it made any sense.

"What is it?" Emile asked, coming alongside her.

"There's so much life here."

He surveyed the dark home. "What are you talking about?"

How could he possibly understand? The power Kalfu had bestowed on her defied explanation. It was as if the world, past and present, opened up to her. She could look at a building and know its entire history in the blink of an eye. The same was true for people. She could study a person's face and see every joy, every sorrow.

The information came in a rush of pictures, not all of it was clear, but the emotions saturating every image gave her an understanding of the person—their triumphs and tragedies. Those tidbits were powerful enough to manipulate anyone to do her bidding. Whether through intimidation, bribery, or making promises she never planned to keep. She understood how Kalfu imposed his will on so many; she'd become like him.

The soul didn't have to be alive for her ability to work, either. She read the dancing ghosts around her as easily as the living, and their hopes and fears could be used to bind them to her will in the same way Kalila had done to those buried in her swamps.

"Lexie?" Emile stepped in front of her. "You okay?"

She scanned the land once more as the ghosts melted away. "Just getting a feel for the place."

"Is she around?"

Lexie tapped into the power Kalfu had given her. It wasn't much different than her old energy, but when she called on it, the results were instantaneous and the images sharp. The power amazed her at times, and the more she used it, the more she liked having it.

ALEXANDREA WEIS WITH LUCAS ASTOR

She sent her energy out, searching the area for Emily. In a rear corner of the home—the old kitchen—she perceived a presence. A lump of black, darker than any ghost on the plantation pulsated with anger and a need for revenge.

"She's here." She faced the house. "Back left corner."

Something else came to her—a human element. She could detect the flow of air in lungs, the slow, steady heartbeat, and extreme fatigue radiating from the man.

"Will's with her. He's alive."

A rush of emotions hit her—joy, excitement, sadness, fear— they bundled together in a ball and settled in her stomach, drawing it tight.

Later, when he's safe, I can fall apart.

Emile opened the back door of his black cruiser. "I have men parked on River Road outside the gate waiting for my signal."

He pulled out a black pump-action shotgun and a flashlight from the back seat. He checked the safety on the shotgun and then set it on top of the car.

She wanted to laugh at his faith in his weapons. They would never stop a spirit such as Emily.

"Give me twenty minutes, and then you and your men come in and get Will to safety. Leave her to me."

Emile yanked the revolver from his holster and clicked off the safety. "You've got ten, and I'm going with you. Then my men are coming in and getting your ass, and Will's, out of danger."

Her first reaction was to challenge him and insist he give her the twenty minutes she'd asked for, but then an odd sensation erupted in her chest.

An overwhelming calm trickled to her limbs, and with it an image of Emile handing money to his brother, Remi. With the money, he passed along information. Lexie heard whispers: dates and locations of police raids and pleas for Remi to avoid arrest.

"You told Remi about police raids, informed him about places to avoid, so he didn't get caught dealing drugs." She tilted her head, soaking in the information her power gleaned. "What would your fellow officers think about that?"

Emile backed away from her, his reaction hidden by darkness. "How ... where did you get this information?"

She detected his uncertainty and knew he would do as she asked.

"I will go alone, and you will give me my twenty minutes." Her voice came out flat and cold, sounding foreign.

It was the first indication of the changes taking place in her. Until that moment, she'd never felt different.

"What's happened to you?" Emile cringed, not hiding his distaste. "This is more than just getting Will back."

"I've woken up. I'm not going to be pushed around anymore." Lexie collected her dragon cane from the front seat of the car.

He handed her his revolver. "Renee is a suspect in three deaths and dangerous. I want you to take this."

Lexie balked at the gun and plucked the flashlight from the top of the car. "I won't need it."

He nudged the gun closer. "The only goddamned reason I'm agreeing to let you go in first is because you promised you could deliver Renee without incident."

"I don't need a gun to deliver Renee." She held up the cane. "I have this."

Emile sighed. "Please, Lexie. For my peace of mind."

She wanted to argue but thought it better to appease her friend, so she put her cane and flashlight on the car and took the revolver, securing it in the waistband of her jeans.

The moment she retrieved her cane, Lexie sensed something

different in the air. Tendrils of curiosity from Emily reached out to her. She sized up the spirit's power as it stayed in the shadows of the home. Then, like swatting at a bug, she blocked Emily, shutting down any chance she had to assess Lexie's skills. The incident swelled her confidence; she was stronger than Emily, but she also had to be smarter.

Emile put his hand on her shoulder. "You have twenty minutes to find Renee and coax her out. Then me and my guys are coming in to get her and you."

She concentrated on the prophetic graffiti on the window, expecting to feel a jumble of nerves in her belly, but all she detected was the cold force of her newfound power. It shined within her, resembling black oil in the sunlight.

Would Will notice the difference in her? The restlessness in her soul awakened as she pictured the look on Will's face when he learned what she'd done.

Emile waited by the car as she strode across the wet grass. The lights from River Road faded behind her, and the darkness of the plantation house loomed.

"You're a glutton for punishment, dear girl." Magnus walked next to her, frowning as he swung his cane.

"Where have you been?"

"Waiting until you were clear of the prying eyes of the other men on the road. I figured seeing me might be too much for them."

"I want you to do what you can to help Will when we get in there." The boggy ground squished beneath her tennis shoes as she trudged toward the house. "I need him out of the way before I deal with her."

"You'll need me at your side to help with Emily."

She stopped and confronted her ghost. "No, I don't. I'm a lot more powerful than you think."

"Yes, you simply ooze confidence just like that overbearing cad who loaded you up with his blackness."

His fiery gaze bounced around her face as if searching for proof of Kalfu's influence.

"I was there. I saw what happened to you, but no matter how strong you may be, I know Emily. So don't think you can toss me aside."

Lexie wanted to remind him of his place and wipe the ever-present cruel grin from his lips, but she let it go. First, she had to save Will, and then she could deal with Magnus.

"Fine. Stay. I can't fight you and her."

They climbed the sagging steps from the ground to the long porch. Above them, birds' nests of twigs and straw sat tucked into the eaves and exposed beams.

Lexie inspected the boarded-up door and a nearby window, looking for a way in. "We may have to go around back."

"Nonsense," Magnus argued. "Wait a moment."

He slipped into the wood sealing the front door.

She reached out to check on Will with her gift, hating to waste another minute apart. His breathing remained slow but steady. Why wasn't he upset or scared? Was something wrong with him?

Dammit, Magnus. Hurry up.

About to give up on him, she heard a thumping on the other side of the window to her right. She went to investigate. The wood covering the window moved.

The gap was tight but big enough for her to squeeze through.

She set her flashlight and cane aside. Just as she was about to climb into the window, Magnus reappeared.

"That should do it."

"How did you do that? I thought you couldn't move things."

He adjusted the lapel of his coat. "It would seem your gift has changed a few things for me. Objects are easier to take on, especially doors and windows."

After wedging her shoulder under a gap in the plywood, Lexie worked her way through the board around the window. When she finally crawled onto the dusty floor inside the house, she struggled to keep from making any noise.

Once on her feet, she wiped the dust from her hands and reached outside to retrieve her baton juju and flashlight.

Magnus's essence shimmered next to her. "They're in the back of the house."

The cane jerked in her hand, encouraging her deeper into the home.

Lexie tiptoed from the window, her eyes assimilating to the darkness. Shadows were everywhere, but none of them were spirits.

She tripped over something. "Fuck."

"My dear, your flashlight."

She switched on the light and a slim beam stretched ahead. The damaged wood floors had a thick layer of dust, and broken desks, metal chairs, and the shell of a few computers lay scattered everywhere.

Punched out sheetrock, hanging fluorescent light fixtures, and fallen vinyl ceiling tiles had erased all the old-world charm. Up ahead, piles of office furniture, and rising at the back of the long foyer, a pair of intact twin curved staircases climbed to the second floor. Then the beam of light dulled, and her flashlight blinked on and off.

Lexie knocked the flat of her hand against it, and when the light came back on the disarray of modern furniture pieces had disappeared.

The room dazzled with mahogany settees, benches, and love

seats draped in red velvet. Long Oriental rugs of cream and burgundy covered shiny, intact hardwood floors. Ornate wallpaper done in silver thread, with intricate images of life along the Mississippi River waterways, shimmered in the light. Crystal chandeliers, dripping with scintillating teardrops, descended from the ceiling, washing the entrance foyer with candlelight. The ticking of a gold-faced grandfather clock to the right distracted her, and then the laughter coming from the top of the stairs made her look up.

On the second-floor landing, two young women, with flowing dark hair and in the bloom of youth, peered over the railing and giggled. The vibrancy of the bright yellows and pinks in their antebellum dresses danced in the candlelight.

The soft strains of violins and french horns drifted by.

Lexie followed the direction of the music, and a party blossomed around her.

Men and women in formal attire held up champagne flutes, their cheers blocking out the chorus of a waltz. Humidity touched her skin, the heat from the crowd dotted sweat on her brow. Cigar smoke mixed with the body odor of others, the mildew in the home, and the mustiness of old clothes nauseated her. Faces were blurs of light, and the conversations she picked up only snippets with a word here or there. The room spun, her equilibrium faltered and then her flashlight snapped off.

"Lexie, what is it?"

The beam of light once again shone on the abandoned room strewn with discarded office furniture.

"I saw … I'm not sure."

Magnus raised his head to the second-floor landing. "We're being watched. The dead are all around us."

They moved beneath the grand staircase, her flashlight checking every nook and cranny.

She listened intently to every *creak* and *crack* the old house made. The vibes in the air tingled as if electrified by lightning and the temperature dropped. They were getting closer to the black presence she sensed by the car.

"She's up ahead," Magnus whispered.

"How do you—?"

Ripped from her side, Magnus got sucked into a dark corridor toward the rear of the home. He called her name as he vanished into the blackness.

The last vision she had of him was a twisted figure, feet and hands joined together as he folded over on himself, and his face contorted into a ghoulish, widemouthed scream.

Lexie made a move to go after him, but a hand held her shoulder, urging restraint.

"You ever play chess?" Kalfu materialized in front of her.

His jeans had a light coating of dust on them as if he had been traipsing through the house with her. He focused on the corridor where Magnus disappeared.

"You sometimes have to blind an opponent by doing one thing when you mean to do another." He nodded to a hallway to the right. "The path least expected."

"What about Magnus?"

"You don't need him; you have me." He tapped her flashlight, and it went out. "Stick to the walls and stay out of the light."

She could not see a thing in the darkness. "Why are you helping me?"

"I'm protecting my investment."

Then Kalfu disappeared.

Lexie set off in the direction of the hallway.

Cobwebs assaulted her, brushing against her skin and face.

She stopped and frantically wiped her body down while

picturing a hairy, creepy crawler with sharp fangs nesting in her hair.

Keep it together!

She resumed her path, still batting away anything tickling her arms.

When the hallway opened up, she hugged the walls as instructed. Up ahead, beneath an arched entrance, lights flickered.

She slipped inside the archway. Several white candles arranged in a circle sat on a bricked floor and burned beneath a peeling white plaster ceiling. Outside the candles, white bread, white eggs perched on mounds of white flour, snakeskins, and white rice.

A magic circle.

Made for protection to keep whoever inhabited the ring safe from the influence of spirits conjured during a spell, this particular circle had the placement of items backward, allowing the energy to pull something in, and not keep it out. Whatever spirit summoned, would be trapped in the ring.

Her baton juju trembled. The dragon head changed from its marbled wood color to a deep green, but the staff remained unchanged. The head moved, and the creature blinked. It raised its head and stared at the circle, flicking its red tongue.

She followed its gaze to the center of the circle. A symbol, drawn in white flour seemed familiar. After hours of staring at the decorated shot glasses in her shop, she'd come to know it well— the symbol of Damballah.

Damballah's energy. It's why she needs the cane.

Lexie checked the ceiling and walls in the room, hoping to find something she could use to her advantage. Capped pipes poked out from where a sink had once stood. On the opposite side, wiring and the coil from a gas line used for a stove remained.

She scanned for any sign of Emily, but the black mass she felt before had left the kitchen. The place was empty.

A cough came from behind an ajar pantry door on the other side of the circle.

Lexie stood motionless. Someone was in there, they were weak and hurt but didn't have any magical power.

Will.

Lexie hurried toward the magic circle to rescue her husband, but the cane shook violently almost sending her to the floor.

Powered by Damballah, the baton juju could not cross the circle. It would be sucked in and lost. What did she do? Toss the only weapon she had to use against Emily and save her husband?

"Such a dilemma," a woman's craggy voice said. "Your husband or your cane?"

A figure moved out from a doorway. Lexie waited, holding her breath.

Renee Batiste stepped into the room.

Her hair wild, frizzy flowed behind her, and her eyes glowed with a black fire. In a white dress with red turban and a red sash around her waist, she reminded Lexie of the first day they had met at her cooking school.

"I knew you would come." The voice was not Renee's. She sounded whiny and vile. "You have been so easy to manipulate, Mambo."

"Emily Mann, so we finally meet." Lexie tightened her grip on the cane, fighting to hold her rage in check. "What did you do with Magnus?"

"He's safe in his world with his wife." Her coarse chuckle floated in the air. "You never knew the little vixen. Silly girl. She thought she was a mystic and had the power to speak with spirits, but she was a fraud. She stole Magnus away, and I vowed to make her pay; to make them both pay. And I will, after I'm done with

BOUND

you."

Lexie stepped to the side, keeping a watchful eye on Renee as she drew closer to the circle. She needed to keep her talking. Maybe it would distract her.

"Why me? What did I do to you?"

Renee stumbled but caught herself. Lexie got the impression the woman struggled against the spirit holding her captive.

"You took Magnus from me." Renee wandered around the circle, avoiding touching the edges. "I was in heaven living with his ghost in Altmover Manor all those years. After I died, I made sure the proper spells were read so my soul could remain in the house forever. No one saw me or heard me. I just wanted to be near him. And then you came along. You took Magnus from me, burned down my home, and took my cane."

Lexie glimpsed the partially opened door behind Renee. Her body ached with longing—she was so close to Will but unable to see him. She wanted to lunge across the circle to rescue him, but she had to play it smart or they both would end up dead.

"You left the cane to me. In your will, you left it to the new owners of the mansion. That was Will and me."

"I never imagined a mambo would show up in Maine. I thought the cane was safe. The power it held protected so one day I could return and claim it. In a matter of days, you undid a lifetime of work."

A *thud* came from the other side of the pantry door.

"Looking for this?"

Renee yanked the door open and Will toppled onto the floor.

Bound and gagged with black rope, the suit he'd worn to work that morning had blood stains on the lapels of his jacket and sleeves.

The sight of the blood enraged her. In a fit of fury, she set

271

out across the room to get him, but the cane roused her from her desperation and kept her from falling into Emily's trap.

Will raised his head to her.

His lower lip was swollen and split, he had a black eye and an ugly black bruise on his cheek. His injuries almost sent her to her knees. Her hand on her chest, she gulped in air, and then her gaze shot to the bitch who had hurt him. She imagined ripping Renee's heart out with her bare hands, and when done, setting her ass on fire so she could delight in her torment.

"Do you want your man back?"

Emily's harsh voice rattled around in Lexie's head, fueling her hatred.

"I'll give him to you, just give me the cane." She slinked closer to the circle. "If you don't, you will watch me tear your husband limb from limb. Then I will make you lick up his blood before I shred you to pieces."

The cane in Lexie's hand shuddered, or was it her? She wasn't sure. All she saw was red rage. Her every muscle tensed, ready to charge at Renee and dig her nails into her eyeballs.

She sized up the distance between the circle and Will. The markings took up most of the floor, making it impossible to get to him. She had to buy time to come up with a plan to save her husband.

"Why do you want the cane?" She kept a cool disregard in her voice to hide her anger. "The baton juju can be of no use to a ghost."

"Ghost? Do I look like a ghost to you, girl?" She patted Renee's chest. I've got the power of Kalila, Jacques, and Titu. All I need to complete the *once was* spell is the power of Damballah in your cane."

"What about my power? Why did you take it?"

"I didn't take it. Maybe the voodoo spirits are angry and

stole your power to show you how pathetic you are." She eased away from Will, leaving him on the floor. "After all, you've done nothing with your gift. You're the most powerful priestess in the city, yet you help no one, change nothing."

Lexie's anger splintered apart. Emily's words hit home, tapping into her greatest fear—had she been a good mambo?

"But I have helped people. I've made a difference." She attempted to sound convincing, but her wavering voice gave her away.

"Have you tended to the sick or needy? Rescued the downtrodden, lifted up the helpless?" Renee stood weaving, her eyes as black as coal. "You have done none of the things the Queen did. You're not fit to carry her baton juju."

The cane answered Emily's taunt with a burst of power. It radiated an extreme heat into Lexie's hands along with a swell of confidence.

"If you were mambo, you would destroy lives and bury the city under a dark cloud."

"I'll bring a new order to the world. Something it will never have with you." Renee took an awkward step forward. "You only bring chaos to every life you touch."

Lexie arched her back, growing impervious to Emily's words.

"You'll bring nothing but evil! I will make the world a safe place. I'll protect life; you will annihilate it."

Emily laughed, and Renee's body stumbled into the circle, thrust forward by the expression of air.

Suddenly, the air changed. Humid and dense, it weighed on Lexie's skin.

Emily hissed as she stood inside the circle. "Once I have your cane, I can rule as mambo through this host."

"For how long?" Lexie noticed a trickle of sweat on Renee's cheek. "Renee can't be your prisoner forever. Her body is weakening as we speak."

"All I need is time to find a way back from the dead."

"There is no way back from death."

Renee's lips twitched upward in an awkward half smile. "Kalfu knows a way. He has promised I will come back and rule as mambo with Magnus by my side."

Lexie's fingers tingled.

Checkmate.

She suppressed her smile as her dark power swelled, encouraging her to make a move.

"What makes you think Kalfu will help you when he's already helping me?"

Renee's brow furrowed slightly, and the black fire in her eyes dulled. "I'm his devoted servant. He doesn't want you."

Lexie held up her cane. "Then why have the eyes changed. One white and one black—Damballah and Kalfu reside in me."

She edged closer to the circle, and the staff shook with such force she could barely hold it.

"I gave myself to Kalfu. I have more power than you can ever possess. I'm alive, unlike you, and I am Mambo of New Orleans. Is it any wonder the spirits prefer me?" She stopped at the edge of the circle, sweat beading her upper lip as she fought to hold the cane. "I have the cane and Magnus. You will never replace me."

Renee tossed her head back and shrieked at the top of her lungs. She flew out of the circle as if carried on wings and lunged at Lexie.

Lexie threw the baton juju against the wall to keep it as far away from Emily's circle as possible.

The cane fell, hitting the floor. Renee instantly let go of Lexie and went after it.

"The power of Damballah is mine!"

Seconds before Renee latched on to the cane, Lexie threw her arms around her waist. She used all her might to ram Renee's head into the metal pipes jutting from the wall.

The blow knocked Renee out, and she collapsed on the floor.

Lexie had to move fast. She only had seconds before Emily left Renee's body. She had to get her as far away from the cane as possible.

There was only one place to take her.

She grabbed the woman's wrists and dragged her toward the circle.

Right as she reached the edge, Renee's eyes flew open.

"No! Not without the cane!"

Chapter Twenty-One

The moment Lexie and Renee breached the edge of the circle, an explosion of white light engulfed them.

A deafening roar filled the blinding radiance, and Lexie let go of Renee and covered her ears.

The sound vibrated in her bones as she tumbled in the light. Hot air rushed past her cheeks and the tumult intensified into a painful blaring. The heat became unbearable. She could not breathe and gasped, hungry for air. She prayed for her torment to end.

Then, everything came to a sudden stop. Her momentum ceased, and she floated as if suspended in the intense white aura. The air cooled and lovingly curled around her arms and legs, holding her in place. Even the light faded and when she opened her eyes, stars, thousands of them, twinkled in the night sky.

Something hard came up under her back, and in the distance, she recognized the sound of rushing water—a river perhaps. She touched solid ground and rolled over to her side, thankful the ordeal was over. Or was it?

Beneath her, thick planks of black wood led to a crisscrossed railing. She stood and peered over the side. She was on a bridge, but there was no rock face, or deep caverns, just a wall of black clouds around her. At the bottom of the great expanse, a teeming river flowed.

There was something odd about the water. It had a milky white color and shadows swimming below the surface, leaping in and out of the rough white caps.

A loud moan made Lexie spin around.

On the ground a few feet away from the end of the bridge, a woman lay curled in a ball. Even with her back to Lexie and her head tucked to the side, she could tell it wasn't Renee Batiste. This woman had brown hair, not black, and wore a green ballgown with lace about the sleeves and a high collar.

Lexie carefully went to her, anxious to discover who the stranger was.

When she rolled over, Emily Mann's small brown eyes stared up at her.

"So you can't hide behind Renee anymore, eh, Emily?"

Emily gathered up her gown and sprang to her feet. "You stupid girl, I wanted to bring you here. Once I cast you across this bridge, you will be out of my way forever."

Lexie glanced back at the bridge, a nudge of fear creeping into her voice.

"This is the bridge to blackness?"

"None other."

Emily's haughty manner was reminiscent of what Lexie had seen Magnus do a thousand times before.

"This is Damballah's world—the creator of water and life. His shadow spirits—creatures who bind the soul and the body to create life—live in the white water of the River of Shadows." She came closer, and a familiar black fire lit her eyes. "Kalfu helped me capture a number of them from the river and release them into your world. It's how I created the rain, dead rats, and awakened the dead. As long as the shadow spirits remain free, chaos will continue."

Lexie backed into the railing, searching for a way out, but she was trapped.

"You need to return the spirits to the river and make things right again."

Emily ventured across the black beams of the bridge, closing in on Lexie. "Only Damballah can return the shadow spirits to the river, and once you're gone, and I possess his cane, he will not be able to act against me. I will rule all."

"And do you think people will put up with you as mambo? Bow to you? They will despise you and look for any way to destroy you."

"Who cares about the people?" She came right up to Lexie, baring her buck teeth. "They're insignificant."

"Not to me." Lexie raised her chin, not about to let the callous witch intimidate her. "A mambo must care about her people, nurture them, and guide them on their journey. You will never be what they want."

Emily shook her head. "What does Magnus see in you? You're not as pretty as the others, and he had quite a few. I should know. I was an expert at finding the right type for him. Pretty, timid, petite but with a shapely figure, and blonde hair. He adored blonde hair."

Lexie smirked, eager to unsettle her opponent. "Just like Francis."

Emily snarled and backed away. "That bitch deserved what she got."

"And what about Jacob? I know what you did to him. How

you buried him. Did it make you feel powerful, Emily, to take a man's eternity from him?"

A hard slap stung Lexie's left cheek, sending her back into the railing.

She held her face, stunned Emily had stooped to such a blow.

The shadows dancing in the white water below stoked a black fire in her soul. Hate in the form of a nocuous blob slicked with every hurt, betrayal, and injustice she'd endured ascended from the deepest recesses of the blackness Kalfu had given her.

"I gave Jacob what he deserved." Emily squared off in front of Lexie. "He took his life because he murdered Magnus. I sent his soul to Altmover Manor for Magnus, so he could spend eternity making Jacob's life hell."

Lexie curled her hands into fists. "You had no right to change his fate."

"Fate? Fate can be manipulated by magic. Why do you think I studied voodoo all those years? I wanted to learn how to bend fate to my will and bring everyone under my control." She fixed her hand around Lexie's throat. "I moved heaven and earth to make sure my spirit remained after I died."

Lexie never flinched, and never raised a finger to fight her. She'd discovered her weakness, and it was time to lower the gauntlet.

"No matter how hard you prayed, how much you tried to change the wind in your direction, you're still here, Emily. Still fighting to get Magnus's attention. All the magic in the world can't make a man fall in love with you, but you already knew that. You decided if you couldn't have him, no one else could."

Emily's grip tightened on her windpipe.

It was getting hard to breathe, but Lexie remained calm. Kalfu's power multiplied inside her, expanding and growing stronger.

"You don't know him. Magnus never loved anyone, but he will love me. We're the same. We feed off the same hate."

"He's not that man anymore." Lexie glared. "He's changed."

"He'll never change."

Emily raised her other hand to strike, but Lexie summoned her strength and the darkness inside her answered.

A lightheaded feeling accelerated into an empowering rush. The quickening followed every nerve pathway, generating tremors in all her muscles. Alive with power, she grabbed Emily's hand, which was slowly cutting off her air, and squeezed.

After a cry of pain and a stone-cold glare of disbelief, Lexie forced Emily's hand back against her wrist.

But Emily fought back and wiggled free. She pushed her weight into Lexie, attempting to send her over the railing and into the River of Shadows.

The harder Emily struggled, the more powerful Lexie became. Unable to budge her from the bridge, Emily landed blow after blow on Lexie's stomach, chest, and face.

But Lexie felt nothing. With a right uppercut, she flipped Emily around and pinned her against the railing.

Emily squirmed, desperately punching into the air. "What's happening? Where is my power?"

Lexie's hand slid around Emily's neck and lifted her in the air as if raising a soda can.

"Looks like you have a problem."

Her feet dangling above the black boards, Emily clawed at her hand and arm while Lexie carried her to the center.

Emily's eyes bulged, she kicked at Lexie as she saw her fate approaching.

"Kalfu, help me!"

Near the middle of the bridge, Lexie stopped when a bright

pillar of light formed in front of them.

It bent and swayed as it pulsed with energy.

Emily quit fighting and relaxed in Lexie's grip. "You have angered the great spirit Kalfu," she croaked. "I am his servant, and he will save me."

The light expanded, widening and taking up the entire bridge. A shadow formed in its center. It appeared human, walked with a casual gate, and as the umbra approached Lexie and Emily, it grew bigger. By the time the unusual shade reached the size of a man, it stepped out of the light.

In blue jeans and white T-shirt, Kalfu strolled up to them.

Emily's enthusiasm paled when she regarded his clothing. "What have you done? Where are your long coat and red vest?"

"Forgive, my dear." He bowed his head, and his clothes changed.

His jeans became fitted dark pants while a long black coat covered his T-shirt. A red vest appeared and a white ascot knotted up around his neck. His shiny high black boots and long dragon-headed cane added the final touches.

The spitting image of Magnus from the portrait in the living room of Altmover Manor, he even had the same tousled blond hair.

Emily's eyes soaked in the slick recreation, adoration oozing from her being.

"You've come to help me." She latched onto Lexie's wrist. "Banish her across the bridge, Kalfu. Finish it, and you will rule the universe."

The spirit's outfit changed back into his jeans and T-shirt. Kalfu lifted one side of his mouth with a cocky grin.

"I don't want to rule the universe."

Emily gaped at him. "What?"

"Who needs the universe when I have a mambo. Once Lexie

pledged herself to me, you were no longer needed."

Emily grunted as she fought hard against Lexie's grip.

The black fire in her eyes had died, and from what Lexie could detect, so had her power.

"You—you can't mean that. I've done everything you asked of me. You said you would make me—"

He rolled his eyes and passed his hand over her mouth. Emily's voice dried up.

Her pupils dilated as she clawed at her throat, hoping to resuscitate her voice. But despite the frenzied open and closing of her mouth, she never uttered a sound.

"She must be cast across the bridge by you." Kalfu pointed at Lexie. "To absorb the power of the others, she must be sent across the bridge to blackness by the one who challenges her."

Lexie eyed the dark swirl of clouds gathering on the other side of the bridge. What she felt there scared her. It was a cold, dank place where souls wandered without faces, memories, or even names. She might hate Emily, but did she hate her enough to send her to such a hell?

"Do not hesitate."

His deep, menacing tone surprised her.

"Enemies never hesitate to destroy each other. And she has been your enemy all along, Lexie Arden."

"Even the Queen showed leniency with Bloody Mary."

"Bloody Mary did not attempt to destroy Queen Marie, only you." The smoky quality of his voice returned. "If she'd dared challenge such a powerful mambo, Queen Marie would never have hesitated. Now do it."

The darkness in her center mushroomed into a nova of black light. It spread out to her fingers and toes, feeding her fury. The shards of doubt she held on to receded, sealing Emily's fate.

Lexie tightened her grasp and carried Emily the last few steps to the center of the bridge. Emily's helpless flailing quickly siphoned whatever energy she had left.

At the center of the bridge, a wall of wind blew not from the side but rose up from under the bridge. The temperature in the vertical line of air changed drastically from comfortable to unbearably cold. It marked a boundary Lexie sensed she dare not cross.

She fixed her gaze on Emily's small brown eyes. She wanted to make sure her face would be the last she ever saw.

"This is for Titu." She held Emily's limp figure higher, putting her nose right up to the wall of wind. "I cast you across this bridge to blackness, Emily Mann. For all your sins, may you never know peace."

She hurled Emily's soul to the other side. The black clouds closed around her like a pack of rabid dogs, obliterating any trace.

A single shrill cry came through the barrier of wind, but it created no guilt or remorse in Lexie.

The scream finally died, and then she knew—Emily Mann was gone.

She closed her eyes; thankful her ordeal was over.

Then a strange vibration tickled her feet.

The planks below her shuddered.

Lexie stepped back, not sure where to go or what to do. The shaking increased and a few boards ahead of her bucked in place. She wheeled about, convinced she had landed in the middle of an earthquake.

Kalfu, waiting by the end of the bridge, casually took in her attempt to stay upright.

She hurried to the railing, holding on for her life. "What's happening?"

He calmly rested his elbow against the railing, grinning up at her.

"Wait. You'll see."

A beam of brilliant light shot up from beneath the bridge and caught Lexie. It zoomed from her toes to the top of her head, holding her prisoner. She could not move or cry out. The light gathered in her chest, building until it burst streams of white energy into every atom of her being. She could sense every molecule, every cell, how the blood flowed through her veins and arteries, the air in her lungs, the strength of her muscles—each layer of her body flashed through her mind.

But then the light got sucked back down into the bridge and out of her body.

The quaking of the boards beneath her stopped.

The loss of such an intense rush sent her tumbling to the bridge. She lay on the boards unable to move, aching all over, but at the same time, experiencing intense jubilation.

Lexie pushed herself up, and when she raised her hands and examined her palms, the change astounded her. She reeked of energy. Much more than she once possessed, it also felt different. Where had it come from?

"It's what Emily Mann stole from your friends." Kalfu strolled up the bridge toward her. "The power of Kalila, Jacques, and Titu resides in you."

In her mind, she could feel them: the motherly essence of Titu, the charismatic leadership of Jacques, and Kalila's dark strength. Their power intertwined with hers, becoming part of her.

A ribbon of white light shot out from her center. Overjoyed to see her old energy return, Lexie hoped it meant her life would get back to normal. She'd missed the way she used to be, and her connection to Magnus.

The ribbon swayed, not acting in a way she remembered. Traces of black appeared alongside the white. The colors twisted together and soon resembled a barber's pole. The new black and white ribbon stretched out from her chest, and her senses came alive.

"Now you serve both of us. Part of you belongs to me, and part to him." Kalfu eyed the river below. "Damballah never shares his toys, so this could get interesting."

Before she could blink, he vanished.

Left alone on the bridge, Lexie went to the railing and gripped the wood. With the current of two opposing forces bursting in her, she lost herself in the breadth of power at her fingertips. She could move mountains and conquer any kingdom with the flick of her wrist. The sensation intoxicated, but also frightened her. With such power came extreme responsibility.

She'd barely taken up the heavy burden of being mambo; now, the game had changed. The acute senses she possessed would make her life more difficult, but it would make sure no one on the council ever challenged her again. Would it be worth it?

Then Lexie's stubborn nature raised its head.

You may be all-powerful, but how do you get your ass off this bridge?

Her gaze drifted to the valley below and the River of Shadows. She examined the sleek clouds on either side and then frowned, stumped for a way to get back.

About to head to the end of the bridge, something touched her ankles.

The gray Maine coon cat from her shop stood at her feet, rubbing against the leg of her jeans.

"Where did you come from?" She picked up the cat and held it. "Got any ideas on what to do next, Toto?"

The black and white ribbon in her center nudged her chest, creating an urgent tingle. It drew her to the side of the bridge.

Still holding on to the purring cat, she proceeded to the base of the bridge.

Right next to the end of the railing, she found a path inlaid with iridescent oyster shells leading down to the river.

The cat hopped from her arms and stood next to her, staring up with its bright green eyes.

The cat's behavior initiated a trickle of alarm. "What is it?"

A blast of warm air crashed into her, sending her into the railing. Lexie only registered the loud whoosh, before everything transformed into a streak of white light.

Rolling and twisting in the wind, her terror intensified. All the power she had at her disposal was suddenly useless.

How do I get back to Will?

Chapter Twenty-Two

Magnus peered out at his silent world through cell bars made of clouds. Dragged away from Lexie's side, Emily had banished him to his supernatural dimension and locked him in a jail reinforced with her oppressive power. He'd attempted to reach out to Lexie, but Emily bound his hands with black rope, blocking his ability. Trapped in the cramped, foggy prison, he felt like a man fighting against quicksand. Magnus paced his cell, staring at the bars while every horrible outcome for Lexie's fate rolled through his thoughts.

His frustration compelled him to the door. He had to do something to free himself. Magnus threw his shoulder into the bars, testing their strength, and then he rammed into them again and again, desperate to silence the endless hum of hopelessness in his soul.

Then, at the moment he was about to give up, a strange sensation came over him. The crushing desolation in him lifted. The thick, gray clouds making up the walls of his prison bunched and then parted, gaps appeared in the bars, then they thinned and faded.

He could not believe it. The sign meant Lexie had somehow bested Emily, or at least weakened her power, allowing him to escape.

He rushed to the door and pushed it open. Once outside the cell, he glanced back. The prison walls parted in places, and erratic shadows covered it in others. Soon the mist distorted the door, and it disappeared becoming part of the landscape. Magnus could no longer find the jail in the sea of clouds ebbing and flowing around him.

The black rope binding his wrists frayed and crumpled, falling into the mist covering the floor.

Exhilaration raced through him, but try as he might to connect with Lexie, he could not. She was still out of reach, and his jubilation soon dwindled to despair.

A flicker of gold, twinkling in the weak light of the mist, appeared to his right. The gold formed an outline of a woman's ball gown, and then the details of the dress and the woman wearing it revealed themselves.

With her long, glistening dress swooshing from side to side, Katie stepped forward.

She remained the way he had last seen her in the flesh: her honey-blonde hair piled atop her head with the twin doves nestled in her curls. Her hands still bound in black rope, and a gag in her mouth, she appealed to Magnus with her twinkling blue eyes.

He rushed toward her and freed her hands, letting the rope fall into the mist. He removed her gag and tossed it away.

"Magnus."

Her arms went around him, and he detected the slightest whiff of her favorite gardenia perfume.

For a moment he went back in time to a happier period in his life when he'd first married the Southern beauty.

"We must hurry from this place."

Her innocent, girlish voice brought him back from the past.

"Emily will come back for us."

She took his hand, urging him to flee, but he never budged.

"No, my dear. Something has happened. Emily's powers have faded. She can no longer hold us prisoner."

Her dainty features crinkled. "I don't understand. What has happened?"

Magnus extended his arm, hugging her waist. "Mrs. Bennett has saved us."

"Mrs. Bennett? You mean the woman I saw you with before. The one who spoke to me."

An uncomfortable twinge awakened in him. "Ah, yes." He cleared his throat, unsure of how to proceed. "She has been working with me to help defeat Emily Mann. I sense she has succeeded."

"That dastardly creature." Katie glowered at her husband. "I never cared for her when she worked for you. The woman used to always look at me with daggers in her eyes." Her sweet smile never wavered when a slight wrinkle marred her creamy brow. "How do you know Mrs. Bennett?"

Apprehension raced through him. How did he explain about Lexie and her world?

"She's an important person in New Orleans," Magnus said in an upbeat tone. "A leader of her people. I have been working with her as a spirit guide."

"You? Working with a woman?" Katie's wide-eyed astonishment made him grin. "I find it hard to believe."

"It wasn't my choice, my dear, but she and I have become quite a team."

"I wondered where you've been all this time." She cuddled

against Magnus. "I've searched and searched for you, my love. I'm glad we can put all the unhappiness behind us and finally be together."

Magnus wished he could avoid the scene to come, but he had no choice. He had to return to Lexie and send Katie on her way. He hesitated before confronting his wife. How could he explain all of this to his Katie?

Lifting her chin, he admired the softness of her smile. The childlike enthusiasm she exuded in life had stayed with her. It was one of the things he fell in love with, and something he still missed.

He took her hands, longing to feel their velvety smoothness. "I haven't been with Mrs. Bennett for long, but I am bound to her in a way that is hard to explain."

"Bound to the living? Why? You belong to me. You're my husband."

Her voice reeked with the impatience she often showed when she didn't get her way.

His annoyance sprang to life. "I was your husband, but death has parted us. What the universe deems for me now is something new. I have no control over it!" He checked his tone. "The same way I have no control over where you go. Wherever it is, you have to go on without me."

"Leave without you?" Katie stomped her foot, rekindling images of their fights together. "That's not fair. We're supposed to have our happily ever after."

"We had it, in the year we shared as man and wife." He touched a ringlet of her blonde hair, remembering how soft her curls once felt. "There are many things I did, things I said to you at the end that I very much regret. I wasn't a good husband, Katie, and I'm sorry."

Katie's dainty mouth expanded into a panicked grimace as she grabbed the lapel of his coat. "It feels like you're leaving me forever, Magnus. Tell me it isn't so."

He kissed her lips one last time and then took a step back. "I wish you every happiness, my dear."

A single tear rolled down her cheek. Magnus wanted to wipe it away but didn't.

He waited for one of her outbursts, the kind she had when things didn't go her way, but no furious shouts erupted. She brushed aside her tear, and when she raised her head, a trickle of sadness came alive in him—his Katie was ready to go.

"Do you think we will ever see each other again?" She retreated into a gathering of clouds.

He put on a smile, needing her last memory of him to be a good one. "If fate is willing, perhaps one day."

The vibrant gold in her gown dulled, and the rosy color of her cheeks faded. Her creamy skin dulled to gray, and the effervescent light in her eyes went out.

"I will pray for that day." Her image changed into a translucent apparition when she said, "I love you, Magnus."

And then the last remnants of Katherine Blackwell dissolved into dust.

He waited in his world saddened by their parting. She'd been the last link to his life, and when he let her go, he also let his past go with her. What he had ahead of him with Lexie mattered most.

The fog closed in around him as Katie's last words replayed in his mind. He was glad he had them to carry with him through eternity. What else could a ghost ask for?

Gray clouds grew thicker, solidified, and changed into walls. A cement floor rose beneath Lexie's feet, and a peeling plaster ceiling closed above her. Capped pipes pushed through the walls, and then the smeared flour symbol for Damballah presented beneath her white tennis shoes. The circle of candles flickered around her, and then she found herself back in the kitchen of Devereaux Plantation.

Lexie sucked in the humid air and frantically searched the room for Will. She took a step toward the pantry door and tripped over something.

Renee Batiste lay at her feet, breathing peacefully, with traces of flour in her black hair.

A groan from the corner of the kitchen made her raise her head.

Will sat perched against the pantry door. Still gagged, with his hands behind his back and his feet secured together with rope, he saw her and slouched.

"Will!" She hurried to hug him, but he groaned when she pressed on his shoulder.

She sat back on her knees and untied the knot securing the gag. "Are you hurt?"

He spat the gag out and coughed. Blood trickled down his chin.

Lexie died inside at the sight of his blood and wiped it away with her thumb. She touched his black eye, wanting to take away his suffering, and never let him go again for fear of losing him for good.

She gently curled her arms around his neck, the stink of sweat and blood on his skin filling her nostrils.

"I was so scared I'd lost you."

With one arm, he pulled her close. "You'll never lose me, baby."

Before she could protest, he pushed her back. "What the hell happened to you?"

She went around to his back and worked the rope free from his hands. "No time for that. We have to get you out of here. Emile and his men will be here any second to arrest Renee."

"One minute you were dragging Renee into the circle, and the next you were gone, disappeared completely. And then, seconds later, you came back. Am I crazy or did I really see that?"

She went to his feet and got the last of the rope off him. "You're not crazy, but I'll explain everything, later." Lexie cupped his cheek. "Did she hurt you?"

He took her hand and kissed it. "No. I got banged up when they tossed me in the back of a car and brought me here."

"Did you see anyone else working with Renee?"

Will shook his head. "Someone put a bag over my head in the apartment when I got jumped from behind. I never saw anyone until I fell out of that door and saw you with her. But I'm sure there were more of them. There had to be. She couldn't have taken me out on her own." He let out a long breath. "Lexie, please tell me before I go mad, where did you go when you disappeared?"

Bouncing beams from a few flashlights intruded on their moment.

"Freeze, police!"

She raised her hand, blocking the glaring light as a big man with an enthusiastic smile came rushing up to her.

"Thank God." Emile dropped to his knee. "I thought I'd come storming in here to find a massacre. You guys okay?"

Behind him, three plain-clothed officers, their guns drawn and badges shimmering on their hips, cautiously approached Renee.

Will squeezed Lexie's hand. "She stopped Renee."

Emile lifted Will's chin. "Good thing for you I've got an ambulance on the way."

Will held up his hand, signaling he needed some assistance to stand. "I'm not hurt. Just bruised a bit."

Emile and Lexie helped get him to his feet. She put her arm around his waist, and was thankful when he leaned on her for support.

She silently vowed to treasure every minute they had together. But when the click of handcuffs traveled through the kitchen, Lexie turned to a groggy Renee and forgot about her husband.

She took a step forward to go to her aid.

Emile put up his hand, holding her back. "Let my men handle it."

Renee writhed on the floor as one of the men patted her down for weapons.

"What ... what is it?" she called out. "Where am I?"

Lexie shirked off Emile's hand. "It's not her fault. Emily's spirit forced her to do those things."

Emile never let her go. "She can tell her story to the DA, but there's so much evidence against her ... It doesn't look good."

"You know what they'll do to her." Lexie confronted him. "She doesn't deserve that!"

Will put his arm around her, and she caved into him. "Let Emile and his men do their jobs."

"Mambo," Renee garbled when she caught sight of Lexie. "Mambo, help me."

Lexie stood by as the men dragged Renee from the kitchen. Her pleas for help carried through the house, shaking Lexie to her core.

"Steady." Magnus came to life in front of her. "Get your husband home, and then we'll tackle Renee."

Lexie glanced at Will as he spoke with Emile, and then noticed something odd—neither man registered Magnus's presence.

She lowered her voice so the others in the room couldn't hear. "They can't see you."

"It's how it should be. Seeing me only confuses matters." Magnus touched his chest. "The ribbon between us has returned. But it's a different color and stronger. What happened?"

"That doesn't matter now. How did she get to you? I saw you pulled away, and then you disappeared."

"She overpowered me and imprisoned me in my world. I tried to reach out to you, but she blocked me." He narrowed his eyes. "When I'd about given up, her power disintegrated, and I could return to you. Does that mean she's gone?"

Lexie gave him a sad smile. "I banished her across the bridge to blackness. She'll never bother either one of us again."

His shoulders sagged as if relieved of a heavy burden. "Of all the women I hurt, I never considered her to be one of them."

"Your past is creating a strange future for both of us, Magnus."

"Truer words were never spoken, my dear." He glimpsed the men not far from her side. "Your husband is looking for you. We'll talk again." He dipped his head and faded away.

Will stepped up to her side. "What is it? Do you sense something else?"

Her arms went around him, holding him tight. "No. Everything is good."

"Let's get you two out of here." Emile put his hand on Will's sore shoulder. "You're gonna need a doctor."

Will winced. "I need a shower and a drink. No doctors."

Lexie helped a limping Will out of the kitchen.

She made him stop at the edge of the magic circle so she could collect her cane. With the flour smeared all over the floor by the officers, and the candles blown out by the activity, she sensed the energy in the circle had died.

Grateful for the return of her baton juju, she gripped the dragon handle. The power of Damballah crashed through her, but the zing she always got had changed. It wasn't a warm flush as in the past. There was something else mixed with it—an icy chill she'd never experienced.

"Your cane?" Will squinted in the low light. "The eyes have changed."

She tightened her grip on him. "It's nothing."

Not until the moment Will had seen her cane, did she question if he would see the same change in her. Would her darkness show? And if he did find out, would he still love her? The ocean of consequences closing in around her would eventually drag her under if she didn't find a way to free herself. She didn't have a clue where to begin or even if there was a lifeline strong enough to save her tainted soul.

After a brief interrogation by the police, Emile took Lexie and Will back to their apartment.

"I'll be in touch when we find out more," he told them after helping get Will up the stairs. "I want you two to lay low for a few days. I'll keep a squad car out front just in case."

"In case of what?" Will implored, easing onto the sofa.

"Renee had accomplices, probably thugs who were employed by Bloody Mary. They may come back for revenge."

"Damn it, it wasn't her." Lexie scrambled for a way to make him understand. "She would never have lifted a finger against me. When are you going to get it?"

"Hey." Will's hand reached for her. "Give the guy a break,

huh?"

Emile went to the front door. "I get it, but right now I'm more worried about you two. You're witnesses. I need to protect you for the case we have to mount against her."

She bit her tongue.

The world still had laws and protocols to follow. No amount of magic would change the practical nature of man.

After seeing Emile out, and securing her front door, Lexie directed her attention to her husband with his feet propped up on the sofa

"We need to get you cleaned up."

She helped him up and with her arm around him, guided him to the bathroom.

Lexie eased him against the sink and gently got him out of his suit. The sight of more bruises over his ribs sent a sharp jab through her.

"These aren't just from the car, are they?"

He lifted his arm and checked the bruises. "Well, they sure weren't gentle with me."

They were alive and safe, but things could have turned out differently for both of them. Deflated by the weariness of fretting over her powers, Titu, and now crushed by what her husband had endured, Lexie hugged her arms around Will, held on tight and cried into his chest.

He stood against the sink, holding on and rocking her gently in his arms. Will would whisper to her, assuring her he was fine, but she didn't believe him. When she pulled away and wiped her eyes, the bruises were there as an ugly reminder.

"I wish I would have never come to this city." She sniffled and shook her head. "If I'd stayed in Boston, we would be—"

Will tugged her to him. "We'd be right here, together. Whether in New Orleans or Boston, you'd still be mambo, and

I'd still be yours. Geography doesn't matter when magic's involved."

She kissed him, thanking the heavens for sending her such a wonderful man.

Will returned her kiss, his hands pulling at the hem of her shirt and pushing down her jeans.

"What are you doing? You're hurt."

He wrestled her T-shirt over her head. "I want to feel you next to me. All I could focus on from the moment they took me was how much I wanted to be with you. Every second, all I thought about was you."

Lexie kissed him again, convinced she would never love anyone as much as her Will.

She stepped out of her clothes and ran a shower for the two of them. In the tight stall, she nestled next to him. The water beat down on her body chasing away the last of the cold in her bones.

It took a little maneuvering, but she washed away the grime and blood dried to his skin. Lexie counted the bruises all over his back, side, and down his right leg. In time they would heal, but she made sure never to forget the image of them, ever.

Settled on the sofa in their robes, she kept touching his black left eye and battered lower lip, wishing she could use her power to make it go away.

"I'll be fine, baby. They're just bruises. Nothing's broken."

They both shared half a bottle of scotch before crawling into bed overcome by their exhaustion.

Safe in his arms, Lexie finally relaxed, knowing her ordeal was over.

"Will you ever tell me what happened?" He nuzzled her neck. "One minute you were dragging Renee across the floor, the next you were gone."

In a calm voice, she related her story. About the journey to the bridge to blackness, her confrontation with Emily, and her banishment to the other side. She skipped the parts about Kalfu. He had been through enough for one evening. Best to save her pledge to Kalfu for another day. When he was better, or when she could find the courage.

"Wow. You had a busy day," he mumbled after her story had drawn to a close.

Lexie nodded against his chest. "Yep."

"What about Magnus? Did you send him off with Emily?"

"No, he's staying with me."

"Why?" The curt reply teemed with anger.

She sat up and stared at him. "Why? Because he's my spirit guide. We're bound to each other. I can't be a good mambo without him."

Will let out a long breath and rested his good arm behind his head. "Maybe you should give it a try? It was better before when I didn't see him. After meeting him the other day … I can't say I'm happy about your relationship."

Lexie couldn't believe they were having this conversation. "He's a ghost. How can you be jealous of a ghost?"

"He's the ghost of a man. A really bad man from all you've told me." His lips curved into a grimace. "I'm not sure you should spend so much time with him."

She sunk down next to him, her mind reeling. It wasn't like she had a choice in the matter.

"What if you don't see him anymore? What if I can guarantee you won't run into him again?"

Will remained quiet for a time. She wished she knew what he was thinking, but no matter her ability, his thoughts eluded her.

"I guess I'd feel better if I didn't see him, but not much."

With a relieved sigh, she hugged his chest. "Then you won't see him again, I promise. I never chose Magnus; we're stuck together, and I couldn't send him away if I tried."

"I'm not comfortable sharing you with another man … or ghost. But to see him every day would make things impossible." His arms closed tighter around her. "It's all over, right? Things will go back to normal now, won't they? No more murders, vengeful spirits, or over the top voodoo spells?"

She yearned to tell him it was far from over. A dichotomy of good and evil lived within her, and one day, they would fight for control of her soul. But he didn't need to hear it, not yet.

"Yes, Will." Her voice shook as she spoke. "It's all over."

The thick stubble on his chin tickled her cheek. "When I was in that pantry, I kept thinking of all the things I wanted us to have. Things I'd never get to see."

"We have our whole lives ahead of us."

He shifted on his side to look at her. "Then let's start living. I want a baby with you. I want a house, a family, and something real to hold onto."

"I want those things, too."

"Good, because I vowed if I ever got out of that damned pantry I was buying you that condo in the Warehouse District and getting you pregnant right away."

She sat up, bowled over by his admission. "We've been trying."

"But not in earnest." He kissed her, a long deep kiss. "I want a new life together. Tell me you want the same thing, baby."

"Of course." Her voice didn't match the exuberance of her words. "I want you, the baby, and the fancy condo."

Her arms slipped around him, but a conflict raged within her. How could she raise an innocent child? Would the child be like her—half light, half dark? Or would it belong to Kalfu?

Drowning in anguish over the woman she'd become, she held on to him, desperate to be consumed with something other than her thoughts.

Will caressed her hips as they eased the nightshirt up her torso. With a tug, he worked the shirt over her head and threw it to the floor. His lips skimmed down her neck to her right breast, and she savored the excited tingle rising from her belly. He teased her nipple, while his fingers slipped between her legs.

She rocked against his hand as he eased two fingers inside her.

He whispered, "I love you," in her ear as he spread her legs apart.

She closed her eyes as he sank into her. Tendrils of pleasure ran up her spine as he moved in and out. For a brief moment, she forgot all about Kalfu and Emily Mann's shrieks as she cast her across the bridge to blackness.

The horrid images faded as her body tensed. With her orgasm building in her muscles, Lexie let go and handed herself over to Will.

When her release overtook her, she moaned into his chest, her mind blissfully blank.

She stayed nestled in his arms, listening to his breathing as he drifted off to sleep. But the window of relaxation their lovemaking had afforded quickly closed. Images of the black and white ribbon plagued her, resurrecting her restlessness. What lay ahead for them?

Afraid to wake her husband, especially after his hellish experience, Lexie climbed from the bed. She checked a snoring Will and then plucked her nightshirt from the floor.

After sneaking out the bedroom, Lexie left the door ajar to keep an eye on him as he slept. She didn't want him out of her sight again.

In the living room, eerie moonlight from the courtyard shone through her balcony windows. On her way to the kitchen, she tripped over something.

She caught a glimpse of her ruined altar, but the melted white candles and crushed herbs didn't reflect her new existence. In the morning, she would build a new one and make changes to balance her newly acquired abilities.

On the kitchen counter, Lexie found the half-full bottle of scotch. Maybe a drink would settle her nerves. She sucked back a swig and took the bottle to the sofa, hoping to catch a late-night movie.

At the coffee table, she felt around for the remote under the scattered plans and diagrams left after Will's abduction.

"Check under the cushion."

The voice came from the column of light forming in front of her. It swayed hypnotically until a woman materialized in its depths. In a silver muumuu, and matching turban, she stepped from the fading light and held out her open arms to Lexie.

"Titu!" Her heart soared. It was a moment she'd hoped for since learning of her friend's demise.

"I wanted to see you one more time, child."

"One more time?" Lexie's joy evaporated. "What do you mean?"

"I've come to say good-bye. I can't stay, no matter how much I would like to." Titu's loving smile slipped a little. "You must come to terms with the two masters you serve. They will each try to rule you but remain strong. Strength is your greatest gift. Remember that."

Lexie collapsed against the sofa. "What do I do, Titu? I thought I was helping to get rid of Emily Mann's ghost, to set things right, but I'm afraid I've made everything worse."

Titu drifted closer, the bright light behind her filling the room. "You will have to figure out these problems without me. You have a great deal to do, and much more to learn. Your sacrifices will be great, and your challenges overwhelming at times, but know I will always be proud of you. You've become the mambo I always knew you'd be."

"How am I to accomplish anything without you to advise me?"

The light around her pulled back, and the room darkened around Lexie.

"You have others who can help you; those experienced with serving two masters. And you also have a ghost to keep you on the right path."

The light dimmed, growing fainter. Titu's image faded with it.

"Thank you, Titu, for believing in me."

The spirit mouthed words Lexie could not make out, and then she disappeared for good.

Her grief took her breath away, but she held back her tears. She'd cried enough for one lifetime.

Chapter Twenty-Three

Two weeks later, the sun shone through the balcony windows on the boxes piled high along the walls of her apartment. She'd been packing for two days, ever since Will surprised her with keys to their new condo in the Warehouse District.

"Where you want this one?" Nina asked as she held a box marked *dishes*.

Lexie nodded to the smaller stack of boxes she had reserved for breakables. "With the rest. I want to make sure Will and I move the delicate stuff and leave the rest for the movers."

"Still can't believe you're doing this. I thought you loved living above the shop."

Lexie put on a brave smile for Nina, hoping to hide her inner turmoil. All that mattered was making Will happy. It was the only way she knew to silence the guilt haunting her.

"Will and I want to start a family. Living above the shop with a baby isn't the best idea. Plus, the new building has pretty tight security. Will wants better protection for us."

"You're sure about letting me take over the lease here?" Nina took the box to the other side of the living room.

"Why wouldn't I be?" Lexie finished taping the box containing her voodoo books. "I've got a newly renovated three-bedroom condo waiting for me. And a view of the river to die for."

Nina stacked the box next to the others while giving Lexie a thorough going over. "I never thought you gave a damn about river views and fancy condos. You seemed happy here until … all that mess."

Lexie's forced smile slipped a little. "Will wants it."

Nina's intrusive gaze pecked at Lexie's confidence. "Are you okay? Lately, you've been out of sorts. Preoccupied."

"I'm worried about Renee. I still haven't heard from her attorney."

Nina retrieved another empty box. "The paper reports they're going after her for first-degree murder."

Lexie's overburdened spirit sank deeper into despair.

"Yep. They didn't buy her story. She has no memory of the murders, says she blacked out. The court is appointing a psychiatrist to see if she's competent to stand trial."

"A lot of people in the voodoo community want her head on a spit."

"None of them will make a move as long as I protect her." Lexie threw the spool of packing tape on the floor.

"Yes, since the bad juju has left the city, the rains have stopped, and the ghosts have gone back into hiding, no one questions your authority anymore." Nina took the empty box to the sofa. She put it down and picked up the dragon cane Lexie had left there. "What happened to your cane. The eyes have changed."

Lexie sat back on her heels, surprised the young woman had noticed.

"I dropped it and damaged one of the eyes."

Nina put the cane down and peered around the room. "What do you want me to tackle next?"

She was about to give her shopkeeper a suggestion when something on the wall distracted her.

A shadow moved out from behind Nina. Lexie followed the stealth outline of a man as it disappeared into her kitchen.

"Packing?" Nina snapped her fingers in front of Lexie's face. "What do you want me to pack next?"

Disturbed by the shadow, Lexie kept one eye on the wall as she faced Nina. "Can you see to the stuff in the pantry?"

"What's up with you? You keep doing that—tuning out." Nina pointed at her face. "And you look like you haven't slept in weeks."

Lexie gave Nina her full attention, wanting to allay her suspicions. "Got a lot on my mind is all."

She needed to find an excuse to get out of the confining apartment. She went to the pile of empty boxes and picked up a few of them.

"I'll take a few of these to the atelier and see what I can pack up there."

"Aren't you going to keep using it for client readings?"

Lexie hurried to the door. "Yes, but there are some things I want to bring with me."

Before Nina could say another word, she made it to the back door and dashed down the stairs to the courtyard.

Once her feet hit the pavement, she dropped the boxes and opened her inner sense. She could see Nina in her apartment, going through her pantry, picked up the conversations of tourists on the street, the chatter in neighboring shops, but no shadow presence came to her.

Lexie had a seat on the bottom step. She'd never seen such an apparition in her apartment. It meant the creatures taken from the River of Shadows were still in the city. Thankfully, no one else seemed to notice them—not even Magnus. All was not back to normal.

She pushed off the step, already weary with the work ahead of her, and gathered up the boxes in her arms. While strolling toward the atelier, she went over everything she'd read on the shadow spirits, which wasn't much. The river and its ghostly residents were considered more folklore than fact by many texts about voodoo.

A gray blur ran in front of her, scaring her to death.

"Dammit!"

The gray cat sat at her feet.

"What are you doing, you …?" She remembered the same cat on the bridge, rubbing against her leg.

The fur along the creatures back undulated. Its eyes burned bright, changing from green to amber.

Lexie dropped the boxes in her hands, terrified.

The cat never moved as it tilted its head watching her.

Light slithered in from the corners of the patio, clinging to the ground as it rolled up to the cat. Within seconds the cat, covered in a cone of brilliance, disappeared. The rays climbed higher, to the height of a man. It fanned out and formed a shape.

The light dimmed, sliding down from the top, and a human head emerged.

Lexie stood a few feet away, questioning if Kalfu had decided to appear, but the black part of her center did not respond to the creature taking shape before her eyes. But the other part of her, the white, came alive with excited tingles.

Steaks of light scurried to the outer edges of the courtyard and seeped back into the cement's crevices. A towering man in a white suit stood in place of the cat.

His ebony skin glimmered in the rays of sunshine filtering down from the sky. His round face and bald head seemed familiar.

"Ah, my dear Mambo."

His throaty voice had a singsong quality not native to the city.

Lexie rifled through her memories convinced they had met. "I know you, don't I?"

He smiled, his pearly white teeth gleaming. "I am Damballah. I'm inside you; I'm inside of all things."

Lexie took a step back, frightened and relieved at the same time. Then she remembered the cat. "It was you. The whole time. At Altmover Manor, in my shop, on the bridge? You were there."

He nodded, acknowledging his deceptions. "I've always been with you. You've felt my presence, my light."

She touched the center of her chest. "Then you know about …?"

"Kalfu never plays fair." He perused the courtyard. "I knew when he set his sights on you by luring Emily Mann back from the dead, he would try to erase my power from your soul. So, I found a place to keep it safe—your Mr. Blackwell."

She stared at him in amazement. "You put my power in Magnus."

"He's an intriguing fellow and an oddity among ghosts. I hope you appreciate what I've done bringing the two of you together."

She stood, unable to speak, overwhelmed by his disclosure.

He moved closer and pointed his finger at her chest.

She gasped as her center opened without tapping into it. It surged with heat, and then the ribbon of light snaked out. Small and wispy, it gravitated toward his finger.

Shocked at laying her eyes on something she'd only seen in her mind, she went rigid when the intertwined black and white tendrils became more pronounced. The reminder of what she had done dampened her enthusiasm.

"You must be careful, Lexie Arden." He lowered his finger and the ribbon hastily retreated. "You have two masters to please, but only one of us will win you in the end."

A flurry of wind from all four corners of the courtyard blasted toward him. White in color, it wrapped around Damballah like a tornado, obliterating any hint of his dark skin or white suit. A whirling cone rose above the pond and then in a single poof, dissipated into the air.

Lexie scanned the blue skies above, but there was nothing left of the smoke or Damballah.

Something rubbed against her leg.

The gray Maine coon cat was back, sitting in the same spot as before, glaring up at her with its disarming green eyes.

It trotted off to the back of the courtyard and disappeared into the shadows.

She bounded through the atelier door, breathing hard. The converted garden shed had become the one place she felt comfortable in the past few weeks. More and more she retreated to the workshop to escape rude customers or Will's constant plans for the new condo and hoped-for family. Now, she felt it might be the only place left where she wouldn't run into spirits.

"It's getting harder to hide from the powers that be, dear girl."

Magnus arrived in a corner as she plunked down on the

bench at her worktable.

"Did you see what happened in the courtyard?"

He flung his coat out behind him and had a seat across from her. "I had my run-in with the man in the cat a while ago."

The constant burn of anger in her gut exploded. "And you never bothered to tell me?"

Magnus stiffened. "You had a choice to make." He held up his cane, showing her the black and pearl eyes of the dragon. "And you made it, but it's not what you expected, is it?"

She rubbed her hand against her chest where the intertwined wisps of black and white had surfaced. "I've got it under control."

"Not from where I'm sitting." Magnus put his cane to the side. "You can't keep what you're hiding a secret forever. People will find out."

She sat back, agonizing over how others would react. "They'll fear me when they do."

Magnus drummed his fingers on the table. "No, they will hate you because they fear you. I should know. I used to enjoy having people fear me, or the power I wielded."

"But if I share what I am with anyone, they'll use it against me." She rubbed her forehead, her insides raw. "I will turn into the kind of mambo Bloody Mary was. I don't want to intimidate people; I want to lead them."

His fingers stopped and he showed her a tentative smile.

"I think you will find it's hard to do one without using the other."

"Lexie!" Nina called from the courtyard.

She left Magnus in the workshop and rushed outside.

Nina waited on the balcony, holding up her cell phone.

"It's Emile. He says he needs to speak with you."

Lexie's senses came alive, and energy reached out, probing for why the detective would be calling. The raised voices of men, and the lightest essence of death came to her. She hurried to the stairs.

She reached the balcony and grabbed the phone out of Nina's hand.

"Emile, what is it?"

"Lexie, we have a big problem." His dejected voice sent her stomach into a tailspin. "It's Renee. She's dead."

"Are you sure you want to do this?"

Emile stood before the entrance to the viewing room in the Orleans Parish Coroner's Office. The steel doors had *Admittance with ID Only* in red across the front and a call button to the right.

He removed the badge from his belt and held it up to a camera fastened above the door.

Death mixed with a medicinal aroma drifted past her nose. A brief queasiness blew through her but quelled when an unexpected tingle stirred. The darkness became aroused by the atmosphere of death.

"I have to echo Emile's sentiments," Magnus muttered next to her.

She patted the visitor ID. "You said I needed to see her."

"I meant pictures." Emile pressed the buzzer. "I never intended for you to come down here and identify her."

Lexie waited as the doors opened.

"Are you all right?" Magnus stuck close to her side. "You seem very at ease for one about to see a dead body."

She glared at him and sucked in a breath, captivated by the nauseating smell.

"Renee had no family, and you admitted there's no one to

identify her body," she said to Emile. "The least I can do is make sure it's her."

"After she kidnapped your husband and tried to kill you?" He shook his head as he turned the door handle. "If you're going to be sick, let me know."

She kept her chin up. "I'll be fine."

Magnus angled closer to her. "Liar."

Emile put his hand behind her back, guiding her toward the door.

"Your husband would have my hide if he knew I was letting you do this." He held the door open for her. "And don't faint on me. I might not catch you in time."

The intolerable cold in the small, square, windowless room tickled her skin, but she found it comforting. Beige tile covered the walls and in the center, a metal table with a white sheet covering someone underneath. The outline of a woman's body, her breasts, and wide hips, rattled her.

She approached the table, and the darkness in her vibrated with excitement. She should have been terrified, having only seen the dead bodies of her father and grandmother—both times had been dreadful experiences—but all she felt was calm.

Emile put his hand on her shoulder. "I'm going to pull the top of the sheet back to reveal her face when you're ready."

Lexie's mouth went dry. "Okay. I'm ready."

Ever so slowly, the white sheet slid back. First, the tendrils of her black hair surfaced. It was still damp as it sat bundled on top of her head. The sheet lowered a little more, and the ashen color of her forehead peeked out. Her closed eyes and long lashes came next, and Lexie moved closer waiting as the woman's high cheekbones, nose, and lips finally came into view. The white of her lips bothered Lexie. She remembered Renee always having the prettiest red lips.

"I disliked the woman." Magnus went around to the head of the table. "But I never wished this for her."

Lexie studied Renee's face, a swell of guilt came over her. "You said she asked for me before she died."

"She wouldn't tell me." Emile left the sheet resting right below Renee's chin. "She insisted on speaking to you. Said it was a matter of life and death."

And now she's dead.

A knot formed in her belly, at odds with the pervasive apathy of her darkness.

She gazed down the length of Renee's body, searching for some clue.

Magnus dipped his head in front of her. "What are you looking for?"

Something under Renee's chin caught her eye. A cut, nothing deep, but the odd angle of it gave Lexie pause. There was more going on here than Emile was willing to admit.

"You never said how she died. Only she was found dead alone in her cell."

"It's an ongoing investigation."

Emile's tight-lipped expression aroused Lexie's curiosity.

"I can't share the details with you because—"

Lexie grabbed the sheet and yanked it back, letting it slide down her throat, over her chest, until it came to rest on her hips.

"Damn it, Lexie!" Emile scrambled toward the table and snapped up the sheet.

Her hand went to her mouth and she stumbled backward from the table.

"My word," Magnus mumbled.

From her neck down, her blue skin had an array of carved geometric shapes, wavy lines, and almost cuneiform symbols. Her white breastbone gaped under a few of the cuts, while her breast looked as if they had been peeled away to make some of the complicated designs. Every inch of her shoulders, chest, and abdomen had been sliced, leaving little of her skin intact and exposing all the red muscle underneath. Despite the refrigerated condition of her body, the aroma of rot coming from the black edges of some of the symbols rose to Lexie's nose.

Despite the encouragement from her dark power, she wretched, fighting not to vomit.

Emile put his arm around her. "Let's get you out of here."

His touch agitated her black side, and Lexie arched her back, shirking off his arm. She had to remain strong, and could not be seen running from the morgue.

"No. I have to do this. I need to find out what these symbols mean."

"We already know." Emile's gaze swept over the body. "It's called a devouring spell. The same one used on Gus Favaro. But Mr. Favaro, unlike Renee, was found in the swamps."

Magnus crept closer to the corpse, getting a better view. "These symbols are very intricate. I suspect this isn't the first time the murderer did this."

Lexie kept her focus on the carvings and away from Renee's face. "Are you sure this is the same devouring spell?"

"Our anthropologist at Tulane, Dr. Rebecca Soter, confirmed it. I also reached out to Harold Forneaux for a second opinion."

The mention of his name stirred her irritation. "Why him?"

"Harold is a well-known practitioner of black magic."

"And the same man who wanted you to step down," Magnus whispered in her ear.

"What is this devouring spell?" She went around the table, studying the carvings. "I never heard of it."

"It's a sort of revenge spell." Emile shoved his hands into his trouser pockets. "The symbols are meant to mark the person as a traitor and slowly kill them with magic."

"But she didn't die from magic."

"No, she didn't." Emile went to Renee's head, pushing Magnus aside, and pointed to her throat. "The coroner thinks she died of asphyxiation but found no strangulation marks on her neck. He won't know for sure until he conducts a full autopsy."

"Do you know anyone other than Harold who can perform such a spell?"

"Only a few." Emile stood back from the table. "But they all have alibis. And none of them were anywhere near the prison when she died."

"Did any of the other prisoners see anything?"

"Saw nothing and heard nothing. The last check before the guards found her was three A.M. The body was discovered a little after five."

"I know what you're thinking, Lexie." Magnus floated up to her. "But you're not a police detective."

Lexie focused her attention on Renee. "Do you have any other clues?"

"No. I wish we did." Emile gathered up the sheet. "The carvings remind me of several other cases I've handled. People we've found in the swamps. Perhaps the person or persons who committed this crime comes from there." He stretched the sheet over Renee's head.

"But why Renee? She didn't betray anyone." Lexie's anger lifted her voice. "She's innocent of ever—"

"She wasn't innocent! She killed my aunt." Emile unclenched his fists and flexed his shoulders. "When you came to power, and she renounced all her ties with Bloody Mary's network of scumbags, it sounded too good to be true. Maybe the guys she hired to do the murders and kidnap Will were trying to keep her quiet by killing her or paying her back. Who knows."

The disclosure made Lexie feel more useless than ever. Here was another life she should have saved. Why didn't she see Renee was in trouble?

"I should have done something to stop this."

Emile took her arm and escorted her to the door. "You've seen enough."

Lexie glanced back at the body. "She never gave you any hint there was someone after her?"

Emile pushed down on the door handle. "The only thing she talked about was wanting to speak with you."

The darkness's sway ratcheted down as they left the frigid room, and her burgeoning guilt replaced the emptiness it left behind.

Once outside, the explanations Emile gave for the crime ate at her. The entwined pieces of her power throbbed in her chest, begging not to let this go. There was more to Renee's death than the police envisioned, and somehow, her newfound powers sensed it had to do with her.

Magnus moved in front of her, blocking her way. "Do not even consider getting involved in this."

She ignored her ghost and faced Emile. "Is there any way I can help find out more about who committed this crime?"

"No. Let us handle it." Emile tensed and ran his hand over his mouth. "But there's another possibility you need to consider." He guided her down the corridor to the morgue entrance. "Someone may have punished her for backing you as mambo. Titu told me some in the voodoo community weren't happy you were chosen."

His words only magnified her misery. The power she'd gained was meant to silence her detractors and squash any possibility of rebellion. What more did she have to do to prove she was mambo?

She reached for the wall, overcome with a bout of nausea.

Magnus was instantly at her side. "You need to sit down. You've gone pale."

"Are you okay?" Emile's arm went around her waist, holding her up.

Her knees buckled, and a warm rush came over her. "I'm going to be sick."

Emile hurried her to several waiting chairs.

Right after she settled into a chair, Lexie vomited up the cup of coffee she'd had for breakfast.

It splatted on the floor and sprayed ugly dark yellow stains over her white tennis shoes.

Magnus leaned over to Emile and whispered, "Call Will."

Emile pulled out his cell phone.

Lexie groaned as she pictured her husband's reaction. She didn't want to worry him; he'd been through enough.

This is all I need.

Chapter Twenty-Four

"**A**re you insane?" Will set a mug of hot tea on the coffee table in front of her. "What were you doing at the coroner's office in the first place?"

He rechecked her forehead, muttering under his breath.

She wrapped her hands around the warm tea as she sat on their sofa. "There was no one to identify Renee's body, so I decided to step in."

"If you wanted to identify her body, then why didn't you call me. I could have gone down there and spared you from seeing her."

Lexie sipped her tea. Her nausea had calmed, but she still didn't feel right. "I couldn't ask you to go, especially after what happened to you."

He sat next to her and patted her knee. "Well, I think it's more than she deserved."

Lexie set her mug down, bracing for Will's reaction to her next proposal. "I have to find out who did this to her."

Will's fingers tightly interlocked, his knuckles turning a dusky white.

She put her hand over his, hoping she could make him understand. "Renee wasn't responsible for what happened to you or me. It was Emily Mann."

Will stood, combing his hand through his hair. He paced in front of the sofa.

It wasn't a good sign, but Lexie kept her voice calm as she presented her argument.

"Emile said there's a possibility Renee may have died because she backed me. A lot of people weren't happy with my appointment."

He came back to the sofa and settled next to her, cupping her face. Then a stern expression creased the corners of his eyes.

"I want you to stay out of this investigation. I know you, and how you love to go looking for trouble, but you must let Emile's people deal with it."

She eased back, her stubborn nature refusing to back down. "I have to find out who else opposes me in the voodoo community. If I'm going to assert myself in my role, I have to learn all I can about my opposition."

He gripped her arms. "Please, listen to me. We have both been through enough. I don't want you chasing after murderers and drug dealers. I want to know you're safe at home in our new condo with a security guard downstairs and an alarm in our unit."

By the emphatic way he spoke, Lexie knew better than to push the subject. They had been through enough, but she wanted to make sure nothing bad happened to either one of them again. She had to keep digging for answers: otherwise, they might never be safe.

She patted his hand. "I will let Emile's people handle it."

His sigh let her know she'd made the right decision. Will picked up her mug and handed it to her.

"Here, drink this. You're still pale."

She sipped her tea and her queasiness flared. "I must be getting a bug."

"Perhaps you should see someone." He sat back on the sofa, keeping his eyes on her. "You haven't seemed yourself lately. You've been distracted a lot, and I hear you up almost every night watching television until the early morning." He hooked his hand around her thigh. "Why not let a doctor take a look at you? See if it's just nerves or something more?"

Lexie put her mug down, an uneasy tickle rising in her throat. "A doctor? But I don't know any."

"I have just the guy." Will patted her leg and stood, sounding like his old self. "His name is George Paulson. He's got a practice in the city."

Lexie crinkled her nose as he went to the kitchen. "How do you know this man?"

He halted and glanced back at her "He's a client. How else?"

The moon cast white tendrils of light across the black water in the fountain as Lexie sat at the black iron table on her balcony. Unable to sleep, she'd come to her favorite spot to soak in the sounds of the French Quarter and forget about the questions plaguing her.

Despite the late hour, the city still hummed with the far-off laughter of tourists, the distant thump of loud music coming from Bourbon Street, and in the air, the faintest aroma of a potent curry concoction from a neighbor's kitchen. The strains of a solo trumpet coming from the courtyard close by rose above the din, easing her troubles.

She gazed out at the courtyard, enjoying the respite it provided. A shadow moved across the cement. A man, or the outline of one, glided toward her as if on a determined course. He had no color, no defining features; just a figure in the moonlight.

He stopped below her balcony.

Lexie swore he raised his head to her. Then he disappeared.

Magnus materialized in the empty chair across from her. "Why are you still up? You need to sleep."

"I can't sleep." She rubbed her arms to stave off the chill in the air. "I keep thinking about what happened to Renee and wondering if it will happen to me."

He sat back, tapping the handle of his cane with his long fingers. "I know. What you feel, I feel. For example, that display at the coroner's office today. I'm still reeling."

She rolled her eyes. "Will wants me to see a doctor. He even called and made an appointment for me."

Magnus settled in his chair. "He's eager to make sure you are well."

"But I'm not well, am I?" She closed her eyes and rolled back her head. "I keep thinking of what's inside me. How do I solve this? How do I get rid of the darkness, or will the light leave me and then I will be all Kalfu's? It's like I'm waiting for a bomb to explode."

"You're not going to explode." Magnus paused as a refrain from the trumpet swirled around them. "You're too valuable to the light and the dark. In the meantime, you must take care of yourself. Get some rest."

She cast a wary eye to her ghost. "You don't strike me as a someone who should be handing out health advice."

"Since the moment we met, my only goal is to make sure

you never end up like me."

"If I become a ghost, please don't let me scare the shit out of people."

Magnus chuckled. "If you ever do become a ghost, you will probably scare the shit out of me."

Dr. George Paulson's bedside manner consisted of telling bad jokes and sucking air through his prominent teeth when not speaking.

A round man with a thick head of brown hair and deep-set brown eyes, he poked and prodded on her belly, listened to her lungs, and after checking her throat, stood back from the exam table.

"Everything looks good." He pressed his thumbs under her eyes. "You've got some dark circles, probably from not sleeping, but physically you're fine."

Lexie wrapped the thin patient gown around her, feeling the cold in the room.

"I told Will I was fine. He just worries about me."

Dr. Paulson went back to a metal desk in the wall of the small exam room and had a seat on a rolling stool.

"Any other symptoms you can think of?"

She browsed the tall cabinets above a small sink in one corner, along with a selection of tongue depressors and Q-tips in glass jars. "Distracted mostly, and a little irritable."

He picked up her chart from the desk, nodding as he listened to her.

"I've had a lot on my mind lately."

He selected a pen from the top pocket of his white lab coat.

"All perfectly normal when you have a busy life." He made a notation on the chart. "And when was your last period?"

Her mind went blank, and then as she counted back the days, a distressing shiver rolled through her.

"Ah, a few weeks ago."

Dr. Paulson raised his head, a slight gleam in his eye. "More than four?"

She gulped and nodded as her heart rate picked up.

"Any chance you could be pregnant? You didn't list any birth control under current medications."

She bit her lower lip, her sinking feeling growing stronger by the second. "Sure, there's a chance, but I seriously doubt it. I've been so stressed. It doesn't happen when your stressed, right?"

Dr. Paulson got up from his stool, a slight grin on his face.

"It can happen anytime." He walked up to her and patted her shoulder. "Let me get the nurse in here, and we'll do a quick pelvic to make sure everything is in order, then we'll run a urine test to confirm if you're pregnant."

He left the room and Lexie sank into the exam table. Pregnant? Holy shit! Her initial response was absolute joy, but then the horror of the past few weeks resurfaced, and her delight plummeted. How could she think of bringing a child into the world, especially after what had happened to Will? Any child she had would be a target, not to mention how her current abilities would affect it.

Then a thought struck her. If she was pregnant, how did it get past her ability? Attuned to everything around her for weeks, a baby growing inside her womb would have registered at some time.

"Okay, lie back on the table." Dr. Paulson entered the room with a round brunette dressed in blue scrubs. "This won't take long. Then Beverly will get a urine specimen from you."

323

"Dr. Paulson, I don't think this is necessary. I'm sure I can't be pregnant."

He gave her one of those indulgent smiles she remembered getting from her pediatrician as a kid when she didn't want her vaccinations.

"Let's just make sure, shall we?"

With her feet settled in the stirrups, Lexie cringed as she waited for the uncomfortable portion of the visit to end. Dr. Paulson was gentle enough, but his intermittent "Hmm," revved-up her mounting anxiety.

"You can lower your legs," he told her, popping off his gloves. "I'm going to do an ultrasound on you."

Lexie sat up, grasping the top of her patient gown. "Why? You think I'm pregnant?"

He patted her knee. "Let's just see what we see, and we'll talk after."

Escorted to another room in his maze of an office, she yearned to call Will. His voice would give her encouragement. She even wished Magnus was with her, but he'd decided to wait discreetly at the entrance to the building.

An ultrasound tech named Mandy, also dressed in blue scrubs, helped her onto a slender table, and covered her with warm sheets. She then lifted her gown and applied warmed blue goo to her abdomen.

Lexie chewed the inside of her bottom lip as she waited for the tech to begin the exam. "Is there anything wrong?"

"Not at all," Mandy said in an upbeat tone. "We always do these kinds of ultrasounds. Gives Dr. Paulson a better picture of what's going on."

Mandy worked in silence, moving her transducer around on Lexie's lower abdomen and staring at weird gray images on her monitor, which made no sense to Lexie.

Mandy's lips pouted, and she squinted at the screen. A sliver of concern rose in Lexie. She reached out with her ability to read the woman's emotions, but all she got was a profound sense of surprise.

"Let's rotate you a little." Mandy put her transducer down and repositioned Lexie on her left side.

Back at her screen, Mandy once again scanned Lexie's lower belly, but her expression never changed.

The sinking feeling she'd felt in the doctor's exam room escalated into abject terror. Her ability snapped into overdrive, and Mandy's unsettling apprehension became hers.

Something is wrong.

An hour later, she sat across from a thick oak desk covered with hundreds of pictures of babies ranging from newborn to a few months old. All the cherubic faces smiled back at Lexie, amplifying her agitation. She entertained the thought of having her baby picture added to the ones on the doctor's desk, but then the icicles of cold within her stirred. She wasn't pregnant; she could sense it, but then why all the fuss?

The loud *tick-tock* of the second hand on the clock behind his desk grated on her nerves. If she didn't get answers soon, she was going to run shrieking from the office.

She distracted herself by perusing the framed college degrees and assorted specialty certificates on the wall to her left, and the thick stack of patient charts piled on the floor to the right of the desk.

The door to the office opened, and she damn near bolted out of her chair.

"I looked at your ultrasound results," Dr. Paulson announced, walking into the room.

Lexie clutched her purse. "Is there a problem?"

He flopped in his thick desk chair and opened a manila file in his hand.

"You said your cycle has been normal up until the past few weeks, correct?"

The dark in her came to life. "Yes. Everything's been fine."

"No surgeries, no problems of any kind before now?"

A tightness formed in her chest brought on by the insistent black snaking through her system.

"No. Nothing."

He made a funny grimace and then flipped the file on his desk around to her.

"Do you see those two spaces on your ultrasound?"

Lexie stared at the photograph. She could make out two white patches where his finger rested, but nothing else.

"Yes. Is it something bad?"

The black ribbon inside her cinched tighter, taunting her. She put her hand to her mouth fighting a bout of queasiness. Whatever the doctor found, she suspected the dark power inside her was responsible.

"Nothing is wrong, but there's nothing there." He sighed and dropped his gaze to his desk. "Those two empty spaces are where your ovaries should be. When I did your physical exam, I should've been able to feel them, but I didn't. It's the reason I ordered the ultrasound. This is something I'd expect to see in an older woman after having her ovaries removed surgically. But you say you've never had surgery, and everything has been fine up until now. Which makes no sense. It's as if your ovaries have disappeared."

BOUND

Outside the doctor's building, on the sidewalk next to Prytania Street, Lexie paced the pavement. Her heart shredded into a thousand pieces as what she'd discovered settled over her.

Her chance to bear a child, to have a family and a future with Will had been taken away in one irrevocable move. She knew the culprit; she'd guessed it before the doctor had told her the devastating news, but now what would she do? Her husband would be destroyed, and never see her as a complete woman again. He would leave her, she knew it. All her dreams, every good thing she had planned for in life with her husband, Kalfu had taken away without warning. Why?

"You're upset." Magnus showed up, hovering close to her. "What did the doctor say?"

When she saw his aristocratic face, something snapped. Lexie sank to the bench by the entrance, overcome with sorrow.

She dropped her purse on the sidewalk. "I can't have children."

Saying the words made what had happened to her finally sink in. An avalanche of tears crested her eyelids, waiting for that last blast of emotion to send them over the edge. When the first teardrop landed on her cheek, she was helpless to stop the rest.

Magnus stayed, watching over her as strangers ambled by.

When her weeping slowed, he gasped. "Your cheeks … they're black."

She wiped her eyes and stared at the black streaks on her fingers.

Black tears.

The final proof she was Kalfu's. The black tears stilled her grief. She'd chosen to give herself to the master of darkness to save her husband; now, she would lose him because of it.

"We should call Will," Magnus whispered.

The image of confiding in her husband clouded over with the blackness residing in her.

"No. I won't say anything." She brushed the last of her tears away and with a shaky hand picked up her purse from the ground. "He'll leave me if he ever finds out."

"Nonsense. He loves you. He would never leave you for this. He's bound to you."

Bound? A flurry of anger swept through her. How could any man be bound to a woman who was an empty shell? The life in her had been gutted and stripped. What remained was her empty carcass. Something only useful to the dead, not the living.

"You are bound to me; Will is not."

He stood over her, his voice drenched with obstinance. "Not all couples are meant to have children. You simply tell him you have a condition preventing you from carrying a child. He will understand."

"I don't have anything." She stood from the bench. "Don't you get it? I had something taken away. Something sacrificed. He took this from me as payment for his power."

Magnus's thin lips pulled back into an angry sneer. "When?"

She trembled all over as she recalled her meeting with Kalfu. "The moment I committed to him, or after that night with Renee, I'm not sure. Titu warned me there would be a sacrifice. And he told me it would be revealed in time."

"What will you do?"

She wiped her cheeks again, making sure to remove all traces of the evidence. "What can I do?"

Magnus rushed up to her. "You must talk to Will. He will ask questions when you never get pregnant. He might want you to see other doctors. Then what?"

Her stomach balled up, squeezing the biscuit she ate for breakfast up to her throat. "I'll deal with it when the time comes." She gulped back her despair. "Whatever happens, Will must never know about me. I don't think I could survive it."

Chapter Twenty-Five

The four large windows overlooking the river let in the bright afternoon light and allowed a breathtaking view. Lexie admired the ships navigating the turbulent waters as Will chatted with a client on his phone.

From the windows, she crossed the shiny hardwood floors to the kitchen, her dragon cane tapping as she went. She ran her fingers over the smooth black granite countertop, then examined the white cabinets, stainless appliances, double sink, and newly installed refrigerator.

The kitchen's luxury hinted at their future, but Lexie wasn't thrilled about her new home. The only sensation registering was the icy touch of darkness still holding her hostage.

Several boxes Will brought from their apartment waited by the entrance. With the big move days away, she considered the bare beams in the ceiling and the freshly painted walls. Would they ever be as happy here as they'd been in their cramped apartment?

"I understand, Mark, and we will have the bearing wall done by the end of the week." Will came to the kitchen and rolled his eyes. "You can call Owen about the deadlines if you want. But I'm sure he already has your notes."

He listened some more.

Lexie walked across the living room floor to him, putting her thoughts in order.

"I will, Mark. Talk to you soon." Will hung up the call and came up to her. "Sorry, baby. Antsy client." He kissed her. "Now tell me what Paulson said."

"I'm not sick." She smiled, trying hard to make it look convincing. "He thinks I'm stressed."

He let out a long, relieved breath. "So everything's okay. I was worried there was something wrong."

She gazed into his eyes, willing back her tears. How could she ever tell him the truth? The harrowing experiences he'd undergone as a result of her struggle for power proved Lexie had to do all she could to protect him. No matter how much it hurt.

"Everything is perfect."

Will's relieved smile made her feel like a worthless shit for lying to him. He tossed his arms around her, and Lexie closed her eyes, asking God to forgive her.

"Let me show you the woodwork I had added to the master bedroom." Will pulled away. "And the tile work in the bathroom is over the top."

Right when he took her hand, his cell phone rang. He checked the number and held up his index finger.

"One minute. Let me take this call."

He ventured back to the scenic windows, leaving her in the kitchen. Lexie decided to check the final renovations without him and made her way along the hall off the open living room.

The master bedroom had similar scenic windows facing

Canal Street. Not quite as stunning as the river, but Lexie preferred the skyscrapers and high-rise rooftops to the lure of the rushing water.

The wood cabinets Will insisted on adding would sit above their king-sized bed and replace their night tables. The sleek room with its white carpet and oak baseboards lacked the cozy feel of their current bedroom, but Will assured her their condo would have the same appeal as their French Quarter apartment.

A cold breeze sailed past, and a slight odor teased her nose—the scent of a fresh forest, green with spring.

"I must compliment you on your performance."

He stood in front of the window while a misty halo around his figure blocked out the sunlight and cast a long shadow across the white carpet.

His jeans and T-shirt replaced by a tailored white suit, almost matching the carpet, she could not help but compare his clothes to those of Damballah.

"I had hoped you might crack and tell him the truth." Kalfu winked at her. "But you're made of sterner stuff."

The taunt in his smoky voice filled her with disgust. She'd never give him the satisfaction of seeing her weak. It was a wedge he'd use against her one day. It was time to face her opponent with the same placid demeanor as a seasoned chess master.

She kept her voice low and steady as she spoke, belaying the turmoil tearing her apart. "You could have told me at the time what you were taking, and spared me the medical bill."

"Ah, the lady has a sense of humor." Kalfu clapped his hands. "Most who have sacrificed to be with me aren't quite as composed as you. There are tears, lots of them, and a few pleas for mercy, but I have to admit your reaction was most unexpected."

Lexie checked the anguish buckling her knees and stood as if she'd shoved a rod up her back.

"Why my fertility? Considering all the other options, I'd like to know your reasoning."

He strolled across the room to her, his hands behind his back.

The black in her center fluttered as if drawn to the spirit who had placed it there.

"Everything I take from a person isn't something they miss, but something they think they need. I am showing you a child will only hamper you, and keep you from becoming a legendary mambo."

"Marie Laveau had children." She folded her arms, concentrating on the cool exterior with which she meant to deceive him. "Many as I recall."

"And in the end, they tarnished her legacy. But you will be spared such a fate."

She raised her head, meeting his gaze. "Is that why you're here. To gloat."

"I never gloat." His hand swept down her figure. "You've changed. I can feel it. My flavor has blended well with yours."

"Your flavor? Interesting choice of words."

"Apropos for the city we are in, is it not?"

Lexie's hate for the spirit swelled, strengthening the grip of his blackness. "And what will your flavor do to me? Make me do horrible things?"

"Darkness is not what drives people to do bad things. It adds to the essence of what is already there."

He moved closer, his calculated stride resembling a stealth hunter in the brush.

"With you, the darkness has intensified your light, which will make you a formidable mambo." He placed his hand on her chest. "I'm sure Damballah approves of the changes I've made."

In response to his touch, the black and white ribbon in her center twisted tighter, struggling against each other.

"Damballah didn't act very impressed when we spoke last. In fact, he told me you were dangerous."

The statement took him off guard, and his composure slipped just a little, but it was all Lexie needed to uncover the weapon she would use against him

"He visited you? How odd? He never sets foot in this world." His sly grin reappeared. "I doubt you will see him again, and as for the comment about me … I'm far from dangerous. I'm the one who helped you in your hour of need. Where was Damballah?"

She raised an eyebrow. "Maybe he couldn't get a word in with you around."

He came up to her, his fingertips lifting her chin. "Your mouth is a creature all its own, Lexie Arden. Careful how you address me. I'm not as forgiving as Damballah, and definitely not as kind."

"I saw your kindness with Emily. You turned on her just like you'll turn on me one day."

"I'll never turn on you, Mambo. I plan on keeping you by my side for a very long time."

She wilted at the concept of remaining his. The black swirling in her wanted to take control, she could feel it, but she had no intention of becoming his entirely.

He raised his head. "Your husband is coming. We will speak again."

In a swirl of mist, he spun into a cone of glistening light and then disappeared.

The sunlight beamed into the room through the scenic window once again, and the shadow receded.

"There you are." Will strutted into the bedroom. "Looks

great, huh? It was worth the extra week of waiting to move in. The lights from the city at night are breathtaking from here."

She nodded to the window. "Yes, you can see everything."

"Are you still happy about moving?" He circled her with his arms. "No second thoughts about leaving the shop?"

How could she play the role of the happy homemaker when Kalfu's black influence spread through her system like cancer? For Will, she needed to pretend to be content.

"The shop will be fine with Nina."

He arched away from her, a surprised frown on his face. "That's new. You've always been so protective of the shop. What's changed?"

She tensed, unsure of what to say. She went to the bedroom door leading to the hall.

"I'm just broadening my horizons. I've been thinking of spending more time away from the shop and going out into the community." Lexie ducked out the room, eager to get away.

Will pursued her down the hallway. "The community? Since when?"

Lexie reemerged in the living room. Will came up to her and she patted his chest, wanting to appease the annoyed smirk settling over his features.

"It's something I'm expected to do."

"Goddammit!" His tone quickly turned condescending. "I want you here, safe and away from anyone who may want to harm you. Not out gallivanting around the streets where any lunatic can hurt you."

She rubbed her forehead, quelling her anger. "I have a role to play, and that involves interacting with the people of this city."

"No, Lexie. On this point, I'm putting my foot down. You want to tend to the community, do it on your cell phone or at the shop."

Her fury awakened her power, and her voice thundered throughout the apartment. "Don't ever tell me what to do!"

A stunned Will took a step back from her.

Regret shut down her fury. She'd lost control and let the energy in her dictate her reaction. Sickened at the look on her husband's face, she eased closer to him.

"Will, I'm sorry. I shouldn't have said that."

He went to the bar and picked up his jacket. "It's fine." He shrugged his jacket on and grabbed his keys. "I have to get back to the office. I'll see you later at the apartment." He stormed out the front door without glancing back at her.

She hugged herself, rocked by her guilt. How could she have let her power get the better of her?

"You shouldn't have done that." Magnus materialized at her side, his gaze on the condo door. "You need to make things right with Will. You can't drive him away."

She put her hand over her center while the black ooze slowly retreated. "What is happening to me?"

Magnus's lips pressed into a tight line. "Not what, my dear, but who."

Perched on a box of books, Lexie held an iPad in her hand as she went through the metal shelves packed from floor to ceiling with T-shirts, glasses, plastic voodoo dolls, and different tokens in her cramped storage closet. For days, packing for the move had preoccupied her, and she'd neglected her business. But the respite in her storage room gave her time away from Will, and her customers, so she could think.

The constant remorse she'd suffered since leaving Dr.

Paulson's office had relented, but not completely. It hurt more at night when she lay in bed agonizing about the future, and Will's reaction when he eventually found out. The ever-present cold easing through her system was another cause for concern. She could feel it surging and ebbing like the tides of the ocean. She considered herself an upbeat person until then, but the weight of her worries had taken their toll. Her moments of happiness ended up singed by darkness.

Out of the corner of her eye, a shadow appeared.

Willowy and resembling the lithe figure of a woman, it hugged the walls and slipped behind the door.

"Yeah, you assholes are becoming a growing concern."

"Talking to yourself again." Nina walked into the room. "Or is this a private conversation between you and your ghost."

Lexie checked off another box on her iPad. "Why aren't you out front?"

Nina came up to her, a bold smirk on her lips. "Still in a crappy mood, I see."

She lowered the iPad and stared at the young woman. "What do you want?"

Nina straightened up and wiped the grin off her face. "There's someone here to see you. She calls herself Madame Henri."

Lexie reached out with her ability and searched the shop.

The white energy hit her instantly. In her mind's eye, she saw Madame Henri, in a black dress with a matching black shawl, turning her nose up at a stuffed voodoo doll.

Lexie put her iPad on top of a stack of boxes. "Did she say why she's here?"

"Not to me." Nina marched out of the storage closet.

Lexie chastised herself for being short with the young woman. She needed to try harder to keep her snappy behavior under control.

After retrieving her dragon cane, she set out to meet with Madame Henri.

She walked through the red door to her shop, and the hum of activity greeted her.

Customers crowded the floor, browsing the display cases, hunting through the T-shirt racks, or reading from her bookshelves.

Across the room, standing by the register, Madame Henri gave her a brief smile.

A nudge from the black within her warned Lexie this wasn't a social call.

"Madame Henri, what a pleasant surprise."

The older woman's black eyes darted to a few customers perusing the shop. "We should talk in private, Mambo."

She showed Madame Henri down the narrow hall to the back of the shop. In the kitchen, she offered her a chair at the small table and went to check the coffeemaker.

"Why have you come to see me, Madame?"

Madame Henri settled in her chair. "I know the past several weeks have been difficult for you with Titu's death, and then Renee's murder, but council business has been put off for far too long. The tragic deaths of Jacques and Titu have left openings on the council which must be filled. We show the voodoo community we're weak when we remain disorganized. We must appear united to keep the peace."

Lexie gave her a curious once over. "I would have thought you wanted the council to remain in limbo."

"I prefer order and balance. Reestablishing the council is a first step to regaining that balance."

Lexie rested her cane against the counter and selected two mugs from a cabinet above her head. "Who would you suggest for the council? Many will be afraid to join us after what happened."

Madame Henri's light laughter rose around her. "Never you mind about that. There are plenty of ambitious practitioners in this town who would be more than happy to risk their necks for a seat on the council. I will make some calls and come up with a list."

"Then I will be happy to go over your list, but let's steer clear of the ambitious ones." Lexie tipped the coffeepot over one of the mugs. "I think I'd prefer members who are more interested in coming together than promoting their agenda."

"Wise words." Madame Henri took the mug of coffee Lexie held out to her. "But I'm afraid you will soon learn everyone has an agenda."

"Even you, Madame Henri?"

"Even me." She blew on her coffee. "Titu told me she expected great things from you. I can see her faith was well founded. You have a good heart and a thick head. You'll need both to be a wise mambo." She put her mug on the table. "There's another matter. I've received a number of reports from other priestesses in town—the shadow spirits are still with us."

Lexie put the coffeepot back on the warming plate. "Yes, they were stolen from the River of Shadows below the bridge to blackness."

Madame Henri gave a curt nod, acting impressed. "What do you know of the River of Shadows?"

"I've been there." Lexie picked up her mug of coffee. "I've stood on the bridge to blackness and seen the white waters of the river."

Madame Henri crossed herself. "Then you've endured more than me." She waited as Lexie sipped her coffee. "Have you seen the shadow spirits in the city?"

Scattered pictures of the dark figures in her shop and apartment danced across her mind.

"Yes, I've seen them."

"As long as they remain in our world, chaos will return. Your duty is to find a way to send the spirits back to the river."

Lexie held back her rebuke. Didn't she have enough to deal with?

"I'm not sure how I can do anything. I've been reading—"

"You must use your ability." Madame Henri stood from the table, her gaze dropped to Lexie's cane. "You have a great deal of power at your fingertips. It's time you applied it."

Doubt curdled her regard for the priestess. Was this the reason behind her visit? To test Lexie's power.

"How can you be so sure about me?"

Madame Henri came up to her. She placed her hand on Lexie's chest.

Her touch awoke a spring of warmth. It engulfed every part of her, and the respite it gave, eased the grip of the darkness on her soul.

Lightheaded, and for the first time in weeks, filled with profound peace, she stared at Madame Henri, confounded by the ability she wielded.

"Power is not your problem." Madame removed her hand. "Use what you have to bend the spirits to your will."

The black rekindled, blending once again with the white light in her center. Her peace disintegrated

"Which spirits?"

"The two you serve—Damballah and Kalfu. Both are powerful masters, but you are your own mistress. Remember that as you struggle to appease them. It will help guide your way." She paused as if listening to an undetectable voice. "I must go. I will have a list of candidates for you by tomorrow."

A crumb of hope came alive in Lexie. After weeks of despair, the morsel wasn't much, but it was enough to make her want more.

Before the older woman could get away, she reached for her arm. "Madame, what do you know of serving these two masters?"

"I've been where you are." She revealed the slightest smile. "We will talk again."

Lexie stood dumbfounded as the older woman walked out the room and down the short corridor to the shop.

When she disappeared behind the red door, Lexie rested back against the kitchen counter, grateful she wasn't alone anymore. She still had questions about her fate, but they didn't seem so overwhelming.

Anxious for space to move, she stepped through the french doors leading to her courtyard.

Outside, she breathed in the nippy late fall air. Sunshine covered the high-pitched roofs of the Creole townhomes around the courtyard while the happy laughter of tourists drifted in from Royal Street.

A shadow hovered on a balcony to a neighboring home across the courtyard, bending over the railing and then disappearing when the sun came out from behind a cloud.

"Why are you out here?"

Magnus rested his back against the yellow stucco of her building, his gaze overlooking the pond.

She went up to him. "You didn't happen to hear my conversation with Madame Henri, did you?"

He nodded. "Every word."

"She can help me." Her voice ballooned with excitement. "I could feel it when she touched me. She's like me—dark and light."

"She's not quite like you. You are still struggling with your opposing forces."

Lexie folded her arms as a ray of sunshine shone down on her. She basked in its warmth, and then the icy touch of her darkness roused from its brief respite.

"They're vying for control. Fighting for who will win me."

Magnus scoured the courtyard as he moved away from the building. "It seems to me what's happening inside you is a reflection of what plagues this city."

Lexie twisted the wedding set on her left hand. "How do I marry the two opposing forces and restore order?"

He came up and stood next to her. "We will find a way."

For some time, she felt alone in her battle to bring the forces teeming in her to heel. It brought some comfort to her raging river of doubt to have Magnus by her side.

"I've been sitting on the sidelines waiting for things to happen, but I must make them happen. I have to find a way to take control."

Magnus tipped his nose upward, appearing smug. "You sound like me."

The comparison made her smile. "I am like you in a way. You're bound to me, and I'm bound to the darkness inside me. Life will never be the same for either of us."

"Every leader needs a touch of darkness to rule, my dear girl. You have found yours."

She rubbed her hands as she considered the future. "And will it help me?"

Magnus gave her a cruel grin and drifted toward the kitchen door.

"We shall see."

ABOUT THE AUTHORS

 **Alexandrea Weis** is an award-winning author of twenty novels, a screenwriter, ICU Nurse, and historian who was born and raised in the French Quarter of New Orleans. Having grown up in the motion picture industry as the daughter of a director, she learned to tell stories from a different perspective and began writing at the age of eight. Infusing the rich tapestry of her hometown into her novels, she believes that creating vivid characters makes a story moving and memorable.

A permitted/certified wildlife rehabber with the Louisiana Wildlife and Fisheries, Weis rescues orphaned and injured animals. She resides with her husband and pets in New Orleans. Weis writes paranormal, suspense, thrillers, horror, crime fiction, and romance.

www.alexandreaweis.com

Lucas Astor is from New York, has resided in Central America and the Middle East, and traveled through Europe. He lives a very private, virtually reclusive lifestyle, preferring to spend time with a close-knit group of friends than be in the spotlight.

He is an author and poet with a penchant for telling stories that delve into the dark side of the human psyche. He likes to explore the evil that exists, not just in the world, but right next door behind a smiling face.

Archery, photography, wine making, listening to jazz, blues, and classical music, and helping endangered species are some of his interests.

www.lucasastor.com

Made in the USA
Columbia, SC
06 May 2018